A. L. KENNEDY

Serious Sweet

VINTAGE

1 3 5 7 9 10 8 6 4 2

Vintage
20 Vauxhall Bridge Road,
London SW1V 2SA

Vintage is part of the Penguin Random House group of companies
whose addresses can be found at global.penguinrandomhouse.com.

Copyright © A. L. Kennedy 2016

A. L. Kennedy has asserted her right to be identified as the author of this
Work in accordance with the Copyright, Designs and Patents Act 1988

First published in Vintage in 2017
First published in hardback by Jonathan Cape in 2016

penguin.co.uk/vintage

A CIP catalogue record for this book is available from the British Library

ISBN 9780099587439

Printed and bound by Clays Ltd, St Ives plc

Penguin Random House is committed to a sustainable future
for our business, our readers and our planet. This book is made
from Forest Stewardship Council® certified paper.

for V. D. B.
as ever

'The endeavour, in all branches of knowledge, is to see the object as in itself it truly is.'

Matthew Arnold

A family sits on a Tube train. They are all in a row and taking the Piccadilly Line. They have significant amounts of luggage. They seem tired and a little dishevelled, are clearly arriving from somewhere far away: a grandmother, a father, a mother and a daughter of about twelve months. The adults talk quietly in Arabic. The grandmother wears a headscarf, the wife does not.

Although her adult companions are quite dowdy, the girl is immaculately flamboyant. She has spangles on her perfectly white shoes and wears hairclips adorned with the shapes of butterflies. She shows colours upon colours. There is a complicated pattern of embroidery across her cardigan, like flowers and like stars. She sits on her father's lap, with her back to windows full of autumn and declining light and she faces out at the rest of the carriage, and is self-assured, interested, genuinely charismatic. She fixes passengers with a quietly adult gaze and grins.

The girl has extraordinarily lovely eyes.

On her hands, her plump knuckles, the side of her throat and on her cheek and forehead there are recent injuries. Some are just scabbed abrasions, while others are more significant. Nothing has finished healing. It seems clear that something dreadful, perhaps explosive, has caught her – not badly, but badly enough. Some of the damage will make scars inevitable. The rest of her skin is as silk and downy and remarkable as any young child's would be, but she has this persistence of wounds.

She practises waves – sometimes shares them with her grandmother and mother, sometimes with strangers who cannot resist waving back. Her force of personality is considerable. And she plainly assumes she is special and a focus of attention for only good reasons. And it ought to be possible that she is right in her assumption, that she always will be right. It will take repeated outside interventions to remove her self-assurance and happiness.

But this morning she is authoritative and waving, delighted. Whenever a passenger smiles or waves back, her relatives seem both proud and on the verge of dense emotions which could overwhelm. The adults' obvious tensions and their sense of things unexpressed have rendered them mysterious to other occupants of the carriage – both mysterious and a source of quietly intimate concern.

The mother, the father, the grandmother – they keep themselves busy, offer their daughter healthy titbits and drinks from a variety of bags and packages. They have games also. They have tiny cloth books and a nice toy animal a little like a horse. They are as prepared as anybody can be.

06:42

THIS WAS – *OH dear God* – this was not what he'd – *nonononono.*
  Shit.

Jon could feel his shirt dampening with a panic sweat, his jacket heavy and encumbering. He wasn't dressed for this, for this problem, this level of problem.

'I'm doing my best. Really. Come on now … Please …'

He was holding a bird.

Although he didn't want to.

He had a bird in his hand.

And it would be better in the bush. Ha ha ha.

Although it couldn't be allowed anywhere near the sole currently available bush – that bush was the problem.

The innuendo is a problem, too. But I'm ignoring it. If you ignore an innuendo it may go away. Unlike a problem.

'Just … Just let me. I can fix this.' Actually, he wasn't remotely sure if he could fix this.

He was quite possibly lying. To a bird.

It was very young, the avian equivalent of a fattish toddler, or chip-fed adolescent maybe, and was fighting inside the curve of his left hand while Jon tried what he could with his right to make it happier. It wasn't happy now, of course. It was biting him, clenching his left forefinger with its beak in a display of determined impotence, small bravery.

5

He didn't want to upset it.

But he really couldn't leave it alone – not in its current condition.

But not leaving it – rescuing it – was already making him late. The creature was sapping his morning, draining his schedule to dregs before it had started. And he could have done without this, to be frank, when his day was already arranged to be challenging, punishing, fatally flawed, to be easily toppled by an incautious sodding breath. So to speak.

Today is the day when I get what I deserve.

I think. Possibly …

As if anybody human, any human body could stand that.

So to speak.

But, even so, one would have to do one's best with today, whatever happened. One always had to do the best one could – one being the only one available.

But then again one might be failing already to do any good at all – birds were sensitive, animals generally were sensitive and birds in particular could be overtaxed and flat-out murdered by simple shock. He might be killing it.

But he didn't want or intend that … Which was a point in his favour.

But probably his lack of expertise would guarantee he screwed this up …

Too many buts – which isn't like me. I'm the man who takes away the buts. I'm known for it – slightly. I can remove them from any public statement, press release, precis, report, discussion document, Green Paper, White Paper, any note on the back of an envelope, if you insist that you need me to help you and are having a delicate day, well, I'll do what I can … I can, in theory, make having cancer be, well … still having cancer, but also, somehow, a favourable outcome if I'm given enough time. I do have that skill. I don't want that skill, but it does seem to be required that Jon Corwynn Sigurdsson should hook out any sense of obstacles in the world and paint over any action's possible consequences. If you feel that you can't quite like some part of reality, I'll step in and rephrase it for you.

But I would rather not.

And my actual duties lie elsewhere. Very much so. In my opinion.
It makes me tired.

Jon shut his eyes to let his head settle – like covering a parrot's cage to shut it up: so much noise to so little purpose …

I can rewrite anything, but we are – in this situation – talking about death and that does tend – even in commonplace birds – to be viewed as a negative outcome.

The blackbird shivered – which might be a bad sign, Jon didn't know.

Nobody normal liked having a death on their hands. In their hands. In hands which, as it happened, seemed insufficiently evolved for this type of thing – too close to the ape: his had unsightly knuckle hairs and a deficit of manly dexterity.

One's construction disappoints oneself.

Plus, this would be an Unforgivable Death, which was worse.

Pregnant women, dogs, horses, some cats, all chimpanzees, most children, the sprightly elderly, men with good hearts, pretty women, brave blind people and promising youths from troubled backgrounds with Oxbridge scholarships – and endearingly courageous baby birds – these are beings whose Deaths may be regarded as Unforgivable. Heart-clenching photographs across multiple media platforms may emphasise their tragic stature by showing them in earlier moments of unwary hope. (If a horse – for the sake of argument – can experience hope.) Their troubling loss may inspire campaigners, legal reforms, the provision and naming-in-their-honour of community facilities, or new diseases. Or else the provision and naming-in-their-honour of replacement horses.

The chick produced another urgently shrill lament – these were emerging at unpredictable intervals – pleas that were larger than itself and accusing.

Then it bit him again.

'Oh just … Look … Please …'

We preserve the names, create the laws and the memorials, so that Deaths which are Unforgivable can also appear to serve a purpose. Although obviously it is we who do the serving. The dead and their deaths cannot serve – they are only a removal, an extinguishing. Nobody – this is an unwieldy example, overdramatic – but nobody died in the Holocaust in order to provoke a compensatory outbreak of human-rights legislation. That wasn't their aim. Nobody threw themselves into the corpse mud of the Somme in hopes of inspiring commemorative artworks. And yet ... These thoughts emerge, because we long for hopes and meanings and want them to spring forth from bitterness and permanently modify Again *by adding* Never ...

This is simplistic as an attitude and could be quite dangerous in its ultimate effects. It could lead us to encourage suffering in others because it might conceivably give rise to quite ill-defined and therefore inspiring good. It could lead us to embrace the fruit of various poisoned trees. It could lead us to plant poisoned trees ...

But no Death *is anything other than* Unforgivable.

I would have to be morally bankrupt to suggest there was such a thing as Forgivable Death. *And I am not morally bankrupt — not entirely. Although others may be. Maybe. It may be that I'm saying others could, on occasion, misplace their moral centres and subsequently rank fatalities according to a graded scale, descending from ... let's say* A Death of Shattering Importance Occurring to a Person of Celebrity Status *to* Inconsequential Deaths, Tedious Deaths, *and then* Distasteful Deaths *and on towards* Necessary and Solemnly Welcomed Deaths. *All would be* Predictable Deaths. *Even the unforeseen can be predicted, its proportion of reality quantified — the emotional distancing and coarsening suggested by this type of quantification being perhaps undesirable. Conversely, taking the deaths of others lightly, or approaching them purely in terms of public relations, or a contest between cost and benefit, might not be something one ought to judge harshly and could indicate — rather than a spiritual lapse, or defect — a sensible effort to impose a form of triage on a busy compassion schedule.*

I could retain a proper reticence and yet still make an observation along those lines.

An observation about others. Not myself.

'I'm not a bad person.' The bird seemed unconvinced. 'But I am ... I'm late. And I can't be. Today is ...' Another sweat broke over him. 'Today is today and is full of ...'

Shit.

This was Valerie's fault – because she'd changed things. Her patio was usually an area of grimly straightforward vegetation, potted clumps of foliage that didn't mind her smoking at them. Now it appeared she'd decided to harbour a blueberry bush. Or somebody had given her this blueberry bush – *much more likely* – and she'd dumped it out here in response.

She'd dumped it where it would be dangerous.

She'd dumped it where it would act as the bait in an unnecessary trap.

Which meant the entire scenario was indicating the character of the bloody woman just clearly, massively – it absolutely showed the way she always was and would be.

The bird flexed within its confinement, its tiny efforts and huge distress managing to impregnate his fingers with yet more clumsy guilt, despite his efforts to be helpful.

He was aware this indicated his own character – a child's terror, animal fingers – just as clearly, massively …

'It's OK. It's OK. I'm making it better, you better. Honestly.' He'd been speaking to the creature throughout – this fawnish, biting blackbird child – ever since he'd heard it calling. He'd run outside from the kitchen and into the dawn, found the bird struggling, punishing itself, in the especially dense jumble of netting left at the foot of the blueberry's far too ornate planter.

Must have been a gift. She wouldn't have bothered with something that needs any maintenance, not voluntarily. Unless – is it stylish this month to eat fruit fresh off the bough, or currently held to prevent appropriate ageing, or to offer defence against cancer?

Christ, she can be appalling. Although I shouldn't say it.

'Sorry … Sorry …' Jon apologised, made efforts to sound soothing.

I do realise I ought to hate less.

In general, in my wider life, hate has grown to be almost a hobby. I walk between the rented fig trees of Portcullis House and hate. I practise quiet and detailed hate at weekends and in leisurely moments I wander the Natural History Museum and can no longer guarantee to really see anything, so thick is the fog of hatred that I peer through as I rush on and this is inappropriate. It helps no one. I acknowledge that.

'Sorry.'

And in my current position, I mustn't, mustn't, mustn't, hate anything or anyone because proper animals register negativity. Complete animals, as opposed to people, understand even the earliest traces of loathing and they hide and run and fly away from it.

Besides, I can't be all covered in hatred — wet with hate, can one say that? I can't — not today. I mean, I can't hate anything today. Today is about — possibly — the opposite of hating.

So — even if I didn't have to anyway, I need to think gently, feel kindly, or else my bird will know.

Not my bird. I don't own it.

This bird.

My responsibility. Not owned, but owed.

Which would make a nice sound bite, polished up and delivered with humility — a stirring phrase to lift the tempora and mores, in as far as anyone still remembers what that means …

'Oh, for Christ's sake!'

Above him, the mother blackbird bulleted past, keeping neat to the crown of his head, threatening, letting out hard chips of alarm in rattling bursts. She sounded like the din from escalating assaults on some type of thin crockery. She hadn't hit him. She was pretending that she would, though, because that was the most she could manage. She was displaying a violent kind of love.

'I'm … will you … will you both … I'm doing what you want. I promise … I …'

Once he'd understood the situation, he'd run back to Val's mildly louche kitchen — greasy handles on all of the drawers — and found some scissors before scurrying out again to cut away the horrible green tangle from around the bird's fretting body. This initial rescue had left it free from the net as a whole, but still personally bound by these nasty plastic strands and he'd had to pick the poor creature up, hold it in his palm, coddle it securely and snip, gentle, snip — *Christ, if I'd cut a wing or something, crippled it, condemned us both to*

a subsequent mercy killing, an Unforgivable Murder ... and that could
still happen, it still could, awful, awful ...

Jon's free hand had gone seeking about fairly blindly with the
scissors' threatening ends and had hoped to catch and then cut
the constrictions around the animal's breath, the palpable hysteria,
as it wriggled with bleak strength, resisting his grip.

The thing gave another chirp of surprisingly loud dismay.

'I won't eat you. I won't.'

He found it was odd, if not moving, to hear an identifiably
childish note in the call. This seemed to be a rule in nature: that
when we are properly, deeply troubled – birds, chimps, horses,
humans, things with blood – we all become children, we all wish
for our parents, scream for our mums, whether their aid is available to us, would be useful to us, or not.

'I won't hurt you at all. I promise. Promise.'

The blackbird's mother swooped again pointlessly, but louder.

This whole horrible situation was entirely the result of Valerie's
being Valerie and doing the wrong thing. She had an instinct for
wrongness. The netting on the blueberry bush was the wrong
netting. Jon wasn't, strictly speaking, a gardener but had seen the
stuff you're meant to put over vegetables often enough. The bore
of it, the diameters of the loops – he was unsure how you classified
anti-bird protection – the denier, density ... it was meant to keep
out even sparrows, surely. Any reasonable person would deploy it
with the aim of repelling assailants, not garrotting them. But Val
had covered her sodding blueberries with what had to be the
largest possible grade of the stuff – this gaping hazard to all and
sundry. A drift net for anything feathered. Was she eating birds
now, fresh off the bough? Was that guaranteed to put a bloom on
post-menopausal skin? What had she been thinking – if at all?
She was a woman who could be quite gloriously unburdened by
consideration. Anything slimmer than a tomcat and in search of
blueberries would simply plunge straight into the hazard and be
caught and alone and yelling and bewildered.

That was the trouble with animals – their lack of understanding
created dismay upon dismay: theirs and then one's own to follow.

One looked at them and saw oneself and then became foolish and overwrought.

'For crying out loud! If I was going to eat you, I would have! Wouldn't I!'

It was an outlet, sometimes, the shouting. Not that Jon often shouted.

'Shh, no. Sshhh. I didn't mean it. I'm not angry with you. I'm not angry at all. Don't worry. Please. Don't worry about me.'

Neither attempting to soothe the bird nor losing his temper with it seemed to alter their mutual positions. Both blackbirds, in fact, were beyond the scope of his communicative abilities.

Which Val would have pointed out. She had a good ear for a punchline, a knack for summarising failures.

'Sorry. Sssshhhh. I'm going to ... This will ... it will ...'

Experimentally, he tugged at what he thought he had successfully reduced to only an opened length of plastic, its structure defused – the end of the problem. Jon pulled a little harder and an unpleasant, spurred thread began to emerge from his fist, no doubt sliding around the blackbird's chest first, moving over and under its wings. He could feel the creature shudder. The transmissible burden of horror in this was remarkable.

As a response to the unfamiliar contact, the chick – quite naturally – shat hotly on to Jon's trousers, leaving a long purplish streak. The colour of stolen blueberries, the first fruits.

Then it called even more poignantly than before – Jon could have done without that – and the mother answered, dipping past his ear in a sweep of outrage. What was she saying? Was she trying to reassure, already in mourning, uttering menaces, vowing revenge, shouting advice? She had muted the usual calls of other birds in the vicinity, made them withdraw to a cautious distance.

Their silence had begun to sound judgemental as the drama continued – even though Jon had succeeded, apparently. There didn't seem to be anything further left to encumber his captive. 'See? Ssshhh. That's ... It's ... I did tell you ...' He tried to check all was well. He'd never get hold of the thing again if he'd ballsed this up and it was still afflicted when he let it go ... You wouldn't want to contemplate a fellow creature getting strangled slowly by its own motion, by its growth ... or else getting crippled ... stuff like that ... deformity and gangrene.

The upside being that Death in something deformed and gangrenous would be a Desirable Death.

God, I'm a bastard.

No, I'm doing my best. I have done my best.

He angled the feathery shape this way and that, peering between his fingers and attempting to inhabit his sense of touch with sufficient concentration to locate errant strands.

Nothing appeared to be wrong any more.

I think.

'OK. OK, then. That's fine.'

Somewhere the mother was watching, loathing him, loosing off further hard strands of complaint.

Jon murmured to her offspring, 'It's all right. It really is. Silly. Weren't you ...?' In a sort of croon he hardly recognised.

'It's all right.'

He breathed. A slight shake hampered the progress of his inhalation and then eased. He'd stopped sweating. The muscles in his thighs relaxed. He pondered his slightly ruined trousers, the darkish, white-streaked stain on the incompatible blue of the cloth.

Then he gazed around himself, sighed outwards.

The block of yellow light that had been splaying from the kitchen doorway had become entirely invisible once the dawn strengthened into day. Nevertheless, a soft blueness, a gentleness, remained here and there in the shadows as he studied them. And there was an atmosphere of accessible beauty. If he'd wanted, Jon could have smiled. But he only looked, carefully looked, let himself see and see and see and inhaled again and held the breath, both air and peacefulness thick in his lungs.

And beyond him there was a dense inrush of stillness.

It locked.

Safety was happening, the imposition of comfort at something approaching seven in the morning. And the disappearance of every motion.

Jon could smell the river: the relative proximity of exposed mud and spring greenery, dirty life going on beyond Valerie's home. (A desirable Georgian property not entirely unfamiliar with dirty life. *She only does it to annoy, because she knows it teases.*) But there was no sound, not a bit. He could believe that the trees by the road outside, the neatly restless waterside gardens, the shifting and searching of silt feeders, the willows thickening out on the eyot, the push and lap of the current, were perfectly held at a stop. And the early brawl of cars on the Hogarth Roundabout, the unending overhead slither of jets, the climb of the sun, the virulent spinning of everything necessary to this particular April Friday – it was everywhere suspended.

Just now.

Just for now.

Even the mother blackbird was silent and unmoving.

It was as if simultaneous fears – the birds' and his own and the world's – had created a mutual understanding and therefore a pause to take stock.

And then Jon blinked.

Which broke the moment.

Reality tumbled on again.

'Well. OK. Then ...'

And he let go, came quite near to a sigh, opened his hand and watched for the whole wide instant during which the chick didn't leave him and its dark gaze rested on him and shone.

A schoolboy hope appeared in Jon that perhaps the animal was grateful to him and would stay, perch on his finger, groom its disarray.

Oh.

But it left him.

Oh.

Naturally.

Oh.

It lurched up in a flurry of speed, crying in a manner which implied it had been wounded most severely at the last. Yet it was patently fit enough to escape him and entirely free and saved. He had saved something.

Jon watched the bird dart hard up into the small box of sky fixed there above Valerie's patio walls.

Oh.

And then it was as gone as gone. The mother, too.

His palm turned cold.

His usual tensions reasserted.

A panic arrived, or something like that, something like being nervous but in the absence of one's nerves, something like being stripped of interior wiring and feeling one's gaps. There it was. Here it was.

I think I may have to be sick.

Half a dozen parakeets slipped by above him, high enough to show in silhouette. They had harsh wings and tails drawn to a long, narrow point – one could imagine – by sheer speed, the violently straight flight. And they produced this din – *tsseuw, tsseuw, tsseuw.* They made a noise like wives.

No, I withdraw the remark. They sound like the fear of wives, the fear of one wife, my fear of one wife, of my wife, my fear of my wife, of that wife.

Tsseuw, tsseuw, tsseuw.

I don't, I don't know. I don't know about wives, or parakeets. I ought to know what they sound like, but I don't. I could be mistaken. I have an ape's hands and no wiring. I am a tall child in a man's suit and unfit for purpose.

Tsseuw, tsseuw, tsseuw.

And now I am late, really. And I've got to have time today, I've got to make time, because then I'll be able to … There are things that I need to finish and they shouldn't be rushed.

But I think I'll manage. Truly. I swear. I'm going to punch a hole clear through my schedule and everything, so that I can breathe and operate as I should and I'll make it possible to see and see and see what I do next.

Tsseuw, tsseuw, tsseuw.

The sound of being laughed at.

Here it is.

Tsseuw, tsseuw, tsseuw.

Yes, here it is.

06:42

BECAUSE LYING IN bed when awake was inadvisable, she'd come up here to see the dawn arriving. The council left the Top Park open, even at night. The qualities of the view it offered made constant access a must. People felt they might have to nip round any time and check on the metropolis where it lay uncharacteristically prostrate at their feet. And wasn't it flat – the city – when you saw it like this, so plainly founded on a tidal basin, rooted in mud? Strangers would remark to strangers about that. Inhabitants of the Hill didn't need to, they were used to it. They could stroll along, perhaps through music – the Hill is a musical place, people practise instruments – and they could hope for the startle of a good London sunset, the blood and the glitter of that splashing on banks of distant windows, making dreams in the sky. Or else they might get the brawling roll of storms, or firework displays, or the tall afternoons when the blues of summer boiled and glared like the flag of some extraordinary, flawless nation. Even on an average day, the city needed watching. You shouldn't turn your back on it, because it was a sly old thing.

She'd wanted a sunrise. Or rather, she'd wanted to be out and it had been very early and she'd had no choice about what she would get – at dawn the sunrise is reliably what will arrive, you can be calm about that, no fear of disappointments. You're all right.

She'd cut in and taken the broad path, safe between distantly dozing trees, no shadows to hide any bother. A woman by yourself – you didn't want to feel constantly threatened, but you'd no call to be daft about things, either. You don't like to put yourself at risk. Well, do you? No, you don't. You shouldn't. At risk is no way to be.

Then she'd gone round past the silent tennis court and headed – with fair confidence, even in the dimness, because she was here a lot – headed over the oily-feeling grass to the absolute highest point on the slope. Foxes had been singing, screaming, somewhere close.

It was traditional to hate foxes, but she wasn't sure why. She guessed it was a habit to do with guilt. They always sounded injured, if not tormented, and that could get you thinking about harms you'd done to others in your past. The foxes perhaps acted like a form of haunting by offering reminders of sin and that was never popular. Or perhaps there was no logic involved, only free-form loathing, picking a target and sticking with it.

She enjoyed the warm din of the foxes, the bloody-and-furry and white-toothed sound – it was intense and she appreciated intensity. This was her choice. In the same way, the Hill was her choice. The open dark had given her a clifftop feeling as soon as she came within sight of the big skyline. It provided the good illusion that she could step off from here and go kicking into space, swimming on and up. Below her, opened and spread, were instants and chains of light apparently hung in a vast nowhere, a beautiful confusion. It was easy to assume that London's walls and structures had proved superfluous, been let go, and that only lives, pure lives, were burning in mid-air, floating as stacks of heat, or colour, perhaps expressions of will. What might be supporting the lives, you couldn't tell.

Then, during the course of an hour, the sun had indeed pressed in at the east, risen, birds had woken and announced the fact, as had aeroplanes and buses, and the world had solidified and shut her back out. It was like a person. You meet someone at night and they won't be the same as they will if you see them in daytime. Under the still-goldenish, powdery sky, buildings had become just buildings, recognisably Victorian in the foreground and repeating to form busy furrows, their pattern interrupted where bombs had fallen in the war. These explosive absences had then been filled with newer and usually uglier structures, or else parks. There were also areas simply left gapped. They had been damaged and then abandoned, allowed to become tiny wildernesses, gaps of forgotten cause. Rockets had hit in '44 – V-1s and V-2s. Somewhere under the current library – which wasn't council any more – there'd been a shattered building and people in pieces, dozens of human beings torn away from life in their lunch hour. It didn't show. There was a memorial plaque if you noticed, but other human beings, not obviously in pieces, would generally walk past it and give it no thought.

She was the type, though, to give it thought. She had an interest in damages, you might say: damages and gaps. They could both be educational.

Other places were more peaceable. She could pick out church spires and the cream-coloured Battersea chimneys of what had been the power station. Further off, thin trains pushed themselves to unseen destinations and details blurred. The far distance raised up shapes, or hints, or dreams of impossible coasts, lagoons and mountains. Mirages crept out from under the horizon. And somewhere, the crumpled shape of the Thames hunched along invisibly towards the coast.

It wasn't a bad morning. She wasn't a morning person, but she could still like it. The parakeets were lively already and sleeking about, flaring to a halt and alighting, an alien green that never was here before, bouncing and head cocking in dull trees. They were something from the mirage country beyond the rooftops. Initially, there'd only been a pair of them on the Hill, but two was all it ever took – think of Noah. One plus one equals more. They were teaching the magpies bad words.

By this point – almost seven o'clock on an April Friday – the standard architectural landmarks were on offer: the complicated metallic cylinder rising up near Vauxhall, the vast stab of glass at London Bridge, the turbines rearing uneasily over Elephant and

Castle, the shape of a well-turned banister marking Fitzrovia … each of the aids to navigation. And then there was the toy-box clutter of the City, a slapdash collection of unlikely forms, or the vaguely art deco confections at Canary Wharf and, dotted about, the distant filaments of cranes that would lift more empty peculiarities into the undefended sky.

These were the self-conscious monuments of confident organisations and prominent men – everyone of less significance was forced to look at them and reflect. Insignificant people gave them nicknames purposely comparing this or that noble edifice to a pocket-sized object, a domestic item: mobile phone, cheese grater, gherkin. If you couldn't make them go away, or prevent new ones appearing – these proofs of concentrated power, silliness, silly wealth – then you could declare them ridiculous. You could be pleased to hear of their design flaws, their structural defects, their expensively unoccupied floor space. It did no good, but it could make you smile.

You could try the same with other sections of reality. Sometimes.

Sometimes the art of naming could subdue hostile territory for a while. She'd once visited a friend – more a friend of friends – in hospital. The room he'd shared with two others had been high enough to peer across Chelsea. Some former inmate had left a meticulous drawing of the landscape, every roof in silhouette, marked across an elongated strip of card. The detail was obsessive. Each building was identified and given historical, or scurrilous, footnotes.

As she'd had very little she could talk about to her friend's friend, she'd drifted into remarks about the unknown artist. She'd said that someone must have spent week after week here being very ill, or very bored, or dying and trying to keep useful by leaving a present behind. Her friend's friend had, at that time, been in the process of dying, although he was taking it well.

It had been one of those days when her tact had failed her.

Now she wondered if the Hill could find somebody who would make them all a similar long, thin chart to explain their outlook and keep them right. It would be both useful and appropriate. In summer, when residents loitered outside in the early hours to smoke, paced on front paths and in gardens, leaned against doorways, sat on steps, then the place did have a hospital atmosphere: slippers and nightgowns, quiet nods in passing, half-awake stares and faces still pillow-creased, soft. They all needed a therapeutic map they could walk up and learn from, alter, perfect, garnish with added footnotes as they wished. It would be a thing of power.

Or they could go on as they were – half knowing, recognising, deducing.

Or they could make things up. She could do that. She was good at invention, often unhelpfully so. She could quickly feel definitive and point to Over There and then announce, *That is the listening post that records our affections, there is the confectioner's workshop devoted to making models of our souls – they do it with spun sugar, souls never purchased, only taken as gifts, or eaten – and that's the Depository of Regret and there is the doorway to the Furnace, guarded by a clever dog.* She could reel off all sorts of nonsense like this – no worries over whether you wanted it or not.

In bleak moods, she just would prefer that all the signature constructions, the grand gestures, were rechristened factually: the Shinywank, the Spinywank, the Fatwank, the Flatwank, the Weirdwank, the Overlooked, the Understrength, the Pretty, the Petty, the Squint, and the Sadwank.

Why not be straightforward?

But she wasn't in a bleak mood today. In conversation, she might – it was true – have said, 'I will meet you under the Spinywank – right beside the station.' But she'd only have meant it in fun. She might even have thought it, but kept quiet. She would have been able to remember that some people don't appreciate terms like *wank* and so she would have waited and had a thinkthinkthink, checked to discover if she ought to skip the cheap laugh and be more standard-issue instead. That way you wouldn't cause offence. Although you might discover later that non-habitual swearers were up for it on some occasions and pleased by bad words from others when the time was right. Hard to tell by looking. You had to test the waters without drowning, slip in gently for a bit of a dip. To be cautious, then, she might have said, 'I will meet you on Friday, right next to the tower – at London Bridge Station.' And added no flourishes.

She'd have been happy, though, however she phrased it. She'd have been happy in any case.

I will meet you.

It's a happy statement.

It's a good promise.

And it had joined her birthday as a pleasant thing to bear in mind.

It's my birthday.

This is her first birthday.

She is forty-five years old and having her first birthday.

This has been her first birthday for quite a while, in fact, longer than average, to be honest.

I'm spinning it out. Just try and stop me. You can't. Bet you can't. This birthday is all mine.

She's made it as far as her continuing first birthday and is trotting further on. This is an excellent thought.

She has a collection of premium-quality thoughts which she likes to count through. She has scenes and moments she remembers deliberately. This is her equivalent of maybe passing warm pebbles from hand to hand, smooth and reliable, or her version of the rosary, her misbaha, her mala, her komboloi, her worry beads – everyone worries and why not have beads? She counted out invisible fragments and wished they were more obvious, better at saying to other people, *Just leave me alone for a minute, because I am busy with wanting to feel all right.*

There's no fault in wanting that.

There's no harm in milking your birthday. Even if it did happen more than a week ago – so what?

My name is Meg. It's my fucking birthday.

She feels that she's justified.

How often, after all, do you have your first birthday? Usually not more than once.

Fine, OK – it wasn't a birthday, it was an anniversary.

My name is Margaret Williams, Meg Williams. My name is Meg and it is my anniversary. One year.

But birthday was a better word for it, because telling yourself *first birthday* could remind you of when you were a kind of celebrity at rock-star level, but too young to enjoy it. When you got born you were immediately good news. When anyone saw you they smiled. They gave you stuff. They wanted to hold you and protect you and be kind. You could dress like a mental patient and not utter a sensible word, but that was OK, that was cool, that pleased people and they purely wanted to know more about you and find out your needs. If you messed up then somebody else washed away your problem and you only had to *be* and that was enough to satisfy. You being you was a bloody treat for anyone who caught it.

One is the age of automatic celebrity.

Who wouldn't want a share of that?

One is spotless and has no baggage and can do no harm. It has only the ghosts of things to come – each one of them carrying a happy promise.

She didn't, in the usual way of things, enjoy thinking of the future – the future had an unmanageable shape.

But when you were one, you had this big, noticeable, smiling future – it was right there for you, straight ahead and held to be inviting. You had promise and it wasn't meant to disappear, not until you were older. You were a promise. To others as much as to yourself.

A nudge of emotion started to seethe up from her feet and she hoped that the early dog walkers didn't come too near and notice her slightly crying. The Hill was a chatty area, you might not get away with tears – you'd have to protect yourself against enquiries.

Really, she ought to head home and get warmed and out of her pyjamas. Outings undertaken with wellingtons and a coat over pyjamas were viewed as an acceptable morning practice in many households around here. The Hill didn't judge. Car jaunts of an evening could use the same dress code. If you had a car. She didn't any more. And there was work soon and something else before and she had to get ready in a number of ways and the bus schedules had become mainly theoretical of late, which meant she had to be responsible and set aside more time for journeys. She should shower and make ready and chase straight off to be where she should and then onwards to do her job and serve a purpose.

This was another good thing to have in mind: she was employed and her employers found her useful and wanted her to keep appearing as agreed and paid her and provided a workforce kettle and mugs – free to all staff – and encouraged community-building traditions, like the rota that meant each last Friday in the month someone had to bring cake.

It occurred to her that the pressure of her approaching turn as a bringer of cake was OK.

But, then again, it was a pressure.

When a cake failed it ruined the mood for the whole of the office and finished the month sadly. Success in the cake area was therefore important.

She'd have to buy one, because she couldn't bake, not reliably. Baking the cake, anyway, would invite hysteria. If it was a dreadful cake from a shop, you could blame the shop. Your own dreadful cake – people have to be polite about it, but they don't want it and you being around in the aftermath of your rotten cake provision means that co-workers have to sneak off and ditch their slices. Then you'll end up catching sight of binned cake wrapped in paper towels, but still obvious, or cake troubling pigeons on the window sills, or anywhere really, it would depend on how resourceful your co-workers at GFH were, and the more resourceful they were, the more energy they'd have to waste in jettisoning your disaster which was your fault and the entire mess would be so deeply humiliating that it didn't bear considering.

So she shouldn't consider it.

She should acknowledge instead that it wasn't a big deal and she was being melodramatic.

Nevertheless, she'd been testing shop cakes once a week to be sure she'd avoid catastrophe. How good they were depended quite depressingly upon price. She wanted a relatively cheap cake. She also wanted a cake that felt innocent and as if some experienced relative's hands had formed and finished it – plain but delicious and heartfelt. She wanted to give people something kind and simple.

That wasn't available.

The cheap cake was horrible. The expensive cake tasted of greed – of greedy bakers.

She couldn't win.

Who knew cake was such a bastard?

It wasn't the major issues that tripped you up – glorious suffering and mayhem were oddly easy to discuss. You could similarly try not to be embarrassed or pursued by your very many inadequacies. But ridiculous, obsessive anxiety about virtually nothing: that was shameful and so you didn't mention it and so it festered.

I am letting myself be harassed by eggs, butter, sugar and flour.

She should buy chocolate for Gartcosh Farm Home. Chocolate cake.

Chocolate always worked.

A cake could be nasty, commercial, impersonal, slightly toxic – if it was chocolate, it worked anyway. This was some kind of rule.

Foolproof.

Perhaps.

You couldn't be absolutely sure, because maybe it would be possible to make the people at GFH finally tired of chocolate. It was a bit of an open goal when it came to providing treats and so it occurred very often.

She shouldn't be boring.

She shouldn't trash a path to joy for everybody.

She shouldn't ruin chocolate for everyone forever.

Jesus, this was hard.

Cake was hard.

No.

She was out of the park now and on her way back to the flat – her strides fast with patisserie-related tension.

No. This is crazy.

She paused at the kerb, as if being cautious about suddenly appearing traffic, although no sign of any such thing was even distantly approaching.

I cannot be bullied by cake. Not even real cake — by theoretical cake.

She sniffed, frowned, stepped into the empty road.

What I should do is get a chocolate and another one …

No.

NoChristfuckshitforshittingfuckssake.

I mean, really.

What she should do was not think about it.

Starting now.

Not think about chocolate cake without traces of nuts.

And no gluten.

And no alcohol.

Organic chocolate.

Chocolate that helped starving villages and put orphans into schools, that built the schools, that saved lives and nourished communities and made strong women sing and wise men love them.

No one could argue with that.

Although there was no need to fuss or think about this. Not about cake.

It was just a fucking cake.

Which should be chocolate.

Why the hell were they all so demanding?

Making people bring cake. Which sadist thought of that?

Not that it wasn't a good idea.

It was nobody's fault but her own that the prospect of cake provision could burrow a hole through her head within seconds and let all the sense drop out, have her imagining accidents: choking, allergies and sickness, these swiftly followed by her sacking and destitution, homelessness, begging and death.

Just a cake.

Just the threat of a cake.

So don't think about it.

She should move herself forward to something else.

She should pick one of her shiniest, best things. Pick a warm thought, a true one.

I will meet you.

She opened her gate, walked up the path to her front door and undertook to ensure that while she waited for the doubtful bus and then something unpleasant beyond it and then work – she did like her work – she could have that promise, kept safe.

I will meet you.

Fear or no fear, the thought was with her – all the way in.

I will meet you.

It was so dangerous with hope that she'd only consider it in little rushes, for fear of worrying and pulling it apart. For fear of fear and the way that her fear would breed further fear. One plus one equals more.

I will meet you.

But it was with her, anyway.

My name is Meg and I've passed my one-year anniversary and I have this with me.

I will meet you.

Meg could feel it was almost certain that if somebody parted her ribs and looked inside, there would be a light to find because of this. Because of all this.

It was with her.

Here it is.

A middle-aged woman sits beside the window in a café. Behind her there is a chaos of children and parents – some kind of community group outing. Mothers and fathers chat tiredly around one large accumulation of tables while their charges ramp and squeal. Beyond the window there is weather: grey horizontals of rain and battered leaves being tormented along gutters. The park across the way is a riot of lashing and tearing green. Only the woman is still. She stares through the glass with a kind of absence, a type of seriousness, which keeps the children from approaching her, even though they are unstoppable everywhere else.

The woman sips from a mug of something and turns back to the sheets of white paper on her table – these three squarish sheets with black handwriting across them. She studies them and, from her expression, it's impossible to tell if they are keeping her attention because they are wonderful, or dreadful.

Then she smiles.

Jon had vomited quietly, neatly, into Valerie's downstairs toilet, flushed his evidence away and then ascended in search of clothes.

Throwing up had been calming, although weirdly impersonal.

On my back and the back of my shirt – right through my shirt – I'm clammy.

I need to change completely.

Something with which Val would happily, delightedly agree.

Jon had padded up to the second floor and barely begun combing through Val's subsidiary wardrobe in the Rose Room – *her term, not mine: bloody Rose Room, bloody ridiculous* – when his phone rang. Predictably, he flinched in response.

Even though it's not her.

Even though she would anticipate and relish my being curious – it would please and not disturb her – and she no longer has the right to shout at me.

How lovely. Now that I think of it. This lack of shouting.

At present, Valerie was allegedly at or near what she'd described as a villa in the Bahamas, enjoying the exotic wildlife of the Inagua National Park. That's what he'd been told.

She hates wildlife. Presumably whoever she is with has a thing for sandflies and flamingos. Won't last.

Although perhaps her current escort has – in fact – a thing for shouting. People do. People do flock towards all kinds of harm, shouting included.

Or else if the damage is something they haven't chosen, they'll choose to own it, as if that might help. That could have multiple implications for any relationship – a person might end up trusting cruelty, marrying cruelty, craving it. And, bearing this in mind, any sensible human being might actually have doubts should any other human being greet him with apparently consistent warmth. That initial human being – the first human being – who has grown into doubts might think to himself, Yes, but am I wonderful? Really? Or am I a new knife she's chosen to run her wrists across? Is that what she intends for me? Am I a weapon? I really would rather not …

And – as someone who might myself be fond of predictable hurts – wouldn't I be better off and happier with someone harsh?

And wouldn't this produce a state of permanent emotional incarceration?

Which is what Valerie would highlight as an example of morbid thinking.

His phone stopped ringing but retained an air of business left undone.

Then again, why did Valerie choose me, if not as a mortification, a morbid pleasure? I was a pain she could love to find intolerable.

He rubbed his face, as though rearranging the outside of his head might tousle his brain and leave him refreshed. Then he wondered if he'd washed his hands enough after trying to deal with his trousers.

Shit.

In every sense.

His phone began again.

And shit.

And this is not the bloody Rose Room, it's the Spare Room with Foolishly Expensive Hand-Blocked Wallpaper in a Relatively Vile Pink. But that would take too long to say. I do see her point. She isn't a woman to waste words.

You don't need a lot of words in a shout, they would spoil the effect.

Unless you're tirading. She sometimes branched out beyond simple yells and screaming — embraced the tirade.

I do not often shout.

I do not tirade. Not ever.

I am lots of nots.

And, since Valerie, what do they see — women — when they look at me?

Exactly the correct amount of harm?

An opportunity for shouting.

Or is it me that has a thing for shouting?

In any case, shouting from Valerie wouldn't be at me, not these days. Not now. Not at me, why at me?

The phone tickled and asked in his jacket pocket — knowing, smug. In the end, they both knew that he'd have to respond.

But it won't be her.

Why still anticipate it? I won't even be crossing her mind — not if she's ... She won't be awake. Or if she is, one might say that her wakefulness would be for the usual reasons and therefore wouldn't make her think of me.

Nevertheless, he did mainly expect to see her name on his caller display when he checked it.

Nope. Sansom.

He didn't want to speak to Sansom. Although a call this early would indicate a level of urgency to which Jon should respond, he didn't wish to. He wasn't in the mood.

And never mind early phone calls — vis-a-vis the time it would take to get himself from here into the office, it wasn't half early enough. It was past seven. He truly did have to get on and step lively.

It was only that liveliness seemed beyond him.

Nope, Sansom.

The phone continued to pester as he forced it down into his pocket again, despite its complaints. Then it stilled.

Like drowning a puppy.

He smiled and went back to fumbling Val's coat hangers as if he were a burglar.

Less a burglar and more a pervert.

Since his trousers were spoiled with both bird shit and inexpert rubbing at bird shit and his shirt was unpalatable, Jon really did need something fresh he could wear.

He was sure that he'd left some clothes here. A few things. She might well have given them away, though. She might well have burned them in the Aga, shredded them, had them fired into outer space, who could predict ... She could on occasion possess a magnificent spite. Really. He wasn't being unpleasant about that — her imagination was genuinely impressive in many areas.

Mine has been trained to be no longer there. In many areas.

Up to a point.

So today I can make a disinterested search of Val's house without distraction ...

She'd be disappointed if I didn't search.

33

The hangers were heavy with her winter coats, several of her pensioned-off evening dresses and winter outfits he recalled and – *yes* – a couple of men's suits.

Neither of them was his.

A couple of men's suits. The suits, in fact, of a couple of men. That blue should be illegal and that one looks like it was issued by a work-house – faux Edwardian labourer. Spare me. His week's spend on moustache wax and beard-care products would be more than a labourer earned in a year. And, yes – he will have a moustache and, yes, he will wax it. Twirled ends, I bet.

And there were shirts. Four ... no, five shirts. Ghastly shirts and ghastly in two different ways. He surmised that numbers one to three belonged to the blue suit, which belonged to a moron who thought that deep cutaway collars could be worn in civilised society – *youngish, probably works in finance, how fat does he anticipate having to make his tie knot ...? What would that prove? Dear me ...* And then there were these two unaccountable efforts from yet another man: not-bad point collars, but silk and in colours and oppressive patterns which strongly suggested a last dash for sex before taking the friends of one's twenty-something daughter out for tea becomes an acceptable way to express one's desolation. *Oh dear again. It's always sad to see a past mistress finally losing her form.*

Passed mistress.

Still, it truly doesn't hurt any more. It does not hurt me. I think. As far as I'm aware, the pain isn't waiting, or boxed, or numbed. It has departed. It has upped and left – in this, as in all things, my pain preceding me.

He'd undergone a sort of nerve death, obviously, over the years – the same pain repeating consistently and therefore disappearing in almost every way, if one were to discount all its more lateral symptoms.

And this isn't any kind of pain I'm feeling.

Strange to have one's grief lifted when one no longer minds if it's gone or not. And to find that I simply feel as if I'm wearing slightly better shoes. I wouldn't have wished so hard to be free if I'd known it was this unimpressive. Assuming that I am free. Not sure. Does being divorced equate with emancipation?

The phone chimed and shuddered against his chest, indicating a volley of texts and – no doubt – emails, very probably from Sansom. No one else should have any reason to be in touch. The department was no more or less besieged than usual, not in any real sense.

And Sansom's reasons for trying to reach him would not be real. Sansom wasn't real.

He's like the hen-night version of his profession – not that I'm familiar with hen nights. Went to a stag night once – for twenty minutes. Sansom is as convincing as the lady who appeared and pretended she was a policewoman to no avail, before disrobing. He's like a pre-striptease phoney fireman. I believe that hen nights have firemen. I'd imagine that fake male nurses would give out a number of mixed messages with regard to sexual orientation and the onset of diseases … And military uniforms might suggest PTSD. Who would want that? Would that be sexy? I can't say.

I can say that Sansom is a Hen-Night Special Advisor. Or a Stag-Night Special Advisor. Both. He'll swing in whatever direction is necessary. Loyal as a tick.

He closed the wardrobe doors. Then decided to leave just one open – so she'd be sure that he'd been there. She always closed her doors – afraid of moths.

No spare suit means I'll have to trail back home and then change before work. Can't be observed in disreputable trousers. We don't stand on ceremony, but even so … I can't proceed in unhappy trousers, not with hard-to-identify mishaps having left signs on the inner thigh, for God's sake. And my shirt's an irritation … but, even if the sleeves were long enough, I couldn't wear the shirt of a debt-happy child, or a dick-happy failure or somebody lurking behind a moustache. That can't happen, not today.

I cannot contentedly wear the shirt of some man who's been making love to my wife. My ex-wife. I don't think that's an unreasonable position.

And then the phone butted in again, ringing. Jon was old enough to remember when being away from the office actually involved being away from the office.

It was Sansom.

The concept of deferred gratification was unknown to Sansom. Jon reached out the mobile and pondered it.

What? What is it? What could I possibly do for you? And why?

Which wasn't a permissible attitude and Jon would have to do better, but the scent of Valerie's perfumes, their weird mingling of discordant notes and the threat of past occasions – they were combining to throw him off.

I'm not sad. Not injured. It's equally clear that I'm not delighted, not even content … I'm uncomfortable, I do know that … Is it nostalgia …? Neuralgia …? Indigestion …? Delayed shock after the struggle on the patio …?

And here was Sansom's name in annoying, shiny letters on the caller display.

Apologies Mr Sansom – Andy – for my failure to maintain the high performance standards we always do seek to achieve. I will be with you shortly. I am currently experiencing an unwilling recollection: the temperature of the interior of my wife's mouth – you know how it is. Quite possibly you know exactly how it is.

No. She would only have tried Sansom to make a gesture and she and Jon had moved beyond the stage where any gesture could be necessary almost a year before Sansom had even taken up his post.

Or, more precisely, I believe this to be the case, but could be mistaken.

Dear God, I feel weird. Am I just tired? I don't sleep. I should be tired. End of the working week – early start to get in here and then leave again on time, because I'll have no chance in the evening … I've a right to be tired.

Seeing him there in the corner of rooms – embedded and feeding. Why is a thing like a Sansom necessary?

He pressed the appropriate key, lifted the phone to his ear, let himself pour Sansom's hectoring whine into his head.

Yes, here it was, the usual tepid rush. Like spittle. Like drool. Another's mouth infecting yours.

Her mouth ... all those movements ... and the words ... mine, too, as well as hers. She felt contagious and I volunteered to be infected.

Sansom continued. And you had to reply, because that was your duty in most situations, both professional and private. You were the replying type of man, you were of service – or if you weren't and an informal resolution of your perceived failings was not possible and your customer was still dissatisfied then they might apply for an independent internal review by contacting – please God – someone other than you. 'Sansom, what can I— Well, I—' Sansom was forcing in a drumming pelt of injured something or other. There were shades of accusation.

I haven't failed you, though. I don't fail in that context. I do the job. I am relentlessly effective in that regard. That is what I am for. Sansom is not what I am for.

Jon fended him off, 'But that's not my, not strictly ... not broadly my—'

Apparently, the Member for Wythenshawe, Frodsham and Lymm had, once more, gone astray. The man seemed to have been preprogrammed by forces of such exquisite and bizarre malignity that Jon could only ever think of him as the Mancunian Candidate.

When I imagine her mouth, when I imagine her at all ... or my living here ... it's hard to say ...

Sansom was whining at speed. *Like a mosquito, perhaps sandfly, even. Definitely an arthropod kind of man is Sansom.* And, according to Sansom – which was no guarantee of reliability – there had been a mishap late last night at the barrel-scraping end of some standard hotel jolly. Which was the reverse of being anything to do with Jon, particularly now.

The point is, my issue is .... that I am – to a degree – feeling something. This sensation ...

Jon tried to summarise and, by doing so, move on and away from bloody Sansom, 'So he was verbally unwise, yes? That's not really news ... Your Honourable Member generally—'

The Honourable Member is generally a fuck-up. What was it the last time, the last incident? The man is a walking Fat Finger – a soft, thick accident waggling about and sure to thump itself against what it should not …

Ah, yes – I remember – 'Beware the Hun in the sun.' The last time had been in Leipzig. Fact-finding trip for comparison of this with that, or that with this – heaven forfend that MPs should achieve the same result by exchanging emails, phone calls, Skypeing, no one should ever be caused to miss an excursion. You could tell the Mancunian had prepared it – his bon mot – hooked it out as suitable for the occasion and therefore gone heartily off-piste in an address to several hundred sophisticated polyglot Europeans whose water glasses knew more about social grace and twentieth-century history than Mr Manchester ever would, even after some type of wholesale brain transplantation. The paper coasters under their water glasses could have beaten him at chess.

Chess … what am I thinking? Anything – animate, or inanimate – could beat him at chess. The coasters could have beaten him at rock, scissors, paper – at hangman – at snap.

He's got the right idea in a way. Voters are justifiably scared of clever politicians. They'll never like or trust you, never respect you – but if they can laugh at you, whether fondly or despairingly, you may prosper. Be a buffoon. But not too much of a buffoon. Don't bury yourself in the part. There is a line it's possible to cross. And Parliament's gift to Timperley would usually cross it, because he wasn't faking – he was both a genuine moron and stridently addicted to attention. One of the little-boy types who says what he hopes will earn him a spanking, because spanking is attention of a kind.

And God save us from a sly buffoon, we have no defence against that.

'Sweet Jesus, really? *Baby's got back.* He actually said that. And this woman was …?' Jon tried to enjoy hearing a problem that was not his problem. And to enjoy reciting it back even more. 'So to summarise, in the run-up to a general election, a white, male Parliamentary Undersecretary of State has insulted a black, *female*—
Yes, it was an insult, that's why it was taken as an insult, it could hardly not have been … Because it was grotesquely discourteous, why else? And—'

Two things about Sansom – he wouldn't let you draw breath and he lied to the wrong people. Which is to say, he lied all the time. The ends of his sentences didn't even match their beginnings, so hard and fast did he reshape the narrative of each trouble that beset him. You couldn't help a person if they wouldn't acknowledge reality – reality was all you'd got and, left unplaced, it would inevitably bite you. Swearing on your mother's grave that the world did not have teeth and wouldn't harm you made no difference. The hot and manly thrust of your sadomasochistic ambition went all for naught.

If I knew what I was feeling … One can't have nameless emotions, surely … They must eventually declare themselves – neither vague, nor trifling, nor tendered in a spirit of mockery. Surely …

'Sansom, you wouldn't be calling me if it hadn't been taken as an insult. So white, male and so forth has insulted a black, female activist who works for his own party and is … substantial in mass as a person … which was ungallant … And is this true, anyway – what's your source?'

Sources … if one can trace things to their sources, they must surely then become identified, identifiable …

So is the source of my emotions my wife?

Ex-wife. She's my ex-wife.

That would be the important question. Does my, as yet, unclassified emotional disturbance derive from her, or has it flown in from elsewhere?

'He was recorded doing it …? Well, isn't everyone? Isn't everyone now recorded while doing everything …? He at least wasn't overheard by a sober off-duty policeman of impeccable reputation, decorated former serviceman and tirelessly devoted to a number of charities …'

Jon ambled down Valerie's staircase as he spoke, its skewed angles marking it out as original. If anything lasted long enough, it got twisted.

Always makes you think you're falling, or about to.

And, as his telephone reception became exquisitely weak, he peered at his image, caught in the shine of the living-room door.

Original again – oak, two-panelled – polished by centuries of various substances until it had a deep and browny-goldy finish, the subtly uneven surface further enhancing the impression that it was a slab of very tranquil, well-aged liquid set up on end and then graced with a doorknob.

The one thing I miss about this place – the doors.

I can picture myself being desolate about the doors.

Although I'm not.

Emotions were like pine needles in your carpet – you'd think they were cleared and then another would work its way up and sting you, then another.

But you can look at a needle and see it for what it is. The bloody things are explicable.

His face, wavering in the sombre woodwork, was definitely grinning. He didn't look remotely annoyed.

And not bad for fifty-nine. Seen worse. Possibly. Any unbiased observer might be kind. Any kind observer might be ... willing to look away.

His arms – *spidery* – were distorted, his body's long outlines flickering as he moved. But it wasn't disturbing.

I never truly got the benefit of being tall. And yet people say it's a good thing. I was told recently that it's good.

'I was joking, Sansom ... No, I was joking ... I made the policeman up ... He does not exist ... He is a fiction.... You know about fiction ... Audio, or video ...? Magnificent. The Internet loves camera phones, where would we be without them ... You know I can't help you.'

I don't want to help you, but I also can't. My loyal and effective service may not be inhibited by the taint of comprehensive commitment to any particular interest or philosophy. We don't even share a minister. Be your bloody age.

My dad would say that – be your bloody age. Another tall man, Dad – not a clue what to do with it, either.

First time I came back from school – home for the holidays – and he'd decided to be short around me. My own father. I made him stoop. That could never have been right. I should have said so. One can't, though, can one?

Jon slotted himself down the steps again, jogtrotting.

Is that what I feel? Rushed? Am I thinking of all of the everything I still have to do?

'Sansom, you know that especially now I can't help you. And I have to make that very clear. If you are not satisfied with my response, I genuinely regret that, but there's no more I can do. By which I do mean precisely that there's no more I can do. This wouldn't alter if we were in the same room. And you shouldn't have texted me and I hope that you haven't emailed or that if you did, you bore the clarity of my position in mind.'

The Honourable gentleman currently under discussion is of a party and I cannot be of a party. The Honourable gentleman is subject to nervous difficulties, but that's none of my business in the sense that you require. The Honourable gentleman once made a moderately painless speech to an audience of which I was a member, that's all. The Honourable gentleman's dogged insistence that my subsequent presence on other occasions would ensure smooth sailing and the free flow of elegant locutions is based on a false assumption. He believes that every time he opens his mouth in public and precipitates a catastrophuck it's because I wasn't there. This is untrue. He doesn't fail because I'm never there, he fails because he always is.

'To repeat, I can't help. I can't ... But I can't. Particularly now. We're deep in the period of sensitivity and everyone has to be unimpeachably well balanced. Like a Toledo blade, as I used to be told. Acting as your Parliamentary Undersecretary of State's lucky gonk isn't being impartial, now is it ...? We're in purdah. At least, I am. And I can't *just be there* when he makes obeisance before the press ... I have my work to do ... As a suggestion, it's untenable in the particular and in principle and as a request. And beyond which, if *he* gets a gonk they'll all want one.'

And since when did a Parliamentary Undersecretary of State get anything much beyond the headed stationery?

I am here to serve, of course, I am a servant ... It becomes, though, difficult ... It becomes, in an environment where change-bunching *is a concept and we have to believe in and pander to such a thing as the* garden-fence effect *and* cascade *is deployed as a serious verb ... It becomes difficult. I think I reached my tether, its end, became aware that I was tethered and did not like it, when I encountered my first* zero-based review. *I do not wish to be involved with the thing which is a* zero-based review. *Zero is an ugly word. The name of the Greek philosopher of all things lost to despair should be ... Nemo Zero who lived in a burning barrel, close by the Abode of the Crows ... I should mention him at some point – see if anyone admits they've never heard of him.*

I think I should do that. I think so.

But then again, I can't hear myself think. On occasions.

And then again, I don't like it when I can. On occasions.

'Sansom ... Sansom ... Sansom, would you like to explain yourself to my minister who is currently a little busy, what with that ... that whole, what was it ...? Yes, that whole upcoming general election distracting him from his usual devotion to your well-being and that of every other special advisor, no matter their department. Regards, by the way to your minister, I thought he did terribly well the other night and it was a tough situation for him.'

Always be nice about a special advisor's minister. Their minister is the nipple at which they suck – he, or even she, will bring out the mammal in them – and they can't help being fond.

The Mancunian is, perhaps, Sansom's minister's ugly and wet-brained child, the one they couldn't sell to the circus – which is to say, not to a circus other than the one he now calls home: not to a proper circus that insists on its staff having skills – like tumbling, or eating live rats. All of which is not to be pondered.

'Talk to him, to the Honourable Member ... Then talk to him again ... Don't talk to me ... Talk to someone who *can* help you. Please. Not me. I'm someone who can't. Deep breaths, take deep breaths ... I'm so sorry ... Yes, you could ask my minister and if he were to tell me that I should assist, then I would try to see how we could do that.'

But he won't, because he isn't insane. I know there was something of a precedent set in Scotland, but purdah really should be purdah – I mean, it does matter a little, to democracy and so forth.

'No, *deep* breaths, Sansom.'

It had been a while since he'd hung up on somebody who was swearing.

It felt good.

He paused at another door. His reflection bowed slightly and flexed its knees.

He nodded to it, watchful, but it didn't take offence. He winked. *Some men have the face for that kind of thing. I don't.*

And he did need to be gone now. The plants had been watered, trousers must be fetched, borrowed, purchased, the office was … it waited. Things waited.

It's only my servant's nature, my servility, that means I'm here at all.

Val must have encountered – *have come across, have had … there really were no verbs that didn't end up leering once you'd put them in a sentence with Valerie* – she must have been the innocent acquaintance of some other person who knew how to fill up a jug with water and then empty it out at horticultural locations, repeat as necessary. There had been no call for him to be the one. She'd made it his responsibility on purpose.

Because she knows it teases.

He trotted his way down to the hall, switched on her alarm, then pulled open – with wonder, bliss, relief, something – her front door and stepped outside. Then he duly swung the impeccably painted wood, pushed it back into its impeccably painted frame. Her forbidding selection of locks were duly thrown, expensive levers operating as required. His phone rang again and he could almost take the small din as a fit celebration of departure.

And it wasn't Sansom.

And wasn't any other kind of pressure or disturbance.

Thank God. Or almost that.

'He got me … Yes, Sansom got me, Pete … I'm sure. I'm sure … Yes. He should know better. But they never do. And we're an anachronistic, smug elite when they don't need us and we should all be working in Croydon, what few of us are left, and then when they want us … Would be what I might say, but I don't and didn't. But one could.' It was Pete Tribe from the office. A promising man,

43

Peter. 'And he shouldn't have bothered you, Peter ... He shouldn't have bothered me. I've just got rid of him – one can always hope – and I'm on my way in and don't worry about it, you did the right thing – only I have to change my trousers, so I need to go back home ... No, no ... Of course ... We don't have someone with a remit to provide gangsta slash hip-hop references in support of the notion that he was in some manner ... The trousers? No, I was at home last night, but now I'm not ... No, not that ... I'm in Chiswick ... At Val's ... No, she's not here ... No, it's ... No ... I'll be in as soon as I can ... No, not that ... Yes, bye.'

Jon turned at the brewery corner – sucking in the malty air – and started to lope for the Underground. Val's had never been that handy for public transport. All this nonsense meant he was late and the Tube wouldn't cut it, time-wise, and the rush hour was going to cripple any cab's progress – if he could even find one. She'd made him have to deal with the rush hour. That was bad of her.

Peter will naturally mention my trousers and Chiswick to others, to the denizens around him, which will make for an inflammatory combination.

Once the sticky type of word got round, it stayed round and rumours of a sexual nature were the tastiest for onlookers and the most adhesive.

No, not that.

His current predicament had nothing to do with women, or a woman, in the erotic sense.

No, not that.

But everyone would assume. They thought he had women, that he had some ludicrous stable of complacent partners and rushed from one bed to another dispensing sex.

No, not that.

If you trace things to their sources ...

During his marriage he'd been taken as neuter, treated like an invalid – patronised by some and softly avoided by others who didn't want his assumed deficiencies to infect them. And those men who knew his wife in the sporting sense ... some were brash with him, some guilty, some gentle. Being married to an adulteress taught you a lot about human nature.

After the divorce very little had changed, although he'd seemed to be accepted as less contagious. And he'd been able, for a few translucent weeks, to identify even the most covert of the colleagues she had encountered, come across, had ... Each of the men had displayed an underlying tension he could only assume was caused by fears that Valerie might now intend to marry and then betray them.

Although I must not exaggerate. It wasn't so many men. Not that many. It was only enough. I suppose one could frame it in those terms. It was enough to satisfy her needs, which I was not.

Beyond that stage, there were pats on the shoulder, rueful and complicit looks, invitations involving pubs, or coming round for dinner to get a change of air, meet the wife and kids.

Jon had sidestepped each offer of hospitality and been punctual, reliable in his working life – which was to say the whole of his life, pretty much – and had given no indications of internal crisis.

What I feel ...

Well, if I don't know at present it doesn't matter ... Except it does feel ... I do feel ... as if I have misplaced something of importance and forgotten what ... And Christ knows, I haven't and can't and mustn't forget anything today ...

It's as if I am ill ... as if my skin were someone else's ... There's a strain ... the obvious strain ... which I hope is not obvious ...

And then, it had been on a Thursday morning – he'd never taken to Thursdays, they weren't as generous as Fridays should be – *today is an exception but could rally* – they weren't as workman-like and peaceable as Wednesdays, Thursdays were bitter ... On a Thursday, he'd discovered he'd been turned into this whole new figure of fun.

The word had been put round. A number of words, to be accurate: Lucy, Sophia ... words such as those words. And I was declared a divorcé now off his leash. One and all have since assumed that I am, in some manner, taking up where Valerie left off.

Not that she has left off. Not that I am presently left on.

Jon was far from the river by now, had passed – surely and inevitably had passed – the usual priggishly well-trimmed Chiswick hedges and lopped trees at a pressing but sustainable speed. Which was to say, he did have to assume he must have done that. He was no longer on his wife's pavement, was able to realise that he'd travelled quite a way ...

I started by passing the brewery – that recollection is clear – Valerie still gets a ration of free beer to make up for the ambient scent of brewing. Not that she's a beer drinker, of course. Unless terribly pressed. I think she sometimes cooked with it.

Then after the brewery there must have been streets ... There were, are streets ... houses ... mature magnolias ... anal-retentive privet and masonry apparently covered with royal icing ...

His head shook, perhaps only internally, as if he'd been dunked in water and was trying to rid himself of some flowing, cloying burden, the way it filled his ears.

Chiswick High Street is a bit of a walk from Val's, it takes ... usually not as long as it seems to have taken ... But I am, at present, in the high street.

But something, lots of somethings, come before that ...

But I can't recall them ...

Which is too many buts again.

But I'm here ... The laws of physics dictate that Chiswick must therefore have existed as I passed through it, but was somehow unaware.

He couldn't quite explain how this had happened, but his head – and the rest of him, all the way down to his feet, his totality – was already in the high street and this change of location had taken place apparently in one blank instant and yet – he examined his watch again, as if it would be helpful and informative, when in fact it was only scary – his journey had also definitely taken far too long. He had significantly misplaced himself.

I ... I should be feeling concerned perhaps ... I'm not that, though. I'm not that, either ...

He flagged a cab, resigned to the fact that the traffic would murder him and only compound his problem, which was lateness, rather than the problem with his interior, which he couldn't identify, and the problems with his exterior which were … They were just …

Their name is legion. Their name is Rebecca and Lucy, Sophia and … Christ.

His heart pattered. 'Tothill Street, please.' And he set his fingers to the cab's door handle almost as if he doubted it would be there.

The driver nodded a consent and Jon climbed in, his limbs more unruly than necessary, right hand clutched around his brief-case as if it were a safe support.

Like gripping the armrests on your seat when your plane hits a storm front – you're holding on to what may drop and kill you. Something to do with our history as apes – we used to be fine if we hung on tight, so we keep on clinging to ease our tensions.

Of course, if the entire tree was ruined and dropping with you, then you'd be better off letting go …

'Actually, sorry … I have to get some trousers.' No one but Jon needed to know that and the back of the driver's head seemed to reflect this truth eloquently. 'That is … I'll … if you can stop when we see somewhere … Damn … no, there won't be anywhere open … Unless … you don't know somewhere …? An early-morning trouser …? Provider …? I mean, that's … thanks. Tothill Street.'

Jon forced his spine, his intentions, to stop craning forward. He could get there for half-past eight – behind schedule, but before nine – and this would pass and would be OK, if imperfect. He preferred to be in before the busyness, but it would be fine. He was a professional of some rank – he could have done better after all these years, but had a not unnoticeable rank and could deserve the confidence of those with whom he dealt. That was understood. He would overcome the trouser issue. It was not unethical to ask a staff member, maybe, to go and purchase … No, it had overtones. Could one tell a female subordinate the length of one's inside leg? Or outside leg for that matter?

In my proper context, I can make decisions. But I'm not in context, I'm in a cab.

Could one ask, then, a male staff member, someone with trouser experience from a male point of view …? No, it wasn't a prudent use of public funds.

Civil servant squanders man hours on fashion-buying jaunts.

Deputy Director experiences … what? Wildlife mishap. Midlife mishap. Late-life mishap. Trouser debacle.

Deputy Director Jonathan Sigurdsson suffers ambulant blackout in Chiswick – cause for concern.

He couldn't work out how he'd ended up in the high street. That was surprising. He didn't like to be anywhere surprising.

It's not to do with women, though.

No, not that.

St Martin's Lane, near Wyndham's Theatre: a purple balloon is carried by light breezes over the heads of pedestrians and then moves safely across the busy road. As it goes it drifts lower, rolling softly over the bonnet of a passing car. It finally drops almost perfectly by the feet of a man in his thirties, quite formally dressed, who is standing at the kerb. He picks up the balloon. He straightens and stands, holding it between both palms. He smiles. He smiles so much.

07:58

JON LEANED HIS cheek flat to the cab window as London stuttered by beyond it. He was halfway to the office, but no further. Matters were conspiring, according to the cab driver, who also found himself unable to comment on whether they'd be lucky, or crawling and stalled for another half an hour, if not longer. Cunning and manful dodging along alleys had resulted only in their being trapped by the apparently psychotic helmsman of a large delivery van in a space within which only bicycles or mice could possibly manoeuvre.

'Smug, aren't they?' the driver remarked.

'I beg your pardon.'

'Times like this they get smug – the cyclists. Not so smug when a lorry hits 'em. I'd make them take a test and earn a licence. For their own good.'

'That's certainly an opinion.' Jon let his eyes close and carefully made himself think of Berlin earlier this year and seeing Rebecca.

Nice. A consolation. Necessary. And important to spend time.

A holiday for them both. One day, the Sunday, he'd bought them a boat tour on the Spree – bundled up for the cold, the quite kindly March cold – and he'd leaned his cheek flat to the barge's chill window as they passed by the Bode Museum, the building fixed in the water, right at the edge of Museum Island like a high round prow, an impossible vessel. Waves patted the stonework at its foot, sneaked and rolled and faltered prettily.

Light in blades on the water, bridges menacing only softly overhead and then a broad European sky. The Fernsehturm spiking up into crisp blue – looks like Sputnik after an accident with a capitalist harpoon, a speared ball, a penetrated curve, although remarkably asexual, unsexual ... then again, stainless steel and concrete aren't notoriously arousing. Never were – not even for Young Pioneers.

I'm not obsessed with sex. Other people are obsessed with my being obsessed with sex.

The Berlin TV Tower – prop for some never-made Bond movie, as fatally dated and inappropriate as everybody's visions for their futures turn out to be. Für Frieden und Sozialismus *– as if either was possible anywhere. Few things say 1960s East Germany like the Fernsehturm, still laden with suggestions of circular ripples emanating from its globe, expanding rings of peaceful and anti-fascist socialist know-how that pushed nobly – with appropriate self-criticism – through the brown-coal-scented air – that particular Braunkohl bitterness – broadcasting the one true faith and a kids' show about the Little Sandman who sent boys and girls off to sleep. Instead of picking them up in Stasi vans and sending them off to other, less pleasant places. Or inviting them to variations on a theme of suicide.*

East's a beast and West is best.

I could be that simple, then. I could. I was clear-minded.

We all like to be clear-minded and simple.

The Terrible Enemy is different now. And the same. It serves the same purpose.

We like to repeat our themes – like good opera and bad television.

But do I now dwell amongst the least beastly?

Where are there not beasts? Encouraged and permitted and condemned beasts ...

I never would have suited the Foreign Office.

And the FO only recruit the cream from the top of the churn. Or the shit from the top of the water. I'm neither I'd hope, although I could be mistaken.

Plus, I sound foreign ... I have an unsuitable name. And that would be one of my repeating themes.

Good opera, bad telly and worse propaganda ... Of which I watched a great deal, along with the Sandman show, when I was a student – over in Berlin and fastidiously observing. I've always been a man for details, can't get enough of them. Not a spy, not a bit of it, not really. An observer. Product of an unsentimental education.

It's the least you can do – watch.

Watch it all tumbling down like the Wall – Berliner Mauer, the Anti-Fascist Protection Rampart. Never a good sign when your wording tries that hard to fight reality, it suggests the beginning of your tumble. Yes, it does. It always does.

But I'd rather watch beauty.

And is that a denial of reality, or an attempt to embrace it? I think I am too tired to know. I hope I am too tired to know.

That day with Becky, trying to be on holiday with Becky, I watched the city moving, everything moving – details, details – as we motored on. Mild to uncomfortable guilt – the usual – that here she is, an adult, and I'd been so often held back in the evenings and still working when she was a child, when it was time to talk, to be, to set my own dear baby safe in her bed. Night night.

I've missed a lot.

School concerts, parents' evenings, the time she fell off a pony and scared herself, the times when we should have talked.

I missed the lot. Almost.

I've missed my life, I think. I think that might be true. If overly emotive as something to mention.

Regrets apart – and I do always pack them for holidays – in Berlin I was having a good day. In terms of weather. An airy afternoon ahead for hands in pockets and brisk walking, arm-in-arming it along Unter den Linden, wandering about in the theme park and high-gloss purchasing opportunity that central Berlin has become. Poor old Mitte – freedom has done some ridiculous things to you.

Which isn't what I was thinking – I was full of how much, how so much I like being arm in arm.

And that weekend she hadn't let me yet.

But on the boat Becky had taken his hand. Their barge had sway-glided on while an instructional narration had attempted to intrude via the tour-guiding headphones that he'd refused to wear. And Jon had closed his eyes against the glare, or to prevent the leakage of his own variation on a theme of stupidity, or to prevent glancing across at his only daughter's disappointment in him.

But then she had taken his hand.

Always the same way, but always more – she is always more.

The stroke of her forefinger at his wrist and then the warm, soft enquiry when her hand closed over his knuckles, when her thumb slipped under to find out the heart of his palm and make it rest.

Beautiful. A lovely shock.

Not that it was remotely unheard of. They took each other's hands quite a lot. She'd just surprised him on that occasion because they'd spent the weekend fighting until that point: Friday evening on the plane was unhappy, their Saturday had been spent bickering in the Old and New Museums, the National Gallery, the Pergamon Museum – they liked their culture rigorous and swift, or at least he did – then there was unease in a restaurant, and this morning: fighting, fighting, sulking, fighting and sulking. His fault.

'You booked it on purpose, Dad.'

'I didn't, Becky.' She was right, though – he'd chosen the Hotel Sylter Hof on purpose. 'I didn't choose it on purpose. The place was recommended and it's nice?' When he was on the back foot, everything emerged as a question. Especially questions. 'Don't you think it's nice? But afterwards I did notice, I checked and I saw that it was ... that there was ... is a history to the place. And I didn't change it to somewhere else. I mean, it's not happening now – it's history.'

Which fundamentally contradicts everything I believe about history and she bloody knew it.

'And it is ... I have to say ... I mean, Rebecca, Berlin has a past ...' *I sounded like an utterly patronising moron.* 'There's no getting away from it without not being in Berlin. And we are in Berlin. So I didn't change it. Because it's nice. As a hotel.'

She always understood when he was lying, when he could do nothing else. 'You can't help it, can you? Being miserable. You have to be.'

Becky didn't add *Mother was right*, but he heard it in any case – the way that only dogs can hear those special whistles when they're called to heel. 'I'm not miserable. I'm interested. I like to keep on being interested.'

'Implying that you think I've stopped learning. I'm not interesting now I'm with Terry?'

'Not at all.' She glanced at him, appraising, while he bleated, 'No.' She always knew.

That was the first of Saturday's spats. And she had a perfectly valid point: it was probably not fair to pick a hotel – albeit a perfectly acceptable hotel with good reviews – primarily because it stood on the site of what had been the Jüdischen Bruderverein until its forced sale in 1938. And a forced sale did leave an atmosphere of a kind – the pestilent kind – and then, because those intoxicated by the use of force develop a taste for irony, nurture a specialist and heavy-handed brand of humour, the building was taken over by the Reichssicherheitshauptamt Department IV B4 – the department responsible for 'Jewish Affairs', which oversaw the seizure of Jews' homes and possessions, the removal of their German citizenship.

If there's a department for you, then you must be a problem. A solution to you must be sought.

So he and his daughter were, yes, sleeping not quite where Adolf Eichmann slept, but where he worked, where he and his administrators, his planners and implementers, his civil servants worked. Becky and Jon had been eating their warm little kaiser rolls – warm little Berlin *Schrippen* – and their hot boiled eggs that morning inside the shadow of a building where human beings in clean and orderly surroundings had proved unable to connect their paperwork with other human beings elsewhere, or with reality, or with pain.

Unable, or unwilling, or uninterested.

Consenting to one hell, so they could avoid another.

Most likely there had been a canteen back then, maybe other warm little Austrian *Kaiserbrötchen*, other *Schrippen, Schwarzbrot*, maybe eggs.

Perhaps not always eggs, perhaps not butter, what with the rationing.

The place had been bombed in the end, like so much of the city. Lord, hadn't it? He and Becky had already explored the sharply modern and forward-looking riverbank development on foot, its immaculate geometries laid out there between the restored Reichstag and the railway station.

The RAF reduced that whole area to a town planner's dream – wall stubs and rubble, only the Swiss Embassy left standing and that by chance. It's still there now. And who can guess what it remembers, where it echoes. Not that Speer hadn't thought he should wipe out the streets himself and start again – build a temple to bloodshed, a monstrous dome as big as a fake mountain and colonnades and boulevards for parading. The things leaders need to help them feel truly like leaders. And anything's possible once you've cleared away inconvenient residences and residents.

Efficient and muscular administration would be required if one were to achieve a plan of such ... A legion of servants would have to serve.

What remained of RSHA Department IV B4 had been torn down in the sixties. And a number of people must have planned and some other people must have given appropriate permissions for and some further people must have built and then maintained and some other people must still be making the customary inspections of what now stood in its place. It was a fairly pleasant hotel in which to house temporary visitors who might be unaware of the site's past and might also not be infected with fatal levels of obliviousness, although no enquiries were made into guests' moral character, there were no formal vetting procedures and acceptance of bookings was based solely on apparent ability to pay.

Jon hadn't slept properly during his Friday night at the Hotel Sylter Hof. This was partly because, stretched out in the dark of an anonymous bed, he could still hear, to a degree, the neat ruffling of terrible file cards and the clean peck of ribbon typewriters, summoning in filthy things. They disturbed. As did the thoughts of easy canteen chatter, boredom, office gossip and faraway corpses.

He had lain and checked – fastidiously – that he was the man he thought, who tried to do his job well and to think well, while keeping his grip on wider historical perspectives. Jon always tried to remember how wrong life could go, because that was in his nature and also because, possibly, he came from the humanities. He'd been a European-history specialist. And hiring graduates from the humanities had once served a purpose for the civil service: it had perhaps intended to gather a workforce used to doing more than bouncing along the surface of a subject – or even personnel not unfamiliar with the concepts underlying humanity. Specialists could be called on when necessary: accountants, mathematicians. That had been the way.

IT providers ... they were specialists, although Christ knew what purpose they specially, actually served – it seemed one simply fed them money and, some while later, they converted it into insecure shit, uninformative shit, unworkable shit and, in general, shit. And economists – why did you need them? Economics was not a humanity. It was not now, as currently practised, a science. It involved little more than submission to a cult. It made him long for maths, the inarguable truth and perfection of maths.

And he'd always hated maths.

The only mathematical form that I can appreciate is music. Which transcends maths – and a person has to be transcendent somewhere ... even me.

Howlin' Wolf wasn't thinking of maths when he played. He just felt it. He could feel.

'Heard the whistle blowin', couldn't see no train. Way down in my heart, I had an achin' pain. How long, how long, baby how long.'

You could see what he felt, know it, share it, taste it.

It was pure in him and strong.

And Howlin' Wolf was also an orderly man and a good boss – in him that was compatible with letting feelings out, with letting himself out. He could burn and sweat and shudder and wail and wail and wail when he needed it for the music. He could keep safe otherwise.

And he could feel the blues. Deep blues.

Which is, naturally, not about safety. But he squared the circle and certainly circled the square.

Jon felt that he was an orderly man and a good boss – his assessments did not undermine this belief.

Perhaps it is the blues I am feeling.

Jon grimaced swiftly. *Like hell. I am all square and no circle, no matter what I try.*

But I'm not a bad man. In my own way. I am not.

This is because I keep asking myself if I'm not. And I listen out for ribbon typewriters in the night. And I do, I do, I do what I can.

Typewriters, as we know, are these days the most secure option. They produce traceable, hard to access, discrete documents. The Russians ordered up thousands straight after Snowden. India followed. Germany. Wise beasts everywhere have shipped them in.

Taptaptap.

Peckpeckpeck.

Me, too. Back at home.

Tocktocktock.

The sound of modern caution.

The sound that I don't hear at work.

Only in my dreams.

Taptaptap.

I am sorry for the hotel, Becky. I am sorry that I have these blues — these uptight white overcomfortable blues … and that's the worst kind, baby.

But the hotel hadn't really been his problem — not his pressing problem — the fight he started with his daughter on the plane had troubled him more. That's what stole his sleep.

It was so plainly imbecilic as a course of action: get your only child alone and immediately criticise her boyfriend. No, not immediately. I mentioned that her shoes were great and that she looked well and wouldn't this be fun and that we didn't often get the chance. Then I started in with the ill-advised comments. Just after we were allowed to unfasten our seatbelts. Idiot.

'You don't like him.'

'I'm not … that's not what I'm saying.'

'No, it's what I'm saying. You're barely civil to him. What about at my birthday party?'

'At your …? I wasn't … Did I do something wrong at your birthday party?'

'You didn't say one word to him.'

This seemed unlikely. Jon scrabbled back to an afternoon of blustery wind and having a headache on Becky's little balcony, feeling sick due to unforeseen events – lots of her friends inside and shouting. It was good that she had so many friends. Otherwise you'd worry. Loud friends. 'I … Didn't I? It was an odd day. I think. Stuff was going on—'

'At the office. That office eats you.'

'I'm nearly done.'

'Nobody stays as long as you have, not any more. You could have retired. You could be resting. You could be doing something you might like.' She'd begun to change the subject and for some reason he hadn't let her, even though stopping her was insane.

'Well, you don't …' A gulp when he swallowed – this was his throat attempting to prevent him from screwing up, yet on he went. 'You don't … It's that when you're with him and with me, when we're the three of us and having a meal, or something of that sort … I notice … It's that …'

'It's that what?'

And he shouldn't ever mention this, except she is his daughter and he does, he does, he does – in his veins and in his breathing and in his blue and buried heart – he does love her and that makes her happiness matter. 'It's that when you're with him you seem not to speak. You stop saying things.'

'Go on.' Her tone a clear warning that he ought to jump out of the plane before doing any such thing.

But on he had stumbled. 'Darling, it's just that I have been around, alive, for a while and seen relationships – I'm not talking about mine, this isn't anything to do with mine – seen what happens when the man does all the talking, when either partner does all the talking. I've seen what that suggests has happened already between two people … what it means when the woman can't get a word in sideways and the guy …' She was condemningly quiet and so he continued to dig his own grave – speaking while she did not and aware of the irony. 'My generation of men, we had a hell of a job getting it right – the feminism thing – but we tried, we absolutely, not all of us, but we backed up what women were doing and we had no maps and that was – I'm not saying we did well – but that generation, men and women, attempted to change how partnerships went, or some of us did, and it wasn't, it wasn't about beautiful and intelligent women with wonderful futures sitting next to blowhard young men and *just listening* as if they haven't a thought in their head—'

'Blowhard.'

'I don't mean it as an insult. It's not an insult. I was a blowhard, too. It's automatic. He's twenty-four. If you're under thirty and have a penis, you're a blowhard. It'll pass. It doesn't make him a bad person.'

'So what does?'

'He isn't … I don't think that he's a …'

But I do think that he is a bad person. I kind of am completely certain that he is a bad person. I am aware that everything about him bespeaks a lack of consideration in many areas and with Rebecca in particular – the more intimate they are, the more he will harm her – and this makes me want to stab him in his balls and then his throat. I want to watch him bleed to death in agony and silence. Sorry. I do, though.

That is the shape of my moral high ground. I would claim it in less time than it takes me to draw this breath as a place of irrevocable mountaintop sacrifice.

'Becky, I don't want him to hurt you.'

'Because I wouldn't be able to tell if he was without you explaining? Because I'm a moron. Because I'm like you.'

Because you're in love with him. You're in love.

Moron is uncalled for.

You love him and he makes love to you and steals tenderness from you unsweetly I bet and by the time the shine's gone off it, please Christ you haven't married him. Or had a baby. It will end badly and I'm trying to spare you that.

Moron is …

His body sinking as it would if the engines had failed them and yet just as it was, where it was, only stirring gently in tranquil flight.

A baby.

OhGodababy.

Go on – ask if she's pregnant – if she's being careful. That's the only mistake you haven't made.

Moron was fair comment.

And she'd spoken very softly, been at the edge of inaudibility as the plane grumbled evenly around them, but he had perfectly heard when she said, 'Not everyone doesn't notice when they're being tortured.'

He'd been nauseous for the remainder of the journey, got through customs and out of Berlin Tegel by the application of grim effort, almost as if his daughter were not there and he were managing alone. They'd checked into the haunted hotel – marble and cream foyer, chandelier, you couldn't complain – in an ache of isolation – at least he had ached – and they'd not said *night night*. No kiss. He hadn't even felt secure in mentioning when they might join each other for breakfast the following morning, as they ground up in the lift to their rooms. So he had to rise early the following day and sit and drink endless tea until she'd appeared and did sit facing him across his littered table, did smile, but only enough to indicate that he wasn't out of trouble yet.

There was mercy, though. Eventually. By the time they were there on the Spree.

'Dad, I have to, ahm, do this for myself, you know?' Her hand making small contrapuntal squeezes at his while she spoke. 'Terry's better to me than you think. You have to believe me about that and try and be civil.' The boat kicking merrily under them for a playful moment, then pressing on.

He'd rushed into the promise, 'I will.' One he couldn't keep. 'I will. I'm sorry. I've been getting anxious.' Inside a pocket of his coat there was the flinch of his phone as it gathered a text, the small noise that warned him of incoming communications. Becky glowered at the interruption and he blurted, 'I'm not answering. I won't. I'll turn it off, even … if you want.'

'Do what you like.' She undoubtedly knew this would always drive Jon to do what she would like. 'Dad, I don't need the lectures about women.'

'No. I realise. It's presumptuous. I simply … The only country in the world where there's a majority of women in a parliament is Rwanda. Rwanda. That's when women get power, real power – if the men are either dead or in prison. Convicted genocidaires. A high percentage.'

'Could we not talk about genocide.'

'Sorry.'

'It's not that I don't get it. And I care. And I made a donation to that place you said I should.'

'Did you?' Turning to look at her and realising that his expression would be this dreadful, fond open smile, this doting that probably seemed absurd both to observers and Rebecca. 'They're good people. The money goes where it should. If you can afford it.'

'I gave them fifty quid – it's not going to render me homeless. Can we just sit and enjoy this and then have lunch. Not on the boat and not in the hotel – somewhere we can relax. I'll buy you lunch.'

'No, I should.'

'You paid for the holiday.'

'And the depressing hotel.'

'And the depressing hotel. Do you understand that I hate it when you're sad and that I would rather you weren't and when you volunteer for it – what am I meant to do?'

'Nothing. You don't … I don't expect …' Having to stare down at this nesting of hands at his knee – hers and his – rather than face her and become … something else she would hate because it would look like sadness, when mostly he got wet-eyed over good fortune rather than injuries and his good fortune was her and that was the issue currently in play. 'Please let's, yes, pick somewhere for lunch and have a nice meal before the plane and then … I really did, I really have, I really have enjoyed this time. I appreciate it.' Nodding and breathing raggedly.

And she'd kissed him underneath his left ear, softly clumsy like a girl and this had torn his last level of restraint and made him sniff. And he was nodding and grinning and uneven in his heart while she'd released his hand – it was cold once she was as gone as gone – and she'd worked her arm in behind him, hugged his waist, and leaned her head snug to his shoulder. Berlin had progressed outside in blinks and smudges and he'd kept nodding and nodding while Rebecca fitted herself to him until they were comfortable.

He'd let his cheek drift over and away from her, find the glass and settle. And his daughter was wonderful and that was something very plain, along with how remarkable it was that two wrong parents had produced the beginnings of such a person, given her enough to build upon.

And his daughter rode a bicycle to work – cycled in London – which was reckless of her, crazy of her, and yet unpreventable.

And any slighting references to cyclists became, therefore, provocations that outstripped his ability to express outrage – an ability which had atrophied into, at most, a show of pursed lips and perhaps firm but appropriately crafted comments, delivered at apposite moments, or kept in reserve, kept in perpetual reserve.

Nonetheless, as he waited for the cab to progress from Chiswick to Westminster, Jon pictured the way he might grin as he stepped from the taxi and dragged the driver out by his lapels, ears, by something available, and punched him, threw him into the path of oncoming traffic without a helmet or relevant licence, because there was no relevant licence, you don't need a licence to be crushed.

As he racked up another three inches towards his workplace, Jonathan Sigurdsson cleared his throat, 'What do you reckon? Much longer?'

'No idea, mate. Not a clue.'

'Ah, well.' Jon rubbed his thumb across the pads of callous he was growing on the fingertips of his left hand – small areas of invulnerability which were helping him learn to play the guitar. Rhythm and blues. He felt that was a style which might forgive his lack of skill. And his love. It was a place to indulge his love with an entity which would neither care nor take advantage.

It's an outlet.

D7 – *that's a troubling chord to form. It makes me all thumbs and no fingers.*

Done D9. I can manage that, get into it quite smoothly. Which was worth it. I think. It's useful. Sounds useful. But putting everything together ... the transitions ... and by myself ... I have a book, but I am by myself ...

I am aware that I'm no good.

But it is an outlet.

The traffic did not move.

His phone started ringing.

09:36

IT WASN'T LOST on Meg – the humour of steering herself about from one hospital to another, her semi-regular trips. Although the Hill wasn't really a hospital and maybe only seemed like one because of her thinking and where she was with her life just at the moment.

Where she was this morning was a genuine hospital: mall-style food court with a range of options, frequent opportunities for hand sanitising, slick floors that seemed to anticipate the spillage of shaming fluids. There was none of the medical smell she still expected from medical buildings: the disinfectant reek that used to set the scene so unmistakably, used to make the whole of yourself clench, even if you were healthy. Nowadays you walked into any of these places and there was only an aroma of cheap coffee and beyond that perhaps the scent of a low-class office block or a cheap hotel. The overall banality of what you were inhaling made your surroundings seem less professional and therefore more frightening. And then maybe there were traces of something nastier that you didn't quite catch, not fully, something to do with used bedding and uncontrolled decay.

And she was frightened – more in her body than her mind, but both communicated, she couldn't prevent it. Back and forth, they whispered, they bled.

As she'd climbed the stairs – the lifts here always seemed unclean and were too obviously big enough to contain trolleys, biers, bodies – her muscles had seemed to soften and become unhelpful.

And then there was the form to sign and the multiple confirmations of her birth-date – as if she might have changed into somebody different from one end of each corridor to the other.

In the waiting room where she finally paused were the usual telly and posters pledging to do nice things very nicely and threatening that any violence would be met with prosecution. One woman was already there with – it was only a guess – her supporting male partner. A second outpatient sat between uniformed and, most likely, less supportive female warders. It took a moment to notice the second woman was handcuffed to the warder at her left.

The warders chatted desultorily. They wore cheap and shapeless black pullovers and trousers which were ill-fitting. They reminded Meg of a trip she made once to a number of foreign countries as a student – excursions involving unwise hopes for excitement. Those in authority – their uniforms, their slack pullovers – had seemed scary and shabby and odd in the same way as these guards. The more notorious the regimes, the more their uniforms gave the impression that power was power and was unmistakable, but rested, somehow, with amateurs who'd get things wrong and make a point of not caring about it when they did. The idea of possibly being oppressed by people who didn't bother to iron their trousers seemed somehow to make the threat of harm more harmful, or just more insulting. It suggested the way that important things worked might not be logical, or civilised.

Handcuffs in a hospital didn't seem civilised.

Fair enough, when it was time for the woman to head off and be examined, Meg watched as the unattached warder hooked out long-distance cuffs – a significant length of heavyish chain there between bracelets. It was tangled and the officer tutted while she sorted it out, shook it like a badly behaved length of washing line.

Meg made a point of meeting the prisoner's eye in some effort at empathy. There was a moment of interchange, but it would have been hard to define what passed.

Solidarity.

You never know how you'll end up. You never know, do you, whether you'll be in civilian clothes and not look like a prisoner, but nevertheless be chained to a stranger who doesn't talk to you and who will soon probably see you half naked and be watchful in case you try to run away. If you're honest, you'll admit how close bad stuff always is to you and even feel it brushing by your cheek.

Half naked and running away. Imagine.

The party was summoned – one prisoner and one prison officer – and twenty minutes dawdled by while those left behind – the other warder included – sat and let the telly explore current property values and opportunities for investment. The clock provided was louder than the TV.

Tick, tick.

Then there was the noise of doors opening and feet. The pair had been released – at least from the examination room – and sat on the chairs placed out in the hall, chatting now. It would, Meg supposed, be odd not to chat after having done what they had done together. She took the back and forth of it as a sign of civilisation. The prisoner spoke softly about unjust accusations and the officer's replies were warm with amusement.

The next woman was called out, leaving her partner (still supportive) to wait behind.

Nice that he came with her.

Or weird that he came with her.

Or suffocating that he came with her.

That patient took twenty minutes, too, and then reappeared, gathered her man, held his hand. What must have happened to her meanwhile had left no visible trace.

The TV now spoke about a charity giving support to deserving cases, cancer cases.

And there was no cause for alarm – neither on screen, nor off.

Nothing beyond the usual causes for alarm.

This was no big deal.

And yet also a big deal, a big unavoidable deal, because Meg's turn was next.

Breathe in faith.

Tick, tick.

Breathe out fear.

Tick, tick.

Doesn't work.

'Hello, Meg. My name's Kate.' That was the nurse. She was cheery, outdoors-looking, Caribbean and clean-handed, neat nails.

What I would say or do if she looked infectious, I can't imagine. And she's not going to touch me, anyway – the gynaecologist will touch me. I am just taking the nurse as a symptom of the regime and being optimistic, that's the thing. I am not feeling powerless.

So. The nurse's name was Kate and Meg's name was Meg.

And Kate's knowing your name and you knowing hers couldn't help but involve you in an admission that you were here and that you had to stay and had to go through it all again. You had to walk round and into the room, as if you were volunteering, as if you weren't a good friend to yourself and wouldn't dodge this all and run away.

But at least you knew Kate's name was Kate.

And thank God she didn't call me Margaret. Or Maggie. Being either of them for the whole of this would do me in, it would really.

'You can hang your coat up on the hook there.' Kate smiling and indicating a hook on the back of the door, as if its availability was great news and it was, indeed, a bit of a departure – you're used to just piling everything on to the chair. That's the chair which comes later. Within the track for the drawable curtain, behind which you undress, there always is a waiting chair.

You don't remove your coat because you want it round you.

I don't want to be here, not today.

There was another chair in here, over by the desk – in the administrative area of the examination room. This chair came first and so Meg sat down on it and answered questions offered by someone who was probably a student doctor and whose name escaped her when he said it – all long and fluttery and spoken in a gentle accent of some kind – unfamiliar. She couldn't quite see the whole of his name badge. She guessed that he was perhaps

Greek, or else hoped he was Greek for unexplained and irrational reasons.

A childhood in sunshine, classical inheritance, the roots of European medicine. That could all be an asset for us both. Cheery thoughts. Wherever he's from I would like him to be cheery. Please.

And he has clean hands and neat nails. Two tidy-handed people looking after me, both of them possibly used to better weather.

Breathe in fear.

No.

Breathe in faith.

No.

No.

No.

He asked about her physical regularity and fitness.

This part left Meg feeling inconsistent and unwell. As usual.

Then it was time for the nurse, for Kate.

The nurses were trained to call you by name and bond with you, because what would happen next was degrading and they didn't want it to upset you. It would upset you, no matter what they said, but they made this effort to improve the theory of your situation. The nurses never asked the questions, not unless they were nurse practitioners.

Or, really, they just asked the questions that weren't important enough to be written down.

Nobody asks the important questions.

And now it was time to stand and walk to the next chair – the one in the corner, behind the curtain.

Kate offered, 'How are you?'

'I'm fine.' Meg's voice came out dry and half-swallowed, resentful. 'Hello.' Which wasn't fair on Kate who was being actively kind.

And this was only Meg's early-morning-and-get-it-over-with kind of check-up which was no cause for alarm. It shouldn't be missed, but needn't make her stressed.

It's hardly any kind of a procedure and I don't have to mind it.

I do, though, I bloody do. I can't forgive it.

Kate ushered Meg over towards the curtain, the chair, still smiling, 'If you undress below the waist and maybe pop your sweater off, too, because you might get hot. And then you wrap one of those sheets around you before you come out.'

Meg proceeded as she was told and did not deviate and this was a relief, this lack of choice. She wanted to smile, as if she was happy two women could get each other through something horrible. There was no mirror so she couldn't tell, but she felt as if her face was mainly looking savage.

The nurse left her and Meg drew the curtain – although why bother when everyone was going to see everything soon? Why was undressing allowed to be delicate when nakedness incurred an immediate audience?

Beyond the dull mauve and green of the drapes, Meg could hear that the specialist had arrived. He told his colleagues that he'd needed to take a call and check on something … the something was inaudible. It was of concern.

Meg bent to remove her shoes, blood distantly roaring in her ears at the unexpected upset. Her body had decided to be nervy and easily unbalanced. This wasn't her fault. Then her jeans went, then her pants – she folded them on to the chair in a small stack, innermost item closest to the top, as if she might get extra marks for being tidy. There was this sensation of childishness in her fingers which, because she was in an adult situation, made her stomach tick and become wary. She slipped off her sweater as instructed, even though she knew what happened next would make her cold for the rest of the day. Every time, it was the same.

Still, around her waist with the strange, unwieldy sheet – so white and yet also a bit second-hand-feeling – and then out from behind the curtain she stepped in stockinged feet. It took four five six steps to reach the final chair, the one with the dressing pad laid out ready across what there was of its seat. Then she set her body to the thing, shelved herself, found the foot rests, the knee rests, dealt with the awkwardness of one size not fitting all.

I would rather not. Today I would rather not. This is not a cause for any drama – but today I would rather not.

And when this is suggested, you loosen the sheet until it's opened and simply resting across your outspread lap as a rug might if you were reading at some fireside in some cosy evening on some other day.

It's good to imagine that.

It hides you from yourself, but no one else.

The gynaecologist appears wordlessly, glove-handed, positions the instrument tray, pats the sheet so it dips, less taut, between your legs and covers you more completely. This seems an automatic gesture. He is either preserving your modesty for another ninety seconds, or would rather not look before he has to, not at you, not there.

Yet surely he's used to it. Staring into women. Bored of it.

I would be glad if he was bored of me as a person, while being interested in me as a condition, my condition.

He will be exploring me as a doctor does and not as a man does. He will not be touching me as a man does.

As a man, he is calm and projects a straightforwardness you can find as pleasing as anything would be for the next few minutes, ten minutes, maybe fifteen or twenty at the most. Tick, tick. And it might as well be him as anyone who asks you those last important questions – all of which are repeats of the previous important questions, in case the student hadn't asked them right – and if you could please move a little further forward and that's excellent and now he is raising your chair and adjusting your legs so that he can see and see and see.

I would rather not.

Through the first insertion – which is undertaken by the student – the nurse stands beside, stands on guard, and sometimes says, 'You all right?' And this is a pathetically necessary question, although your answer won't be written down. There is pain. It is a not manageable pain: it is a racing away and running and lunging pain.

You say, 'I'm all right.' Your voice emerging in a state that proves itself untrue.

And the student comments on the way you are constructed, which is imperfect, and the insertion of the speculum doesn't quite work and has to be done again. The gynaecologist takes over and you realise that you haven't been able to check his hands and so you don't know if they're clean, or nice, or anything. His face is ruddy, beefy, butcherish and so perhaps his hands are also coarse and to do with meat. And this worries you – as if you could stop him now, or say anything about it, even if you did see and see and see something you don't like.

And your eyes are closed, but there is a trickle of ridiculous crying that breaks across your cheek, tilting back into your ears and you remember being a kid and lying in bed and reading a worrying book – some silly book – and having this exact same sensation of prickling, progressing sadness.

You have cried since. But the tears have taken other directions, or you have perhaps not given them your full attention.

The gynaecologist tries to open you again. 'You're very tense.'

The procedure isn't usually this clumsy.

You feel at fault.

'If you could relax.'

You grip the armrests as if you are falling and try to breathe at all.

The crying continues.

Deep.

The gynaecologist attempts a factual distraction. 'It's from the Greek, you know: *kolpos* – vagina – and *skopos* – to look.' He tries again and manages less badly.

'You tend to the left, you know.' This in a voice which is almost fond. Bizarrely fond. 'I am sorry.'

You hear yourself say, 'It's OK.' And it is not OK – and especially not today – and your lying about it makes this worse and there is a sob.

Deep.

He dips his head – balding, that pink tenderness of a balding crown: you should focus on that …

He looks through the eyepieces of the instrument, equipment, device and there is a video screen that is – at the same time – showing you to the student with the quiet eyes and the long name which might be from the Greek also. The student is trying not to be there and he is almost succeeding – he is ashamed for you. He is, nevertheless, staring at the screen and the shades of pink, the glistening which is you, deep in where no one can normally find you.

You don't think it's unreasonable to want to hide.

In faith.

Out fear.

So-hum.

So-hum.

Breathing is supposed to keep you calm, but also it keeps you alive and so you are not calm, because you are alive and being alive is never calm.

And you are going back in your mind, going somewhere too close and too certain and too clear, somewhere in a time which should have vanished but hasn't.

Something catches – something the man is doing to you – and it makes you flinch.

'Sorry.' You are aware that he probably doesn't enjoy causing you pain and are ready to believe this is why his voice sounds irritated when he tells you, 'Nearly done.'

'Mm hm,' you tell him back. 'Mm hm.'

Mm hm is the opposite of so-hum.

And it betrays you, your letting go into grief. Even though nobody asks, not one person asks the most important question, or writes anything down, you know that your crying means they can see how you are, who you are. No one says anything and you don't say anything and still it's plain that you have been damaged and are still damaged and cannot be fixed.

The gynaecologist tells you, 'There is thinning and there are changes: menopausal changes rather than your previous kind. We'll send off the tests, but it looks clear.'

And you hear this as an announcement that your last chance to be a woman has already gone.

But the laser has got rid of the bad change in you, the precancerous change. The tick, tick in your head from the presence of that can now fade ... If you really are clear ... And you're nearly done and this is a simple procedure and you'll walk back out beyond the door and there'll be a little queue of other women waiting their turn – women for whom this will be nothing and shrugged off and only a mildly inconvenient section of an ordinary day. Or a wonderful day. The rest of this twenty-four hours might be amazing for them. They are outside and sitting and waiting with the loudness of the clock and its tick, tick and it might be tapping away the time between them and forthcoming miracles.

And there could be miracles for you also. Up ahead and beyond this now which is now. You try to think this.

But you are fully weeping when he finishes, when it is over.

There is that last shock of withdrawal and then you're done.

You cannot sit up and be reasonable as fast as you would like.

Kate the nurse tells you to take your time. No one else tells you anything.

The gynaecologist has nodded and drifted away, perhaps left, you can't see.

You lean back against the angle of this final chair and you are aware that you are sobbing, that something is still happening to you, even though they have stopped being in at you, being there and fiddling, being all over you and not stopping.

There is an amount of sympathy from Kate and murmurs from the student doctor and you can hear them both and you would rather not.

You do not want to.

This is, this is the stopit, I love you, stopit, I can't, I love you, stop it, you don't love me, you don't love me, you don't, you shouldn't and stopitstopitstopitstopitstopit under my breath where he couldn't find it, in under my breath.

In faith.

Out fear.

He found everything else.

You do not enjoy being hurt.

But you have been hurt.

I can't help it if I don't like this.

It keeps you naked, even after you are fully dressed.

I don't like this.

In some stupid and nasty way, you have stayed naked for a long time.

Stopit.

He isn't here but he might as well be.

You would rather not be reminded. That would be your preference.

Stopit.

There's the shape of him in me.

You would rather not be reminded that you have gone on and lived – not lived wonderfully, but still lived. You've kept on for all of this time, been naked but keeping on, and you must therefore be remarkable.

Stopit.

You are remarkable and therefore you walk – gently walk – back to sit on the chair in the corner – *where bad girls sit at school* – and you draw round the curtain and you wipe your face using the tissue which the nurse pressed into your hand and you are therefore reminded, therefore remarkable, therefore reminded.

Stopit.

I know that the shape of me is bigger than the shape of him.

I do know that.

You are remarkable and reminded and gentle and pressed and a bad girl in a corner and not living wonderfully, but still living, has made you tired.

And you are trying to press your heart into your hand, so as not to be naked – and if you could do that you would be remarkable, but you can't – and the nurse talks to you through the still-drawn curtain, 'All right, Meg?' and she reminds you that you're not.

But you open your eyes and have to answer her, 'Mm hm.'

And you do what you have to, you keep on.

And this feeling – it doesn't go away.

10:57

BY THE RIVER, on the South Bank, a bleak day is punching between angles of concrete, sheering along walls to gather up pressure and speed. Heavy cloud is grinding overhead, fat with blue-black threat, although it may not rain. The February sky and the water are sorely depressing each other. The Thames is high and has turned the colour of wet iron, it is making a muddy and rusty heave up from its estuary, from perhaps a troubled sea.

Pedestrians are sparse and hurried. Some carry umbrellas they'll find impossible to use in the bankside winds. They carry them anyway. There is still ice in the chinks and seams of the pavement. The heat of the year hasn't woken yet.

Running along the line of the kerb, dodging, comes a youngish man, his arms outstretched, long hair flaming upwards darkly. His anorak is loose, broad-sleeved, and catches each gust of wind.

For long moments he is his own sail.

From time to time he leaps.

The air snags away his voice, shreds it, but sometimes it is still possible to hear that he is whooping, laughing.

But something in his tone suggests fury.

What few people there are avoid him.

Jon had masters. This was an unfashionable way to term his position, but he was a servant and that did imply masters, which had further implications. Although, strictly speaking, he served the Queen. He worked, after all, within Her Majesty's Government. So he had a mistress, then.

Always the women.

But he was hired out, made available for the sake of practicality and the functioning of a stable and democratic state. He served his queen by serving the ministers who served her. He was the servant of servants.

A passed-around servant of servants, hand to hand.

His phone twitched. Another text, one of a series. But not Sansom-related.

He replied. Or rather, composed one compact and effective message, thought about it, erased it, paused to make another, adjusted it and then sent his final draft. He had to tuck his briefcase away safely between his feet and stand in a doorway to accomplish this. He sent another text. He frowned.

Jonathan Sigurdsson, the king of felicitous rephrasing.

Well, it is a skill.

He texted again. One letter.

He ignored the shake in both his hands, retrieved his briefcase and then strode out briskly again. It wouldn't do, somehow, to rush, pound along the street, release that flavour of desperation. So he never did, never had in the recent past, except for that one time … Still, being brisk was permissible. It projected a firmness of purpose. Which he did have, both as an individual and as one of his kind – the men who make ideas into realities, who translate words into provisions, schemes, systems, ongoing experiences, lives.

Tell me what to create and I'll make sure somebody creates it. Or at least investigates its creation.

Promise, cross my heart. Just let me loose and I will do it – I know how.

Jon was heading for Tothill Street again after a jaunt involving the purchase of pristine trousers. (Which wouldn't fit that well – he had a longer leg than average and a deep, but narrow waist, in conjunction with what was termed a hollow back.)

Not hollow inside, not exactly, which is a mercy. Although that wouldn't quite be a feature one's tailor would see.

Not true — it's just what any proper tailor sees — it's why he tucks you up in special cloth and tries his best to make you look substantial. He understands that you need help.

Jon was aware that he suffered from areas of sagging — afflicting both the trousers and the man. But at least his bird-struck pair had been dropped in at the dry-cleaner's and he was operational again.

10.58 — I've only been gone half an hour: that's not bad for a round trip to buy temporary corduroy trousers. I am, as we must now all say, customer-facing and therefore unable to spend a day on show with — as previously established — a potentially lascivious inner-thigh stain.

My customers wouldn't like it — they would make assumptions.

Always the women.

Even when it's not.

But these are terrible trousers. Or acceptable, but unsuitable for today. The best of a frightening lot: pink corduroy, gold corduroy, yellow corduroy, powder-blue corduroy, purple ... Christ ... it was either that or even more horrifying options in linen — twenty seconds after you've got inside it, linen's like wearing a week-old handkerchief, you can't win ... The predictably garish choices preferred by gentlemen of influence. Serves me right for trying to shop in Mayfair, where it's hard not to be imprisoned by the Henley Colour Chart: camp faux-schoolboy ensembles, and hopes of faux-hooker girls to totter along on a suitable chap's arm or thereabouts, heels sinking into the turf — the valueless values to which we must aspire ...

Says the man who gets anxious if he has to buy a ready-to-wear shirt.

I opted for navy corduroy in the trousers. It was the only sober choice.

And my new shirt is relatively awful, but at least fresh. Blue overcheck tattersall in brushed cotton. I took so long about the trousers, I'd lost the will to choose anything better. Too short in the arms and too loose in the shoulders, but it doesn't make me seem unreliable or predatory, which many of the others did ...

And flannel is soft.

As if that would matter ... Only it slightly does, somehow.

It really does.

Mild rash on my forearms − nerves − which don't actually enjoy the texture of brushed cotton, but that can't be helped.

He was very breathless, which was not a good sign.

But all is well. More than. Everything is fine. Navy cord. Everything is saveable. I have unused capacity for saving. And that's fine.

He briefly attempted to remember the name of the retired policeman in *Gaslight* − the one who rescued Diana Wynyard from Anton Walbrook's dodgy foreign husband and his tricks with her mind. Jon had always loved the moment when the old copper gave a yell, 'I've saved you!' and slapped his own thigh. That's how Jon remembered it − 'I've saved you!' − someone saying this and being as certain as anything and happy, right through to his boots.

It's all fine. I'm on track.

I'm in navy cord and a suit jacket without the suit trousers − an orphaned jacket which only agrees with the shirt and barely that − town and country having a fight across all of my surfaces, but I'll do. I may almost pass.

And he wasn't too hot. Not flustered.

He did have these small red prickles of something on his skin − despair, unease, panic. If he rolled up his sleeves he suspected he would somehow give himself away and this was an ugliness to add to all his others.

But perhaps they could be forgivable. And at least I only give myself away − I do not offer myself up for sale.

And I was efficacious in the office before disappearing, I didn't just dash in and out inexplicably. The team is happy and they know that I am happy, or have assumed that I'm happy, in as far as they care, or should care, about whether I'm happy or anything else. We are each of us sculling quietly along in purdah. I can be in both navy cord and purdah ... And brushed cotton.

I smell like the inside of the shop. Brisk and powder dry and gentlemanly.

His heart did something not unpleasant in his chest.

I am two kinds of gentlemanly brisk.

I didn't buy a tie to match my ensemble. My original tie is now in my briefcase like a guilty secret and I am going about with an unencumbered and unbuttoned collar.

I can do that.

Every available tie in the shops showed something one's meant to shoot: grouse, pheasants, hares. Although nothing that depicted miniature poachers, burglars, travellers, ravers, Rastas, happily married gay couples, birds of prey.

He consciously changed his case from one hand to the other so that he could break his train of thought.

It's OK.

Nothing is actually irritating me.

I am fine.

Today is fine.

Purdah is fine.

That period of grace within which our masters — but why not call them customers …? If they want me to be customer-facing, then they have to be customers … If they want to be all neo-liberal about it, then they can be customers. It suits them. So. Our customers cannot currently demand and insist quite as they usually do, because they are busy defending themselves against losing power, busy being loudly scared on our behalf, busy having all the usual public emotions, while still other customers do much the same and heartily defend themselves from every natural and unnatural shock that might creep in and thwart them, bar them from righteous success, from finally gaining control of their ambitions. (Or rather giving their ambitions full scope to roam.) Enchanting though all of our possible futures might be, we cannot currently offer our customers anything more than rudimentary assistance. All that remains — sadly, mainly — is to measure up their futures, plan the ways we'd cut our cloth for them, trying to ensure their hollowness won't show. This is impossible, but not something we aren't used to.

Which means these are easy days. Should be.

We prepare ourselves for what This Lot will do if they stay in government. We prepare ourselves for what That Lot will do if it turns out they get to play with the special toys. And then we must ponder The Other Lot. And we must even consider the chances of — angels and ministers of grace defend us — Them. Or even Them. We spend time in consideration of Them.

We explore whatever more and less grotesque conjunctions and alliances may be expected to arise and the minority hopes and promises these might unleash. We treat manifestos as if they were written on thrice-blessed tissues of silk, employing a distillation of truth made visible with an admixture of brave men's tears and each word dusted dry with fine powder derived from noble children's bones. We take each listed vow as binding. As binding as a woman's love. If I might say that. And then we calculate the weight of every promise, we judge the urgency and hidden implications of each dream. Just so we know.

I mean, we do it all nicely for them — so they can rush in on that happy post-election morning and squabble about who gets which room at Number 10: inner sanctum, outer sanctum, sofas or easy chairs, Cabinet Room, White Room, Ground Floor, First Floor ... Which spare bathroom can they convert ...? They'll cobble together a Cabinet within the next forty-eight hours ... remember who's been promised what, which oversqueezed peach has been twice and thrice promised elsewhere ... And one sentence must follow another, put a shine on the Queen's Speech, so that it can be rushed off to hit the goatskin and be all ready for Her Majesty's Voice ... Goatskin ... Written on sodding goatskin — says it all. Or rather the Queen says it all — once it's been presented on bended knee ... Which also, as above ...

How many years did we have a prime minister who could barely turn on a computer and who slightly worried when he did ...? The machines made him feel inadequate — as if God might one day leave him for another source of information.

But we work on.

And when anything goes wrong we won't be surprised. We have our models, we can foresee.

Much good it does us when nobody listens.

Much good it does us when the central collation of data will always seem to come between God and His elected and give rise to the contradiction of core aims and objectives and also create disproportionate expense.

It is disproportionately expensive for our masters to know anything.

It is disproportionately expensive for our masters to be informed and therefore culpable.

It is disproportionately expensive for our masters to be culpable.

And yet they are still, of course, culpable. Forever.

And now they are forever uninformed.

But we continue to inform them, to toil for them, as if it matters what we do.

I continue to toil also.

There's a sort of nobility about that.

There's a sort of stupidity about that.

And after the election some of those I serve will leave and others will arrive – for various reasons, innocent and malign. And I may be ageing, but it seems the new intake is each time not only younger, but more ignorant and happier and more steadfast about its ignorance. They have found it to be their bliss. We must try to inform them – that's our duty – but, because they don't like it, we no longer inform them very much. They insist on attending only to their demons – internal and external – and to their familiar spirits who whisper better spells than ours into their ears, draw flattering conclusions.

Their visitors from the outer world: industry, finance and so forth – Business – these are the sources of all wisdom.

They are the Neighbour's Dogs. A bank, say, lends us someone to talk with, work with, as a new neighbour might ask us to walk, or feed, or please just keep an eye on their dog. You get used to the dog, you know it, you take to it – and then your neighbour has to be your friend. Because of the dog. Whitehall is cluttered with Neighbours' Dogs. They roam the Estate, shit in the hallways and bark.

Makes me tired. Knackered.

Cynical.

No, this isn't cynical. This is so far from being fully cynical, I promise … So far from a full awareness of failings and wrongs.

And change will be instituted – inflicted on all but those who institute it – because there must always be change, especially where it is least needed, least expected, least wanted, because that's where change will catch the eye. My masters like to draw a crowd.

My customers like to yell beside their barrows, squeal in their prams.

Still, it always felt like coming home, this walk to his department. And this had made a kind of sense when he'd been weathering the marital home, avoiding its issues. But with his Chiswick existence now fairly far behind him, he was still overfond of his desk, cherished his mouse pad with its picture of Beauly – a view from Phoineas Hill over Strathglass, to be more accurate. It was a present from Rebecca. With green hills kept too far from him, he could feel most relaxed when he was strolling through the suitable bustle of his professional precincts, or seated and thinking, devoted to his calling, inside a place where he might strive to do good.

He could have that aim.

Becky's wrong – the office doesn't eat me. It has eaten me. I was swallowed up long ago.

But that wasn't so bad, not really, and he was coping with and moderating the challenges of his day. The taxi from Chiswick, defeated by traffic, had dropped him at the far side of Parliament Square and he'd been only negligibly late.

He'd walked the small homecoming distance to his department, thankful that he had an overcoat to wear and hide his shame.

Now my coat is hiding corduroy, brushed cotton and my heart.

A man's got to have a coat.

Anorak or parka with a business suit – it was a rotten combination, made you look like an estate agent or a copper, and yet one saw it all the time. A declaration of defeat.

And over there on the opposite pavement: grey overcoat with a flash black velvet collar, something approaching a blue suit beneath and caramel-coloured shoes, for God's sake. Inexcusable. Pacing about and speaking intently into his phone as if the world depends upon him when it doesn't. I know him. And it does not. He whispers in ears. Thinks he's an intimidating figure, and that he is large in the world, but that isn't so. He'll drop through the fabric of how things truly are and the world will heal over him like water and not a sign will show he ever was.

For some reason the street had looked a bit off, a bit unkiltered to Jon as he'd first rounded its corner – it had seemed weird. It still did. There was something too bright about it, or else too grey – it had badly adjusted colours ... badly adjusted something.

God. I'm in a strange mood – joy with phases of fury. I'm going feral in my dotage. It's the kind of thing one might anticipate if I'd been sent out on secondment to the UN. That place breaks you. It's not old enough, not enough layers and labyrinths and customs to keep you locked away from rogue motivations, to temper your impulses and moral imperatives. But here – here one can be expected to render acceptable counsel, be open to the necessary pressures, lie down beneath them and have faith that all is well.

Parliament has a long-established mind designed to supersede your own. Its brain has grown into suitably baroque coils and undulations, redundant organs and strange structures of unclear purpose. It dominates – like the will of a grand old beast, like a God set apart from God.

When I'd get a new team member, I used to tell them the story of the Eastern monastery where a cat was always tied up outside the hall while the monks meditated. Whenever a cat died, they'd find a replacement and tie it up. Across centuries. One novice asked why. He was told the community once owned a playful cat which had troubled the monks as they tried to worship peacefully and perfect themselves. So the animal was tied up when they needed calm. And what was once practical and necessary had become a habit and then a tradition and then a sacred necessity. Now no one would think of meditating in the absence of a tethered cat. At the end of the story I used to say, 'Beyond the obvious implications – try not to be the cat. Don't let them tie you.' I haven't bothered for a while.

No one would ever send me to the UN ... Why would they? Why would I think of that? Off the leash in New York and looking for blues connections – being ashamed of myself in the corner of no-longer-smoke-filled clubs ... Ridiculous.

He was almost at the office now and could picture the wide and automatically opening doors – two sets, like an airlock. And they'd installed these little gates in the foyer that snapped away and back when you tapped in your key – like gaining access to a provincial railway station.

The decor inside was more reassuring – not luxurious, but of definite quality and in the neutral tones currently preferred by homebuyers and classy landlords. If you paid attention to the standard of your surroundings, you could be reassured that what went on here was of value. Why else have such charming natural wood features and detailing?

Like Portcullis House – never mind the misguided artworks and the flyspecked conference-room ceilings, just look at the wonderful doors. Solid. Generous. Borderline baronial in a modern way. Five hinges apiece, they'd withstand a siege.

His own department looked pretty – it wasn't all bumpy layers of nicotined gloss white, dangerous gas fires and khaki linoleum. There was no sense of continuity with the nobility of the war effort and a nation in its prime, because you no longer continued to drink rusty civil-service tea from the war effort's teal-coloured cups.

Or that could be one theory.

One can hardly complain that one is comfortably appointed.

It had to be admitted that Jon was virtually ambling by this point, his thought dragging him back and tangling around his ankles – his thoughts, or his morning's efforts. As he approached his office, the tribes of the political quarter were out on display. The middle-ranking dads: inelegant, fading, ends of their jacket sleeves compressed by the cheap elastic of their unwise cagoules. They smelt of Badedas and escalating fear. There were only a couple just now, but they'd be out en masse later, collecting the lunches they'd bring back to eat at their desks – a heartening change from the canteen, a breath of air, enough exercise to remind them they don't get enough exercise.

I shouldn't be out of breath, shouldn't be weary. I try my best – a sort of improvised training programme in the flat: weights that I bought online and a mat for what would be termed floor work, I think. Last week Carter told me he was buying a scooter – we're about the same vintage. Our age-related panic emerging in different ways. He will zip around on his scooter, fantasising – one shouldn't say, but even so – about milk bars and seaside violence, or angora sweaters tight over Wonderbras, and cappuccinos in glass cups.

Which is completely unfair – and making sexual assumptions.

He most assuredly just thinks that a scooter would be easier to park and soon he won't have to ferry paperwork about and will be released into the world. More time for the garden, the grandchildren – the bloody scooter.

I am a greater absurdity. I try to bulk up muscle mass to alleviate the worst of the … slackening, wrinkles, crêping at joints and when I bend … how unappetising I am to myself when naked. How appalling for anyone else to have to see and see and see.

And no mantel full of grandchild photographs – we had Rebecca late and lonely and after what we've taught her about marriage one can't really expect …

Becca, please don't have a baby. Not yet. Not with him.

Do have a baby. Children are wonderful. They are beyond description. But not with him.

None of my business and the more I fixate upon them, the more likely my fears all become. This is axiomatic. As I no longer feel it's my professional duty to point out.

A woman passed him, talking quietly as she wandered. She was one of Westminster's distressed, all of whom were impressively, theatrically Other: dirty white hair and long fingernails, coats fastened above further coats, multiple grubby bags in hands and either aimless or passionately darting.

I have a theory that they offer a physical demonstration of each regime's health. At some subconscious level they respond to and act out our ambient political tensions. Visible anxiety in the street people seems to coincide with Budget announcements and emergency debates, votes of confidence. Recess leaves them tranquil, while a major tussle with the Lords provokes twitches and random laughter, an increase in the number of bags and other carried belongings.

That's only anecdotal – someone should prepare a thorough study, it might be worthwhile.

There were tradesmen nipping fags outside the café: work trousers, company logos, ignoble and yet indispensable skills on hand. And here were the tourists, stunned with jet lag and epidemic unfamiliarity, hesitant gaggles of them.

The tour buses park in our street. The drivers rest up here, having released their interested parties to snap photos of Big Ben's mildly leaning tower, or to queue for access to Westminster Abbey – pay your entrance fee to pray in a place of worship which could lend sophistication to your pleas. No guarantees, but who can say? Or I suppose that I don't mean the abbey lends sophistication – it now sells it. The abbey is customer-facing. Healing services available. No cats.

The grasping, the failed, the crazed, the obviously stupid, the sweat-soiled and annoyingly necessary – they were what Westminster saw of the world, of the other ranks bumbling and labouring and muttering through.

'... Immortal, dreaming, hopeless asses ...' That was it. Stephen Crane. I used to read him a lot. '... who surrender their reason to the care of a shining puppet ...' That's what Parliament sees in the average voter. And it sours us. How could it not? These visible voters' failures make Westminster fail them, make Whitehall fail them. We are their fault.

And no children here, nothing beyond adult description, adult use ... This is no place for youth unless it's suited up and toured about in little parties of prematurely middle-aged chaps: being shown the world they can walk into once they've got their degrees in Presumption, Prevarication and Economics.

Here is democracy, children – in its palace, in its unnatural acts.

And he looked at the better-informed faces passing with that Westminster Expression, the Estate Expression: a certain gravitas, a pinch of visible intelligence, alert attention and – above all – irritation. Westminster found all that was not Westminster – and much that was – deeply irritating.

Here it is.

But here I am, also.

The first set of doors opened to gather him inside and away from the street.

Home.

And then the next.

Even more home.

He nodded to Albert on Reception: *nice man, has a daughter going up to St Edmund Hall, of all the colleges to choose.* Her future had both delighted and terrified poor Albert. *He comes all the way from the Ivory Coast to Tooting and now she'll end up at Teddy Hall – which is much further.*

He's right to be scared – he will lose her. She will come back to visit and still be far away.

Like me.

When I arrived off the train from university, I shook my father's hand. I kissed my mother as if I were meeting her for the first time at a party – acting the prematurely middle-aged chap.

In Mother's case that was perhaps not altogether a bad thing. I might well have seen it as a repayment for past favours. Dad didn't deserve what he got, though.

But being in your teens is about being savage and too savage to notice it. If you're lucky.

Or was that whole hand-shaking incident earlier? After I'd gone away to school?

Jon slipped through the snap of the gates.

Probably it was both and on any number of other occasions I'd much rather forget. They wanted me to be successful, Mum and Dad, and success was a country they'd never been to and wouldn't visit. Society Street was a neighbourhood unlikely to harbour it.

At least the whole nonsense didn't put them into debt. I was a scholarship boy, me, and then I could round off my future with a grant. Every Good Boy Deserves Funding. The fenny winds and greens of Cambridge, so much softer and bicycle-paced than the Other Place. And enjoying the Wren chapel – lovely plasterwork – that chapel replacing an earlier model, repurposed as a library – from one sacred pursuit to another – knowledge to knowledge, that making sense, that making of sense …

And one tried to fit in.

One acted, along with all of the others attempting to be successfully socially mobile. The least bad of the alternatives.

Behind a book, on paper – then I was at home.

I was most at home.

The words, the knowing – they could hold me and let me walk all the way from Old Court to New Court and be safe. And Lord, the relief in the God-awful squalor of seventies' student fashion – the concomitant lack of expense.

It was going away to school that did the damage. Years of keeping my secrets from the others, the ones who belonged – not mentioning family holidays taken at Blackpool, Uncle Angus who bred turkeys in his yard and sold dead cars, nothing about my address, my house, the provenance of my Sunday suit, the provenance of my tottering accent, the quiet strain in every possession – and the lying and lying and lying about my life and heart and soul.

Good practice.

Not that I wasn't seen through and found out.

Not that I wasn't in danger of being adopted as a pet, an inverse asset. Particularly at college.

Good practice, all the same ...

I can't complain.

It would be ungrateful.

As Jon had made it to the lift, Findlater joined him – *Oh, really ... Is that absolutely necessary? Why Findlater now?* Any lift containing Findlater felt overfilled. Although he was not a substantial man in any sense.

Amazing that someone so shallow can be so full of shit.

'Jon.' Findlater fired off the kind of smile that chaps of libidinous capacities send each other as a confirmation of shared pursuits. He made one feel smeared with something. 'Jon, how are you? How's the photography?'

'It's ... I'm in two minds.'

That's almost always true.

'Well, if you get any good results, please do ... Art photographs ... Yes? I suppose digital won't give you the quality? And anyway, you'd want to develop them yourself. You are an old-school man, aren't you?' Another contagion-bearing grin.

Old school in the sense of old-fashioned. In the sense of who-knows-what imagined scenarios. Not in the sense of ties. That's ties in the sense of collars and colours and not in the sense of cats. Christ, I have a headache. When did that happen?

Jon had no interest in photography, but had once bought a drying frame for his post-marital flat in his lunch hour. This was intended to help him escape from complete reliance on a laundry service or, worse still, a launderette. It would mean that he could, as his mother would have put it, *rinse out his smalls* and leave them to dry on the frame thereafter. He didn't want the care of his underwear to involve anybody else. He didn't even have a cleaning woman – why should he? He wasn't a messy man, he was self-contained. Findlater had misunderstood the frame, caught sight of it as it lounged in a corner, waiting to be taken out to the Junction and the penitential but convenient one-bedroom hutch where Jon now stored himself in workless moments.

Findlater, ever curious in unconstructive directions, had eyed the frame like a barn owl eyeing a mouse. 'What's that, by the way?'

'Drying frame. Our breakdown should be ready by Thursday at the latest. And if yours is ready then, too, we'll be ahead of the game.'

'Good, good. Drying frame, eh …?' Findlater had manufactured a louche pause. The man was helplessly married, but enjoyed being discontented, liked the idea of straying while lacking the spine required to try it. He had a habit of driving up round Acton for a not good reason.

He told me once that Acton was the place for sighting Japanese schoolgirls. 'You see them in flocks up there. And they look … exactly like Japanese schoolgirls.' The man's expression one of mingled fear and rapture. The Japanese Ministry of Education does run a school in Acton. It does that in order to aid the Japanese community – rather than with any hopes of aiding Findlater's masturbatory fantasies.

And I am sure that Japanese schoolgirls do look exactly like Japanese schoolgirls.

Christ, the poisonous waters that gather in the shallows of the masculine heart.

Do people expect that of me? Do they assume I am always panting inwardly for this or that of women, semi-hard thinking set on a constant alert? Are there confidential evaluations that are certain my primary focus is elsewhere?

If Findlater were genuinely predatory then Jon would have taken pains to do something about him, put a word in – several – called the bloody Met on him, made sure of him, stamped him out, but the man was just pitiable.

It takes one differently pitiable man to know another.

I am, at least, not a lonely husband, hunched in a damp car pretending to read the paper, palms in a sweat, or loitering over authentic bento snacks in some Actonese café, hoping for a glimpse of kilts and knee socks, coy laughter, whatever fantasy sustains him through evenings with Mrs Nancy Findlater and her withered Elizabeth David cuisine, Hampstead Bazaar tunics and boxed sets of The Good Life *and* To the Manor Born.

The lift's upward progress seemed cluttered and languid to an unreasonable degree and Jon reflected again that he should really try the trick of pressing the DOOR OPEN button along with his floor of choice in order to whisk himself aloft without stopping.

Or else you're meant to hold and press DOOR CLOSE. I've heard both offered as short cuts – tiny opportunities to practise selfishness. And the efficacy of the procedure is possibly a myth – like the idea that hitting the button at a pedestrian crossing will make the traffic stop. In a statistically significant number of cases the button is only provided to placate and has no effect. Quite often, your one accessible response to a situation is engineered to simply occupy your time while you wait for what was always going to happen anyway. It's an enforced displacement activity.

Like voting.

Jon realised that he hadn't spoken for a while and that Findlater had become unpalatably expectant.

Just as he had when he saw the drying frame. 'A drying frame …'

'It's a drying frame, yes. I need one. Now that I'm settled in.'

The horror of genuinely leaving a wife had scampered across behind Findlater's expression and was then replaced by a cut-price sort of glee. 'Photography?'

'No.'

'Photography. To dry the prints.'

'Not photography.'

'I wouldn't have thought it of you.'

'I'm not asking you to think it of me. Thinking it of me would be inaccurate.'

But people love to be inaccurate.

Which is why people like me are required. I am pathologically precise and therefore useful. I ought to be seen as useful.

Jon counted off the floors and sent thoughts in the direction of the fellow-travellers who had diluted the awfulness of Findlater: *goodbye, man with water-blemished shoes – goodbye, Palmer, I like you – and goodbye, the woman with the highlighted hair whom I don't know but see around – goodbye, man with two sticks – goodbye, woman who is markedly overweight and limps, perhaps as a result, or else who cannot exercise because of her limp and is therefore overweight, one shouldn't judge, but she is really fat – oh, and goodbye Findlater. Yes, Findlater, go, yes. Just leave me be, OK, with one last grin and …*

'I'll see you then, Jon.'

'Yes, yes. You will. You will.'

Do I echo because I am hollow, or because I am a captive animal under stress and reassured by repetitions?

And then he was alone. Ascending.

So why does this all seem to be a fall?

A girl is balanced on her mother's shoulders, being gently bounced but also held secure. She is laughing. Her father is there also, strolling along, and an older brother who holds their dad's hand. The boy is not of an age to find that burdensome and swings their shared grip contentedly. They are walking west together along the King's Road on a mild autumn day which has been rainy but is now fine and therefore shining, dazzling: azure overhead and sparks underfoot. The family all have the same pleasantly dishevelled corn-coloured hair and a harmonised sense of taste. They look like artist adults of various sizes, people of comfortable wealth but with an access to imagination. Their summer has left them tanned, lean, unified. Everyone's shoes are supportive without being ugly, unusual without being garish. Nothing is home-made but it could be, it could come from a home in the 1930s with lots of leisure and access to quality materials and craft skills.

The daughter on high is wriggling with happiness and twisting round to see where her grandmother – the woman is surely her grandmother – is following along behind: another lanky, graceful, contented shape, corn-and-grey hair swept up in a stylishly untidy bun. The grandmother is talking into a banana, holding it like a telephone receiver of an old-fashioned kind the girl has probably never seen. The woman is nodding and chatting with complete conviction into this piece of fruit and the granddaughter is finding this hilarious, but also not right. It is not accurate in a way which seems to worry her profoundly. There is something impermissible about such a thing taking place. If this can happen, what else could suddenly be real, although this is not real, although it appears to be, although this is not?

The girl giggles and frowns and shakes her head and points waggingly at the phone which is not a phone and her mother reaches up to stroke her, soothe her daughter, who keeps on laughing, frowning, laughing. The daughter also shouts, over and over, 'Make it stop. Make it stop. Make it stop.'

11:30

JON DIDN'T REFLECT upon this – genuinely did not – but he'd obviously made a gross error. Under pressure from several quarters he had acted in a manner that invited unintended consequences – not all of them good – and this was unpardonable, but any regrets at this juncture would simply compound the error with a waste of effort.

He'd screwed up.

He'd done so in an attempt, he supposed, to avoid screwing up.

Bespoke service: letters handwritten.

He'd still been with Valerie when he drafted the first advertisement.

Heartfelt.

That was cut immediately. He'd never wanted to feel a thing, especially not there. He needed to be businesslike and light.

Letters handwritten to female requirements.

Sounded sexist. And overly sexual. He wasn't volunteering himself to write porn. Erotica. That was the term now, wasn't it? For non-pictorial thrills. Ones that don't insist anybody should be employed in a horrible job.

How men can watch that stuff … to look … to forget the performers …
And I wouldn't be a literary performer.

And not erotica, either. I can't write that. That's another horrible job and I do not wish to do it. I couldn't. I can't.

And erotica, they could get that anywhere. Christ knew, Valerie had a whole shelf of the nonsense: her not-quite-joke at his expense. He had read it. Slightly. Strange that she might be stimulated by considering so many things that she would loathe to do in life. Pain and unfairness as agents of arousal.

If that were true, naturally, I'd have been priapic for decades and I haven't and I'm not, I'm not, not this monster of the kind we're meant to be — rape threats as idle chatter and demanding every woman should be nude and pretending we have to be scoundrels as a matter of course. That isn't what a man should be.

I check online, Out There, because it's wise to keep informed and why not take an interest in the generations who may be paying for my palliative care — should the need arise. I listen. I am rendered unhappy by what I see and hear.

Letters handwritten to your requirements.

Which couldn't work, either — he'd known the ad would have to be gender specific. Jon had no interest in writing for men. He'd been selfish in that regard. In all of it, really. His pleasing others was not altruistic, it was a means to an end.

Wanted: Woman to whom a man can be anonymously nice. Opportunity for same unavailable to him in current circumstances.

It was worse than adultery, admitting that you couldn't like or be pleasant to your partner and had forgotten if the problem started with your own distrust or theirs. A betrayer can distrust — a betrayer, of all people, would know they should.

Letters handwritten to the discerning lady's requirements.

That had seemed potentially patronising and archaic — plus, it was likely to attract the type of women he wouldn't warm to and he'd hoped there could be a degree of warmth.

Letters handwritten to the discerning woman's requirements.

Which might seem ridiculous, or amusing, and those who found it amusing and even replied in kind might be the ones he wanted.

If he wasn't, instead, simply swamped by the pompously lovelorn.

So he'd qualified the thing with more information. Factual.

Expressions of affection and respect delivered weekly.

He thought he could manage weekly and it would be good to establish that as a ground rule – no escalation and yet also no dwindling away.

No replies necessary.

This was intended to imply an interaction which was at arm's length.

Although it would also suggest that I'm satisfied with nothing, with throwing myself down a well over and over and hearing my echoes, inside and out.

Terms on application to Corwynn August.

That bit was easy – he was born in August and his middle name was Corwynn. He'd never been that fond of Jonathan, it took too long. And Jon, rather than John, was unavoidably pretentious.

And Jon Sigurdsson … Well, Jesus Christ.

J.C. Sigurdsson having ridiculous echoes in that direction also. Valerie always enjoyed them – even threw a couple of nails at me once, as close as she ever came to DIY: 'Get back up on your cross then, you bastard.'

He'd picked them both up and held them and not said, 'I'd need three.' Another moment to recall that not everyone loves accuracy.

Not everyone loves. Not everyone wants to.

But this would be possible, it could be, this writing thing.

So.

Bespoke service: letters handwritten to the discerning woman's requirements. Expressions of affection and respect delivered weekly. No replies necessary. Terms on application to Corwynn August.

And he'd added the address of a Mayfair PO box he'd rented, the box number given as that of an apartment to add obfuscation.

The whole effort had amounted to thirty-three words in the end, which one wouldn't have thought would be the equivalent of high explosive.

Not that it detonated right away. He had been careful. His first trial ran out across Ohio through classified ads in a number of affiliated papers.

I believed that I was picking Ohio at random: far enough away, English-speaking and yet offering variations … On reflection, I was remembering a bungled Ohio execution – lethal injection. For some reason it stayed in my mind: a Department of Rehabilitation and Correction taking almost half an hour to chemically asphyxiate a man. Thirty minutes of smothering to death.

The name of one's department either outlines your agenda and ethos, or acts as a permanent reproach. My department has changed its name three times since I joined it. This bespeaks unease, if not confusion, if not a prolonged divergence of intentions from reality. This bespeaks an oncoming tumble.

Despite its associations with Distasteful Death, Ohio had still been a reasonable choice for his pilot study. And there was no cause for alarm if – or rather when – correspondents seemed unsuitable. He had replied to them politely, pleading lack of capacity, the emotional requirements of the task, fatigue, and had then ignored any subsequent communications. That worked. That worked 100 per cent of the time.

It all worked.

Because Jon did get replies. There were people – women, he believed they were women – who still wanted delay to be part of a conversation, who wanted to hold paper held by other fingers first, who wanted more than packets of data firing intangibly about in a blizzard of sales pitches and perversions and gossip and cruelty and largely imbecilic surveillance and planned indiscretions.

Jon provided each woman with twelve letters, unique artefacts, unrepeatable – seen only by him and by her. That old-fashioned kind of security. That old-fashioned kind of anonymity.

And it all granted him the baffling realisation that, for some, England was a land expected to supply delicacy and style,

gentlemanly ardour. Crisp sheets and clean cuffs and the movements of cloth against cloth against skin, gracious, permitting,
trusted and fragile.

And old-fashioned. Old school.

*That I specialise so easily in being an anachronism could start making
me feel decrepit.*

Bizarre. It's all bizarre.

I'm not even English. I pass. It's easy to pass.

*But I wrote letters for each stranger and hoped to catch her at the
brink of foreplay so that I could be there, too. Or somewhere like it.
Permanently arrested passion in Zanesville and Akron – and twice in
Columbus and once in South Euclid.*

And much the same for me – in London.

So terribly unwise.

He'd settled on those five women. He'd tried his best.

*And I nearly gave up before I unleashed the whole mess. It took me
three weeks to hammer out the opening attempt. So much stored-away
softness that I thought I'd have on tap, I thought I'd finally be able …
but I wasn't.*

My dear, my dearest, my darling, sweetheart.
Love's words are the weariest, nothing but stale.

*One woman asked me to call her Slim and requested descriptions of
holidays we hadn't taken, and never would, near English landmarks. She
helped, because she wasn't demanding or off colour. She presented herself
as real to me and was generous and therefore made my letters real enough
to work.*

Always the women.

*I invented a trip for us that involved a high tea more perfect than ever
there has been, the scone-laden event taking place within a stone's throw –
not that one should – of Windsor Castle. And then there was stroking her
cheek on the train while mild green acres licked our windows, showed no
blemish – trees straight out of Constable with broad shade and dozing
sheep, a lake not so blue as her eyes.*

*Eye colour is important. They don't have to send a photo – and if
they do I only have their word for it that the picture is of them. They
can be who they like for me, without me. But eye colour, there's something*

true about that, whether they're lying or not. Mentioning it means we can face each other and earnestly enquire.

Which I thought was a good and necessary thing when I began.

I think Woman 4 was elderly. She called herself Nora and posted me a black-and-white baby photo of a small blurred form with a quizzical bonnet thing on its head. And a list of outdated movie stars she'd admired. I enjoyed her. I pretended that her husband had died in the war – or a war – and that she was used to and deserving of a romance she could hold on paper. Love letters to tie with a ribbon and keep. I ignored the signals under her replies that she was married to someone retired and angry who was an ugliness in her house.

Once he'd overcome his stage fright, Jon had sent twelve letters each, in pretty much exactly twelve weeks, to five experimental subjects and nothing untoward had happened.

I was listed under Trades and Services.

The box had filled with long and narrow envelopes of the American type. He had winnowed. He had decided. Then he had written. And then he had checked the box rather keenly for replies, anticipating requests for this, that and no other. And he found them. Along with later modifications required from his content and style, which he did respond to within reason. There were also – he should have guessed – mirroring offers of regard and deliveries of tenderness. It was faking, but beautiful faking – certainly faking on his part – all unburdened by concerns for any future.

Inked out between two countries, he was faking satisfactory affection.

By the end of the eighth or ninth week of that initial trial, there was what he might have termed an easing between his shoulders and across his chest and a growing sensation of useful-ness. And when his hands touched his wife – muzzy under the quilt at late hours – when he touched her … when he touched Valerie, something about him must have changed, because she let him, he was allowed. A kiss or a caress in passing while they used their separate bathroom sinks – were busy with preparing – this didn't become commonplace, but it also didn't inevitably emerge as a failed apology on his part, or the start of an argument.

A sign that you're over, a couple's inability to use the same bathroom sink. One could see it in the plumber's face as he fitted the side-by-sides.

And Valerie would reach for Jon. She would glance at him and pause and be puzzled. 'Have you changed from that dreadful barber?'

'I'm sorry.'

'Don't apologise. But he was a dreadful barber.'

Jon had his hair cut by a slightly secretive gentleman from Guanxian, now resident in Marylebone. The man did a good job and was incredibly cheap. Valerie had liked the idea of Mr Lam's reclusive habits – they ensured his exclusivity – but she had been repelled by his inadequate charges.

'I don't know why you ever used him.' She had been spooning at the marmalade, but had stopped, which was unfortunate because he wanted it. Her undecided hand, the clotted spoon, they put things stickily in limbo.

Jon had adjusted his glasses in the way that one does when one would prefer the world to be more bearable, 'I wasn't … What? I wasn't apologising, I was saying sorry because I didn't hear you.'

'I *said* …' She'd been facing Jon across the breakfast table, setting down her piece of partly marmaladed toast as if it were a token of love from some diseased former suitor. '… I said have you got a new barber?'

'No.'

'You look different.'

'I'm not different.'

'You look it.'

'But I'm not. I haven't even had a haircut from my old barber. I'm the same.'

Valerie had studied him for a moment and then given him his first sight of an expression with which he was now very familiar.

The complicit stare that tells you – I know what you're up to and you haven't got away with it.

Because he *was* different, he did look it and his difference was beginning to show.

It was predictable that he couldn't spend lunch hours and early starts and extra-late finishes being sweet, just sweet, only that, across paper – to Slim and Patty and Nora and Robyn and Clare – without changing.

This feeling … a definite emotion … not specific, but definitely … this constant … ever since …

And there came, of course, a morning when he'd woken and his reach had been already anxious and seeking and then holding tight around his wife – his wife, for Christ's sake – hard against her and a mew of insistence, growl, groan, some kind of noise he was making while his face searched in at her neck and his legs moved under, over, clasping, and there was no objection.

Until he realised.

Until he woke fully.

And could not proceed.

Which was a problem.

Which was – to a perhaps significant degree – the root of her actually leaving him in a permanent way.

Or rather requesting that I leave. The house was hers. Her mother married it.

That moment when he pulled his head back, flinched away and she saw his expression, what would have unfortunately been his honest horror at finding her there in his arms.

So absolutely a problem, yes.

Then – which I didn't think of, or more properly which I ignored as a possibility … Then, it was predictable … Then the letters went on and the feeling also, or feelings, of usefulness, light-heartedness, content.

And these were also months – and then over a year – of increasingly vehement separation from the flesh-and-blood human being to whom he was married and with whom he lived. Then the mess of the divorce and then going off to be in the Junction. There was no absolute need for him to pick the Junction, rather than elsewhere. It had simply seemed correct to pack oneself off to somewhere hard and mortifying …

And then …

He tried an advertisement in Australia, the results of which proved uneventful, stable.

And then …

Another ad was floated out in *The Village Voice*. The *Voice* women seemed too demanding, too degrading, too often demanding to be degraded and to degrade.

And then …

He'd tried the *TLS*. It was closer to home and therefore, Jon hoped, less tiring and more sympathetic. He'd looked – this might really have been quite unlikely – for sympathy from readers of the *Times Literary Supplement*.

And then …

The vetting people found me out.

They uncovered my hobby and my – which could have seemed alarming – dead letter box. I suppose a PO box could be described as a dead letter box, mail drop, something fishy.

But that was all right.

That part of the matter was all right.

I could explain. And they didn't even seem to be overly concerned. There were so many worse things I could have been doing. Having a mildly irregular personal life … well, Val had ensured my – by extension – irregularity for years, in her way.

Silly that she'd been so girlishly keen I should get promoted and yet always managed to undermine my suitability. Not that I didn't produce my own failings – a certain light missing from my eye. Or else an illumination of the wrong sort.

I was only now – as far as vetting could see – being irregular in my own right. And in a mutually consenting and adult manner.

Although money did change hands … leaves a nasty taste at certain levels … but it also reminded those concerned that we were being impersonally personal. I'd charged £120 for a dozen letters. Or $120. In fact, I ended up giving most of them a baker's dozen for the money: that one extra lent the arrangement an atmosphere of generosity. And I donated the money to charity and retained my paperwork in that regard, although questions of paperwork didn't arise. The operation of appropriate oversight had uncovered letters from women, clearly replying to letters from *me – letters of an affectionate nature. I simply agreed that I did, yes, receive letters and that I did, yes, write back to the women, because why not?*

It seemed shameful to have solicited the interaction and so I didn't mention the ads. There were just three women in evidence, I think – they were all that was mentioned. I was dealing with five at that time, but I didn't say – or six, in fact. Or, no – I had escalated to seven. I was sending letters to seven women at that point. Some of them were writing back, three of them were writing back, because why not?

I suppose I approve of the letters having been intercepted. I should be subject to the standard checks and safeguards intended to ensure the suitability and probity of public servants. There should always be oversight and it should be rigorous. I couldn't help but wonder, though, how they did the deed, if they went to the shop after hours and picked the surely inadequate lock on the box – derring-do and balaclavas? Or did they compel its opening by official means – flashy badges and officially severe haircuts? Did they give that usual smug impression of actively defending the realm with every self-important breath? Or did someone insinuating have a gentle but determined word and rifle through my correspondence on an informal basis? It doesn't matter, of course. They could find out what I was doing, because why not?

I was receiving and sending letters to women, because why not?

Lucy, Sophia and so forth: no one involved could suggest why not. No one tried to.

They interviewed me.

Without enthusiasm.

I explained that I was corresponding with women as company. That was all. I said that I was courting. Smirks from over the desk when I used the word.

Courting.

I was not indulging in physical contact. There was no possibility of blurry photos in the Sunday papers, there would be no use of the word 'romps' … More smirks from the desk confirming they'd never have expected romps from me – all I would be capable of was courting, harmless dicklessness.

There was no plan to use the PO box to betray – as they might have put it – my country. Nobody asked, but if they had I would have mentioned that I was in favour of saving my country.

That was pretty much it.

And so I kept on courting.

Because why not.

HR consulted thereafter.

And then Harry (the poisoned) Chalice ambled along and sat on the corner of my desk.

Was I happy? he felt moved to know. Had the divorce been a difficult time? No, really, he wanted to know – had I minimised its ill effects? Had anything conceivably to do with him created a sexual compulsive, a fantasist traitor, freak? (He didn't quite voice the thought, but one could see it passing.) Did I feel a period of leave might be of assistance?

Humiliating, naturally, that our chat should be semi-public. Unpleasant to be thumbed through in one's own – and only real, as it were – home.

I told him that, yes, I was happy, or at least not unhappy. I told him the divorce had been ... had been a divorce. It was simple in the legal and practical sense: I got to leave Val and Val got everything else.

I had been the one to call and tell Becky I was separating from her mother and she said, during one of my pauses, 'I'm glad.' And I had to resist pointing out that my daughter doing this made me feel I had wasted two decades and more of my time.

Not that I'd told Chalice this.

I also didn't raise the fact that Becky being there at the far end of my phone and inadvertently insulting me had nonetheless reassured. Her existence meant not a breath of my marriage hadn't been worthwhile, hadn't led to something lovely. But the combination of elements – slight irritation and tenderness – was confusing and made my voice strained. She had thought for a moment that I was crying. She was mistaken.

Chalice hadn't much to raise about the letters per se.

The official position on courting was that if it didn't bring a department into disrepute, or endanger the defence of the realm and so forth, then my conduct was acceptable, if odd. It would be oppressive and unjust if one's sexual behaviour were constantly under scrutiny – there were guidelines about privacy and inclusion ... Chalice flicked out the little suggestion that, nonetheless, my access to promotion would now cease. But everything about me already meant that I'd stalled. And being stalled makes me happy. Which is taken as a very bad sign, too.

(I'm still great in a crisis. That's agreed, that's axiomatic. I excel — as long as its somebody else's crisis.)

Should my multiple courtships transform into multiple liaisons, then my situation would be reassessed — Chalice said. I would be revisited and supported — as if I were a sickly aunt.

I assured him there would be no multiplicity. It was clearly very easy for him to believe me.

There he was on the corner of my desk, swinging one leg, one Church's loafer, cutting the air back and forth, as if this was fun, relaxing fun. There he was having both a word and fun. He wanted me to see how he was expertly grilling a professionally efficient and yet privately worthless man and enjoying the process immensely.

Or I may have been projecting my own low opinion of myself on to a superior. He did seem to share it, though. His mouth did seem both unavoidably amused and contemptuous. He was being deliberately, lightly, shaming.

Harry Chalice having a word.

Not having a word anywhere quite private enough to be respectful and you know the way with lack of privacy …

The word was good and the word was passed and the word was elaborated upon and the word then roamed about.

So I am known for women.

And I didn't go on leave when it was offered.

What would I do without work?

And I did keep courting.

What would I do without doing what I do? What would I do? This was allowed.

But, yes, since then I have been known for women.

Always the women.

But it's not that.

A man runs out of White Horse Street and turns left into Piccadilly. The day is fine, although autumnal, and his overcoat is open, showing a suit with its jacket also unbuttoned and then a pale shirt, a disordered tie. His coat-tails lash about with his own motion, as does his scarf. He is in his late fifties, perhaps early sixties, and yet there is something much younger in the way he pelts, something of a boy he may never have been. He is dressed appropriately for Mayfair in tailored shades of quiet blue, but his recklessness attracts attention as he rushes and dodges in amongst pedestrians and then across the first two lanes of traffic between him and an entrance to Green Park. As he paces and frets on the central reservation, clearly anxious to proceed, it is possible to see how happy he is, visibly happy: the bunching of one hand in the other and the sweeps of fingers through his hair, the apparent welcoming of excess energy in his limbs. Something about him approaches dancing.

The man, then, wasn't running because he was in flight. It seems more likely that he ran because he had become somehow uncontainable. He may no longer know where to put himself and so he is hurrying into the nowhere which is motion.

His scarf, in a dark, quiet pattern, perhaps silk, lifts with a breeze and he allows this, apparently enjoys this when it touches his face. A couple, perhaps tourists, join him in his uneasy waiting and he stoops to tell them something emphatic. Whatever he says is perhaps not unpleasant, but does elicit a type of shock. The pair flinch very slightly.

At his first opportunity, the man darts into the road, barely clearing a cab, and is over, out of danger, back on the pavement and then sprinting into the park, faster and faster.

The tourists watch him as he goes.

Behind him, the street has settled again and resumed its customary state – the Ritz is still the Ritz, the traffic is still the traffic, the gaudy arcades are still gaudy arcades.

By this time the man is deep in the park, a wild form dashing over the tired October grass. The shape of him seems largely joyful.

12:28

SPANIELS MADE NO sense. They were intended to withstand things: ponds and horrible weather and the noise of guns and battering out across moorland and into undergrowth; and they had to scare bodies into flight and then bring them back dead, gripped in their mouths, and you'd think this would make them insensitive and hardy. Not so. They were soppy. Generations of county types and aristocrats had bred legions of canine neurotics: slaves who were deliriously happy to be slaves, codependents who were delighted just to touch you, pieces of outdoor equipment that forgot every command in jovial frenzies of sensuality, who craved the scent of decomposition and also blankets and affection and – when it was arranged, or they could sneak it – sex and sex and sex.

Gun dogs told you a lot about the ruling classes.

As she walked, Meg was being followed – padpadpadpadpad – by Hector, an older springer spaniel to whom bad things had happened and who was therefore even more than naturally clingy with anyone who was halfway decent to him, averagely gentle. Meg was heading to the ladies' bathroom at her place of work – Gartcosh Farm Home.

Gartcosh Farm Home was nowhere near Gartcosh and it was not in any real way a farm. It was a home to the animals it defended, but did not wish to be. Its aim was to send all its residents back out into safe keeping in the wider world.

Meg was, this morning, choosing to ignore the wider world. She was additionally trying to ignore her body while it resented its earlier loss of dignity.

And I feel his weight on me – that's the thing. After all this time, I can still feel how it was when he was there and it was starting. He can still ruin my breath.

She was glad of Hector, although aware he was being especially attentive because she seemed, to him, injured. He kept reminding her of the chairs in the waiting room and the crying and all that.

I should look on the bright side – at least I wasn't handcuffed to anyone while they rummaged about ...

Telling me that I went to the left ... Why say such a thing? And how far to the left can a person's vagina go? I am not a mine working, I am not a mysterious warren of tunnels, I can't be that fucking tricky to navigate.

There were two ways to cure oncoming depression: to be glad of something worse that wasn't happening and to be amused.

Meg was trying both.

And there was also anger.

Bastard.

Although anger in the absence of its object was unwise, because it turned inward and led you straight back to despair.

Which I do not want. I want Hector. But not quite as constantly as he wants me.

Hector was not allowed into the ladies', because he was a dog and a boy dog at that and therefore it would be weird to have him loitering.

Joke. Sort of. Being amused. Not angry.

More seriously, people sometimes took showers in here – the cyclists took showers, very serious showers – and the work here could be messy and mean all manner of stuff had to be washed off, and nudity could seem inappropriate in the presence of a dog.

I need a shower.

But I have no excuse for taking one – no excuse I'll tell anyone.

I do need to, though, and so I will.

Basically, whatever anyone was doing in the bathroom, they'd want privacy, rather than a spaniel peering at them, or licking the soap off their knees, or being ridiculous in other canine ways which didn't bear thinking about.

Nothing bears thinking about.

My running theme.

I should have it painted on the bathroom mirror, back at home.

I'll open a wrist and do it this evening in fresh blood.

Joke.

Not a very good joke.

Meanwhile, I am actually thinking — because I have to think about something, I can't just be empty-headed — I am considering how enchanted a spaniel's attention can make you feel, especially when he's been denied. Enchanted and guilty. They have the most beautiful-and-tragic-looking selfishness.

And he intended to keep her from harm, from further harm. He knew about harm, did Hector. And his eyes had never left her as she'd swung the door shut across his attention.

He'd also wanted to drink out of the toilets.

Meg had no idea why dogs always loved drinking from toilets — as if they aspired to something more grandiose than a bowl left on the lino.

Plus, they're obsessed by the shit of others.

And Hector particularly can't be in the ladies' because here's Laura, rinsing her sinuses, which would upset any animal with a past. Or anyone who'd like a future free from an image like that.

'It's very healthy.' Water poured from Laura's left nostril in a thin and not entirely clear stream. 'Washes your cilia.'

'I don't have dirty cilia.' Meg stepped rapidly past the unfolding spectacle which she knew was intended as an advertisement as well as a purging of toxins. At least you could suppose Laura wasn't on cocaine.

Or else she likes to rinse the slate clean before she takes it.

Of course, she's not on cocaine. She doesn't 'use' caffeine, even. She brings her own tea bags in a rat-piss-smelling container. She thinks aspirin is a sin.

Then again, she smokes. She lights up and inhales dirty, nasty, addictive, unethical tobacco — not even organic tobacco — and lets its vapours pimp up and down her lungs, calling out new business for tumours.

No use expecting addictions to be sane, naturally.

Meg advanced determinedly towards the emergency-towel cupboard and hooked one out without making any explanation. She then headed for one of the shower stalls as if she did this every day.

'Of course you have dirty cilia.' Laura also belonged to the group of people who wouldn't think to pause a conversation while whoever else was talking pulled a curtain across – *I'm not that fond of curtains today* – and closed themselves up in a shower stall.

'Meg, if you live in London your cilia are besieged by toxins.'

Meg felt besieged, but not by toxins. She had wanted to undress quietly and at her own speed and then to make herself clean, very clean, very fucking clean.

'The levels of some chemicals are illegal in the centre of town. Breathing, Meg. You just shouldn't breathe in some areas. I don't go in any more. I haven't for years.'

She calls people by name. I never do that. That's because I forget names, which is because I don't pay attention when I'm introduced. I intend to do better.

The stall was clean and felt recreational rather than medical. Meg had hung all her clothes up on a line of hooks which had been painted mauve at some time in an effort to make them cheery.

Hooks are useful. I take no offence to hooks. Mauve is not cheery – it is insane, but I take no offence at it.

The water rolled along her limbs and was, quite quickly, warm. It was good, clear, gentle. Even Laura outside with her nostrils couldn't break the moment – the long moment of washing and using the fruit-scented scrub and washing, washing, washing.

'It's like showering, Meg. You cleanse outside the body and cleansing is important inside, too. Meg?'

People appreciate it when you know their name. Unless it creates paranoia and makes them feel they're at a disadvantage. By which I mean, unless they're like me. I'd rather be anonymous.

Meg gave up and answered through the wreaths of steam – steam scented with watermelon soap – that were an indulgence and costing her employer money, but such things are sometimes necessary. 'My cilia are not a big concern.'

There's no point disliking Laura – that will only harm me and leave her completely unscathed. I have to be careful about negativity. So I'm told. I have my instructions and they are detailed and numerous – I am to breathe in faith and breathe out fear and not overthink and … Fuck it – the list's too long. It's too long for today. I don't like today. This has been a rubbish twenty-four hours so far and I would like a new lot.

'And I don't really go into town. I mean I will today, sort of. But I don't need to, not often.' The water tumbled and purled and was a blessing – this must, in fact, feel like successful blessing: comfort and sweetness and clean warmth.

I've been advised that I should be tolerant of others and respect their needs. I also have to be tolerant of myself and respect mine.

'When you start to understand your own body, Meg …'

Meg knew she shouldn't snap at someone, just because she found them ridiculous and they seemed determined to press her, niggle, attract loathing. Meg suspected that Laura wanted to make a reason for some kind of fight, in order to then arrange – it wasn't clear – a workplace mediation, or meditation, or some bonding ceremony: something with levels of manufactured honesty, exposure, unease.

Meg let the shower kiss down, ease out the last of the shiver she'd had in her spine since the hospital. 'My cilia – they don't worry me.' Feeling cold wasn't always about being cold – sometimes it was shock. Meg had never considered that before. Perhaps because she had always been slightly more cold than she ought, always mildly outraged.

I will use her name – she did it to me. There might as well be some type of benefit in being able to actually recall the names of faces I'd like to slap.

'I worry about other things, Laura, but not my cilia.'

'You worry?' This was free-range organic meat and antioxidant drink to Laura. 'Worry's really bad for the skin. And for your immune system. Poor you.' Her tone – a blend of aggression and superiority, concealed by a hippy drawl – suggested Meg shouldn't be out and about without a carer.

And I agree. But only I have the right to think that. She doesn't.

If I pray for her, this will allegedly remove the burden of picturing her being run over by a van. Or the effort of pushing her under the van. But if I do pray for her, I'd only be able to ask God, or the angels, or whoever's supposed to be listening, to grant that Laura ends up – who cares how – underneath a fucking van.

This is uncharitable. And counterproductive, surely.

But then Laura had been overwhelmed by a passionate fit of sneezing. And that had given Meg her chance to finish with the water, dry herself, dress as if her day was starting and had not offended and then emerge. Naturally, she was then subjected to the sight of a chubby, squeezable irrigation bottle being snuggled into Laura's left nostril and compressed until – there was a slight wait, possibly while the solution spurted up and around her brain – more suspicious water flowed forth, this time from Laura's right nostril.

'It's simple as anything,' Laura told her, still irrigating into the sink.

That had to be excessive – it couldn't take ten minutes to sluice one nostril. She had to have waited until Meg had come out and could watch …

People have to wash their hands in that sink.

'I'll think about it.' And Meg had returned – perhaps over-swiftly – to Hector, who had been pacing, huffing and groaning in a small way, out in the corridor. He'd wanted her to hear him and to be sure he was still there.

Hector was currently a handsome creature: long-waisted, primarily white with dots and patches of black. He had a rather narrow white face with black markings – thumbprints and speckles – and black, bewildered ears. Grooming didn't calm Hector's ears. They always made him look as if he'd recently heard dreadful news and still hadn't adjusted.

Hector had perhaps especially taken to Meg – she liked to think so – but he had also made very sure he was generally loved.

He had established himself as a permanent feature in the administration building, where he greeted everyone familiar with a desperate wagging of his lower torso, his tail having been docked almost out of existence by some maniac and therefore giving limited scope for self-expression.

Everyone agreed that Hector's presence settled other dogs as they passed through to the vet, or stepped out for trial visits with prospective owners. And he was pleasant for the humans to have around, either slumped on his rug – he'd seemed to invite the offer of a rug – and breathing gently, or pottering, nudging, leaning, peering up with a confiding, consoling, beseeching expression.

He's a smooth operator is Hector. One of us will get him a credit card before the month is out. Probably me. If my credit rating was better, it would be me.

Although Hector did spend his nights in a pen amongst the other rescue dogs, his profile had been quietly removed from the gallery of candidates available for rehoming.

I wouldn't put it past him to have focused on me, because it's my job to do that kind of thing.

The other dogs continued to be, 'Donny: a placid and patient boy, suitable for a family with young children,' and 'Tosh: he keeps us all laughing with his antics,' or 'Daisy: a loving dog who would need alone time to be introduced slowly at first.' And so on.

The *and so on* involved not only dogs, but cats, rabbits, gerbils, goats, even six battery hens. These were difficult times and difficult times made pets untenable and so GFH – the Gartcosh that wasn't, the farm that wasn't, the home that wasn't; like a riddle or a fairy tale of some kind – was fuller than ever with small lives it had pledged not to destroy (unless they were unhealthy) but which it increasingly feared it could not accommodate.

There's nowhere to put them. Freddy the goat enjoys having more goats around, but they eat like a herd of goats might be expected to and there's one donkey and another on the way – there's not a lot of space for new pens, or new buildings. And even less money to meet more need.

It's like in World War II, people turned out their animals back then as well: they dumped them, or murdered them, and this is that again. There were feral cats in shoals on Clapham Common. Hundreds of thousands of hearts being stopped and trusts broken. This is like that again. It will be like that again.

Meg knew the loss of pets hadn't been the worst thing about the war, but it was still vile in its own way and shouldn't be replaying in peacetime. There shouldn't be families queuing up for clothing handouts and tinned goods, as if they'd been blitzed, and no one should have to abandon or harm any type of domestic friend.

Certain individuals take to it, though – cruelty – and would enjoy it at any time.

Somebody brought in a greyhound last week with both its front legs broken. Ditched by a road, a sandy-coloured greyhound, they'd found it just thrown out like nothing and by a motorway – not a road, somewhere more unsurvivable than a road. The wounds were infected, infested. There was opened bone.

She didn't, despite working in a shelter, have much to do with the animals' welfare, other than indirectly. Meg very rarely met them, rarely saw them when they had no future.

But I was there when they delivered the roadside dog. I saw its face. The eyes. It looked so tired. And it was still trying to do what might please us, but it wasn't managing. It couldn't move as it intended any more.

Meg was an office person. Insulated. When she'd come in to talk about the job and was all nervous at the interview, she'd nonetheless been insistent about that. It was a risk, getting emphatic, but she'd written a script out for what she should say, if and when she met them at GFH, and she'd semi-learned it so she'd have confidence and that meant she could be calm and straight with them. It turned out they quite understood her reasons for wanting to be boxed away. Honesty could backfire, but in this case it hadn't. They liked dented creatures at GFH. They'd hired her. Mr Davis had hired her. She was expected to work for twenty hours a week – which was, conveniently, both all GFH could give her and all that she could take.

They put the greyhound down, which it would have understood as going to sleep. The process would have felt like resting and being offered kindness and the end of pain and wouldn't have troubled it.

I was the one who was troubled: seeing it try to stand. And I was troubled by imagining somebody breaking its legs, either before or after putting it into a car, or into something, putting it into the boot of a car, the back of a Land Rover, a van, crippling it and then chucking it away.

I cannot identify with deciding to break a living creature's legs and so the act sticks in my thinking. I cannot climb down into the mindset of somebody who would do that ... It's a puzzle I return to because it's got no solution. Picking at something with no solution is a nice low-grade kind of self-harm I can really get behind.

But I would rather not have this on-board – not any of this information.

The Emergency Section, the rescue people – I couldn't do their job. I would be constantly furious.

Some of them are. Like David, he does look constantly furious. Except when he's sitting on the grass in one of the exercise gardens and letting the dogs come and make a fuss of him. They can tell he needs affection.

Hector was a master at that: the provision of timely love. He had greeted Meg when she came in, fresh from her hospital appointment – fresh was the wrong word, but it would do – as if she were his best, best girl. He'd nuzzled very delicately at her hands and hadn't bustled. His courtesy had made her unsteady, blurred the room for a moment. And he had kept closer to her than usual ever since, which she wouldn't have thought possible without her wearing him strapped around her in some kind of harness.

He's a proper liability if you're trying to get downstairs – right under your feet every step. Always manages not to trip you, though, which is the way with spaniels. Otherwise there'd be mountains of pensioners killed by them every year. Heaps of dog-owning corpses found on suburban landings and in stately hallways.

But Hector's generally careful – abused animals are. He knows when he's being annoying and he stops then before you get cross. The prospect of a human getting cross makes him craven, sets him sliding along the floor away from anticipated bad stuff to which neither of us should particularly give headspace – bad stuff that happened earlier.

Like in the kids' shows I used to watch – 'Here's one we made earlier.'

Hector the cautious, nervous case.

It's reasonable to be a cautious, nervous case.

And I'm not an idiot. I do know, I have worked it out: people who've been damaged by people go and work with salvaged animals because the animals have also been damaged by people – but they aren't people, so they're OK.

And the animals are also not idiots.

Hector's bright. He's probably brighter than me. He's the lots-of-greats-grandson of that first clever wolf that trotted up out of the dark and lay by some human fire somewhere and looked useful and fond and dependable: a trainable asset.

Smart, but not smart enough to know that we might hurt him.

He does try, though, to be safe. If you're loved, you're safer, so you need to induce love.

Hector is training me to love him.

No need to argue about whether I need a fresh education from a dog with shocked ears and a bathroom fetish. I'm a bankrupt accountant – two words you don't want in the same sentence, or anywhere near your CV. I'm working part-time, because I couldn't cope with full-time, in a home for broken animals … I'm clearly in need of help and advice from any quarter, thanks. I'll have whatever's on offer, thanks.

I should always say thanks, even when I don't mean it, because it is good for me to be grateful.

Borrowing the brains of a dog – that'd be lovely.

And he borrows my scent. If I'm with him all day, he smells of me. He smells of having decided he would like a life with me. He smells of wanting to survive and guessing I could help him do that and I admire his faith and his – patchy, but even so – banishment of fear. I breathe

*this in and out and so does he and I trust him and maybe he does the
same with me.*

And I am grateful for that. Really.

*I am also grateful for the way the trees fit up into the sky and seem
completely right and I am glad of all those other places, fissures in the
world's hardness, where I can find what's right, sweet, harmless.*

There is beauty. I cannot avoid it. In patches. In pieces.

*We convince each other of this – if not the world and I, then Hector
and I are often quietly confident about it.*

*And when I come here in the mornings, he's changed a bit overnight
and started to smell like the kennel and the kennel maids and stuff, which
isn't me. So I reclaim him – he encourages that. He would like me to
decide that our problems would be solved if he just came and stayed at
my house. Most of what he does is trying to make that plain.*

They're clever – the things that want to live with us.

But in my case, the things are probably unwise.

I could be wrong, though. I let Hector decide.

When she wasn't being manipulated by a dog, Meg spent her
days not doing GFH's accounts. She could be near the paperwork,
could even look over the figures sometimes to be helpful, but that
was it. She was officially an absence in the financial-planning sense,
which felt lovely.

Meg was here to keep up with admin, write begging letters
and maintain the GFH website. Admin was just admin, she could
do admin – it required a love of numbing repetition. (Meg loved
repetition. Or else she certainly loved being numb.) And it wasn't
hard to get into web design, learn the basics – coding was supposed
to be fashionable now, all the kids were doing it. It was even less
hard if the one site you had to deal with already existed and was
very simple and you were determined and had a lot of time on
your hands to learn about HTML and CSS, because you had
become – just for an example – unemployable in your original
profession.

Meg wrote most of GFH's rehoming ads and took the display
photos of each inmate. Paul who was tall and from Purley (Tall
Paul from Purley: you wanted to say it all the time in your

head) helped out on the site when he was around. Susan was a gatherer of information and finder of problems. (She was also an ecology bore and fond of discounted designer luggage.) Those two were the other purely administrative staff. (Which was to say, people who never had to deal with fluids or excrement at any time.)

There was Laura, too.

Laura did have to be mentioned. She was based partly in the office – that couldn't be helped – but she knew nothing about computers and wasn't allowed near them, because she fucked things up. Laura knew about empathy and how to screen candidate owners and how to arrange events to generate publicity and funds – at least that's what she claimed and it was fairly true … As Meg knew nothing about empathy and was often able to claim she was electronically busy when consulted about possible events, Laura was kept slightly at bay.

When necessary, Meg spent time updating the information on hard-to-move animals. Recently, the chief exec, Mr Davis – he could be called Peter, GFH wasn't hierarchical – had allowed her to make little films designed to give visitors a better idea of who they might like to have, all new and grateful, about the place and on their furniture and ready for fun and companionship and excursions. This wasn't difficult or expensive and wasn't intended as a fiendish grab for institutional power, as she'd felt others might see it.

Or as my paranoia about others seeing it might see it.

Christ, I'd be better off if I had a stroke, got stabbed in the forehead – then at least some of this crap would shut up, surely. I would leave myself alone.

She wasn't doing badly, though. She could offload her superfluous waves of negativity into the work, try to turn them, make them innocently spin. She couldn't face the animals, was unable to withstand their type of grief, but she was meant to be emotional about her work: it was an advantage. So she harnessed her general outrage and turned it into outrage on their behalf. It was a source of energy. And if she described the candidates – her living responsibilities – with enough energy, then they'd have the best chance of being liberated quickly and fitting their new owners.

The tiny things – hamsters, guinea pigs, gerbils, lizards – they don't give you much to work with unless they're little bastards and it wouldn't do to mention that.

The little bastards are termed sprightly.

I say 'sprightly', rather than 'miniature, violent git who will try your patience'. I say 'cheeky'. 'Vivacious'.

A vivacious gerbil.

As if.

'A little package for a big personality.'

It's justifiable to say that if it will get the thing into the care of kind hands, let them hold it and understand that it's alive and should be able to stay that way, because even unpleasant things deserve to live.

One of my many personal mottoes.

I'm just one great big Christmas cracker, me – stuffed full of mottoes.

And when she worked on the films – the mostly honest and completely well-intentioned films – she'd added some open-source music from a couple of places that were OK with GFH using the material in dog- and cat-loving, not-for-profit ways. She aimed to find a score – *big word for what was just a tune, a couple of minutes of a tune* – a score that set the proper level of not melancholy exactly, but appeal. The filmed sections were appeals.

Here's Laika rolling about on her back and hamming it up and giving a paw in return for a treat, because she's a star and knows a thing or two and how could you refuse her? She's sad without you. You're sad without her.

'Like I'm sad without you.' Meg was at her desk now, having made a cup of powdery instant coffee – that was only her first cup, so she was all right on caffeine consumption – and she was sitting with Hector's breathing leaned tight against her foot, at rest exactly where he liked it. Paul wasn't in today, Laura was off sluicing, Susan was looking into something to do with the wrong kind of hay.

Meg only spoke to Hector when they were alone.

'Because I don't want to seem daft.'

And she moved her foot slightly, pressed his ribs, so that he was aware she was speaking to him and not the telephone. He was perfectly able, anyway, to distinguish between her telephone voice and the one that was for human beings and the one that was for him. Only the last was of any real importance. If she was occupied too long on the phone, especially, he would find it dismaying and ask for attention, come up from under the desk and stare at her starvingly, or set his front paws on her and try to lick her face. (This last was not allowed and would only happen towards the end of a very long call.)

Meg patted her knee and he scuffled up and forward to set his chin there flat, so that his head could be made a fuss of. This was intended to please and calm them both.

And maybe she still smelled of hospital at the moment and of anxiety – traces remaining – and Hector wanted her to smell of him instead.

'It isn't daft to say I'm sad without you. So there. I would say that to anyone who asked me. I am sad without Hector.' Which was, of course, too sentimental a thing to mention in an empty room with a fond dog when you were still slightly hurt in a number of ways and also thinking that you've got the definitive statement now – your menopause is here, pretty much here, and that happens to adult women, it does happen – it's only that you would have wanted to exist as a female person in receipt of tenderness before it did.

It's not that you wanted children.

You never have given children that much thought.

Your biology – tick, tick – had simply been waiting – unreasonably waiting – for a fondness in touch. Your body had an expectation of mercy and it was unfortunate this had not generally been fulfilled.

Meg's hand stroked Hector's warm and silky, spanielly fur – bred for ease of touching, to please. And inside her palm and fingers there was the echo of touching on other occasions – or more likely a hope for her hand after this. She wanted – unreasonably wanted – tick, tick – to be gentle in another setting and another time.

But I'm clumsy.

I might not be able to please anybody.

I might not be able.

She closed her eyes.

I might be rubbish at rubbing a dog's ears.

Hector might not let me know. His breeding is against him and he wouldn't let me know if I was doing something wrong.

She kept on, though, practising the shapes and the intentions of tenderness.

A man stands by the door in the Caterham train as it slows and approaches London Bridge. He is holding the handle of a new bright red pram and putting a slight bounce in it for the entertainment of his child. The pram is of the modern and stylish type, one which is a marked, if expensive, improvement on more traditional models: easier to manoeuvre in crowded shops – or in trains – and raising the baby up high so it can look about. The man is half smiling, bouncing the pram handle, glancing in under the hood, bouncing again.

Another man of similar age – early thirties – stands so that he will be ready when the platform is reached. He says to the recent father, 'It's like a Ferrari.'

'I'm sorry …?'

'It's like a Ferrari. The red.' And the stranger points to the pram with a slight hopefulness, as if it would help him greatly should a pram be able to resemble an iconic and thrilling sports car in a meaningful way.

The father nods, maybe because he would also find this helpful. 'Oh, yes. Like a Ferrari.' He bounces the handle with slightly more vigour. 'It's new.'

'I have one that age.' It's unclear whether the stranger is referring to the pram or the baby.

'My wife's choice.' It's unclear whether the father is referring to the baby or the pram.

The men smile at each other. Their expressions suggest they both feel they have been assaulted in some vast way, but are now redefining their injuries as pleasures.

13:45

MEG WAS WAITING for Laura. When the bloody woman was around, she managed to over-occupy the office, but it was worse when she wasn't there. Laura being in front of you and looking the way Laura looked was horrible, of course: she was all layers of flimsy cloth and too many colours and a bag that would suit a ten-year-old and which matched the shoes that would suit a ten-year-old and had that indelible, burrowing smell of fags and also hemp and perhaps more than one form of hemp. The whole experience could fill a ballroom to its choking point, should you have a ballroom. Meg was glorying in Laura's absence right now, but knew there would be an eventual return to put a kink in every bit of tranquillity generated by the blissful absence.

Eventually, the expectation of Laura became worse than having to sit across the desk from Laura and trying to be happy as she clacked randomly away at her keyboard, or chatted to event-arranging people with floral names, while drinking her herbal infusions and – when off the phone – throwing out strange conversational non-starters.

The trouble with Laura was that beyond being naturally irritating – Meg thought it was fair to say that; maybe not, but she was saying it anyway – beyond being fucking annoying …

Which wasn't fair and wasn't how to approach the problem.

She's not a problem, she's a person.

No, she's both.

The problem was that Laura reminded Meg of being in the support group and the woman who had run it – someone who had also always managed to make Meg feel afflicted. It wasn't Laura's fault that she resembled the group leader, she wasn't even aware that Meg had tried to be in a support group and, frankly, Laura was never going to find that out because she would have loved having the information way too much and it would have unleashed ... Well, it was hard to say: advice about more lunacy Meg ought to try; meditation, or body scrubbing, or t'ai chi. Or else an outbreak of arm patting would ensue, or just ...

All of that stuff gets depressing.

I'm sorted out and getting along just fine. Today was an exception, but not a sign that I'm off the rails. I don't need any more solutions, no more cures. I am in progress. What more can anyone ask? I'm under way.

Being given a solution that didn't work could end up suggesting your problem was permanent, or else that you were the problem. Probably there wasn't any problem. Possibly you were being oppressed by unnecessary cures.

In the support group we were the bloody Sisters of the Unnecessary Cure, perched on our circle of chairs – always chairs – and going nowhere. We had to sit in a circle because that's non-hierarchical. As if I cared. And as if there wasn't a boss. Molly was our Mother Superior, all right – no mistaking that – ruling over the Aung San Suu Kyi Room in a far too faraway and inconvenient community centre to which I will never return. The place smelled of shit, because of the Parent and Toddler Morning Mingle that was in for a three-hour booking just before us. Toddlers can produce a load of shit in three hours. I'd sit there, inhaling kid shit and being stressed after the journey and bloody angry and ...

It was my own fault that I had to travel such a way to get there, though. I didn't want to find anywhere more local, amongst the not massive array of choices. I didn't want to be seen turning up, or discover a neighbour who'd think she had something in common with me and need to talk about it later, come round and hold an autopsy on me in my own front room.

So I went to the Sisters and joined them in their circle of pain – usually seven of them and me – which wasn't enough people to let any air get in amongst us, let it be relaxing, let me coast for a while. Molly would kick off by reading out a piece from a book of special, womanly meditation in her special womanly and extra calm I-love-the-universe-and-it-loves-me voice. Excruciating. I wanted her and the fucking universe to get a fucking room.

Then she'd talk us through one of those going-down-steps-and-into-a-charming-garden bollocksy visualisation scripts, only she had lousy timing about it somehow and so you either felt you were hanging around on your imaginary staircase while waiting for random others to catch up, or else she drove you along your tranquil passageways and over the self-affirming lawns until you began to imagine pursuers, or else your stairs just melted and then you were plunging quick, right down into … I always saw it as a tomb. I didn't get a garden visualised with any success; only a cellar, or a tomb. I mainly conjured up this Gothic arrangement with bones – a sepulchre – and the basic scene got quite ornate. I enjoyed it after a while: rags and costume jewellery scattered on dusty flagstones, footprints of rats. I like rats. You can always trust a rat – intelligent and faithful. Still, I wasn't exactly being invited to explore my fucking happy place – it was more about being forced to hang about in a profoundly disturbing and focused-on-death place. For what my opinion would be worth.

And that's how things ran at the group: listen with Mother, the drop to the tomb and then visions of decomposition and next we had to talk about our week. And pat each other.

Which was the part in particular that got me. Someone would say they'd had a bit of a funny turn in a checkout queue, or a dream, or someone was still with her partner and he'd kicked off and there'd been an incident and it was grisly, just grisly, and turned you clear over inside, but then all that happened whenever a story stopped would be that the speaker got patted. From one side or the other, someone would reach out and pat them on their arm: There, there, dear, we're sorry that you'll keep on being you. It's rotten, but what are the choices …?

You'd never get a pat from my side. None of that from me. I had more respect.

And Molly – who might even have granted her personal pat, if your week had been hellish enough – would pause to raise some tension and suggest to us that she was giving the matter some thought. Then she would say what she always said, which was, 'Thank you.' But with no tone in it. She sounded as if she was sleeping, or computer-generated, or bored witless. 'Thank you.' And next there'd be this bigger pause until someone else could think of a slice of tedium from their previous seven days. Either that, or they'd drag up some honest-to-God nightmare that you didn't want to hear.

Rehearsing the pain until we'd got it perfect. The pain that is sex that is pain that is sex that is pain, but shouldn't be. It should not.

Meg made her third cup of bargain coffee. It didn't taste of much but what it managed was unpleasant. That was OK.

Molly didn't like me. Because I didn't speak. Because I didn't want to. Perhaps also because I didn't pat.

This means, I think, that I am complaining about when they didn't respond to the horrors and also about when they did, which could suggest that I couldn't be pleased by them, no matter what, and that might be true.

They were still wrong, though.

When I got in the room the first day, I knew it would be no use and that if I wasn't careful it would make me feel no use, too, and so I didn't give the pack of them the satisfaction of hearing my specific version of then he did this and then he did that and then on that occasion I did worry I wouldn't make it – I did think that I might die and not mind too much about it – and, by the way, the idea of kissing anyone, trusting anyone, will these days tend to catch me from a number of nasty angles and I think I'll never do it again. I think that I would surely, really die if I genuinely tried, and how can I live like that, exist as this person? *To which there is no answer.*

Molly was unable to answer – not that I asked.

Molly doled out pauses and that regular 'Thank you.' Or if we were really lucky, we'd get a whole 'And how did that make you feel?'

Honestly? That was her best effort? How did being assaulted make us feel? Were we not trying to get away from how it made us feel? Was our problem not that we still very much felt how it made us feel? Was it not fucking obvious how it made us feel?

And fuck that.

I mean, fuck that.

I mean, I am better than any of that.

And my answer in that situation is forever going to be, 'How do you think? How do you actually fucking think it made me feel? How do you think you and your fucking useless autopilot clichés make me feel?'

Meg's spoon stirred away in her tannin-stained communal mug. It served no purpose. Meg didn't take sugar. She didn't take milk. God knew, what there was of the coffee was fully dispersed.

I came there because I wanted to get better.

I wanted to not be about him.

I wanted to be about me.

I wanted to peel away from the sure and certain faith that touching is fatal and kindness an attempt to take by stealth.

And they didn't help.

So I ditched the sessions. After the fourth week, I just didn't go any more. And no one ever called to find out why.

I could have chased up other options, or something. I could have tried again. Oddly enough, telling people who couldn't help me over and over about the thing that they couldn't help on the off chance they might know someone who could and refer me to them didn't really appeal.

I got tired.

She sat at her desk again and knew it was nearly lunchtime and also knew that her lunchtime was happening late today.

It doesn't matter. Molly and the group was three years ago. But if I remember it then it makes me angry. Who wouldn't get angry with rubbish like that? Who wouldn't resent wasting all of a maybe good afternoon with therapy that only ever made you want to hit passers-by when you'd finished your hour, because you couldn't harm anyone relevant – beyond yourself – and nobody there in the group was suitable for stressless punching. They'd be able to identify you later when things went to court.

They made me feel filthy and I don't like that.

I'm not filthy or afflicted.

Meg reached down to scrub at Hector's scalp.

They didn't ask at the hospital this morning. No one even tried to ask me why I was upset.

The dog was out of reach, though – lolled on one side and breathing off and away into a sleep. She forgave him for resting.

I can have a rest, too. I'm a birthday girl – or thereabouts – and I am cultivating gratitude for the areas of my life which are lovely.

I can find them.

I can make them.

Meg had been staring at her computer to no effect for quite a while. A great deal of nothing was getting done.

It's unfair to hate Laura.

She is naturally hateable, but that doesn't mean it's OK.

And she doesn't mean to remind me of Molly or of a minor years-ago disaster that didn't help me with quite different disasters which happened some other years earlier.

It's not her fault.

And I have to work with her.

This means – bugger, bugger, bugger – that I have to be grateful for Laura. In some way. As a remedy for the poison that she brings.

Really?

Yeah. Apparently.

But really?

Yeah.

It's what I'm told can be effective and effective is what I'm after. Effective is what I'm all about.

Said the woman who hasn't answered a single email, or done anything of note in almost an hour.

A message had come in from the Stewart family who would like to meet Roddy, a bull terrier with an especially lugubrious and mildly sidelong expression and a tested fondness for children, but not cats. And don't interrupt him when he's eating.

She replied with an appointment that might suit them.

I can be grateful. I can be grateful that Laura doesn't work here on Wednesdays and I do.

But this is a Friday.

And Friday is a day when she does work here and I do, too.

But I can be grateful that I am putting in a foreshortened day.

But Friday is when I glance – slip, slide – over the accounts, just to help out and save them paying for too many hours of the genuine, real, not-struck-off accountant.

No one has a problem with this. Although I can no longer call myself an accountant, I can still have a look at the week's figures in an accounting type of way. The fact that I royally screwed up my life doesn't mean I have forgotten how to add. For example. And managing the no money I now have to live on is sharpening every skill I ever had, believe me. If you want a manager for a railway, or to run a hospital, ask someone who's living on £750 a month, give or take. Ask someone who's living on less – they'll work you financial fucking miracles. They do it every day. They're either ingenious, or done for – no half measures.

Nobody hires a bankrupt accountant – not in that capacity. I would not want them to. Them trying to would fry my brain. But there is always bookkeeping to look at and I can. If I don't have to, I can enjoy it. If the weight of it is absent and I have no authority. I make suggestions. I am here and capable of suggesting.

And it's not Laura's fault that glancing at figures while she's in the room makes me feel as if she's disapproving and has rumbled me as fifteen kinds of fraud. This is purely a reflection of my own belief that I am not capable of anything beyond screwing up again.

And again.

And infecting all I touch with failure.

Which is why the mental discipline and gratitude are important.

I can be grateful that she hasn't enquired into my past with any vehemence.

I can be grateful that she doesn't insist on being friends with me. I can be grateful that she doesn't pat me.

I am glad of these things.

So she makes me glad.

And I can assume that her mother is fond of her and so I could be – not that I'm old enough to be her mother. Not without some junior-school incident having occurred and it didn't and that's another cause for gratitude.

She's plainly damaged and so am I – we have that in common. Huzzah.

And I can try to like her shoes.

Except that her shoes are vegan creations made out of vegetable leather and bloody tofu. I'm exaggerating. Vegetable leather for sure, though.

I can pray for her.

No, I can't pray for her.

I truly can't.

I can't incorporate the God thing. I'd love to, but it's not a good fit.

Meg's mobile rang in the midst of this demonstration of spiritual ill-health.

No. I'm healthy. That's the point – I am attempting to be spiritual, in my own way, and Laura is attempting to be – I think – spiritual in her own way and I suspect that I loathe her, if I'm honest, because she reminds me of me. That's been known as a pattern of behaviour. It's practically standard practice where I live.

Meg picked up her mobile, took the call, which was from Carole who was asking how the hospital visit went, because Meg had forgotten to phone and tell her.

I wanted to blast away the morning, forget it and go on as if it never was, which is the kind of thing that leads to areas of forgetting – you get these islands of blankness. I used to be mainly made of islands ... But still there's the ocean, the sound of the ocean goes on.

And Laura is trying to manage her own things and, OK, using quite pitiful methods in my opinion, but me too, probably me too. I have to rely on semi-strangers calling me up and harrying me with sympathy, or whatever, and remedies of that type. Laura ought to have my sympathy, empathy, decency.

But then I never get too much decency from me, so why should she?

'Hello.'

And Meg listened to Carole insisting on being given information about Meg's well-being in the way that concerned people did. This was a demonstration of friendship and should be appreciated. 'It was fine ... I'm sorry that I didn't call ...' Carole was functional and a woman and about Meg's age and in an apparently happy relationship – she was therefore someone who felt like several types of threat when you were with her in person. Even though she was nice. She was extremely nice. She was bothering to phone and that was nice.

I apologise to her five or six times in every conversation. Unless it's a long conversation, in which case it'll be more: including the apology for taking too much of her time.

'No … yes … well … but I am sorry, and anyway, and, yeah …' It wasn't quite possible to tell the truth yet. It wasn't quite safe. 'I didn't like it but it was fine and they'll tell me the results in a while – it was ten weeks last time, but it might end up more … and then I'll know.'

There were days when you would hold on to almost any voice and there were days when you wanted a particular one, because you imagined that would be the best to help you keep a grip.

'They seemed happy, though. Nobody had a look round in there and screamed and, I don't know, said they had to cut everything out by this evening. I think visually that it seemed clear, but they'll check the cells to be certain … They're always evasive. That's why you'd pay to go private – because then they'd tell you things. If only to get more of your money. My GP doesn't speak any more except for *Hello* and *What do you think is the matter?* When if I knew that I wouldn't be there, would I? And then all he does is write down what I think the matter is – so really I get to be the doctor and the doctor gets to be my secretary and where that gets both of us is beyond me … Sure, sure, I want them to be certain …'

I want the National Health Service to be certain and to be my pal, like it was when I was a kid and Dr Miller would come to the house if I was really poorly and he'd take time and he was like an uncle, or a friend.

And the point of talking to a friend is that you tell them what's on your mind instead of the first rush, the pelt of irrelevant pieces you throw out to keep things at bay.

'It's waiting, which I don't like. It's that I know I have to wait again and I have been waiting a while with the whole process and the thing today … it was uncomfortable at the time and … you know, I got a bit upset. A bit.' Hector, aware she was getting rattled, had stood and snuggled over to her and was letting her scratch at the crown of his head. He huffed softly, approving. 'No, don't send me a hug.'

Carole was known to offer verbal hugs when no others were available and it was easily foreseen that she would pitch in with the usual if she was phoning after you'd been prodded at, invaded and also threatened – a bit threatened – with cancer, which was to say pre-cancer, which was to say pre-death, which was to say pretty much where we all had to operate every day, but that didn't imply we'd be happy to be interfered with and then forced to remember different threats.

And nobody did ask, nobody bloody asked, nobody this morning fucking asked at any point why I was so upset. Nobody.

I can't shake the fact of that.

I wouldn't have told them, but I'd like them to have tried.

Carole is asking, of course.

Fuck her.

'It's … Thanks … Thanks, Carole …' She was merciless, Carole: she said precisely what would make you cry. Meg didn't think she really needed more weeping today. 'It's … It was only that, you know …' Carole didn't know, because Meg hadn't told her the details. Carole was guessing, but guessing well and Meg could have done without it – the guessing wandered about in her interior, once released, and she didn't like that. Not today. 'It's fine, though. Thanks …' Meg swallowed and made a bad job of it, just as Laura returned.

Fuck.

I need to swear less.

Fuck.

At some point.

'I have to go, though, but thanks and I'll see you tonight, I think. When the other stuff is, or when I've, that's …' Her sentences came out like broken biscuits, spoiled. 'You know …' Meg was tired. 'Yes. We can talk then.'

Meg hung up and was aware that she might appear dishevelled. She pre-emptively announced, 'Laura, I'm fine. I'm fine. I was … telling somebody about that greyhound.' Which sounded a complete lie.

'Oh, yes.' Laura leaned in and – *pat* – shitting, bollocksing, bastarding – *pat* – did the patting thing. 'That was so terrible. I was really upset for ages.'

'Yeah.'

Mustn't be sour about it. Laura's never seen me cry before – I'm not completely weeping, I'm only wet-eyed – and I'm under control now, I am. This is the aftermath of my morning and won't ever happen again. This isn't unmanageable.

She cares about the animals, which makes her a good person and I should cut her some slack. The caring is something of quality that we can have in common and that I can respect in both of us.

Don't ask me if I'm OK, please don't.

She will, though. She's going to, here it comes.

'Are you all right now? Is there something I can do? I have some tea with St John's wort and passion flower.'

Of course you do, naturally you do – you're as big a nailed-together-badly and faking-it monster as I am. Which means you are a victim of some kind and therefore a member of my club, except that I don't want to be a member any more and am getting by fairly well with moving on and cultivating therapeutic rage, cleansing rage, rinsing rage, the energy that's in rage – I like it – and meanwhile you get on with Laura doing whatever the hell works for Laura and let's go with that – you keep over there with that – let's go with our survival strategies for this after-noon and being separate but equal.

'You look tired, Meg. Valerian tea would cure that – you could take a couple of bags for tonight and get a real rest.'

Which is more attention than anyone normal would pay to a woman who treats you curtly at best and can't honestly be hiding how big a fool she thinks you are.

So that's sad. Laura isn't well, or whole, and she is reaching out to me, keeps doing it over and over, and that's the sort of detail I should take on-board and it's an ice-breaker, it is.

When breaking the ice is mentioned it's given a positive meaning. But I find that when the ice breaks I am walking on it and then I drop and I am in bad waters and out of my depth.

That isn't positive.

'What's a wort?' *Shit, that sounded sarcastic. I didn't even know I was going to ask and now I sound like a bitch.*

'Pardon?' Laura was already adopting a wounded air because now she expected an outright refusal, or else a smart-arsed comment.

I use humour to deflect something or other, or everything, or I don't know what, in tense situations. That's what they say – sounds complicated. I use jokes to get away from stuff when I can't run – that's also what I'm told. But who wouldn't? Or maybe I'm running and handcuffed to the humour and it's happy to gallop along, escaping alongside me – it's seen me undressed and unhappy – we're chums.

But not this time.

Meg cleared her throat and concentrated on sounding soft. She pretended, to be honest, that she was talking to one of the dogs. 'No, I was wondering, that's all … Only … I can find out later. I bet worts are good. Saints are good … were good, that would be the point of saints. So a saint's wort … Laura …'

Shut up and just say you'll have the tea.

'I'll have some of that tea, thanks. Yes. Get the stress levels down. And tell me about the sinus thing, again. Could you? Is that for stress, too?'

She'll run with that for ages and I needn't listen. I can just think of what will be my appropriate visualisation, my happiness: no bones, no rags, no dusty engagement rings that have outlived their engagements.

I will meet you.

Not lunch. Last week he said he couldn't do lunch. And not this evening – earlier. At three. Not quite teatime. I'll be hungry before then, maybe. I'll have a biscuit. An unbroken biscuit.

The nerves will mean I'm not hungry.

I should even head off fairly soon, or I'll be late. London – it takes forever to get anywhere …

Having not quite tea far away from here will save the day.

This will save my day.

I will meet you.

There's no harm in enjoying the thought of that.

148

14:38

JON COULDN'T QUITE place himself. He seemed both unwilling and unable to even try. Had he been asked to express a preference, he would have been anxious to recall yesterday's evening in an absolute sense, to wake it and wind it back and put it on again, snug. He would also have requested a dispensation from being inside today's early afternoon. This exact present moment, he would have liked to keep strictly at bay.

Although it was, in a way, his job to make plans, none of his current arrangements were absolutely working. Others' intentions were clambering and sliding and butting in.

Force majeure.

Is what I never am, as it turns out.

I am here and now and would very much rather not be, which is an impossible goal and is therefore causing me distress.

And yet it could be argued – perhaps not by me, preferably not by me – that facilitating government decision-making should – in essence – involve one's impossible goals only ever harming strangers. One should be safe.

I wouldn't say that.

The call from Chalice – *one never does want a call from Chalice* – had come through at ten-past noon. There wasn't an option to simply ignore him and pretend that one had lost one's phone, or else the use of both arms, for a brief but vital period.

He cultivates this unconvincing air of menace, but has enough genuine power to make it real in any case. It's like being threatened by a panto-mime actor and having to like it. I would rather be bullied by someone with a personality. Although I have no particular regard for my preferences, really, in the matter.

Chalice had asked, in one of his consciously forceful murmurs – *which don't work well on the phone, I often want to laugh … a cross between a cut-price hood and the daughter's dodgy boyfriend* – he had asked if Jon wouldn't mind just dropping round to see him and the Minister for Somewhere Outwith Jon's Responsibility. In the Minister's office. No rush. They'd be free for him at any time. Any time now. It wasn't far for Jon to come. Just round the corner. They wanted to chat about Steven Milner. Jon knew Steven Milner, didn't he?

Just round the corner. And one has to go. One has to.

'No, I don't think I do.'

'We thought you did.'

Inside the office, Chalice had been poised by the Minister's shoulder, somehow consciously arranged. It was possible to imagine that he'd intended to appear both physically and mentally agile, alert – this whispering demon balanced at the ear of power. The effect was more disconcerting than authoritative – as if a middle-aged man had appeared wearing leather trousers and was waiting for a positive comment on his choice, hips cocked.

Chalice and the Minister for Something Else (lateish reshuffle appointment, never expected to do anything) had looked up as Jon peeled open the nicely heavy door, offering him the same just-interrupted-but-oh-hello expression once so popular with children's television entertainers.

That was back in the balmy days when no one would ever assume what had been interrupted was wholly loathsome.

And here and now – *unavoidable* – their attention was nipping at him, weaselling in to throttle away the shreds and rags left of a kind idea, the thought of a garden, the possibility of dipping one's hand into water nicely and breathing soft.

They strap one's breath, this pair. If one is already out of sorts, they can steal the air right out from you. The Minister's handshake – it's like being handed a warm shit in a sock. Only on a good day can one resist their extraordinary unpleasantness.

Why Chalice with this minister? They make no sense as any kind of pair. I only like things that make sense.

This is not a good day.

My mental condition …

And while I am thinking of shifty double acts because I can't help it … My mother had this pair of cats – sisters – one minute they'd be licking each other with this bizarre intensity and the next they'd be giving me the clear impression that lesbian incest was none of my bloody business … There is a certain flavour of feline intimacy between our Mr Chalice and this minister who is not my minister and whom I do not wish to see.

I wish, I wish hard as a boy before Christmas, to be in yesterday and a garden and not in a room over which the ballot box looms hotly, this leading me to wonder why Milner would be an issue … Why bother with him now? He'll be the next incumbent's trouble, surely? The Minister for Shake-and-Bake Opinions won't still be here, whoever wins.

And what can I do about it? What should I be expected to do about Milner? Why would they think I would want to touch Milner? Nobody wants to touch Milner. I can't brief, not anyone, not now and not Milner and not for a minister not my own. Not even for my own …

This dragged along, fast and abrasive, like a cutting kite string through Jon's mind while Chalice gestured towards two chairs, set emptily ready. He then promenaded round to sit side-saddle on his own and beckoned to Jon, playing the chummy colleague, the man so securely in charge he might break out into rolled sleeves and banter at any time. 'We thought you got to know Milner slightly after that Heidelberg debacle.' Chalice being gracefully puzzled by Jon's non-compliance, waiting until he agreed, at the very least, to sit. 'The Hun-in-the-sun faux pas.' And he kept on for more agreement yet. Gentle, was Chalice. Gentle like the onset of some disease.

'Leipzig.'

'Really? We thought it was Heidelberg.'

Good cloth in his jacket, but I hate the London cut. He's paid too much for a name on his inside pocket and the pinch-waisted silhouette of a man with breasts. Those cavalry-officer preferences will out. None of it indicates good judgement. Next thing, he'll be wearing the label on his sleeve.

Chalice fixed his gaze somewhere on the wall behind Jon's left ear and semi-whispered, 'We need someone who *slightly* knows him. Uncontaminated by prior exposure and yet familiar.'

Jon's left ear tingled in response.

The Minister continued to not speak, remaining authoritatively distant and – who could doubt it? – mulling thoughts which would be all the more impressive for going unexpressed.

Jon rubbed at his uneasy ear, coaxing it not to be foolish.

And if you don't speak during a meeting then you can honestly confirm – if you absolutely have to later on, when asked by some passed-over backbencher, lop-eared audience member on Question Time*, or so forth – that you didn't in any meaningful sense attend the meeting, never said a word. Just offered your shit-in-a-sock.*

'I was preoccupied with family matters of a pressing nature and cannot recall the conversation, in which I took no part.'

So whatever this is about, it's toxic. And yet he's here ...

Jon offered, neutrally, 'Milner the journalist.'

'That's right.' Chalice began to sound as if he were addressing an especially dim select committee. 'Milner the journalist.'

'I'm not a friend of his, to be precise, even slightly, no.' Jon nodding and realising the Mancunian Candidate, or most probably Sansom, had reached out to hand him some Frodo or other. *And I will be expected to carry my dreadful burden out across the wilderness and then Do Something Terminal About It.*

'Although I would like to help ...' The Minister's desk – Jon was apparently staring at the desk now, *so I must be downcast for some reason* – the desk seemed to be of a very fine quality.

Better than in my department.

The surface has an almost mystical sheen.

And is giving me a headache.

There is an outside possibility that I am mistaken, simply experiencing a new symptom of extreme stress, but we'll set that aside.

When I say 'we' I mean 'I', but I am in need of company and so present myself as if I am a group. I have noticed that others, when under pressure, will often replace 'I' with 'you' – as if they would rather outsource their concerns to random third parties. I think it's a good sign that I don't try to do that. Team player, Sigurdsson. Even if I'm a team of one.

My forearms are itching.

Jon briefly immersed himself in an opaque pause of the sort a man becomes used to producing when his wife is often indiscreet and he must therefore often be diplomatic. He imagined he could feel the heat of his phone, right there in his jacket's inside pocket – he tried to think of it as a lifeline instead of a burden. There was a letter in there, too. Its presence made the phone and the office and Chalice and the bovine Minister seem a shade less oppressive. And even very minor improvements were always appreciated.

While Jon concentrated on yesterday and being with flower beds and secure, he said, 'Milner was in Heidelberg, yes, that's right. We had a drink then. One drink. If I remember correctly.'

'And I'm sure you do. It wouldn't be like you not to remember correctly, Jon. Unless you're tired. Are you very tired? Been overdoing it?'

With my many women? No, I haven't. No, I have not.

'Come in straight from country pursuits?' Chalice eyeing the corduroy trousers with a lack of benevolence.

'No, not that. I was simply … And something happened to my …' Jon breathing for a moment to find his place. 'Milner is foreign stories, isn't he? Not domestic. Trots off to hellholes and pretends he's an aggressive, drunken Brit – asks immoderate questions of one and all, while they are incautiously embarrassed for him, or making fun. Manages terribly well in that regard. Then when he's come round in the morning he notes down what he's heard, or transcribes it, or whatever, and releases it as and when. One of the type who go about shouting from the moral high ground, or at least a good set of steps.'

Chalice produced a smile that would not occur in nature. 'That's the very Milner. You do remember. And his alcoholic camouflage has indeed become, shall we say, ingrained. People don't seem to trust him on overseas assignments any more. He says things the wrong way for ITN ... and his BBC boats were burned long ago ...' He paused to be happy about himself. 'The BBC – they burn more boats than the Byzantine navy ... Another man might move into books, but Milner seems to be unlucky in that regard, too. There's the discourtesy while in his cups, that's a factor – even publishing won't quite put up with it. He seems to call people a *cunt* rather often ... Which one can't, can one? One can't use the word *cunt*. A *cunt* out of context ...' Chalice gave Jon what was presumably space to speak with some kind of expert insight about the sexual organs of women and why they shouldn't be used as terms of abuse, or pronounced by a Jermyn Street sociopath as if they were inevitably infectious.

Pity poor Mrs Chalice. Poor Amanda who never looks that far from screaming.

'I never use the word myself.'

'Secret of your success ...?'

And now I do have to allow him eye contact. Plain and uncontrived – because, sod him, I was already good at this while he was still being taught how to take a salute and order Scousers to shovel horse shit and pinprick the silver polish from the fiddly bits on their breastplates. I've been doing this for a long lifetime and I'm still good at it. Even in my current circumstances. Even in corduroy bloody trousers which are, of course, unsuitable – I do know that. 'I really wouldn't know, Harry.' *I can call him Harry. It's not inappropriate. Especially when he's trying to be East End.* 'I've never used the word.' *All he knows about the East End would be from some heavily curated jaunt into Hoxton, or suchlike.* 'As a word – even in frank moments of intimacy.'

As if I, dear God, get to have any.

'It seems irretrievably degraded, Harry, in a manner that offends. To call someone a cunt ...'

And I would, I would, I would and that someone would be you, Captain Harry.

'... is something I would find doubly offensive, given that it implies there is something essentially wrong about part of a woman's body.'

Designer ale and hand-crafted pie and mash with no one who might alarm him by being too discordant, or calling his bluff – that's Harry's style. A little excursion for a change of air. Like Valerie and her flamingos. But with less screwing.

'I could be mistaken, of course, Harry.'

'That's an opinion, Jon. That's an opinion. And I'm sure it has brought you success.' And Chalice actually, really, truly did lick his lips. 'So.' Before making a meal of getting down to business: the frown, the even more upright posture, the carefully illustrative hands. This was him in operational mode. 'Jon, we'd like you to have a little chat with Milner. Catch him after lunch. We think he's recoiled and gone off-piste, having nowhere else to go, and is trawling on the bottom in home waters. It isn't a matter of party preference – we have good reason to believe that he is feral in all directions. Hardly democratic in the run-up to an election – one drunk deciding the issue by throwing his shit about like an ape.'

An honest ape with honest shit and an honest handshake ...

'Jon, there are too many random elements in play this time. As you know.'

'Is this urgent?' Jon's phone chirruped and ticked – like a mechanical manifestation of guilt.

'We can't have the monkeys running the fucking zoo.'

I like monkeys.

'Is this, though, an urgent matter?'

'Not in the least. But we thought, as you do slightly know him and he is, apparently and understandably, somewhat friendless ... While your workload is low, Jon ... Not that you chaps ever get much rest, we know ... You are appreciated. It's not that we don't appreciate you. There is creative tension at certain levels, but you are ... appreciated.' Chalice halted to let another waxworks smile overtake him. 'We thought that you might establish a common ground.'

'Like a shared allotment.' Jon letting this be audible, because he couldn't prevent it. 'We can talk about our onions together.'

Chalice pressed on regardless – he was the type. They were all that type. Whether they'd trotted about with the Chilly Rivers, or sold yoghurt before they got here, being relentless was seen as a virtue. How else can one shove a recalcitrant civil service up the relevant hill and off the cliff.

And somebody always has to tumble first, go over and soften the landing for everyone else.

I spend my life waving at samphire gatherers as I plummet. I will not mention this.

Chalice would get the Lear *reference, but it would escape the Minister for Nothing to Do With Me. 'The weight of this sad time we must obey. Speak what we feel, not what we ought to say.' I can't go and see it onstage any more – not theatre at all.*

Those inaudible telly actors, they get me down. Which isn't the problem – the words are the problem – the art is the problem – the constant dig of reproaches in most of what I can remember on any subject are the problem …

Chalice had ground on while Jon was rather significantly absent but nodding and fortunately just aware enough to catch: 'I told Milner you could join him for an informal chat. At that little pub – the place opposite you. Around three.'

'Three today?'

'Three today, yes. I know you skipped lunch. That's a dreadful habit.' Chalice made this sound sticky. 'But you can make up for it now. While you're free.'

'But it's not urgent.'

'Absolutely not.'

'I'll … ah …' *Yesterday evening I was sitting by a square pool, herbs planted at its edge and blue tiles holding the water, evening-blue tiles – sepulchral – shining beneath the reflections, the wet ghosts of light, and there was tea in glasses and I liked that. I barely had a headache, almost none. Not a trace of nausea.* 'Then I'll … of course….Three o'clock.'

'We said you were available then.'

Chalice spired his fingertips as Machiavelli surely never did. 'Less bustling than at lunchtime. It does get busy in there over lunch. The boisterous young and freshly-down favour it, I believe. Our new blood. I hear the fish and chips are impressive – for a bar meal.' Chalice gave a tiny, incongruous sigh, business concluded, and stood. 'That's set then.' He didn't extend a hand for shaking. 'Splendid. And if you can tell us how things went.'

Jon focused on standing successfully. 'You want me to tell you today.'

'Preferably today. If you wouldn't mind terribly.'

'Of course.'

'I see him and I tell you about him.'

'Of course.'

And Jon was vividly aware of his feet and socks and the clutter of his shoes and shoelaces, the weight and complications attending each step as he removed himself, nodding to the Minister – *Good to see you, happy to help* – closed the door over, took the corridor at more speed than was necessary just to be out and out and away.

It had seemed not unreasonable thereafter to go astray.

A woman is crying on platform three at Canada Water Station. The sound she makes is unusual: extremely loud, something between a howl and keening, an odd lowing. Although the area is busy with commuters because it is lunchtime, the strange quality of the woman's grief, perhaps grief, means that she is being ignored. Around her there is a bubble of cleared space.

She is middle-aged and plump, Caucasian, dressed in a sweater and thin waterproof jacket, along with loose trousers which would be suitable for jogging or sports in general, although she does not look especially athletic. The woman wears white trainers which are very clean and make her feet appear to be bigger than they actually are. She has a lanyard around her neck which supports a quite large, square tag – identification of some sort, again with a vaguely sporting flavour.

The woman continues to lament, or perhaps lament. Her uncomfortable presence announces itself repeatedly and produces shuffles amongst the crowds, turned heads and an ambient shame, embarrassment, unease.

Two younger figures advance on the woman, one from the head and one from the foot of the platform – they are also women. The shorter of them is white, has a practical air and may have a physically involving job. She wears functional slacks and an anorak, has gingerish hair tied back in a loose knot. The taller woman has an angular, lean face, something Ethiopian about it. She is the more stylish of the two, suited and turned out in a way that would fit a high-end office. She has gone to some trouble with her bag and shoes, they agree with each other nicely.

The pair hesitate when they reach the insulating area, the space cleared around the woman by dismay, the space created by this yowling person. They study her face, which is not so much wildly anguished as puzzled, locked, afraid. It does not correspond with her cries, has not flushed with effort, but only stayed greyish and indoors-looking. They both ask, 'What's wrong?'

The woman continues to yowl and waves the tag at the end of her lanyard as if it is magical. Then she explains, in a voice made tired by its exertions, that she is autistic. Between words, there are sobs. She is aware that she is autistic. That is a truth. She understands that she will not die from having missed her train. That is a truth. She is standing beside a map of the different lines that pass through Canada Water and cannot keep her eyes from it for long, as if it may at any time indicate the removal of a necessary track, a dreadful blank. That will not happen and is an untrue truth. She knows that she can catch another train which will take her where she wants to go. That is a truth. She will not be trapped here for ever. That will not happen and is an untrue truth. Nevertheless, she is lost. That is a truth and an untrue truth. Inside her, truths and untruths are tearing something with nerve endings into pieces and producing terror. She has been howling in protest and for assistance and for the return of her proper train, the one she needs. She needs the passage of time to become different.

The pair talk to her in very low voices, consistently calming: as if they may have children, or like being friends to their friends, or are familiar with anxiety and weakness. It seems they actively enjoy being helpful. They tell the woman the next train that she can catch.

But that train will not be her train.

Still, it will be all right.

But it's not the correct train.

But it will take her home.

The pair are persistent as the woman's fear.

The woman stops sobbing and is stilled, only fretful and slightly irritated by reality as it fails her.

The pair move aside as they undertake to wait for the woman's train. They talk to each other softly. They say, 'Leaving her like that … Everyone ignoring her like that …'

'Disgusting …'

'My mother didn't raise me like that.'

They stay with the woman until her unsatisfactory but necessary train arrives. They make sure that she is on-board it and that she can manage from hereon and will be OK. And then they change their minds and they climb on-board with her and are taken away.

Rather than return to Tothill Street, Jon struck out for Birdcage Walk. He dodged along, slightly stooped, as if live fire were passing overhead. He then cut across and into St James's Park, where it seemed he could straighten.

And he wanted to tread on grass, to be in the care of trees and green shades. And he needed to – *dear God* – really did need to – *sod it* – just where no one would exactly see – *urgently* – he really did need to vomit.

I should be glad this is simply nausea, rather than nausea plus migraine. The migraines make everything seem to be viewed through a translucent screen of Clarice Cliff. And I hate Clarice Cliff – dreadful pottery. Additionally, she looked like a stubby man in half-hearted drag.

Not that it isn't sexist of me to criticise her on those grounds – I wouldn't comment on a male ceramicist in that manner.

I'm not aware, actually, that I know what a single male ceramicist has looked like.

Oh, dear Christing fuck …

This was more a process of heaving and spitting than actual vomiting: maudlin convulsions going on in his torso and producing a watery mouth and sourness and no real improvement.

He was clammy and shaky after.

I need a shower. Must find a moment to nip down and use the office showers. I need to be made more palatable. Or palatable at all.

But he supposed he'd feel cooler and steadier, might walk it off – whatever it might be – here beyond the breadth of plane trees and in amongst the blown daffodils and vacant deckchairs, here with the scent of spring turf being good and clean and animal and rising forcefully, having a strength about it that he could aim to borrow in some manner.

Here and heading for the gloomy pelicans – out of their proper place and ugly, sad-faced.

No, but the overall effect of the park is cheerful: the stridency of blossom, tumults of leaves – visibly, almost visibly, unfurling and so bright. They possess that fiery green.

And if the green is still green, still comes back after winter, after trampling … If it endures …

Jon considered hiring a deckchair, but guessed sitting on one might make him feel too folded over. He was trying to avoid that position.

Besides, I can't stay long — I'd be a mug to pay the hire fee for ten minutes.

Being a mug the required thing these days, of course. Britain is the land of mug punters, fat smokers, of underqualified assistance arriving too late in unmarked vans — full and undisclosed charges payable in advance.

He could have tried moving further up and finding a bench, but he decided — swiftly and borderline violently, an unwarranted savagery in his need — not to do that.

Instead, he sat down in his new corduroys — *well, they are supposed to be for country use* — then he scooped out his phone, turned it off. The thing throbbed once in farewell before surrendering, going dark. Jon returned it to his jacket and parcelled himself up cross-legged on the ground, peered into the grass. He picked out the tiny paths between stems, the miniature clearings and overhung passages. Ant Land geographies.

I would do this for hours when I was a kid. The scale of it cheered me — something smaller than I was — and I was small, small, small. And the overall ambience was restorative.

It comes to you, kisses you, the livingness of things — you have only to wait for it.

That was why he loved the garden so much, the inexplicable garden in Bishopsgate.

'Nobody lives in Bishopsgate.'

'I do.'

For the whole of yesterday's sweet evening Jon had been sitting with Rowan Carmichael in the garden. In Bishopsgate. Where no one was supposed to live.

'I know you do, Rowan. That's what I said, I told them. I said *Rowan Carmichael lives in Bishopsgate, that's why I go there in order to visit him at his home — because that's where his home is located ...* It's address fascism all the time, these days. You can't utter an unwelcome postcode and not be forever cast out. And you're central. No one could say you're not central ...'

Rowan had smiled at him, indicating tranquil disapproval, which was an established speciality with Rowan.

His disapproval is why I seek him out, of course, and would like him to be my friend, would hope that he is my friend. I am aware that Rowan is aware that I am lacking; I therefore find him to be wise and therefore need him.

Who wouldn't want to have the company of a wise and remarkable man? Also a kind man.

And Bishopsgate really is central and has excellent transport links – it simply seems unlikely, that's all. Not blighted. Not like the Junction. Where I choose to be.

Nobody lives in the Junction.

Lots of people who are nobody as far as anybody who is anybody might be concerned … They live in the Junction. They live in the parts of Camberwell which are without beauty in the monochrome air that blew on along Coldharbour Lane and across John Major's childhood, that made him too Brixton and not quite right. Wise in spasms, but not quite right.

I fit in there.

To a degree.

Rowan had pottered to the kitchen to fetch biscuits: shop-bought and not great. He pottered now – had an old man's walk – and Jon could not remember when that had started to be the case.

I am aware – I think I am aware – that Rowan is fond of me despite my failings and that he is therefore remarkable. He has my affection and respect, both of which are useless. Poor Rowan – a man to whom time has happened.

Gets us all in the end – if we're lucky.

It did still surprise Jon when somebody close to him thought he was being foolish, but did not allow this to rouse their contempt: their shouting, threats, or – for that matter – the withdrawal of their sexual favours, should the somebody be his wife.

Ex-wife.

Somehow, she's always my wife, though – more now than before.

And they always were favours, the marital encounters involving sex: never gifts to exchange, agreements, negotiations to achieve a greater good – never the things I have guessed about in letters I have sent by agreement to strangers, never what I have tried to describe until it can become perfected.

In love, I could currently pass the theory paper with most colours flying.

'It isn't the postcodes that matter per se, Jon – they are associated with reality.' Rowan had emerged with, yes, unpleasant biscuits. Ones neither of them would eat. 'London doesn't like reality. We believe we can transcend its limitations.' He set the plate down at the pool's brink.

'Reality is discourteous and should be avoided.'

Rowan nodded, deadpan. 'The trouble with reality is, it never knows when to stop .,.' Then what was an old joke between them became too tender, injured. 'It's intrusive.' Rowan's voice altering, softening, so they'd had to leave a little silence to settle each other and not become glum.

Rowan sipped his sage tea from its comfortable glass, as if he were in a more civilised age, and – being honest – Jon knew that Rowan consistently did still manage to create a more civilised age around himself. For six feet – give or take – in any direction from Rowan Carmichael, you were occupying space in something quite like the Renaissance.

But with Rowan it's all Dante and da Vinci. No Borgias, no wars, no assassinations and Niccolò's empty-souled prince only cited as a warning, not an inspiration. So not really the Renaissance in any comprehensive sense. You always had a downside with the Renaissance: Boccaccio wasn't Boccaccio with no plague. How else would he trap all of his characters outside Florence, force them to tell enough tales to fill a book? The Decameron wouldn't have worked if they'd simply learned their travel route was now impassable due to routine maintenance, withdrawal of maintenance, withdrawal of exorbitantly rented rolling stock, the intrusion of crack-addicted and incomprehensible youths, bent on destruction … It wouldn't have worked as a story if they'd just gone off and thrown yet another party to pass their time. Not enough threat there to press them for truths and details, nothing beyond the perils of a dodgy barbecue, fire pit, hand-crafted alfresco pizza oven.

Which are anachronistic elements to introduce – Rowan always very harsh about that kind of thing. Precision – he insists on it.

Which is unforgivably anachronistic of him.

And I feel sometimes – very often – we are besieged, myself and Rowan. We cosset ourselves, peer out at what's left of our golden hillside palazzo and watch the plague drift in, seed itself. Underneath the phoney scares and distractions there's plenty of threat – it's running with the big and clever London rats, all over the Junction. It just hasn't washed up quite as high as Bishopsgate. Not really – it's only on its way.

I've never been to Florence ... never lifted my eye to the hills surrounding, the purply pink Tuscan hills ... never picked out a villa, a palazzo, where the prosperous, the eloquent, the fragile might once have had themselves bolted away to exempt themselves from death.

Just another bloody conference venue, really.

Like Davos, but with intelligence and lyricism and no obligation to pretend one might wish to help others.

Jon had watched Rowan's smile as it began to seem troubled again and, this time, enquiring.

Bolter – they used to call me that. Easier to say than Sigurdsson.

Bolter in the sense of my being a boy who runs.

Like I run from the idea of human beings succumbing slowly under provocations to fail, the tick of waiting, of daily signing, of the fictitious letters that do not summon them for customer interviews and therefore produce their Failure to Attend. There are a thousand unnatural shocks one can use to produce Closure of Claim.

I also do not imagine Decision-Makers and Cluster Managers sitting in off-the-peg splendour and hitting their Individual Performance Targets.

This is all part of the righteous hudud we must not question, or contemplate, the claim of our particular godless god.

In the lower lands, beneath the hillside, being trapped is the rule and not the exception – you and your stories are held there.

And it doesn't matter.

This would all be terrible if it mattered. So it has to be what doesn't matter.

Rowan was a friend – could most likely and truly be named as a friend: first a jarringly young and clever tutor and then a friend – and friends noticed if you seemed off colour and were indulging in fits of interior petulance and snapping instead of explanations.

My behaviour is unfair. I was always peaceful here. Rowan never shouted, never bullied.

So I should trust him, should have trusted him earlier and ought to at this point.

I should communicate.

But that isn't what one does, is it? If one intends to be correctly English, one must brood on one's list of catastrophes and be disgruntled. One must enjoy complaining, but only to those without power to assist, without the will. And, happily, no one does have the power, or the will to assist. Impotent rage: that's the state to aim for. One must practise self-harm through the forging and hoarding of fears and through the embrace of unfeasible injuries, hotly anticipated. Present wounds should fester and be ignored. This is expected of others as surely as one must expect it of oneself.

The thing was, Jon didn't want to communicate. He did just need to hide inside petty complaining – so he simply talked and talked, made noises about nothing: 'I know – it's property values ... Weren't we ...? Were we? If we referred back to the postcode unreality ... The virulent bubble of property values ...' Jon had paused as his thinking swayed inside his skull. 'That ... on which our economy is poised ... We need landowners to have power, because otherwise where would we be? We'd be in a land where landowners didn't have power, which would be disconcerting. So land must be worth something, everything, and the landowners must get richer and swell until they are Borgias ... new Borgias ... tiny and middle-ranking and towering Borgias ... And we can rest sweetly in our beds, no matter what power we don't have, because our floors and kitchen cabinets and damp courses and gutters and so forth are appreciating in theoretical value, while depreciating in actual value through wear and tear, but nonetheless there is appreciation taking place at fantasy rates in a shinier fantasy world. Unless we bought a council house and it rotted around us, or our neighbourhood fell into hell. Then we're very screwed. And beyond that ...'

Rowan sipped his tea and let Jon run, let him drag himself towards something like tears.

Jon had felt his body becoming breathless and starting a sweat. 'And even if we're not screwed that way, our precious bricks and repointing are only all very well if we don't become homeless through some intervention from the catalogue of mischance, or don't intend ever to move again and won't then find ourselves forced to purchase somewhere else in London for a price which would buy us a small street in Liverpool. Because only London truly matters, it is where our Borgias live, where everyone's Borgias live. Other areas and cities misunderstand power and ownership and must be chastised accordingly until they do better. And ...'And it no longer seemed important to finish the sentence.

I sound angry and ridiculous.

'Have some more tea, Jon.' Rowan's voice amused, but not mocking. 'We consider solutions, though, don't we? Isn't that the best ...? We never allow our description of what might dismay or overwhelm us to dismay and overwhelm us in itself. We assess the available information and generate alternatives ... And we are implacable.' A tired grin after this to acknowledge that he was quoting himself.

Rowan deals with me well, always has – lets me come here and rant. He was always a good teacher, because he's interested in learning – in every sense. He listens, does Rowan – even to me. Not that I'm offering him anything real, or worth hearing.

Rowan spoke to his tea glass, softly, 'Being angry with no one you can find ... No one you can reach ...' Then he looked into the garden's little pool. 'Wouldn't that, in the end, make you ill ...' Rowan's face took noticeable care to remain disinterested while he said this.

Yes, naturally it would. It does. But I want to be angry. I want to be it and feel it. I do. I have to – what's the alternative? If I'm not angry then I'm only scared – that's all that's left, beyond the hating.

I have mislived the whole of my life.

'Yes, thank you, I'll have more tea. In case of apocalypse, take tea.'

Jon did offer his glass and Rowan poured for him – *civilised* – it was excellent, gentle tea, made with fresh sage from the garden, from the raised bed just over there.

An Arabian garden in Bishopsgate.

There were joyfully coloured tiles and alcoves and squared flower beds laid out like a prayer with a pool at the centre. *The heart is a pool which has to be cleansed.* It had been built here for Filya: a present to court her, before she moved in, said yes and got married and did the customary stuff – except that with Rowan and Filya it wasn't customary. They and their garden along with them were – one had to use the term – enchanting.

Jon could remember when the finished courtyard had been revealed – Filya crying and setting her hands over her face while a small knot of people suddenly felt superfluous, because they had been invited to a garden-christening party and it had turned without warning into a public proposal and unashamed sentiment and a slender woman being momentarily quite annoyed about having to consent and kiss and so forth before an assembled multitude. But mainly there was happiness. There had been a great deal of happiness.

Filya, who was Rowan's first wife.

His only wife. And it doesn't seem acceptable to be in Bishopsgate, in the world, when she is not. She would have been about the place, there would have been a knowledge, a sense of her presence, immanent. She'd have left me with Rowan to chat between ourselves, but then joined us for the later evening.

Not in that silly, sexist way – not a toxic, enforced withdrawal from men's business ... It was just that she liked to cook. After work, it relaxed her. She was a neurologist. She saw awful things happen to people, happen to their minds, their private selves, and had greater than average reasons for wanting to create things and hand over health and ... Food's good, isn't it? It makes you able to go on. And I would have an appetite when I was with them both. So we might have eaten dowjic in a while, maybe, or lamb kibbeh, pilaf, lots of small dishes. Home-made and expressing affection. And first there would have been sweet peeled almonds in the garden to assist our conversation, and dried apricots the colour of muscovado sugar, perfumed flavour they had, and fresh dates. And we would have sat in the peace by the little fountain and heard her being efficient with knives and equipment and I would have smelled the heat, the spices, the domesticity, the content. Beneath everything would always be the flavour of content.

Happy households, they have an identical scent. There are variations in the top notes, but the underlying sweetmustysexydrowsy taste that colours your inward breaths is always the same. And without Filya that's gone.

It was her absence, in part, the lack of everything she'd added to reality, which had put Jon in such a vile mood.

And I don't like to see Rowan hurt and he is now permanently damaged, marked. That's what happens when you really have someone who's for you and they love you and they aren't simply this closed loop in human form: your source of pain and your justification for withdrawing and the increased pain they inflict that calls for your attention and the guard you have to keep to fend them off – round and round.

Because it's not that I didn't understand how a couple falls apart. I did see what we couldn't help doing, Valerie and I – we weren't a disaster because we were insufficiently well informed … Just as we weren't, in some ways, cruel.

We were simply beyond help.

I do not personally believe in help.

It was beautiful with Rowan and Filya, though – they conjured belief, produced it.

And then a younger wife who should have outlived her husband gets killed by an unforeseeable aortic dissection. Because everything ends.

She managed just fine being a Kurd and a Sufi and born in Iran and then moving to Gaza when she was a kid … Gaza, of all places … So many things didn't kill her and then she was over. Stopped.

I can't imagine what I would have done: having to be the man who woke beside her that morning and who knew she was in pain and that it was bad and dark and that nothing I could do was fixing it.

She told Rowan it was like a tearing in her chest. She suspected the cause and was frightened, more than sufficiently well informed. She said goodbye a lot, which was a mercy for later but not at the time. She insisted *on saying goodbye. Hands over her face and crying and momentarily furious.*

Is what I was told.

And I could not have borne it.

The ambulance taking however long they take now … Nice people when they arrived, Rowan said, and efficient … And too late.

It wouldn't have made any difference if they'd been parked up ready outside – the situation was unsurvivable. Nobody's fault – unless we involve God, believe that He claimed her. Her blood was just flooding away, and the damage impossible to repair – sewing nothing on to nothing being impossible.

We don't discuss it, but that is what's in the garden instead of Filya – an impossibility.

Jon had crossed his legs, drawn both hands through his hair and bent forwards, hinged himself so that his head was nearly against his own knees. He was doing this more and more often and was sure it must look ungainly and as if he were, to a degree, overwhelmed or else collapsing. 'The whole city will have been cleansed soon: one huge play park for the upper-middle-and-above classes. And where will they get their tradesmen then? Or their servants? Dear me. One will have to bus one's staff in from Surrey, Kent. Dorset. Take their passports and make 'em live in …'

'Jon, is this what you wanted to tell me?'

Of course not. Why the fuck would I care about this? Why the fuck? Why the fuck be nauseous – again and as usual nauseous and should I see a doctor? I get sick. I feel sick too often.

I feel sick when I walk across Eaton Square – been doing that for decades – and see the new pavement furniture, these men who are dressed as butlers and who have to stand about outside the houses. As if there are not enough ways to spend the so much, so much, too much money available to the householders within, or elsewhere but potentially within, and therefore personnel must be made visible and shown to be under-occupied: whole human beings on call in case a bag needs lifting when anybody steps out from a cab, or a door is found closed and so has to be opened.

They are mainly there for doors, I suppose – the fake butlers – they're doormen who can't look like doormen for fear that passers-by would mistake one's house for a hotel. And for fear of passers-by in general.

Probably not even that, it's probably just an ill-informed costume choice. Or an attempt to look like Manhattan – those long, uptown awnings with cheery doormen underneath them, white gloves and peaked caps.

For whatever reason, there they are, set out like breathing bollards.

And a whole tribe of human beings who cannot alight from any vehicle without offering up their packages, making the faces of tired children, expecting that every dreadful burden will be removed, looking out of their windows and over their shoulders and seeing wilderness.

'Jon? Are you not well?'

Jon had been aware that the one thing he shouldn't be here was a bringer of more trouble and that he mustn't be in any way unwell. That kind of vocabulary should not be allowed.

'I'm fine. I'm ... I'm clearing my thinking ... It's ...'

'Take your time.'

And – ridiculously – he'd ended up holding Rowan's hand. He'd reached out and held the man's hand and tried not to find himself pathetic, tried and – being truthful – he'd resisted crying, not because he was brave in any way, or still functional, but because Rowan was the only one there who'd had a true cause for crying.

'Take your time.'

'I really am fine, it's, ah ...'

One's previous aloneness only absolutely clear when one is holding someone else's hand and realising that all day, all day, all day, one has been holding the lack of someone's hand, the awful fact and dreadful burden of exactly that.

'I will, Rowan, take my time ... I've been stupid, is the thing. I have been ...'

I don't care about the doormen, sod the doormen, why think of doormen ... And I can appreciate the wider benefits in the personal accumulation of significant wealth.

Keeps the doormen in business, jewellers, shoemakers ... tailors ...

It's not that I don't possess more than the majority of people do. The statistics on that are clear.

I have a tailor ...

'Rowan, it's ... I see them walking about, these men whose minds have torn away from who they were, away from the world, from facts ... The way they think of themselves, the things they expect to see – they move inside that – what they must have been at some point, what must have ... Men with consciences flapping out behind them like bloody flags.'

'You're not one of those men.'

'I try to think and I can't ... If I'd ... It would be like ... When you have care of a child – and we're all supposed, I think this is true, to have care of children – and you don't ... When you reach in and ... You can't hurt them. You can't be permitted to hurt them. You can't steal what they're going to be because you have appetites and they warm you and you like them, you can't ... There are so many things that you can't, but they happen anyway.'

'You're not one of those men.'

I'm not a man, I'm an old boy.

I went to a quietly acceptable school. I attempted to play rugby – run like a bastard or else they'll catch you – bolting on the terraced playing fields, way up on high, de facto orphans trying to operate sportingly under the gaze of Machu Picchu, or so it seemed. Only we were in Cumbria. Not an especially notable institution, but we had the requisite crests and colours, debates and a cadet corps, traditions and the long, long run and rolls of honour in careful gold leaf under which to eat our meals, a vastly arched war memorial to celebrate our particular and generously given dead and to cover the sneaking of outdoor cigarettes during the rainstorms.

I never have wanted to smoke since I've been allowed to.

And working hard in lieu of loving and being loved and making it all the way to a decent college – more colours: this strange adoration of clashing candy colours amongst the authoritative classes, this need for babyish discordance – and then knowing that cosy, tidy, end-of-the-day relief when the gates were closed for evening beyond the lawns and honey stone, the nation's significant thoughts tucked up behind oak, with No Admittance signs to check the tourists. Toast at the gas fire. Cloistered.

I should have been a monk. Easier all round.

I was taught to be avid for information, accurate. It was implied this would be a gift and of assistance. I was encouraged to be fastidious.

I did have a vocation.

I was—

'Jon?'

Rowan, don't make me think of your hand, of holding a hand, and that without it the undertow that's everywhere will sweep on in and get me.

'Rowan ... The letters they caught me writing ... The love, sort of love, letter thing ...'

I am an old boy. That's what they made of me. I am not a man, I am an old boy. Boys can only cope with so much and then no more.

'It was a preposterous thing to do ...'

But I would come here and see you holding happiness and having it stay with you and I would smile as a grown man should.

'It meant I felt less ... I didn't seem to be so completely ... When I wrote to them, the women, I was ...'

And on paper I was a man who could be of assistance, who eventually had the words for each occasion.

I know that you ought to be loved every day ... You should know how beautiful you are ... People notice but you may not understand what sweetness others find in you and please believe I find you sweet, as sweet as anything ... I was so sorry to hear your news and, if I were there, you would be in my arms and at peace, I promise ... Kissing you was all that I thought of today – the only thought of significance ... In your heart there is so much that's kind and kindness isn't often referred to, only it should be all the time and there's a miracle's worth of kindness in you ... You make sure that others are comfortable and that rooms are centred and it passes them by, but without you they'd be lost. When I open the

175

envelope around your letter, you're there ... My
touch on the paper where yours will be soon, as
if we are holding hands ...

If you would let me I would be more than proud
to hold you, it would be an honour. I don't wish
to sound foolish and don't feel I am being foolish
when I say that it would be my life.

*Sentiment and support. Not sex. None of the vileness of sex. Hardly
any mentions of sex, nothing overt: just these mentions of holding and
kissing and skin and looking. If anyone asked for graphic scenarios,
conjunctions, then I'd be gone. I wasn't angry, only gone. I was giving
tenderness, adult tenderness.*

*I did get irritated once by this one woman – an intelligent woman,
but she was always demanding smut, and so I tried ... And it got
such an immediate response, the dirt. I was encouraged to be abusive –
slapping and urination, ugliness you'd pray your daughter would
never want. I discontinued our correspondence, refunded the fee.*

My aim was the generation and perpetuation of gentleness.

I wanted to write about holding hands.

While intending to never, ever do any such thing.

'It obviously ...'

And Jon slowly, it seemed inevitably, had slid from his seat in
Rowan's garden, Filya's garden, and had kneeled on the terracotta
paving, pressed his forehead against the tiles around the pool – their
placid surface, the idea of the blue and white and crimson soaking
through into his mind and improving its pitiable condition.

'It's not that ...' Jon had stretched his arm slightly behind him
to keep a grip round Rowan's knuckles and hold on. He'd kept
his face hidden and been subject to irregular breaths.

*A person of any quality could stop himself from polluting an emptied
garden with his own self-centred grief.*

Over the wall was a construction site, stilled by the evening.
For most of the previous year it had oppressed the little sanctuary
with successive dins and dust storms that rendered everything
distant and tainted, laid a filmy scum on the water.

The heart is a pool which must be cleansed.

The new building planted next door was tall and cast an unfortunate shadow. There was nothing to be done.

Filya died while the disturbance, the intrusion, was at its worst.

Jon kneeling and eventually sobbing next to Rowan, as if he were begging for something, but he couldn't say what, as if he were on his knees for a confession. He hadn't been able say anything.

I want her last time in the garden to have been nice, pretty, lovely, and it wasn't.

Jon had clung to Rowan's fist and, finally, had managed, 'I have to keep on, but I can't, but I have to ... I thought I had to, but I do no good. It does no good. I stayed in, because I think, I thought I have to ... I can't ...'

And Jon had felt the heave of his ribs, his muscles, beneath this dreadful burden, this minor tearing in his heart, and had understood he was walking out into wilderness.

It had been quite bad.

'This girl, woman, person ... I didn't mean her ... and now she is and ... There's all of this other ... It's all happening at once, all together, and I'm too small for it ... I'm ...' Weeping – there had been a bit of weeping and a reversion to what he had left of his earliest accent. As his words fought to emerge – hot and breaking – he'd sounded to himself like the child who'd left Nairn: a boy filled up with a cleverness and finding no comfort in it.

It had been his cleverness that made him unsuitable for Society Street. It made him have to leave. It spoiled his character with fraudulent self-belief, long before he'd put on the posh blazer, learned the appropriate slang.

Being clever was supposed to help. It's still supposed to help.

An odd storm in a garden – that's what he'd been.

Being in and of the world is supposed to be unavoidable and that means you find out about it and you plant it with sweet things and hopes and ... confessions ...

An ugly fit of spinning shook his head and then subsided.

He coughed. He sniffed.

He did feel a bit better now, here in this big garden, everybody's garden – here in St James's Park. He was better – in some ways, recovered. Apart from the recurrent throwing up.

And he had explained his position – some of it – to Rowan and it hadn't seemed – some of it – insoluble. With Rowan there and listening it had appeared to be a story one could tell.

Although it would be interpreted as a cautionary tale. I am not walking into wilderness, I am running.

No.

It's not that.

The park reasserted itself: tourists, gusty sunshine, his own longer-than-useful limbs.

I can sit on the grass and there is blossom and a luminous green in the April leaves which is compelling, such a mercy, so kind and – even so – I am running into wilderness.

Here it is. It's always here, the wilderness. Maybe the people who like and want to make more of it, maybe they're right.

Here it is. The very place to make an old boy run.

Here it is.

He turned his phone back on.

A man is kneeling in a quiet afternoon shopping arcade. Sun shines. The man is a busker, has his sweatbanded and slightly exotic hat upturned before him to catch donations, has weather-proof clothes and a demeanour intended to be engaging. He is in his twenties, perhaps something older. He is playing a saxophone, holding it high to be sure that it clears the ground. His posture seems slightly strained, but his face is happy and intent.

He is offering a rendition of 'Twinkle, Twinkle, Little Star' with absolute clarity. He is at the feet of a small boy who is caught, it would seem perpetually, between wonder at the instrument's large sound and his urge to press his fingers against the glimmer of its bell, to peer into the breathy depth of that.

A couple, plump and comfortable together, stand just behind the child. He is most likely their son. They are enjoying his enjoyment. They are also a touch embarrassed by their situation. It is unclear whether they or the child have requested the tune. Probably the kneeling in supplication has been added as a flourish by the musician. The child appears imperious about his treat, taking these signs of obeisance as his natural right.

Pedestrians pass the scene without pausing. Heads do not turn as a child is attended to specially and pleased. This happens to children quite often. If he were an adult, the interactions taking place would be more difficult and complex. He is perhaps being ignored by others older than himself, because they are jealous of him, or else as an effort on their part to avoid nostalgia.

15:00

MEG WAS HAVING a late lunch, or early tea. She wasn't meeting anyone.

I am by myself. Apart from some dogs. And apart from some people.

But not one of them is anything at all to do with me.

She had caught the bus that took her home and then ended up allowing herself to loiter and be a bit cold outside the community café round the corner from her house. She was sipping a coffee, because she didn't feel especially like eating. She also didn't feel like spending the fag end of the day haunting her flat.

Bastard.

What I feel like doing, obviously, is making a slightly unhappy situation worse. Why not threaten myself with chucking it all in, giving up?

I am already miserable, so why not be really despairing.

Fretting over what I even mean by 'it all' will set me up wonderfully well for when we do meet.

Because it is still our plan to meet – only we're going to do it all later. Not now.

Whatever 'it all' means.

Everything is going to happen later and not now – the usual.

I will meet you, but sorry not right now …

The usual.

But I can trust the idea of it.

I have to.

I have decided to.

You have to trust something, here and there, and I have decided to trust that our plan really is a plan.

Friday afternoons were unpleasant enough. And here she was, having a coffee she could have made in her own kitchen for no charge.

No – be fair – I couldn't have made a cappuccino. I lack that particular skill.

Among others.

You know, this would, this truly would be a lot easier if I weren't such a whiny cow.

I should just have stayed in at work – said there'd been a change of plans.

But you can't, you can't say you're going out and duly inform the management and tell bloody, fucking Laura that on Friday the 10th you'll be off early and have her give you that 'Oh, do you have a life, then?' stare and then – when it comes to the day – you can't, you cannot, you can fucking not say out loud, 'No, I've had another change of plans. Last week it was going to be lunch today and then a few days passed and the time we'd arranged looked unlikely – although the day was still fine – and so we fixed on three o'clock – three o'clock today – and three o'clock is an odd kind of time for a meeting, but it might suit an odd kind of person, and we are both odd kinds of people … Only now it won't be three, either …'

Six thirty. We'll try again then.

Bastard.

I don't like today.

I don't like anything much about today. It started low and has gone downhill.

I would like another twenty-four hours now, please. I have put in repeated requests and I'd like someone to deal with my problem and make it right.

More caffeine won't help.

Maybe I don't want it to help – maybe I want to feel all manic inside, or spruced up, or …

I get to try again at six thirty.

I will meet you.

But it never works out.

She prodded her spoon about in the froth of her mug while choosing not to think that a tea would have been cheaper and less chemically abusive.

I would rather not suspect that I get cancelled because I'm a terrible person, rather than an odd one.

But I do suspect it.

I fucking know it.

I feel like a terrible person – and that must show, that must be something clear and to be avoided.

I'm currently a terrible person having community cappuccino with some strangers. And some dogs. I can't bloody get away from dogs.

The café had been summoned up inside a remarkably hideous building by an act of concerted will. There had been calls for volunteers and mucking in had happened and now the community had a resource. It offered activities Meg never went to and get-togethers she steadfastly resisted and also sold crafts and produce and hippyish cooking. The place sat between the Hill's two little parks and was, therefore, lousy with dogs during the daylight hours.

She was surrounded by muzzles and pads and sensible, fully inhabited animal bodies. Each sodding dog had those levels of impossibly relaxed aliveness that could be soothing or could be truly bloody irritating if you were an animal too, but couldn't reach that state of ease – couldn't manage what any mongrel, any overbred, pedigree freak could do without thinking.

Bastard.

No.

No one is a bastard.

And at six thirty I will be in a place which is happy and good.

I will trust that – it's good exercise.

The assembled dogs were being loose and jolly round the outside tables, in amongst the lolling bicycles and parked prams. And there were also humans. The ones who wanted to be cosy sat indoors; outside with Meg were the smokers and the hardy types and those who maybe wanted to watch birds – why not? There were birds and, now and then, someone would look at them. Meg didn't know and couldn't care if they were doing so with an expert eye. Why she was outside and not in was a mystery to her – she didn't smoke.

That and gambling – the vices I never quite got.

To her left, a russet-coloured mongrel with a bit of ridgeback about it was flopped down with its greying head on its folded forepaws. Behind her there was a sable and cream Tibetan terrier in need of trimming – she couldn't see what it was doing but could hear its claws pittering and fussing and the occasional murmur as it rummaged under tables, snuffed unwary ankles.

That's a dog being poorly cared for. That's a bad thing on the verge of happening.

Meg briefly enjoyed being judgemental.

Everyone here has children and partners and lives and disposable incomes with which to buy cappuccinos and artisan-made items and jars of urban honey and local ice cream.

Fuck 'em.

This was both untrue and unfair, which was why it felt so pleasant.

Fuck 'em.

Although Meg would stop soon.

I am truly sorry and I truly will stop and get a grip – in a minute.

Meg had spent years being with Meg and knew her to be a foul-tempered bitch who could put a curse on anything she thought of.

Fuck me.

But she was trying to do better.

Fuck me.

She was trying to assume that meetings with her were not cancelled because she had done something wrong. Or else because she was something wrong.

They have leftie concerts in the café … I tend to the left. Which ought to be funny. Singing songs of revolution – as if that does anything, achieves anything. Songs I used to sing – still complaining about last century's battles and hardly any space for those ongoing, picking the Spanish Civil War songs because they've got the halfway lively tunes … 'En los frentes de Jarama, rumba la rumba la rumba la, no tenemos ni aviones, ni tanques ni cañones.' *They always sound dead happy that they've got no planes, or tanks, or artillery. And I'm meant to be dead happy that they could be dead happy in the XVth fucking Brigade more than a generous lifetime ago. They fucking lost, though, didn't they? They hadn't got any planes or tanks or artillery – what were they going to do? Sing the Civil Guard into submission?*

Standing there with the raised clenched fist – well, you've got to, haven't you? – while we all sing 'The Internationale'. I've done that.

Why is liberty never in the English language, what does that indicate?

A breeze crossed the road from the lower park and lifted a little of the dust that prisoners of want were intended to spurn in order to win their prize.

What happens to the dust is that it gets in your coffee. I'm spurning it like fuck – it's still here and doesn't care.

She fussed at the cooling, dun-coloured liquid again as if she was worried the spoon would melt. Then she didn't drink.

I don't drink – that's me. I am a person who doesn't drink. My principal activity is an absence.

Meg turned and faced the park: the tenderly restless trees, branches becoming new, blossom in fat cascades and swags, the world showing itself generous, fluttering, sweet.

Which should be enough.

I am a person who is sober.

I am a positive quantity.

When my head gets this unbalanced I should call someone and tell them and then tip myself over entirely, pour the rubbish out, empty it out, pour myself out, make me empty.

But I'm not going to make a call, am I?

Because I like risk.

Because I am right to hate myself – I am a stupid, stupid cow and I do me wrong.

I also lie. A great deal. Mainly to myself. But I keep on listening.

Stupid cow.

A meeting gets cancelled – you don't get cancelled, it's the meeting – and you go into a tailspin when it isn't your fault and it's only a postponement, anyway, not a cancellation.

We can have an early dinner, maybe. I would enjoy an early dinner. Because I've had no lunch. Running on empty again.

But I'm not empty.

I will meet you.

That's not empty.

But I've had too much coffee – I'm all wound up. Even if the breeze hadn't sprinkled it with gutter dust and toxins, I shouldn't have more of this coffee, or any other coffee, or anything like coffee. I should be drinking some kind of wort.

Christ, I'm ridiculous. Shouldn't be allowed out. Shouldn't be allowed in or out.

And for a moment she smiled, for a moment the blossoms looked perfect: the bounce of them, the contours of infant colour and generous scent.

Times like this – it's like falling down your own personal well, but you can also reach back in there and pull yourself out by the ears. It takes an effort, but you can. Better with help, but I am embarrassed about getting help for this. This is minor. I'm tired and I had a rough morning, that's all. I can deal with it.

And I really shouldn't think about politics and who should, frankly? Who should willingly waste their time on that? Politics is just an organised and expensive way of being furious.

Meg set her mug on the table and walked down from the decking at the front of the café.

Then she stalled, returned, picked up the mug and took it inside to leave it more handy for clearing up. She nodded to the guy at the till and generally behaved as if she loved the place and all its works and anticipated an imminent revolution which would involve the comfortably old-school middle classes being able to have more time for reading and a wider choice of theatre groups and box sets of continental TV dramas.

And then she left again. 'Thank you.' Slipped herself away.

15:23

AS MEG SLOPED down the hill to her bus stop, she was pursued – as happened now and then – by the stain, the taste, of that other Meg, Maggie, Margaret. Thatcher.

Maggie, Maggie, Maggie – out, out, out.

You'd hear people yelling it all the time and agree, but all the same – it was hard not to take it personally as well.

And the last person I'd want to be associated with – apart from me – was her.

Laura said once, 'Well, at least she did something. This lot – they don't do anything. None of them. They just talk. She did something. And she was a woman.'

And I didn't say back, 'Well, Countess Báthory did something – she did something with virgins' blood and murder and definitely, yes, that's doing something. And that Roman woman who poisoned Claudius and a bunch of other people … I should make a list of women who were unpleasant so I could quote from it properly … and Lucrezia Borgia who did something, a shitload of things, I'd guess, but I can't recall … I have a friend who takes an interest in the Borgias, so I read up on them a bit … I have a memory that's shot to hell … I should know, I shot it – that much I do remember … But I can learn. I can learn about all of those women in the concentration camps, the guards – you see them in photos, in those uniforms looking like … it's like a terrible joke … women in schoolgirl skirts who torture people … These are women who did things. Doing things doesn't make you wonderful. Doing – that's not enough, is it? I do things. We all do things. It's which things – what things we do … And being a woman – that's not a guarantee that you'll be lovely. Trust me, I have a vagina and know. And I am not glad that I have it – the thing does not empower me. I do not stare at it in a hand mirror and wish it well and thank it for granting me a lifetime of pleasant experience … But yes, she was a woman and she did things. Yes. For sure. Thanks for sharing. Bloody marvellous. Bless you sideways and back and forth.'

Yes, I didn't say that.

There's never any point in bothering to say that. If you've got an idea that it might be necessary as something to say, then you already know that actually saying it will not be welcomed or understood and you keep shtum.

If you're sober, you keep yourself shut up. Pissed … Well, if you're pissed, then all bets are off.

The trouble was that Margaret Thatcher got her drunk.

Another lie.

I got me drunk.

Meg had imagined that she would die before old Maggie – time was against the former prime minister, but serious drinking, industrial-scale drinking, had been giving Meg the push towards an early finish line that she'd hoped for. She had, after all, wanted to leave – every other option having apparently been knackered.

But then Baroness Margaret Hilda had slipped out via the Ritz and gone before – the heart people said she didn't have stopped beating.

Her soul was lifted free – if people have souls. I think of it catching in the Green Park branches and resting there like a bird, being unburdened suddenly, turning about and pausing to see and see and see.

And Meg – sober Meg – at that point sober-for-two-years-alreday Meg, had stayed alive, moved past her namesake and gone on. Or something like that.

At the time of Maggie's death, Meg was not doing many AA meetings – not doing any meetings, in fact – she was not attending and not exactly accepting suggestions and advice offered by people who were, or any other people she might encounter.

She no longer really encountered people.

She was discontented. She had also just abandoned the self-helpless group that had forced her to sit in a circle with Molly once a week and tried to pat her arm.

A bloody therapeutic sewing circle that was supposed to make me feel like a human being, a convincing woman.

Which I am not. Even a gynaecologist doesn't find me quite convincing – 'Here's some pain, oh and by the way, your life as a reproductive human being is now over. You'll have noticed the little changes – I'm telling you about the Big One. The last one before the Really Big One.'

Although I should leave that now – I should let that be. This morning has gone. And that final morning with Maggie has gone – with no harm to her, only to me.

Meg – still sober, but discontented Meg – had found out the news about Thatcher from the radio and had wanted to be happy.

But you can't be happy that a wandery old lady has died.

She'd played Elvis Costello and sung along and still not managed to be glad.

It had done me no good to outlast her. Or to see the way the world was, beyond her active life, beyond her damage. The place had been steered along unkindly.

Not many pensioners, frail and needful, get to die in a suite at the Ritz, all cosy and dignified.

How many pensioners get to die while being cosy and dignified and never mind the Ritz …?

I tried to be outraged about that, but it didn't make me angry. I wished it would.

I wasn't sad and wasn't happy and wasn't anything – only tired.

The final satisfaction that nature had been meant to provide, the assassination by wear and tear and time and real things – all the stuff politicians liked to ignore – the death that Meg had shouted for in bars and bars and studies and clubs and arguments and bars and bars, in a significant number of bars ... here it was. But the happiness she'd expected to acquire as a result was unavailable.

And next there had been a day and then another and then longer of feeling filthy, somehow, of Meg having this ugliness under her skin and a restless inclination towards darkness.

So she had gone to the funeral, Margaret Hilda's funeral. It was on a Wednesday.

Crazy idea.

And it let her get me in the end.

Meg had anticipated crowds and set out far too early, emerging from Westminster Underground into drizzle and a chill, the pavements mainly empty. Policemen wandered the quiet and quarantined roads, sipping plastic cups of tea, swinging bags of Mars bars and soft drinks. Barriers were in place for the not-there-yet crowd and a camera boom and its tower were set ready at the corner of Whitehall so that a swooping shot could follow the hearse as it passed by.

And there were so many flags, straggling limply at half mast.

The press assembled a nest for themselves: aluminium ladders and long lenses, the ache for an exclusive view – nothing to snap at yet, beyond a trickle of grey-haired tailcoat-wearers heading up from the Tube, along with young men in black suits and white shirts, looking like cut-price schoolboys with carefully shiny shoes.

Coaches began to swing past, filled with apparently dozing men in dress uniform. And there were minibuses – bizarre minibuses, windows filled with hats and fascinators, sparky make-up, gentlemen's well-smoothed hair and brushed lapels, officers' uniforms.

As if it was a wedding they were off to. A society occasion in unfortunate weather.

Which it was, naturally – no more and no less and no more than that.

Occasional soldiers walked from here to there, polished to an unnatural tension. Meg had been surprised by how foolish their thick-soled boots looked – something glam rock about them – and how broad and short the trousers. They were dressed like armed clowns in aggressive hats. This was apparently how Whitehall and the forces displayed official grief – these were its various manners of mourning, as prescribed. And, here and there, a knot of civilians gathered in sensible outdoor greens and tweeds. There was chatter, vehement chatter, the kind of pre-emptive outrage Meg had to suppose was often heard in the drawing-room conversations of those to whom Thatcher was dear. It was the tone of a successful headline: all risen hackles and crazy swings between self-importance and self-loathing, with more loathing for everyone else.

Curious tourists leaned on the barriers and took pictures while a German film crew cruised back and forth, attempting to find anybody who would willingly offer comment to a German.

And there was a scatter of those who loved their country – their idea of their country – in more personal types of fancy dress: the Union Jack coats and handmade badges, the top hats with the photos attached. They straggled around and paced, anticipating. The nation was set out in bitter, brittle pieces – in sparse and crazy pieces.

It was like staring at the essence of all I would rather not be.

It made me sad.

And the cameraman climbed his tower and started to practise lazy dips with the camera boom. And the drizzle drizzled. And the police in the road – being all there was to watch – acted out their cold for everyone's entertainment: taking little dancing steps, clapping their gloved hands together, puffing out their cheeks.

A man in the crowd who had come all the way from Manchester that morning, announced the fact: 'I was at Churchill's funeral, too.' Meg listened while he told her this, uninvited, in the same way he had told a number of other people and would presumably tell more. But not the Germans.

Meg was shivering by the time the gun carriage rattled by, heading for the transfer point – bright metal and black gloss. She turned away from it, turned her back, because that seemed appropriate – this helpless spin of 180 degrees about which nobody could surely care.

And then she wound herself back round again to wait for the actual body of a human being, now deceased, defeated by the end of all power, and soon to be limousined along, much as it might have been in life.

Here would be the satisfaction Meg had wished for.

But there was no satisfaction. Naturally.

The hearse lashed around the bend from Parliament Square, as if in flight from a disreputable public.

Someone threw flowers – and again – as what had been the Baroness pelted past. The blooms landed very short and hit the tarmac: they were something with a dingy green flower, a hellebore. They must have been from a garden and perhaps had some personal significance. The hellebore is poisonous. The flowers are meant to drive out discord and bring in tranquillity.

It all has a double meaning now – what any politician says … Where there is hatred, let me sow love …

Whatever they tell you, exactly reverse it and you'll be right.

Meg – having shown disrespect to the gun carriage – had found herself absurdly and unpleasantly flanked by police. They oozed through the crowd towards her and then stuck – two coppers in tall helmets.

As if I would do what? Leap over the barrier and somersault on to the bonnet of the hearse?

Why be afraid of me?

I didn't matter.

Nothing I did mattered.

And nor did their intervention matter.

Meg discovered a third uniform standing close behind her when she turned her back, this time against the limousine. The uniform belonged to a policewoman who wore a name badge which said she was called Debbie. Debbie shouted, 'Bless her.' She aimed this past Meg's ear with educative fervour as the illustrious corpse shot by in its glossy transportation – propelled at unstately pace.

And that was it.

No more.

There was only cold after, deep cold.

The crowd frittered itself away.

There was a type of shock that nothing was different, even now – that it never would be. The grey and the chill would stay grey and chill.

There was a great disappointment, closing in.

You find yourself disgusting, because you often do and because this time you have wished an old woman to death. Or at least wished that you could.

You are staring at others and seeing they are inexplicable …

You see and see and see and you can't stop …

You have come to watch and be a friend of death, to love it – and, now that you're here, you can feel it take an interest. You feel its scrutiny, digging in sharp – like the attention of the worst kind of police.

Your current police have melted back from you and gone, they are swinging along the pavement somewhere – you can't see them.

Maggie's funeral – it pushes you completely away …

You take yourself away.

You walk through the damp air and find the nearest pub and you ask the lady who's working the optics to set up a double whisky and then another, because you have fallen behind. You ask very politely but inside you are fierce.

You drink among people you cannot agree with – faithful mourners, coddling wine glasses in chilled hands – and yet you don't mind this at all.

Your aim is to not mind anything any more.

You wish to go away.

In every sense, you wish to go far away and have no intention of ever coming back.

Meg had got and then stayed drunk.

It had taken her more than a year to retrieve herself.

Blinds drawn and a minicab to fetch the bottles when you get too scared to send yourself outside, too ashamed in the off-licence. Selling the telly. Selling all manner of odds and ends that your parents kept and cared for and left you so that you could love them – not love death – so you could remember earlier, gentle days.

They left you their house, or you'd have wound up homeless. And even then, you nearly drank the place.

Only a whisker away from the full drop – and no net there to catch you. There's no such thing as a net to catch you, not any more.

And you don't deserve one.

Silly cow, you are.

There's no such thing as anything.

Silly cow, she was, old Maggie.

But I'm sillier.

Letting her almost kill me.

And, since then, Meg had agreed it was wise not to dwell – several people had mentioned this – wise not to dwell on politics and the meaninglessness of hope. She was properly sober now and wanted to stay that way. So she tried not to think of politics, not in any form, songs included.

I fill my head with other things.

I just collect all the good stuff that I see and I save it up and write it down and I try to be grateful. I bear it in mind.

A couple stand in Shepherd Market, a corner of Mayfair that harmlessly pretends to be a village square. The pair are just outside a restaurant and may have eaten a meal together, although it is too late for lunch and too early for dinner. They have the look of people who are interested in each other, who are attentive.

The man is taller than the woman by a quite significant amount and so when they embrace her head meets the height of his heart, or thereabouts. Their attempt to hold each other is a little clumsy initially, the man trying to stoop at first, to shape himself both around and away from the woman, perhaps in the hope of avoiding excessive contact. He may not wish to seem overly forceful, he may not wish to feel overly forced. The woman stays still, perhaps unsure of her response, although there is a calm about her which suggests she is concentrating, perhaps finishing a decision, or pressing herself to particularly take note.

Thereafter, the man straightens his back and their bodies meet, fit, they clasp. Their movements are slow and gentle to a degree that suggests a knowledge of previous injury, or mutual illness. Their hands dab and pat, as if they are hoping to offer reassurance after some past calamity. Equally, they may be attempting to furnish support as some present calamity runs its course.

The little courtyard is quiet around them. No one arrives to visit the stationer's, or the parcels office, the small cafés, the restaurant. The couple's privacy is undisturbed, is extending to touch the prettily painted brickwork that confines them, keeps them safe. Their affection is reflected in a number of windows, an echo of care.

At the end of their embrace – which is heralded by more dabbing, smoothing, a hesitant stroke at the woman's hair – the two part by a hand's breadth and then pause once more. They seem puzzled.

The woman reaches up to cradle the man's head between her palms, slips her fingers loosely over his ears and this causes a visible relaxation that seems to pour downward and into his spine. His face takes on the softness of a sleeper's. She then stands on tiptoe to kiss his forehead and he bows mildly to receive her.

Then they let go, the one from the other. They withdraw.

For a moment the man looks above the woman's head, stares far beyond the high and nicely maintained and drowsy Georgian brick which surrounds him. His expression is one of deep, deep surprise. He has the smile of a man who has stolen something wonderful and not been caught, found something wonderful and not been seen, been given something wonderful and got away, got away, run away with it.

The woman watches while her companion is happy and apparently finds his happiness surprising.

Something about the man's condition means that she takes his hand.

Jon was taking the long way round as he headed back to Tothill Street and a meeting he didn't want. Birdcage Walk, then Buckingham Gate, then Victoria Street – that still didn't add too many minutes, but it was something. Milner was going to be tricky and Jon couldn't handle tricky today, in part because, as he'd told Rowan last night ... As he'd said ... He couldn't quite seem able to recall his words absolutely, but ...

I didn't tell him about the Natural History Museum and I should have.

A place to meet women, I suppose.

It's not that.

I would imagine that individuals do stroll around there and possibly seek out this or that person who seems to share an interest in hawkmoths, or glass models of sea anemones. An opening conversational gambit could be offered – 'Do you like that moth, or are you staring at your own reflection in the glass of the case and thinking you are not at all who you were and that many of the changes have been for the worse?'

I didn't go there to meet women.

The first time, I was simply in South Kensington on a Saturday afternoon and I'd wandered in and been enveloped by the hell of kickingly bored children and of squeakingly overinterested children and the intensified hell of French teenagers. It was rather relaxing. Everything was louder than my head.

And I loved the small display on human evolution – our sad forebears posed dimly behind glass: life-sized and naked and unable to suggest any yearning to use tools, cooperate, learn above themselves, stand upright and prosper. They seemed endearingly devoid of any aspiration.

It became a quite innocent habit to go there for lunch breaks. I wasn't establishing an alibi in advance.

Jon paused in sight of Buckingham Palace and thought once again how disappointing the building was. It always put him in mind of a novelty cake, or somewhere that would have bad room service.

He watched the wide and blue-white delicacy of a spring sky, drifting massively behind the solid pediments of the east façade. He felt the moment when the building came loose from its moorings and seemed to fly, while the high race of clouds locked in place and stood above him, watching him back.

Mustn't be sick.

He tried smiling at a pair of older women tourists, but his expression must have failed him. They turned tail and walked briskly the way they'd come, rather than pass him.

Jon fumbled at his collar, intending to take off his tie, and then realised he wasn't wearing one – that sensation of constriction was therefore entirely illusory and should be treated as such.

Like the palace. Like the sky. Like the progress of my evolution.

He started walking again.

Maybe once a month, if I could, I'd rush out at lunchtime, flag a cab and head for the museum, the warm stone façade. All those mad sculptures of animals, reptiles, the living and the extinct: the monstrous swarm of life carved all over the exterior – terracotta gargoyles defending evolution's temple – I grew fond of it.

I liked walking within work built to last, effort drawn from hope and a need to progress, a joy about it, inspiration drawn from fact … It made me feel furious at certain levels, of course – furious and desperate. But also content.

I would eventually establish a pattern: stroll in past the bony architecture of the diplodocus skeleton, climb the stairs and then call upon the prehistoric humans and their skulls.

They made me wonder. My flat-browed, jut-chinned, hairy ancestors – how did they smell? We progressed to walk erect, but do we still bring with us an animal reek? When did that stop? Or did we already, grunting in huddles, smell like people – like unwashed people who were also beasts? That sweetsharp tang of sweat – yours or another's – that taint, that seal, that gift which stays on your skin, when did we first travel with that? Or have we always? Do we carry the scent of the beasts we still are? Would that be our clue, when we look at those onward-marching illustrations of humanity straightening up from its stoop and being bettered by natural forces, swelling its brain, busying its fingers, perfecting its tongue – would that tell us how little has changed?

Jon's balance, his vision billowed and twisted momentarily, slid like a loosened building. He chose to believe this was an effect of exposure to exhaust fumes and central London's generally pertaining pollution. Probably if Parliament did exile the civil service to the wastes and moorlands of South-east London, it would add years to everyone's lifespan.

His phone rang and – having checked that it was no one he wanted to hear – he slipped it back down into his coat. It protested as it went.

Too modern for my current frame of mind. While all of the other species keep evolving, we simply invent fresh ways to bill each other for being downcast or enraged – rage and despair being all for which we're meant to hope ...

The museum used to please me.

After comparing myself unfavourably with Australopithecus, I'd slope off to the modern bit, the wing where they keep their material archive: leaves, bodies, wings, drawings, samples. I like it there, because it contains no dinosaur remains and is therefore fairly child-free and peaceful – even, at times, apparently deserted. You ride a lift up to its top floor, as if you are boarding a spacecraft full of whatever's left of our good, of the earth's generosity – as if you'll be able to leave and start again with seeds from climate-controlled vaults. It looks smart, futuristic – in the sense of suggesting that we have a future.

And there are interactive exhibits, film displays – quickly spurned by the scatter of more French teenagers as they pass along. And cabinets have been made with real drawers which can be pulled back to reveal displays. The drawers also provide ledges, edges, gaps. One can, as it were, fill the gaps.

Jon unbuttoned his jacket, although it wasn't terribly warm, and let the poisoned air attempt to cool him, ease him. He was sweating. Sweating as he walked was not as bad as sweating while he was examined by a malicious superior.

I wouldn't give them the satisfaction – not one of them.

And I also wouldn't tell them about the Natural History Museum and my visits. I couldn't appear to be a man who might make such visits and then sweat about them. Sweat would constitute evidence.

Because ...

Because ...

Natural history is about evidence. It is supposed to be about evidence, about science, real science. If you want to know the real world and function in it rationally and effectively, if you want to progress, you collect evidence and test it and love it and want more — you have an appetite for it and its intrinsic beauty. Once you have all the information you can currently gather, you collate it and you analyse it and you come to fact-based conclusions. You have used the real world to give you solutions to itself. This is a beautiful thing.

And humans do not thrive without it.

I believe that.

Once upon a time, we won a real war, a world war, with maths: with models and plans and statistics and knowledge underpinning what we did. We weren't always right, but we were the less-deluded side and therefore the less savage. And we won. So that people would not be crushed, or shut up in hells, so that our peace could be filled with human beings living lives to their fullest extent.

That's all I wanted.

That isn't really much to ask.

And it's why I believe that facts are beautiful things.

And ...

Because ...

The thing is, I must not sweat when Chalice looks at me, because that will make me seem to be a man who slips away to the Natural History Museum and who has a small roll of fine paper in his pocket and who rests that prepared paper — small and white and simple, typed on one side, the interior side — who rests that in the cradle of his modestly evolved hand, opens a prearranged display drawer and then slips that paper into one of the little gaps inside, as agreed in advance.

I can't look like a man who walks on while someone behind him opens that drawer and takes that paper and — later, probably later, I bloody well hope later and discreetly — unrolls it and finds it is covered in evidence, figures, raw data, in what have become the most damaging of the leaks which have left the department ...

I have transgressed the Civil Service Code: I have disclosed official information without authority.

But I am meant to behave with integrity, honesty, objectivity and impartiality. I am called upon to set out the facts and relevant issues truthfully and correct any errors as soon as possible. I must uphold the administration of justice.

And they won't fucking let me.

Jon felt that thrill beneath his skin – that sense of being rolled and unrolled himself, reworked, evolved, by each of his attempts at crime, each memory of gathering what his fellow human beings, what the voters ought to know.

It's what the voters are unsurprised and indeed massively bored by, as it turns out. They are not a powder keg and I am not a match. And it's what our current media environment finds indigestible, irrelevant, being more concerned with aspirational spending, aspirational violence, aspirational hate, aspirational fucking.

Please, not that.

So it would seem that deeper digging, further research, more transgression, is required to breach the wall of grubby white noise, to provoke public outrage, wakefulness … And so one develops strategy. One has that in one's nature, one is trained for it … It does no good, but one deploys it, nonetheless.

And, of course, strategy shows – it suggests a mind at work, intentions. It could make people start to hunt for a Moriarty. One worries about that. There is an element of stress.

There are days when one is relieved that anything one releases into the public domain simply fizzes slightly and then disappears, leaves not a wrack behind.

Jon swung into Victoria Street and bolstered himself against simply running and not coming back, or forcing a little bit more of a nervous collapse and therefore bolting over the hills and far away, deep and deeper within the privacy of his own mind.

Off to the cloud-topped towers and gorgeous palaces of my own making.

It's not as if I'm fully operational; I could give minor insanity as my excuse for perceived wrongdoing … But I don't want to live in a world where concern for others and for the consequences of actions and for safety and reality and … Well, why not …? I don't want to live in a world where having a concern for true beauty on a wider and wider scale would be regarded as a manifestation of mental illness.

I want people to be proud of me.

Oh, that's pathetic, though.

But I do, would, do want that.

If they knew, I would like the people whose opinion I care for to be happy when they consider what I have done.

And when they see what I will do.

I am my own department. My own ministry — ministry was always a better and more logical word.

He set his shoulders in the way masters had told him to throughout his school life — an old boy who still undressed and dressed in the order he had been given: socks, pants, vest, shirt, trousers, tie. He walked upright. He could manage that.

I am the Ministry of Natural History. I progress.

15:25

MEG WAS DIFFERENT NOW.

She was different and currently at work on forcing her life to be different. She felt, for example, that it should involve more happiness.

This was all possible, because of a difference she hadn't worked on – one which appeared to choose her.

On the 28th of March 2014, Meg had woken at something like lunchtime inside the flat she had inherited from her parents. Waking was not, at that time, a good or a welcome feature of her life. It made her frightened and regretful. Her first experience of herself in any day was one of disappointment.

Not disappointed in who I was. Or that too, but more I was disappointed to feel I was still breathing. I was clinging on. Again. For more of the same.

The flat she was, by then, kind of camping inside contained what was left of her parents' choice of furniture: 1970s, often brown. The place also contained her mother's choice of decor – occasionally brown, but also cream and beige, although with a brownness about it. And then there were objects and ornaments of various types which had been somehow made existentially brown by continuing exposure to – she had to admit it – Meg.

Over time, the brown had become more powerful and convincing. It had spread. The brown grew to be this mystical shade of bloody doom that inhabited and rambled – a visible curse.

There was something about persistent drinking – home drinking, house drinking, house everything, locked-in everything – that generated brown. The sweating and fretting and regular visits of minicabs and the bottles handed over at the door by ashamed-for-you drivers – wet hands, crumpled money, no further pretence about parties, of just running a little short on reasonable sociable supplies – there was something about each little blow and cut of damage that made everything you touched or looked at become brown.

Even the air – the not-at-all thin, but unpleasantly thickened air. Like fucking gravy, like oxtail soup with madness in it – the madness of dead spinal columns and roll-eyed livestock. It had, by then, taken a shedload of effort just to peer through the interior – brown air, brown walls, brown carpet, brown remaining furnishings and fittings – or even to find anything in what had once been a passable family home.

No, it wasn't passable, it was a good home. It was concerned, attentive, generous, with Sunday dinners and Songs of Praise *on the telly when the hymns still had tunes and you could like and remember them, even if you didn't believe in one syllable, and there had been books and unbroken crockery and no tear in the stair carpet. A decent humanity had abounded. No brown.*

I never got the hang of it on my own. Didn't feel I could belong – not until I'd spoiled it, fouled my own nest.

I suppose I was never quite in phase with it once I got beyond thirteen, but I did my best, while probably not meaning well. And I moved out in the way that people used to when children could afford to leave their parents and, fuck me, I was an accountant and that's a profession and a success story and very appropriate for the daughter of other upwardly inclined people. My parents had bettered themselves, as they say. They did it at a time when that implied you were resourceful, not that you were bad: Mum a secretary in a university geography department and Dad a chemist, in the sense of his owning and running a chemist's shop. (Maggie was another kind of chemist, I know.) And they didn't have anything handed to them. The post-war world opened up for them, sure, and showed them possibilities, but they both had to fight themselves free of jobs on production lines, or some other doomed way to earn a living, a place in manufacturing. They didn't have the hand skills or the mindsset to thrive in a trade – so they went to work clean and came back that way. No industrial illness.

Dad's shop got squeezed out, eventually, when the street around him died, but he was eager for retirement by then – would have enjoyed it, too, if Mum hadn't died.

Dad wasn't why I got the interest in chemicals – and I never involved him or the pharmacy. I didn't sink that low.

Be honest – I would have tried, but his security was too tight.

After a while, just drinking is too hard – you don't have the stamina to match your pace of need. So you intervene with other substances. It's quite logical. It's not like you're a junkie. It's only inadvertent when you find yourself sharing the junkie world, which isn't nice, isn't friendly, doesn't run at a comfortable speed for drunks.

With Mum and Dad gone – when they went ... died, that's the word – when one died and broke the other's heart ... when the other one was murdered by sadness ... After that, I slid. Or else, I slid faster. I slid right out of my profession and out of my own home to deal with my debts and into theirs and thank Christ by then I was too disorganised to sell it, liquidate it, liquefy it – probably saw the writing being pissed up the wall.

So there I was defiling everything they'd left me and the air made of poisoned gravy and everything I looked at being wrong ... I was wrong.

On that 28th of March, she had reached roughly lunchtime and the curtains were closed because that was how the curtains stayed and nothing was especially remarkable about the terribleness of the day. Nevertheless, she'd hit the point when her existence had become no longer possible.

Her life as she was running it – and life was all about running as fast as she could – that life never had been possible, but now it was, for the first time, truly, really fucking clear that she had no future.

There was this moment.

A golden moment.

Like a door that swings open, some remarkable door and it gapes, pauses, examines you and wants you to give a look back and see and see and see – that's all you need do – you see how everything is golden, and then the moment's hingeing round and it'll shut and you're going to be caught on the wrong side and you know that you either have to run – when you're good at running – and you'll get through now, get out to something new, or else you never will. That's that.

You don't know where getting out would take you, or what it might involve.

You do know that your only other choice is dying and that dying might be bad.

Real dying – not the daydreams – doing that might be hard.

And inside the gold of the moment, Meg became distant to herself in a way that was useful. This let her consider calmly that she would either have to make a phone call and ask for assistance, or else head off and fill the grey-ringed bath with the lime-corroded taps (Mum would have been ashamed) and sit down in the water and finally get around to slitting her wrists as she had often planned to, but never quite had enough time for until today. Killing herself had been like a pleasant holiday she'd not been able to arrange because of her busy schedule, what with the drinking having been a very pressing kind of occupation.

I had two professions. I let the accountancy drop – it lacked glamour.

Her realisation had meant she was facing a decision and decisions always required that she should drink.

Only in that moment, that golden moment, she didn't feel like drinking. She didn't want to – didn't fancy it.

This was not usual.

She had an idea that there was, in fact, not anything left available that could be drunk, but this did not diminish the strange reality of no longer being thirsty in her particular way and of being in a state which did not involve the burning and always asking – *pleaseGodletmegoawayagain* – the begging for drink or some chemist's replacement for drink. And strangely – bad practice for an addict – she happened to have nothing chemical to hand.

Still … decisions, decisions … They were waiting.

Meg had felt most inclined – calmly, evenly – towards the wrist thing. There had been an idea, long set in place, to make the cuts lengthwise, along the veins, and get it right and never mind the pain and mess and tediousness of putting up with herself while it happened and then finally she'd be posted out to a peaceful country, no stamp required.

Meg truly in her heart had not wanted to face the phoning-for-help thing. Speaking to someone would always be harder than death – this was obvious. And she had attempted such calls at other times, if she was being fastidious about accuracy. She had called many people up over the months and wanted help more and less truthfully and been, meanwhile, messed about by crying and horrors more or less hugely, while she attempted to say she was never sure what. There was no longer anybody who welcomed her calls, who had enough compassion. There was not enough compassion on earth.

Throw me a lifebelt and I'll tell you it's not the right colour. I'll sling it back. There has only been one moment when all of me has wanted to be helped. I think that's right. Only one golden moment.

People get bored with other people who are harming themselves and unable to stop and who want to go on about it at three in the morning over the phone. That's fair enough.

Then roughly lunchtime on the 28th of March arrived – that small place in the whole of time.

It had made Meg feel tired. Beyond any previous tiredness – and she was usually exhausted – it had yanked all the scraps of strength from her and left her simply wanting to give up and drop – be at peace.

Even the idea of the razor blades tired her – the way they were constantly ready in a stack next to the soap dish, *like a tease, like a promise, like a fire exit that leads into a furnace that is guarded by a clever dog.*

She'd heard inside herself, perhaps outside, a voice like her own saying, 'I'm not doing very well. Please. And I am so fucking tired. Please. Can you help?'

The phone call won.

It won for no reason Meg had found she could really remember since.

Gold doesn't need reasons – or it eats them up and keeps them safe from you.

Gold happens. It's not brown.

Be gratefulgratefulgrateful. Remember to be grateful.

So they tell me.

And I tell myself that they are right.

Perhaps the threat of death had seemed more convincing than at other times and final in a way that was real and could spur her on to self-defence. Nothing was clear.

Golden.

She had dialled the number listed for AA – despite feeling this would be an unhappy choice and irrelevant and wasting a stranger's afternoon. She had spoken and cried and listened and spoken – mostly cried – and felt as a person does when that person is drowning and blazing and drowning and worn out with it.

Golden.

So that was March, then.

And she'd gone back to the AA meetings and had further strangers – and near strangers – walk across echoing rooms to tell her that she was welcome in what she felt was a semi-automatic way, but a semi-automatic welcome is still a welcome and maybe some of them meant it ... They didn't mean it, surely didn't mean it, when she said how many sober days she'd collected, or when people would call out, when there were these scattered voices saying that she'd done well, or that complete strangers were glad she was there – that was just some kind of courtesy thing, that was like a reflex – but when people came up and made an effort and told her to her face they were glad to see her or glad to see her again – weird – glad to keep on seeing her ... That seemed real in some way. And nobody patted either of her arms.

At first, though, she liked to assume that the warmth and concern apparently offered in the meetings was drawn from habit and not kindness. Habit felt safer than kindness. Meg didn't want anything tender happening to her, because tenderness breeds tenderness and leaves you undefended.

They started to greet me by name and ask after details. How are you? That's a detail.

AA is not exactly as advertised in that way – it isn't exactly anonymous.

And it's hard to agree that you're alcoholic because that makes you feel a failure. Not the usual kind of failure – a drunk's always a failure – it's mainly you'd rather not know that everyone else in the alcoholic club allegedly can feel the same ways you feel and think the same ways you think, but they deal with it better and happier and drier. They deal with it dry.

This meant that I had a problem with both of the As in AA.

But there was tenderness.

You can't avoid it.

They can't avoid it.

And you get thankful.

It can't be helped.

Apparently.

Allegedly.

You can be helped.

Apparently.

Allegedly.

And I spent a while clinging almost to that alone, so that I could stay sober.

Apparently.

Allegedly.

Those two golden As.

Apparently.

Allegedly.

Meg, newly sober and clean and starting again, once again, was less thankful and more in self-inflicted agony than anything.

They said the agony was self-inflicted. Sort of good news, because it means you can make it stop. Not good news, because you're not to be trusted and will not do any such thing.

But she sat tight in the meeting rooms and in the echoes of 'Hi, Meg.' Stuck with the whole palaver, all the rest of the ways the not very anonymous alcoholics went about things: clapping and having to listen while other people talked and having to talk while other people listened.

Fucking purgatory.

She held on.

She counted days – clean days, dry days – and announced them to others who were also collecting days as if they were valuable, transferable, pleasant. She piled them one on top of the other, or imagined herself to be laying them down like the bricks of a wall that she wouldn't climb back over again into razor blades and brown.

Having tried AA before and blown it she did expect to make that climb. She waited for the definitive shame of not even belonging with outcasts.

Only they didn't seem that outcast.

And I didn't fail.

I haven't yet.

One year and counting and it feels all right.

She'd got fairly used to recognising the faces of what were almost friends. And they knew and she knew slightly, perhaps, what she was like and found that not distasteful.

All new to me.

There was this day when I laughed and noticed I was laughing and I couldn't recall when I last did such a thing and someone who can't laugh is in trouble and therefore I must have been.

And there was the day when Meg had walked through her own park, the Top Park, and seemingly she could watch the push of chlorophyll, the spring fire rising in a green blaze along branches. She'd seen the drift and scatter of white petals, blushed petals, mauve and pink and cream petals, and been struck, been beautifully punched in the heart, by the presence of everything. She'd kept on walking under surely the most blue on record, a sky which should have been commemorated ever after, a phenomenon of nature. The truth of beauty had given up more truth and then more beauty and then this serious sweet truth, this singing and wordless thing, alight, alight, alight.

*Some kid in a school uniform went strolling through it, oblivious. He
was having a fag and hands in his pockets, not looking.*

That made me laugh, too.

And she had discovered herself kneeling at a certain point,
folded forward on the turf and breathing out and in and this being
an apparently endless and miraculous sensation.

It was all right to breathe. It produced no regrets.

The feeling passed, of course.

The world withdrew to a more bearable distance and made
itself practical.

But that day left a memory which was wholly clean.

There was now an area inside her which was wholly clean –
not just without liquids, without chemicals, substances – it was
filled with being clean.

You could get sentimental about that.

*And, of course, every rescued fucking horrible gerbil makes me think
of saving and being saved and is wonderful in a way, at a level. Although
it gets boring to cry so much, even with happiness. After a while, it's no
longer a treasure, or a sign of growth: you just want to skip it.*

Her progress – if that was the name for it – had carried on:
the work that let her be recovered – as if she was a knackered
sofa – and by the end of April she didn't seem so bad as she had
been and was no longer shaking at all, neither when addressed
directly, nor if asked a question. She could go into an unfamiliar
shop without too much alarm.

Around her, London went brown in her place: Saharan dust
pouncing in and making the breeze taste of broken tiles, of strangeness and thickened views. The screwed-up weather gave her headaches, but nothing like the headaches she'd had before. She could
survey the city from above and pity it for being that little bit
more afflicted than the Hill, the gentle Hill, the quiet Hill. And
when she was out and walking – she did a lot of walking because
it aided sleep – the buildings to either side of her had stopped
leaning over and slyly bullying. She could call on the doctor –
having got a new doctor – and visit the dentist – having got a
new dentist – and have herself looked at and make appointments

for what was overdue and begin to arrange what was left of her affairs. She noticed she was a financially screwed accountant – that wasn't good, but she wasn't homeless, was only being chased by civilised and shrinking threats. The worst threats were those that she built for herself in grey dawns, which was a trouble, but at least they were courteous and often left her alone once the sun was up.

Some things aren't threats – they're memories. It's just that they feel like threats.

It took the police a while to reach me when Dad died. I pretended they believed that I was in shock, apparently intoxicated because of shock.

They didn't believe that. When they saw me like I was, their faces showed the standard levels of contempt and maybe a bit more.

I didn't turn my back at my father's funeral: I was hardly there, instead.

Maybe that's why Maggie's threw me – another bad burial and the feelings creeping up from before, from where I'd left them, not buried deep enough.

I can have feelings now, right when I need them.

This morning I was frightened, right on cue.

Or nervous. More it was just that I was nervous … and I'd slept beforehand. I wasn't scared of my bed, or the dark, or my dreams …

Can't complain.

I can be a going concern.

I have time. I think I have time to do that. I can be happy.

May hadn't been so bad. Meg had gone to the pictures in May and seen a film. She had worried beforehand that the film would be popular and sold out and therefore disappointing when she didn't get in and therefore a cause for getting drunk again. The crowd of others queuing was also a cause for concern – perhaps she would not take to these dozens, maybe hundreds, thousands of happily and easily normal moviegoers. Perhaps they might notice she was built all wrong and decide to throw her out, call the management …

Cast me out of their midst …

My fears do sometimes like sounding biblical – it gives them extra weight when they're especially fucking foolish.

But the showing was not sold out and she bought a ticket and took her seat – which wasn't cheap plastic, or in a circle, or in a hospital … wasn't in a community centre, in a church hall, in a hospital … wasn't in any of the cheaply rented rooms that AA loves – and she'd had an averagely pleasant time, especially during those periods when she was not thinking *I am in the pictures I am here in the pictures I am doing something that people enjoy this is something that I could enjoy I am not sure if I'm enjoying this I am in the pictures I may not be normal I should go I am in the pictures I should leave.*

There are days when I'd make myself deaf, going on. One of the many reasons why it's good that the din is all internal.

She liked when the voices around her in the cinema – those so many others watching the shine of the screen – she liked when they laughed and she also laughed at almost exactly the same time. That seemed companionable and healthy.

And she'd thought about hobbies and gone for walks. She'd looked off the Hill, down at the city where she kept on collecting sober days and collecting her moments, the good ones. It might – right now – be full of moments going uncollected, probably was. It could be purely golden in places, in moments, could shine as it did at night.

She'd begun teaching herself how to cook again, relearning how to slice and stir and eat with her full attention.

And in June she'd seen the advert for the letters.

Expressions of affection and respect delivered weekly.

They had seemed a necessity, not a luxury or a risk.

They had seemed like a genuine sign that reality grew out along a grain and that Meg was travelling with it, following a less obstructed path.

Accepting the offer of letters, chancing that her application wouldn't be refused – that had seemed right.

And I know how it feels to do right – it's entirely unfamiliar, that's how it feels.

She had applied to the PO box listed – her heartbeat making her fingers jump as she posted the envelope – and had then received a polite and prompt request for more information. It had taken two weeks for her to reply. Creating an answer had seemed to need courage she didn't have. Although what it asked was not unreasonable.

While I can write to you without your assistance, offering the truth you deserve and perhaps do not know, my letters will suit you and perhaps please you better if you are willing to tell me about yourself.

I drink. I fall over. I lie down.

I drank. I fell over. I lay down.

I can't say that.

I am good at falling, but currently floating.

I'm Meg and I'm suspended. I think I might be empty now and that's why I can float.

But I can't say that.

Whatever you say will be held in confidence.

Yes, but that still doesn't mean I can tell you that I would like to be somebody else. I can't ask if you'd write to somebody else.

I mean, maybe — I'd guess — you do write to somebody else, lots of somebody elses.

And I want to say I'd like you to stop and just write to me. As somebody else.

I mean, I can't even fucking reply and do you need to know me, really? Can't I be an anonymous alcoholic?

You need not reply to the letters, although replies are welcome. This is, however, not a correspondence.

Meg had stared at the accusing notepaper she'd found in the spare room — probably her mother's paper. *I can't even start to do this, I can't say one word to you.* She'd been dumbfounded. That had been her feeling, right on cue.

Thinking about it makes me sick.

But I have been told to do things that I like, because having a life that's sweeter than before will help to keep me sober. Everything being kinder will make the effort of not drinking worthwhile. This means that I can and must have and do the things I like.

But I don't know any things I like.

And before she'd cranked out a word, her hands had been weighted down by this clear sense of someone being there at the other end of the process, this waiting mind, judging mind, stern mind.

I know what I used to like: drinking and the drugs which make drinking longer and browner and I liked being turned out the way that a final light would be. And inside my dark flat, I liked when the booze taxis came.

And what I'd like now … would be if a stranger might forgive me for all of these things he doesn't know about.

He was already strangely clear, judgementally clear, on the page – this man she quite literally couldn't afford.

What I liked was what terrified me – so I like what terrifies me. You terrify me. I think I like you. I might already like you.

But I can't tell if you're to do with the way I used to be and have to stop, or the way I might end up. What are you? What are you going to be? Will you be something I like that ought to scare me? Will you be someone I need to be frightened of?

Will you hurt?

Would you tell me?

You may call me Corwynn, or Corey, or Mr August, whatever you would prefer, and I will address you as you would wish. I will aim to ensure that everything is as you wish.

In the end, the only reply she could offer to his request for information had seemed very small and lonely, toiling out across the whole of a page in her twisted handwriting. She had to use handwriting – her mother had always taught her: handwriting for personal letters, typing for things that you don't really care about.

Please write what you think I would enjoy. And thank you. And please call me Sophia.

Which was pathetic in general and especially the Sophia part. Particularly that. If you turned round and asked yourself about that, you would find it laughable – wanting to be called a word that suggested wisdom and tasted of class, sophistication, maturity.

All this, when she was a dim, big kid lost in this misleading body and couldn't even manage common sense.

She still was a kid who would leg it, scarper, before intimacy even got threatened.

Well, I do have my reasons.

But Mr August was too far away to touch her and too far away to be bad news. And he was polite.

He was unforgivable and lovely and being lovely is unforgivable and also it made her not run.

I will begin by saying that nothing bad will happen while we're in here together. And please do call me Corwynn, or Corey, or Mr August, whichever you would prefer. Please don't worry about the choices. If you would prefer, you can pick them all. We will be safe together. I can promise you that.

Meeting alcoholics, your tribe, you get used to strangers who still know you, understand. They sit in the echoes with you and talk you through the turns and tunnels, the mine workings in yourself. You get used to that.

This means that someone who guesses you need to be safe, only from reading a note you sent him – he doesn't seem impossible. That good kind of man does not seem entirely unlikely. You try and guess, you try and feel what he'd be like: a man who writes lots of letters? A man who makes his living out of letters? A man who's used to noticing, guessing? A man who reads closely? Lawyer? Therapist? Adulterer? Someone who lies in wait?

But he didn't feel like that, didn't seem like that. And, after we'd properly started, once he was writing by hand and not typing – who types any more? It was lovely that he typed, had a typewriter, was in some place where things were like that: slower, painstaking, private – when I saw the way he wrote by hand ... I could find him better in his words, in the shapes of them, in the lines and dips and dots across his pages, the places where it seemed he might have paused, the paper he'd touched.

And I sent him paper to touch. My mother's paper. My best inheritance.

I knew it would be with him. It would feel his breath.

Please write what you think I would enjoy. And thank you. And please call me Sophia. And thank you again. You are very kind.

There was something about that he understood.

Dear Mr August.

Be very kind.

That's all I would have needed to say, Mr August. Not even that — you were being kind already.

15:47

MEG STOOD AT her kitchen window – Meg, still having her birthday and wishing it might have gone better so far. Meg sober and sober and wholly sober, Meg with the evening still ahead.

She saw the afternoon light colouring the flagstones, the ones she had scrubbed last year when she felt weird and harried one Sunday – they'd given her something to do. They had filled hours and hours with a nice mindlessness. She liked them. They'd been laid out nearest the back door, so you could sit in the sun if there was some. Her mother's idea.

The flags needed to be cleaned again. And the garden required love, detailed and applied affection. Meg was going to tidy and weed it and then she'd plant things. She would grow stuff she could eat – stuff that was healthy. And she'd prune the roses and fill in the gaps she would leave once the weeds were gone. There'd be places she could find that could sell her cheap plants.

It would be satisfying.

She looked through the window, which she polished weekly. She kept busy with maintenance tasks, because they lent dignity and reassured. The glass was almost invisible, but still there: the surface which had taken her father's gaze, her mother's, which had seen them every day.

I still get so scared and I don't know why, or I don't want to.

Here it is.

An older woman, mildly frail and bundled against the weather, steps on to an upward escalator at London Bridge Station. She has a shopping bag in one hand: not plastic, but a traditional cloth bag which is therefore saving hypothetical trees in some distant forest, or the environment in a wider sense. Her other hand holds the lead of a Labrador: a plump and older and honey-coloured dog, who seems a touch unsettled by the escalator and the lifting and rearing of its unforgiving metal steps, its constant shifting. The animal is positioned quite far below the woman on the long and otherwise empty escalator. Its leash is pulled taut.

The dog, only a little, tugs to and fro and the woman tries to turn in order, perhaps, to calm it. Then the Labrador pulls again and gently, gently, this begins to lean the woman backwards in a way that will soon become physically unsustainable.

It is possible to watch the woman and her pet for an amount of time as they begin to have their accident. They are, to a degree, on display. The woman's leaning becomes a twisting, backward sway and then breaks into a tumble that drops her spine and shoulders down on to the metal steps and their harsh edges. As she flails out her arms for support, she loses her bag. Its contents spread, tipping after her. She hits her head. There is an instant when the impact is clear, jarring. She rolls, exactly as she is fighting strenuously not to, down and over her dog – her full weight pressing on her dog – the animal making one high and bewildered noise and then lying flat and, it would seem, frozen in bewilderment. Meanwhile the steps climb away from the woman who rolls again, head over heels. This rolling seems unlikely and frightening in someone of her age and her body seems very soft and very caught by the movements of such a hard place.

And, as this sadness unfolds, people run.

From all over the station, so many people run.

So many strangers have seen this woman and this dog and now they are pelting, racing in from the upper and lower concourses of what had appeared to be an almost deserted, mid-afternoon space.

A man sprints and lunges for the Emergency Stop button, hits it and stills the offending escalator. A woman, about the same age as the one who has fallen, runs down from above, speaking as she does, asking questions with a kind of authority, 'Do you feel sick? Do you know where you are? Do you know what has happened? Can you move? Where are you hurt? No, don't worry about your dog. Not just now. Don't worry about your dog.'

A younger man kneels by the Labrador and talks to it, strokes its head. The fallen woman continues to be concerned about it, as she struggles to sit, dishevelled, trying to gather herself. Shock is plain in her flickering movements, damage and shock. She prefers to be more worried about her pet than her banged head, or her bleeding shin, or whatever else is injured. This is a way of having dignity – to hold cares beyond oneself.

A station employee arrives and he speaks on his radio and seems inexperienced, unsure of where to place his feet, his limbs, but he is trying to be confident and to assist. He pulls across a tape to block off the top of the escalator and pre-empt further confusion. He is thinking ahead. The he leans in and talks to the woman softly.

A dozen human beings who do not know each other are together, doing this one thing, supplying this care for a tumbled woman and her dog.

They ran. They all ran. They all ran beyond themselves.

Something bad had happened and they wanted it to stop.

They wanted things to be OK again.

They all ran so fast.

15:47

JON WASN'T SUITED to pubs. He'd recently begun to dislike them on personal principle. Apart from anything else, the tables never did quite accommodate his length of leg. They gave him knee compression, which must be unhealthy.

And this pub is a tiny slice of Chiswick – same brewer in charge. I would also say that the fish and chips aren't pleasing me, although I'm not best placed with my digestion at the moment and I'm sure they are, in fact, a fine example of their type.

Across two plates of beer-battered hake with chips – Jon's portion hardly attempted – sat Milner, the shine of two lagers and significant additional pre-refreshment brightening his forehead and glinting in the wet hollow of his collarbone. He was pressing what was – according to him – the world's only ethical mobile phone tight against what Jon suspected would be a greasily damp ear.

Somehow that's worse than anything – the thought of his soggy, waxy ear. Which is just a guess on my part. It may actually be a fine example of its type.

I'm OK, though. This is OK. I felt ill and peculiar because I've been awake since four and I missed my breakfast and then I missed lunch. I should eat a little more.

And perhaps I really ought to risk shaming and incomprehension and imprisonment a little less.

Then again …

At half-past six I'll be somewhere with knee room and a lovely view and that isn't a guess on my part and everything involved will be a fine example and not a type. So I can deal with the here and now.

I would like to point out – in the here and now – that I excel under pressure. This has been mentioned in every evaluation I've ever had and was true throughout my marriage, if that's of interest to anyone, which it isn't.

Milner was using the ethical phone to address some assistant whom he clearly viewed as being mentally handicapped by her gender. 'No, it would be in the white file, love. No, darling … No, the big, white file marked … Yes, that's the one …' He was enunciating with a savage fondness as one might to an elderly relative prone to rewriting their will, or else to some senselessly garrulous animal.

I bet he makes jokes about birds that can talk.

Milner rolled his eyes, almost audibly, for Jon's benefit. 'And if you run down the index … Exactly …' He winked at Jon to indicate they belonged in the same long-suffering brotherhood. 'Yeah. So read that to me …?' Milner cocked the mouthpiece away from his face while listening.

The investigator of uncommon influence demonstrates top-flight multi-tasking, yeah yeah fucking yeah. You don't know you're born, mate. Try being at a dinner party and having to ignore the manifest fact that a man you sort of trusted or at least nodded to in lifts has his hand under the table and, of course, on your wife's thigh while you're jamming down your dessert and planning tomorrow's strategies to save the arses of arses. That's what I do, after all – why dress it up, why not leave the arses bare for once? And I coordinate the data arising from overwhelming and over-whelmed change. The data which nobody wants. Except my own individual ministry.

Unlike, for example, the MoJ where it is most especially and stridently the policy to know nothing about anything at all. If there is no news then it can't be bad. And so the politics of faked conviction – in every sense – become the politics of delusion, of delusional narcissism, of assisted suicide, of abuse. Also in every sense.

Although I couldn't swear to that – not being a psychiatrist.

I still do my bloody job, I still assess impacts, consequences, sustainability,
costs and benefits. Facts and facts and facts, so many facts. It remains my
duty to provide them. This is viewed as a betrayal rather worse than pawing
a wife not one's own, or – from one position or another – allowing it.

So why not do what I feel to be proper with my facts, why not share
them wrongly when I am already in the wrong?

But I ought to be right.

I am right.

We do have need of the real world.

I am right.

In this and perhaps nothing else, I am right.

Milner – who didn't make one happy about journalists as a
species – talked on while Jon regretted having ordered fish. It was
probably just out of the freezer. This was nowhere near lunchtime,
so asking for a full hot meal had not been reasonable and Christ
knew why Milner had joined him in requesting another.

You just couldn't see me having something that you didn't. Is that it?
Didn't want to feel deprived, hard done by? Just have a go at living in
my today. Just try it. Today is not unbloodycomplicated …

Jon allowed himself, unwillingly, to hear Milner explaining,
'She's new. They can't keep up, the girls. I just get them broken
them in and—' Milner looked serious in the manner of television
policemen and patronised the phone again. 'Two hundred and
thirty thousand? You're sure? That's what it says? Well, yes then.
Courier me a scan of the whole thing – put it on a thumb
drive – but that's what I need for this afternoon, that page. Email
me when it's done. Use the Hushmail account. Although, by four
thirty everyone will know. That way we catch *PM* on Radio
Four.' Jon knew perfectly well that the *PM* programme was
broadcast on Radio Four. 'If they have any researchers on who
are over twelve, they'll manage something – maybe – depends
on their nerves, and whoever has the fastest hands can run with
the rest.' He rang off and then studied Jon with lubricated belli-
gerence. 'What?'

Jon was unable to prevent himself saying, 'That was an odd
metaphor.'

'What?'

'Fast hands would usually imply boxing, or some kind of contact sport … The running … Were you thinking of rugby?'

Milner speared some remaining chips on to his fork and proceeded to combine eating them with speaking, 'Writer now, are you. Funny. I thought that was my job.'

'It's my job, too. You didn't say goodbye.'

'What?'

'To your assistant.'

'I never do. She would think something was wrong if I said goodbye. And there's nothing wrong. So I didn't. That's reasonable, isn't it?'

Jon noted that his hands were shaking minorly and set them down on the tabletop close to his purposeless knife and fork. 'I …' He found himself exhausted. That was the thing about Milner: aside from his appalling character and appearance, he always contrived to be bone-deeply tiring.

'Is there something wrong, Mr Sigurdsson?'

'There's … No.'

'Every time your fucking phone makes a noise you look queasy. Trouble?'

'No. No trouble.'

'Ah …' The red mouth, glistening lips, opened wide. Milner winked like a music-hall spiv. 'Something up with the love life? Something wrong at work?'

'No. There's nothing wrong.'

In an everything kind of way.

The sparse drinkers and nibblers around about them registered the usual perimeter of Milner-related irritation. He was loud, he was boorish, he was unmissable and apparently gleeful about it. Even across the room it was possible to follow his conversations and be at least slightly repelled, if not alarmed that he might become truly unruly.

For the whole of their rendezvous Jon had tried his best under the circumstances, abandoning deft manoeuvres once it was clear to everyone in the place that the sun was really very far beyond

Milner's yardarm and subtlety would therefore be ineffective. Jon used the word *caution* as if it were a good thing and mentioned a long-standing series of leaks involving quite accurate statistics. He was able to breathe normally while he did so. He raised the forthcoming election as an issue and used the word *sensitivity* as if it were not funny in this context, and had then been very firm about the government's – any government's – willingness to engage generously with serious and reputable journalists anxious to perfect their craft.

I truly did just hear my own voice pronouncing both lifeblood *and* democracy *and slipping only a tiny* of *down in between them.*

Christ.

I may plead that the theatricality of the occasion is getting the better of me. An audience – albeit of Westminster topers – always encourages empty rhetoric.

Reasonable assumptions were made – out loud – regarding the levels of privileged access which might reward and welcome team players.

The man can't be bought off with access – he doesn't want access. If he's ever accepted anywhere he misbehaves until he's not. Milner is a human crowbar – he exists to force things open. The man is a tool.

Beyond that, the conversation swung round to Milner's many foreign achievements and his extraordinary levels of guile, which suited Jon, to be truthful – it meant that he needn't contribute further, beyond offering nods and mumbles.

They drifted on to how interesting ethical phones were and blahblahblah – Jon ceased to listen.

I have done my duty for my queen and country and sod this for a lark.

Please roll on this evening.

Milner being determined to prove himself a busy and significant man, their meeting was blessedly limited. 'Gotta go, Joe. John. Jon without the h … Good to catch up … Unhelpful timing, though, so I do have to rush …'

I did also have somewhere else I was rushing to. Thanks for not asking.

Milner winked at Jon. 'Don't let the bastards grind you down – you look ground, though. Ground as coffee. Ground as dirt.'

Milner's laugh had an unhealthy bubble about it, suggestive of heavy smoking, although he'd given up years ago, as he put it, *so the fuckers don't get me that way, either.* Milner then stood, his paunch defeating his badly striped shirt and allowing glimpses of a distressing belly: wiry-haired and bluish grey.

Jon smiled. He felt as if he had been smiling mirthlessly for the duration and this was probably the case. 'We'll … we must do it again.'

'You're kidding.' Milner wiped at the glisten of his lips with his fat knuckles. 'They can do their own dirty work next time. No need to send you. Not that you're not fun – you're a monkey *and* an organ-grinder, aren't you …?'

It's not that.

Milner tweaked his voice away from a growl and into a smug bray. 'Oh, and I won't shut up. I'm the last of the last who never will. No reason to bleat about Leveson – I don't need to bribe anyone for snaps of posh cocks and nightclub-toilet gossip. I'm an actual journalist. I am the actual basis of a free fucking press.'

'That's …' Jon, still seated, was forced to look up at this creature, to appear in public being belittled and lectured at like a 1950s secretary – taunted by an oaf. 'Unfortunate.' His one hand was clenching, he couldn't help it, but he thought he might still seem placid otherwise and he hadn't – for example – taken up his fork like an angry trident and plunged it into that exposed leer of belly. His calm would count as one of the civil service's many unsung and yet remarkable achievements.

'And why are your owners worried, Sigurdsson? Nervy about the folks out there going all Glasgow on them? The public? No one really gives a shit. The worst I could tell the faithful reader is unbelievable, the best is tedious – all of it makes them feel they've been screwed over and who wants that? Nobody wants reminding they've been fucked. Are being fucked. That's the Great British Public for you – like a Saturday-night housewife putting up with it, like a sad little slag lying back and hoping at least the boyfriend won't wipe his dick on the nice new curtains. They spoil everything, your lot. They've put democracy right off its dinner. Whether the parties parachute more girls in, fanny about with the ethnic diversity, root down the back of the chaise longue and find a coherent pleb, no matter how many muddy pints they gurn behind and cheap snacks and ciggies they hold, how many like-minded freaks they gather ... Whoever they put in the cast, they're always just more of the same old show. Like those bargain buckets of chicken – shitty dead meat to start with and in the end it all tastes the same.'

'You know that's— You can't simply dismiss—'

Milner loomed in and down, breathed hotly. 'And you let them fuck you, too ... You're the closest, you're their old lady, you're Mum. Civil service ... So you service 'em, don't you? You're another one of their shiny garage doors – IN CONSTANT USE.' Another laugh rattled out, spattering lightly against Jon's hair, as Milner swung his torso upwards again and then steered his combined weights towards the door.

His exit was not accompanied by an outpouring of affection from the room.

'And again – no goodbye.' Jon sipped his, by this time, cold cup of tea. His hands performed well while he did so, seemed almost completely reliable.

16:12

OH, FOR FUCKSAKE.

Jon was examining an on-screen document.

Shitting bloody Moses on a bike.

It suggested that anyone's professional life, that anyone's day-to-day activities, might actually involve 'running a discovery'. And that was wrong. That was a wrong thing.

Run a discovery? You want me to run a discovery? You want anyone to run a disfuckingcovery?

This was the kind of thing that made sane parliamentary minds rejoice in the estate's still-patchy Wi-Fi provision. Never mind if you couldn't reach constituents, at least you could steer clear of this.

Page seven also contained reference to Fast Streams and the fact that GOV.ORG as a brand was able to harbour the belief that The Strategy is Delivery.

It's zero content. We no longer deliver anything, we just have a strategy and the strategy isn't a strategy − it's delivery. We deliver an intention to deliver an intention to deliver. Why we don't all suffer absurdity-related aneurysms is beyond me …

Another page − *all of this is in a primary-school font, bloody children's literature I'm reading here* − posed the merry question: What Does This Mean For You?

I'll tell you What This Means For Me, I'll tell you – I won't, but I could – I'll tell you What This Means For Me. It means that you're a moron who only knows how to use not-quite language to not-quite say anything, which is lucky for you, because you have fuck all to say. You're a bloody Squid.

And what is a Squid, children? A Squid is a creature of darkness and the lower depths which renders all around it inky-murky at the least sign of unease. Then it buggers off and leaves you to deal with its squiddy problems.

My world is filled with Squids.

Jon considered his mobile: neat, sleek and inquisitive in his semi-dependable hand. He willed it to be helpful, to provide consolation. None was forthcoming. It was, no doubt, currently telling a number of entities where he was and where he'd been, what searches he'd performed, what preferences he had in various directions.

My preference is to be left bloody well alone.

He was being distracted by a number of factors besides the Squid.

I can't comment on this shit: it's from someone else's people and I shouldn't have to. I can't say a thing. If I started I wouldn't stop. If I could get every holder of an MBA into a burning warehouse ... well, then that would be a wonderful thing.

No, no, it wouldn't. That goes against every principle I still have – that I think I still have.

But one may dream, surely, indulge oneself – unwritten imaginings, no ink necessary.

Jon also had a sensation that might indicate a call from Chalice – or some other Nibelung – was on the way, enquiring about the conduct of Jon's Milner-based liaison.

Then again, they'll have had eyes in the pub. Chalice will enjoy asking for details and knowing that I know that he knows them already and that I also know that. Fuck.

I'm swearing a lot. Even internal swearing can show – Val could spot it. I should stop.

Beyond Jon's desk, the office was fully functional and apparently placid. It was purring along, if not as it should in an ideal world, then certainly as it did on untroubled days. In as far as the departmental definition of Untroubled had been subject to mission creep, through time.

But it all looked fine. Staff members came and went like nicely phrased imaginings. He had a good team. They were engaged, as they should be, in building the long, long memory that any hope for common sense required: adding to an intelligence that could consider and extrapolate, that could govern effectively, that could underpin a civilisation. Jon would seem, on sweet days, to feel the threads of various, reliable, verifiable narratives winding about him as they flowed on and this would make him happy.

I believe in reality: in the trinity of here and now and me. Not in a messianic sense. I believe these three things are connected and should be connected. I believe in the rightness of doing right things and nothing more. Not much more. In this – where else? – I can exist.

The compulsory Sunday services at Jon's school had removed any other faiths, inner and outer. He'd had a not unpleasant speaking voice, even then, and was often asked to deliver Bible readings. That's when he'd first noticed that he echoed – inside and out. And it was when he'd first felt the betrayal inherent in passion, too: the aftermath of nausea and uncleanness after a psalm flared up and lit him, while still being quite meaningless. It wasn't just him, either – the homilies and sermons offered by his betters had also echoed, split open and revealed their emptiness.

And the words of my betters echo still.

He thought about turning off his mobile.

Any text will be bad news. There's no reason for anything lovely, not really. I do hope for better, or for opportunities to be of use. What I'll get will very probably be Sansom having another go.

My phone is not here to help me – it's just trying to guess how I might like to spend my money. It is purring along in its way. Somewhere in its workings, in its extended pattern of thoughts, there are plans to show me other and better shirts than the one I bought this morning – that and new, breathtaking ranges of corduroy.

The back of the device was hot in his hand – *the temperature of an active voyeur, I suppose, or of a readied exhibitionist. It's seen in through my windows – now it wants to flick open its raincoat, show me an offer I can't refuse.*

He felt himself grin.

But I can forgive that. It lets a proper-words and proper-ink-and-proper-paper man, an old-school man, hold on to a solid point, hold tight and when ...

Rowland passed, wearing trousers of a cut at present fashionable, which apparently aimed to highlight the wearer's thighs and cock – his balls, even – in a manner which complimented neither Rowland nor any conceivable observer. Rowland was not unlikely to excel over time. He was a gifted Squid. He had all the necessary modern qualities.

And, I suppose, a suitably unthreatening cock – since he's forced me to be aware of it in detail.

Jon was glad he wouldn't be in post to witness Rowland's triumphs.

I asked him once – he was foisted on me for a while – to Kirkaldy the figures on those possible changes to bereavement benefits between social-security-agreement countries. What precise effect would it have, for instance, if a UK citizen living in Bermuda were to be paid only the Bermudan rate of widow's benefit, rather than the higher UK rate, which could be seen as excessive and unnecessary, given her change of circumstances and lower living costs? Yes, that individual might have made a range of tax contributions while in the UK, but now she was resident elsewhere ... An argument for withdrawal of privileges could be presented as reasonable and fair.

Benefits are no longer rights, they are privileges. We are to forget prior contributions made in any capacity – we are only to regret and be shamed by our greed when we want to reclaim the promised portion of what we once allowed to be held in trust. We should, likewise, never dare to expect any payment from a private pension – that's not what they're for. Whatever we pay for it isn't for us.

For Rowland, this model – of endless wrongdoing and entitlement amongst the crafty weak – was impossible not to embrace. He clearly found it incorporated types of justice that Jon could not appreciate, or indeed administer, and there was hardly a trace of cynicism about his position. Rowland was a man of faith.

We don't have a short attention span in the modern age. It's that we're often bored – which is different. God knows, a great deal of what's presented to us is second-rate, third-rate, inhuman and therefore uninvolving. Our governments, our employments and our entertainments – why wouldn't they make us bored? They could make us incandescent, but bored is more likely.

But that isn't the same as having a short attention span. Claiming that places the blame at the wrong end of the equation – more punishment of the victim – it's like saying that the widow is somehow complicit in her bereavement – soiled by it – simply because it has produced the symptoms of distress and all distress is now deemed a cause for suspicion. Suffering no longer indicates hardship, it indicates bad character and celestial punishment. And if God has seen fit to punish – well, that invites further loss.

Jon checked his texts again, although there had been no indication that anything new had arrived.

What we have is a short memory. For everything. Tell the average mug punter to put a quid in the communal tin, wake him up the following morning and he'll accept without hesitation that asking for ten pence back because he needs it would be a sin.

We forget what – historically – has worked and what hasn't. We forget that's a danger to us and trot on.

Jon couldn't settle. He was relying on his forefinger to prod regularly away, control the cursor that was scrolling down the document on-screen – the one he couldn't stand to read, and to which he would make no corrections ...

I'm not like this. I'm conscientious.

Perhaps I'm ill.

My mind doesn't wander.

Not to this degree.

I still have no idea how I feel.

Other than feeling that my mind shouldn't wander, which is a kind of wandering.

I told Rowland – I ordered him, 'Kirkaldy it.' He'd never even heard the term. 'Kirkaldy it,' I told him. 'Which is to say, subject it to testing according to the motto of that great Victorian and great man David Kirkaldy – Facts Not Opinions. *A neglected Victorian Value, the love of facts.*

'Kirkaldy tested materials. He was a man of the real and unforgiving world where bridges collapse and engines explode and matter fails when it is needed most and kills and harms if it hasn't been properly handled in the first place, if it isn't fully known. He wished to establish reliability and standards ...' I smiled, truly smiled at his ocean-floor face. 'So Kirkaldy it. Comprehensive figures, all eventualities.'

And I paused – because in the pause before the act lies all the peace and satisfaction and security of the world. Passion – yes – betrays. Pausing – yes – is wonderful. It's the test of what's true.

In the pause before the act, I live.

And he looked at me as if I had asked him to cut off his slimline dick and let me wear it tucked behind my ear.

Before I said, 'Only joking. For a start, if we no longer pay their people in full, they'll no longer pay our people in full and they're paying our people more, relatively ... And our widows and orphans still have ransom value. At present ... Respect, at least in theory, for the widow – and indeed the widower – and the orphan still exists. It's all a journey and we're not there yet.'

'It's all a journey and we're not there yet.' Nauseatingly meaningless phrase.

Which meant Rowland adored it. His little eyes flared at its sound and he saved it for later use, I'm sure. He chuckled away in squiddish relief, because imagine if I'd truly asked him to be exhaustive. No one wants contact with actual, undeniable information: it's the equivalent of shit, you don't want to touch it. If information exists then it should be known and it must be consulted. If it's consulted in advance then those we serve will feel constrained by it, oppressed – like having their legs jammed under a pub table. And if information exists to lie in wait, to reproach them in retrospect, point out the wiser paths not taken, or the just plain inevitable failures ... Then it can feel like a reproach, which is upsetting.

Opinions Not Facts — these are our watchwords. Run a Discovery.
Stay Vague. If reality is malleable then anyone can do what they like:
either join the mediocracy, be a mediocrat and pursue nothing much, or
else be a zealot and design impermissible calamities you're sure you can
withstand while others of less worth will perish as they should.

Reassess some human being's illness and then decide it's inadmissable
information. Remove their benefits as a result. Force them to beg from
council contingency funds, relatives, friends — if they have such things.
Force them to fail in payments to utility companies. Force them to seek
advice from a Citizens' Advice Bureau, already under pressure and
employing additional staff because of unprecedented levels of distress.
Force them to seek legal aid for their appeal — if they can get legal aid,
if they haven't given up fighting, if they haven't agreed to beg and starve
quietly. Force them to default on rent payments, mortgage payments, to
risk or to experience homelessness. Advise them badly, advise them
misleadingly and issue threats. In what way does this not release a cascade
of additional expense and wasted time and wasted life in all directions?
In what way …

Oh dear Christ and fuck and fuck and fuck and fuck.

Jon's grasp on his phone now overly tight and not helping.

F*ffffffffff*uck.

The tremor in his grip had transferred to his phone, apparently
by pressure of will, or just pressure of pressure.

I think that I may be beginning to know how I feel and I'm absolutely
certain that should be avoided.

The phone was, in fact, trembling on its own behalf, trying to
let in a call — this part of reality twisting his stomach in nervous
ways he could do without.

I just can't be here any more.

And yet I am.

When he looked at the caller display, Becky's name was showing
and that was nice, was beautiful, there was nothing bad about that.
She didn't often ring him …

Six thirty p.m. and I'll be somewhere else and just now I can speak
to my daughter. I'll manage. I am sustained.

Then again, Becky knew that he usually didn't answer personal numbers when he was at work and so her trying to reach him might imply urgency …

Please not 'We got married on a whim.' Please not 'Dad, I think I'm—'

'Becky, how wonder—' And this noise, simply this noise reaching him, of a young and intelligent woman having been, in some manner, destroyed by something. Just sobs. He told her, 'Oh, darling … what's the …? I'm here. Daddy's here. Your dad's here. I am.' More sobs. Actually, increased distress. 'I'm here.' And then some attempt at words which immediately distorted and ended in heaves of breath. His baby, his child, was breathing in spasms and too far away for him to hold. 'Darling, whatever it is, we'll work it out. We will. I promise.' A sort of howl now. 'No, we will. We'll cope …' It was simply very tricky, though, to help if he didn't know what he was helping with. 'If you could … Is it your health? Darling, are you OK?'

Please be OK.

'No.' Her one syllable elongating and wavering.

Please.

'Well, no, I know you're not OK, but are you well?'

Another gulp of air and, 'Yeah.'

Thank you.

'And your mum's fine?'

Jon was aware he was speaking a touch too loudly and that his upcoming content might be unsuitable for an office that was unavoidably open-plan.

This is our sole concession to transparency, I think – we now have transparent interior walls, due to their absence.

Jon broke out across the breakout area.

Again – whoever imagined such a term wants shooting.

'Becky … Becky, please speak to me, though. Is everyone else OK?'

'Mm-hm.'

Thank you.

'Good.' Jon scampered himself towards the stairwell exit. 'That's good.'

His daughter's voice was snuggled beside his cheek, while his own aimed at comfort, at certainty. 'Becky, whatever's happened, things will be all right, I promise.' And he tucked himself beyond the department's hearing.

We're primates, we have complex social hierarchies which take constant maintenance and that's a bit of a burden, really – even if we don't have to mount and groom each other all the day – and therefore we need breaks away from company. We need to hide.

'Can you tell me what's the matter, darling?'

'—ess.'

'That's good … So … You're OK and Mum's OK …'

And Jon knew, absolutely understood by this point, that no one gets upset with this level of intensity unless it's to do with sex, with love – more properly and horribly with love. And the knowledge of this fragmented and then fought inside his chest, its separated pieces seeming dreadful to him.

'Keep talking to me, darling, I'm here. Take your time.'

If that fucker Terry has fucking done something to her I will genuinely … If he's left her … If he's hurt her … But if he's left her … If she's left him …

Christ, how bloody marvellous. He was such a twat.

'It's Terry.'

Don't blow this, don't fuck up.

'Is it, darling …? Is he … ill?'

'He's gone.'

'Oh, I'm so …' Jon in the stairwell now. He didn't see enough of the stairwell. It was nice: plain, unfrequented, a potential source of healthful exercise. 'I am sorry.'

'He's gone.'

Gone. Then sweet Christing Jesus, there is always hope. Thank you.

Jon swallowed, reminded himself that smiles are audible. 'But that's …'

Exactly what I wanted.

He began again, while a silence rose from the phone – dismal and horrible – the silence of the girl he loved, the girl whose pain he always wished to banish. 'People do fight, Becky … I know you know that … But they do and they say things they don't mean and maybe—'

'He's gone!'

It's good she's yelling. It's good. Good for her.

She kept on now, her volume approaching something painful and making it necessary to hold the phone slightly at bay. 'He's fucking gone because I fucking threw him out because he was fucking screwing someone else. He was fucking screwing Jenny. For two months.'

'Oh, God … I mean … Oh, God.' Jon remembering that first kneedintheballs realisation that what had been loved as only yours was not, that your privacy never was private, that in the shadows other eyes had looked, hands were fumbling, making you dirty at one remove and robbing you in your heart. 'I mean …'

'I had to. Didn't I?'

'Of course you had to. Sweetheart, you absolutely had to. I mean, if you think that was the right thing and it feels right—'

'It feels horrible!' And the crying again.

'I know, I know, I do, I know. Of course. But probably you did have to and nothing is written in stone if you … But you did have to …'

Chuck the bastard out and change the locks and hallelujah.

'I know.'

'You've got more backbone than I did, than I have … You know that, too, don't you?'

Jon Sigurdsson almost entirely lacking in vertebral calcium and despicably overjoyed that Terry fucking Harper the dickhead is out of the picture and now there will be a period when Becky needs me and when we can, we can, we can … I can be her dad. She's letting me be her dad.

'Dad, could you …'

There we go – there it is.

Jon sat on the cool of a step and wiggled his feet for a moment, as if he were dipping them into the shallows of success.

Oh, but—

'Dad, I don't like to ask.'

The thing is that—

'Do, though. Ask.' The step taking on a new chill and seeming to shrug slightly, as he realised, felt her inevitable request nose round the corner and head towards him like a Wild West locomotive on a bend: heavy and high and decided, potentially harmful.

'I'm in the flat. Could you come round?'

'Sure.'

Please. Please don't prove me a bad father all over again.

'Can you ...'

You're going to, but please maybe could you not ask me precisely ...

'Can you come round now? Would that be difficult?'

And under the train I go.

'No, no, not at all. It wouldn't, darling. Of course. You stay there and I'll ... I was leaving early, anyway, sort of ... I mean, now I won't, but ... I mean, I will but for a different reason ... Things are going on, but ... I'll come round.'

'You don't have to.'

'I think clearly I do, though. So ...' *Despising that plummet in my chest.* 'So I'll be round in a bit. Do nothing.' *She was with him for three years. It's not easy, losing three years.* 'I'll bring food. I'll bring ... stuff for the bath ... I mean, nice stuff – not cleaning fluid ... I'll be there. With stuff.' *And it's also not easy being punished immediately for one's uncharitable thoughts.* 'And call again if you need to, we can talk as I'm on the way, and I'll stay above ground so you can.' *It's good, though – gets it over. I hate waiting for pain.*

Why I'm so conscientious – I expect disasters and therefore plan accordingly. In work as in life. If I have to wait, I'll wait fully equipped.

'Really, darling ... Ask me to bring anything you need and I will.'

'No, I'm all right.'

'Well, yeah ... You're always all right. Always. I've always got your back. And I'm on my way. OK?'

'OK.'

'OK, then. A couple of things to do here, but I'm on my way for sure, for sure. And love, Becky, I'm sending love. I am. And bye-bye. Bye-bye.'

'Bye, Dad. Thanks.'

And Jon considered it appropriate to sit for a while longer on the step and rub and rub at his face and close his eyes, because he did not want to see and see and see.

I love Becky.

He rested his head on his knees, folded over the tired and echoing nothing he cradled within, until this made him especially nauseous and he had to stop, right himself and swallow.

It's not that late … I could pop my head in to Becky and then … No.

I won't make it. I can't get up there and then back to London Bridge for six thirty … But maybe for eight thirty … Or nine. I mean, I could get away again … I mean, it's a disaster, but not a complete disaster – for her. I'm not thinking of me. I am thinking of …

Would not seeing me be a disaster? Surely not that. Hardly that. Presumptuous of me to think it would be that.

I'll have to call and say I'm rescheduling again. Text. I'll send a text. I can't do a call. I think a call would make me faint.

Pathetic, aren't I?

I do want to go and be there – at London Bridge. I do.

All of me wants that.

So why am I also relieved now I might not have to?

Jon stood, leaning for support on the banister, watching the steps below him undulate briefly.

I love my daughter.

Maybe I shouldn't love anyone else.

A woman sits in a café on a not unpleasant day. There may be rain later, but it's gentle now and quite mild for October. She sits by the window reading and sipping a coffee. She is in her forties and although she seems healthy there is something slightly gaunt about her. She is carefully dressed: neat black shoes with a moderate heel, business suit in dark grey cloth with a pale blue stripe, pale blue blouse. Everything is of quite good quality but is a touch large for her, a touch out of date. It might be that she hasn't worn this ensemble in a while, took it for granted and then discovered, too late to do better, that it wasn't exactly suitable, or as she'd wished.

Perhaps it's this cause for regret that lends her a noticeable tension. The woman might, equally, be expecting company. That said, she has left a black mackintosh of traditional design folded over the chair opposite and has a book with her – no one appears to be on the way.

There are two waiters on duty – one behind the counter and one with a roving commission – and both of them seem to know the woman in the sense of recognising a regular customer. They do not resent that she has ordered just this small coffee, has ignored the generous towers of brownies, heaped scones, the possibilities of hot dishes. They don't mind that she seems in no hurry to leave.

Then again, it's not busy now. The square outside is quiet, the afternoon is lengthening, even dimming. The day is coming to an end. The place will close soon, as it doesn't cater to the after-work crowd, leaving that to the pub over the way, to the restaurants dotted round about. There would be no absolute harm in the woman staying put until that happens.

She looks at her watch and orders another cappuccino in a voice which is soft, maybe distracted, maybe involved with the book she reads and then does not read, instead glancing out through the window at nothing much. It may be an uninvolving book.

All of these actions on her part have a kind of weight, a significance, simply because she is the café's only customer and therefore a focus of attention.

There is nothing significant in her lifting the new coffee to her lips, then deciding against it, standing, paying the waiter without getting change and walking outside.

Her expression, though, as she opens the door – her expression reflected in the glass panel that lets her see the wet autumn pavement opposite – her expression is one of such certainty and content. She seems to be more than she was. It is remarkable to her.

16:20

MEG HAD ARRIVED late. She had decided that rather than haunt her flat she might go into town and do what AA recommended in case of emergency.

Which is that I should pick up the phone and call someone or go to a meeting. And picking up the phone would involve speaking and I've been speaking a lot today – feels like a lot, feels like I am all spoke out. A meeting is just peaceful – being there in a room with members of your own species ... really your own true species. You don't need to speak when you're that closely related.

And it was humiliating to be over forty and upset about a boy. A man. About nothing much having gone wrong in connection with a man – a man she had very rarely been in the same room with, if you wanted to think of it like that. So why miss something that hardly happens?

But he matters. And it's pathetic that he matters, so I'd rather not mention it, thank you. I will simply sit. In the seat that I clattered into just as the speaker was finishing up, so I have no idea what she said. Everyone looks a bit thoughtful, so she was presumably sharing stuff of the momentous and spiritually insightful kind.

Quite glad I was too late for that. I was more on the prowl for something funny. Or really grim. Either would be cheering. Funny is cheering in itself and grim makes you glad that you're only yourself and not somebody else.

My late and disruptive self.

It's OK that I wasn't on time, though. No one is thinking badly of me, or if they are I don't care. You're only ever late for your first meeting: that's how the saying — I think it's a smug saying — seems to go. AA has a lot of sayings. It can get a bit much — the slogans and sayings and suggestions and steps and the spiritual fucking insight — the assistance. It can irritate.

It always reminds me of Jim — friend of my father's — who had a stroke a while back and they stuck him on a ward with a bunch of old men. Jim didn't think himself old and found this a bit insulting. He also didn't want to look at what could be his future — joining the shambling, babbling victims of their own lumpy blood supply. They scared him. They weren't showing him a good way to be old.

Every morning, volunteers would turn up in the ward and would read to the patients — including Jim — from the Bible. This didn't please him, not one bit. The stroke meant, at first, that he did sort of join the shamblers. But he couldn't move one of his feet, or one arm, too well, so he couldn't get up without help and nobody wanted to help him get clear of the readings. More importantly, he couldn't even babble. He was completely unable to speak. And the people with Bibles kept on.

But after a week, Jim was able to utter his first words — to a Bible-reader.

He said, 'Fuck off.'

Possibly AA works like this — it annoys the hell out of you, talks and talks, and so you find out what you think, you find what you have to say and you get better. Possibly.

Possibly, you look at the shambling and babbling when somebody first arrives and you know you aren't like that any more. You have been spared and want to stay that way. Or else, people tell you their stories and you hear about the chaos inside, which is like your chaos inside — you have the Hindenburg burning inside you always — and that's worse than any stumbling in the street, or dropping bad sentences, slurring, acting as if you are gravely ill when you are only self-inflicted … And you see these other types of people — brand-new people, just-in-the-door people, getting-better people — and you can believe that your trouble could be compelled to pass you by. The bullet came close, it whined at your ear and you felt its heat, but now it's flying on without you. It didn't hit.

Or maybe it did hit, but being here makes the time roll backwards and the lead burrows up out of you and leaves, goes and tucks itself back in the gun.

Maybe this is the place where you can keep on with being alive …

If I do have to or do want to stay alive …

Which I do, I do – I've got things I can be getting on with …

Meg sat at the edge of the rearmost line of chairs.

But most of the things today seem to involve plastic chairs …

She and the chairs were set out in the vestry of a Palladian church on the verge of the West End. There was musty-sweet air about that suggested sanctity, that had the flavour of thought upon human thought attempting to hold out for better things, reaching. That elevated type of straining after God left a noticeable aftertaste, it was there under every breath. It was like flowers, like honey, like old paper – it was practically religious. But thank Whoever that it wasn't, in fact, religious.

If I had to really pray it would stop me breathing.

Tea, coffee and not bad biscuits were also available.

Meg hadn't been here before, because attending afternoon meetings was something she associated with not really having a life.

And I do, I do. I do have a life. I matter. I can be firm about it when I say that I matter to more than just a Machiavellian dog.

It had taken her a while to find the building and there were no faces here that she recognised.

So I can nip out smartly at the end and get away, not be detained by pleasantries.

How am I? I'd rather not tell you and I don't have a genuine interest in how you're doing, so I won't ask. Forgive me.

I am glad to be here, but I do also want to leave.

An older man whose name she hadn't caught was telling the room, in a slightly mumbly way, about something or other – some custody battle with his wife – Meg couldn't bring herself to listen. There were murmurs of sympathy, or comfort, or approval from the occupied plastic chairs and that should be enough for the guy – he didn't need the whole world, surely, to hang on his every word.

She could let her mind be soft and wander, leave the stacks of fading hymn books, the irrelevant psalm numbers posted up and the strangers' pains.

I will meet you.

So so sorry.

It will be seven thirty or possibly eight. Could you do eight? Dinner at eight?

So sorry.

And, as the meeting rolled and worried on, Meg knew she wasn't going to stick her hand up like an eager student and then wait to get picked and then shout out that she'd had a recent anniversary. She wasn't going to say a word. She didn't feel like celebrating any more. She felt as if she was waiting for a distant point to hit her – a point which dodged away and away and away and who could tell if this was a good or a bad thing.

I will not resent him. I will resent a meeting which isn't a meeting for making me finally finish with my anniversary.

Every delay he makes is not forever. It will feel as if it is forever, because people of my sort feel everything bad as if it will go on forever.

And we get worried by joys because we know they're short and when they're gone we'll miss them.

Fun being us, isn't it?

The older man stopped talking and there was a disjointed hubbub of thanks before a very young woman took over, tumbling into some complicated saga about her neighbours.

I don't have to join in, if I don't want. Those in more need can have the time – there's only an hour in the first place ... Why should I stick my oar in? I have nothing to contribute, not a word.

Speaking can be the uncommunicative option. Sometimes, instead of fretting down the night over conversations you can't build, can't have, can't face, conversations you know you'll lose – because any conversation is competitive and you never can compete – you can sit down with paper and write what your best self would say, write as someone who seems better than yourself, write to someone who seems better than yourself. That can work.

So Meg had written – letters.

Letters for Mr August.

Dear Mr August.

She set them out on that paper her mother left: good-quality stuff, lying still in its box on a wardrobe shelf in what had been her parents' room and what was currently the ghost room, mainly empty, mainly echoes upon which the door was shut and shut and shut and had to be shut while she was drinking.

The paper was cream, heavy, serious enough to be intimidating.

The last hands to touch it had most likely been been her mother's. It was a personal stock for responses to formal occasions like anniversaries and weddings, or notes sent after relatives had stayed. Any departure left behind what her mother would interpret as an ongoing desire for reassurance on the part of absentees. Her correspondence had wished well and made requests that whoever read it should come back as soon as possible. Her mother had liked a full house and had never been able to settle, not really, until she'd received a reply of equal vehemence, equal need – something that promised.

So it was paper with a history of wishes and determination and that was maybe no bad thing, Meg didn't know. It was available and it was nice and it made her feel comforted, rather than guilty, and she'd used it.

She hadn't imagined how fast the whole block would be worked away by her efforts. This was partly because the pen-and-paper thing was like life – mistakes were permanent. If you wanted to end up with something you wouldn't be sorry to show someone, then you had to destroy attempt after attempt and keep starting again.

Which isn't much like life, actually. Unless the drinking – the coming round again and drinking again and passing out and then coming round again – unless that's an attempt at tearing up your own stupidity. Tearing and beginning and tearing and beginning – forever.

But I am here now and trying to start again. Forever. Different kind of forever.

Today. Forever inside today – I'm told I can pop it all, my everything, inside these twenty-four hours and that it won't be too big to grip. I try to believe this in the AA way. I'm trying all kinds of things. I am.

I am sitting on a plastic chair and trying to listen while a wife goes on about her son getting drunk at a party for his first time and being terrified he'll now do that every night. This doesn't apply to me in any way — I won't have children.

I do understand being terrified.

I can be terrified of paper.

For Mr August, she'd torn up so much paper. There had been so many tries for a clean start. For Corwynn August. And all the attempts at that first letter were the hardest. They felt like for ever.

I wanted to answer you, because

When you wrote you made me happy

When you wrote it made me happy

You make me happy

I had to answer

She almost gave up. Also for ever. After all, he'd written that she needn't answer if she didn't want to. Meg was paying him for letters, they would arrive anyway. But she did want to answer. Answering Mr August was as right as picking up the phone in that golden moment had been right — it was a right thing to do. She'd felt that for lots of reasons — most of them pathetic, but still there all the same.

And there was the forward-slanting shape to his words, this rush in his handwriting — and his choice of pale blue paper. And it seemed, when she read him, that he was being kind to her — which is what she'd paid for — but it also seemed that he didn't have a friend, that how he was and what he was doing with these letters had been partly caused by not having a friend.

And I'm not the most wonderful human being — I know that — but a person can't do well if they haven't got anything friendly they can be with. Any friend to keep you going is what you need — that's maybe not great, but it's better than no one.

I am better than no one.

I could be really a step up from no one and all right.

And kind people should be able to live, they should be helped with that.

Finally, his third letter had been freshly opened and in her hands, was warm there and clear and had this decency, which was unusual and made you think you would like to have more of that around. And it made her want very much, this time, to write something she would send him.

She'd bought a dictionary from the Oxfam shop in case any faults of spelling might shame her. Her brain felt out of use and as if it would betray her in that area. For this attempt, she'd sat at the kitchen table, which she had wiped down and then dried and then dried again. She'd put out the paper again, tapped the edges of the little stack to make it neat again. She'd sat – on a wooden chair, not plastic. Her mother's chair.

Meg's thumb and forefinger, her fist, her forearm – all of her – was used to keyboards, typing on a screen. If she used paper at all then she was only scribbling lists and notes. And so the special paper – the downy texture of its skin – and the good pen … She could only make them produce unpleasant loops and scratches, unreliable forms that hadn't been part of her since she left school and which had compressed and deteriorated. Everything she wrote looked fraudulent, but made plain the underlying truth – that here was a scrawling drunk, wet writing.

I have the hand of a woman whose cheques came back from the bank – refused. And not often due to lack of funds – it was mostly just that signing my name in the usual way was now beyond me. I could no longer write my name. Not every day, not on demand. Some accountant, me … Some human being …

That whole evening when she first tried to write a letter in the kitchen – it had crumpled into heaps around her. She had nothing but abandoned pages and a sore forearm. She'd written for longer and therefore gone more astray, made more errors. The effort had actually made her muscles sting – the unaccustomed effort.

Like at school – in exams, tests.

This is not a test.

Oh, yes it is, though. Yes, it is.

Everything's a fucking test – forever.

Then she'd closed her eyes.

She'd thought that there must be some family tradition, some sweep and dip of every pen, some length of arm and pace of blood that meant she could write a fucking letter, one letter, be another woman of her family who sent words out in envelopes to please those she cared for.

Those she loved.

This one she loves.

We've got a tradition of paper and love.

Which I do, I do — I do believe. I did then and I do more now. And that can be forever.

It was almost midnight when she'd let some part of herself wade, or swim, or run out into a real attempt to tell him something — full effort — and had felt this rising thin coldness move across her, this strangely penetrating contact which seemed to shock. But it felt clean — wide and high and clean. She was in this new and wide and high and clean space where she would speak to Mr August and be true.

Then she'd opened her eyes.

Then she'd written down what she believed he ought to know — only that.

Dear Mr August,

You are dear and don't make any mistake about that because I don't and don't let anyone treat you badly because they shouldn't. You're dear and if you forget then I'll remember. I don't forget.

I go about my days and I have what you write in my head all the time. It's sweet. It's serious and sweet.

Forgive me for sending this, but you mentioned that I could if I wanted and I do.

You're a good man. I can tell.

Truly.

I think of you going about your days and being in your suit and busy. I hold you in mind. And I hope everything is gentle for you. It sounds as if it's not, or not gentle enough. Do take care.

You said I might send you a photo, but I don't have any good ones. I don't think good ones are likely, not really. It's maybe best if we keep on like this.

The kitchen had swayed in and out of focus as she thought – whole slabs and staggers of time simply falling away between one sentence and the next. The night had turned to morning when she'd done – and all she'd managed to produce was two sides of a single page, filled up with cramped and worried ink.

I got this prickle on my neck, as if he had already started reading, reading me – silly. Embarrassing.

She'd fought to keep her lines level across and across and across that cream-coloured oblong of paper, smooth as a new bed sheet and the shape of a window looking out, the shape of an invitation to look in. She was turning on all the lights that she could – she was trying to be honest. That meant he would really be able to see.

Which you can't help feeling on your skin.

And in the end you say things to each other.

I will meet you.

You say that and he says that and then it's out loud and in the open and so it might happen.

Which is the sort of thing that can make you disappointed.

I think maybe that it always does. Always is the same as forever.

I will meet you.

Serious sweet.

A man sits at the foot of a staircase inside Bond Street Tube Station. He is slightly an obstacle for commuters who want to make the turn for access to trains heading roughly west for Ealing Broadway and West Ruislip, or else the turn for those that head roughly east towards Leytonstone and so forth. This is a busy station at a busy time and the weather up above is hot, violently sunny. This is a Central Line stop – that particular route noted for its sticky air in summer, baking carriages, its general discomfort. Passengers look at each other as if they are both being an imposition and being imposed upon.

The man is not exactly begging, but he is also not a traveller. He is sitting with his legs crossed tidily, a soft bag at his side and a baseball cap upturned beside one knee. He is not asking for money, he is simply being the series of startling absences which is himself. Each of his arms ends just below what might have been a functional elbow at some other time. Thinned stubs of limb can be glimpsed through the loose sleeves of an oversized T-shirt. There is scar tissue, reddened skin, the signs of aftermath. The man's head is bald and covered, like his face, with grafted skin – it looks flushed and painful, it sits in sections and planes which do not meet in quite the usual way for a face. His ears are of the customary sort, as is his nose, but his eyelids aren't quite practical.

People pass him with expressions which suggest that he has injured them, or that he is a type of intolerable puzzle – this man who must at some point emerge into bright light with wounded skin and no eyelids, who must function without hands, who must be as hot and thirsty and discomfited as they are and yet also beyond them, peering in at them from some raw and unthinkable space.

A woman in her forties pauses against the flow of the crowd, bends and speaks to the man whose age it is impossible to guess. Age is one of the things burned away from him at another time and in another place, both impossible to imagine. She talks to him, but also reaches out her purse and folds what is probably money into her hand. Their chatting seems separate from his hooking one arm under his bag's handle and lifting it and her placing what is probably money inside.

It is possible to hear him say, 'I'm just not doing very well at the moment.'

16:42

JON WAS CARRYING soup out to his daughter. She didn't want the soup, but also hadn't eaten all day, apparently, and so he'd heated it anyway, in her dismaying kitchen.

Which is not a galley-style kitchen, it is more a 1970s caravan-style kitchen. Galley is altogether too kind and jolly a word for it. Becky always intended to rip it out and upgrade – maybe now she will.

But I mustn't suggest domestic renovations as something she could do to take her mind off her current ... Even though I'd swap a new work surface and a halfway decent sink for Terry Harper any day.

Jon had taken a cab to his daughter's place, pausing at the first decent supermarket he saw to let himself buy groceries. That would be necessary, he knew – the bringing of food from outside. Jon felt of no use to Rebecca when she was happy, but was glad that – because he understood being sad – he could be helpful in showing her how to accommodate sadness gently.

The first time you're hit in your heart, you stop wanting ... Because you can't have what you do still need, because it's been taken away, your mind and your body together assume that the rest of the world will be inadequate as a replacement for your one dear thing. You no longer want to dress yourself, or wash, because you no longer intend to be out in that vastly disappointing and punishing world. You forget to buy milk. Or, indeed, cartons of ready-made soup that will keep you going when you're stuck in the worst of the impact.

I do remember how the process runs – she's at the start of it and that's horrible.

But one gets through it. One does survive.

In a manner of speaking.

His mind was filled with the idea that even if he managed not to say something impolitic, he was going to drop the soup tray. He was anticipating a fast-approaching future in which he failed to control the spoon, the bowl, the scalding liquid (organic chicken and vegetable) and the thin slice of proper wholemeal bread and the plate for the thin slice of proper wholemeal bread. In the mid-air ahead of him, Jon could almost see his care of her spilling up and then horribly down in a violent mess that caused damage.

But he padded cautiously and safely onwards, in stockinged feet because of her ludicrous wood floors – *easier to bruise than peaches, more vulnerable than intelligent and attractive young women's hopes –* and then he stood by the sofa where Becky was resting. He'd persuaded her to take a bath and now she was dressing-gowned and snuggled and warm-pink-skinned and resting on her side with a cushion bunched under her head. Her hands were curled close to her mouth and seemed wounded, although they were perfect. She was a twenty-eight-year-old who'd recently dropped the twenty.

My girl. My wee girl.

The sight of her sang in him and felt like honey.

To be a proper dad, you do have to be useful.

And, of course and naturally, seeing her pain felt like having his sternum opened.

Opened so I can display where I keep my selfishness.

'Darling, are you awake? I do think, if you could – not to be annoying – that you might try some of this. It's just soup and not much, although you can have more.'

She reached and patted his calf, then simply rested her hand there against his trouser leg. He didn't quite know what this meant.

'I know. It's horrible. I do ... Your freezer, by the way – I filled the freezer. Do you want me to call someone at work?' The hand curled round his shin and held on, as if he might manage to be an anchor in the current disturbance. 'If you could maybe ... prop yourself up a bit and I'll sit next to you and we can … I'll get another spoon and we can share the bloody soup, if you'd …'

And a wail rose from her that could have raised one from him, too, but this wasn't his day for wailing. 'It's OK … No, Becky. I promise. It is. It will be.' He disengaged his shin, while delivering a stream of, 'It'sOKit'sOKit'sOK.'

'It's not.'

'Well, no …' Jon stepped out to set the tray down on the table behind him and then returned to kneel by her and to let her roll and cling to him, sob tight against him. And this was dreadful, but also – well, as he'd said – OK. You did this bit and then you dealt with the next bit and you continued to be alive. 'Baby girl, really. It's all right. I'm here.'

Her clutch round his waist strengthened and he cupped the back of her head in one of his hands. Under his palm there would be the dark swim of bad ideas, the trouble in her head, the inheritance of sensitivity with which he'd undoubtedly cursed her. Becky's mother was more, as one might term it, emotionally robust. 'I'm here.'

Hidden in his inside pocket, Jon's phone pulsed against his chest – a superfluous heart. He ignored it while his daughter's arms stiffened slightly. Then the sodding machine began ringing. 'I needn't answer. I needn't.'

Becky sighed in a way that scalded him and then she purposefully slipped away from her father, recoiled on to the sofa again and curled with her back to him. She didn't speak, because she didn't have to. He had failed her.

Jon lied while he fumbled the bloody phone out and took it in hand. 'Becky, I said I needn't. I don't even want to. It won't be …' The caller display told him it was Chalice. 'I don't … I really …' Nevertheless he stood up, paced to the window, the dark swim of others' unguessed ideas perhaps making his mobile heavier than it should be. Then he did what he had to and let that dark come cruising in.

'Hello, Chalice, yes … The meeting was fine, in the sense of his being intractable – but nobody sane would give Milner anything, he's clearly out of control.... What do I mean? I mean he was deeply drunk and nasty at four p.m. I don't think that's normal ... No, he didn't say much beyond pretending to be Ed Murrow staring out at the gallant Spitfires and urging on the better cause, or—'

Jon looked across at Becky. Becky who was fine, who was excellent, but who didn't know it. Chalice, meanwhile, pretended to be both the Kray twins at once and ear-burrowed for more than Jon could tell him, because there was no more to tell. The rendezvous had been almost entirely uninformative. *They all adore gossip – unreliable information.*

That's all he wants. I'm safe.

He's not throwing me up against a pressman to see if I bounce in some way that reveals my true nature, my leaking hands. He's not.

Jon wanted Becky to sit up and look over to him and then he would be able to mouth *love you* at her and blow a kiss and make her know that he was hers entirely, truly, and that his work wasn't coming between them.

Chalice then did what might have been expected, what a paranoiac might have thought was the result of a malevolent God's special interest, or else a phone tap in combination with an evil mind. Chalice told Jon they should meet.

I can't though. I can't.

And, of course, the meeting was to be at seven thirty.

Which isn't possible. Not at all.

'There's really no ... I mean, calling it a debrief would be overstating how much I could pass on ... No, really.'

His implication being, when he insists, that I can't sort out inconsequential details from matters of weight. Bastard.

'Seven thirty isn't exactly convenient, Harry ... eight ... eight o'clock?'

Eight is worse ... Why am I saying eight?

'I ...' Jon's ribs beginning to feel – he could imagine this forcefully – beginning to feel they were made of some heavy and grubby metal. 'Eight o'clock, then. Yes ... No trouble at all. No trouble ... At your club ... No, no trouble.'

Jon having to listen while Chalice's voice passed on those three tinny little syllables – *at my club*. For Christ's sake, whoever would still say such a thing?

'Fine. At your club.'

Chalice ended the call and Jon was left holding on to nothing much.

He spoke to no one: 'Fine. Yes, fine.'

At my club – the three most irritating words on earth. Just when we'd all moved beyond that kind of nonsense. At least I would like that to be true – clubs being dated, unnecessary and inappropriate in a time of conditionality and sanctions. But none of that stuff ever really leaves us, does it – we always have to function in a world where special perks for unspecial people get clawed back in again.

Upper, Middle, Lower, Under – no matter our class, we must all do our best to incur unnecessary expense. We must be fooled with glamour, or hints of advantage, or passable subsitutes for love – whatever are the most useful and readily available lies – as long as they cost us. We all of us buy something in the end – scratch cards, bespoke jackets, fake portfolios, fake insurance, fake repairs, fake warranties, fake affection, fake chances ... the membership of this or that club.

We're all in the Mug Punter Club. The Honourable Society of Sad Apes.

He soft-footed over to his daughter again and knelt.

Chalice's club looks like a Stalinist fire station and is full of the worst military art I have ever encountered – and military art is an area rich in utter, utter crap.

He kissed the top of Becky's head. He spoke to her and only her and only ever her and was not in any way apologising to a woman currently elsewhere while he said, 'You're beautiful. And you're wonderful. And you're smart and sweet and there is absolutely no one on earth who shouldn't understand that and respect it and if they don't then it means they're no use, they're all wrong, they're just ... They should never dare to come anywhere near you. If I didn't make this clear then I should have – because I know men, I meet them all the time, they speak to me in the way men speak to men, I know their horrible fucking secrets....

277

It's more important even than you think to get a good one. You deserve a good one.'

This did nothing but crank her breathing back up from a soft regularity of grieving and into another struggle, more sobs.

'You will find someone extraordinary and they will be with you, really with you, and that will be extraordinary, too. I promise. I promise. I promise.'

He closed one arm over her, kept kissing her hair.

She was fighting, you could feel right through her how she was fighting and how she was brave.

I can stay here. No need to rush. Here and then Chalice. My duty being done.

He'd left his phone at his side and saw – *Yes, why not? Because this is how today is running, like a contact sport with no rules I understand* – Jon saw that, while Chalice's call had progressed, an incoming text had made enquiries about a meeting at eight thirty, a meeting quite different to that involving Chalice. Chalice's fucking fucking fucking meeting now superseding his prior commitment – a commitment about which he cared, one might say, deeply – and making it impossible.

This was slightly unfortunate in the way that contracting ebola would be slightly unfortunate – contracting ebola and then not noticing until one had already hugged everybody one loved.

Jon replaced the phone in his jacket pocket, having considered and then rejected the possibility of throwing it through a window.

I'm not built for this, not for anything that's happening today.

I'm not built for …

He found one of Becky's hands and kept a hold of it while settling himself to sit on the floor, cross-legged, his back leaning against the side of the sofa, his head pressing somewhere around Becky's spine. He kissed her hand. It tasted of crying.

'Oh, God. We're a pair. We are … Oh, God.' He didn't wail, because – as previously established – this was not his day for wailing.

It would not be possible for Jon Corwynn Sigurdsson to wail.

An older woman rides the 453 bus – the one which will eventually stop and rest itself at Marylebone. She is heading up west and over the river, perhaps: having some kind of Saturday outing.

Beside her on the double seat is a boy child of around seven. He is well behaved in the manner of children with parents of an age to be their grandparents. He has a certain formality. His jersey and coat are neat and he wears newish leather shoes which may be meant for school. His trousers – which may also be meant for school – have anticipated someone more substantial and they make him kick his legs mildly, swing his feet, while studying the generosity of blue material in which he's hidden. He tugs up the orderly crease that rests over his right thigh and then watches it drift back down. He tugs up the other crease and watches again.

After a while the woman holds his hands to still them and, once she lets go, they also drift back down.

The pair are on the top deck of the bus, right at the front. This is where adults let children sit so they can see and see and see. The boy does indeed mainly wonder out at the spin, slip and glide of buildings. From his expression, both the commonplace and the remarkable are equally satisfactory. His day is pleasing him.

At his side the woman maintains an intensity of interest in the child, almost as if he had appeared only this morning and might be taken back at any time.

Then the woman turns and leans her chin on the top of the boy's head, leans and rests and closes her eyes. There is a moment when her face seems to suggest something like an unbearable joy.

The boy looks at the city passing.

Jon had – Jon loved having – this memory of a slight woman darting – not quite pouncing, but it felt like that – darting forward as he'd left the parcels office where he rented his PO box.

He'd known who it was. He knew before she said. He pretended not to, played badly for time while feeling faint and feeling trapped and feeling …

I felt I'd have to leave myself – be elsewhere and my body caught stupidly standing in its socks and brogues and meanwhile I'd never come back.

I'd just leave it – every part of it.

I'm not built for women who dart.

I'm not built for women.

Not for my mother – there was nothing right about me, according to her – not for Valerie … Well, fine then – don't have me. I'll just be in writing. Let me do that, let me be that. Surely to fucking God I am permitted to be that …

She'd called him – *ridiculous* – Mr August. And he'd reacted. *Because in my heart, it's my name.* And then she'd turned shy – as soon as she knew she was right, she'd dropped her gaze. *Extraordinary way of looking at me, she had – she has – as if I'm a sunset, or a … the last of my kind … alone in the glass case already. I truly don't merit that much attention.*

She'd said, 'Mr August?' This utterly frail smile that would swipe the feet from under you if you had a pulse, and he still did, or thereabouts. 'I think you're Mr August. I'm very sorry, but I had to meet you. After all the letters. I had to.'

And he could feel her examining his hands and the small bundle of – *absolutely, there they were* – incriminating letters he was clutching. The week's harvest amounted to three. And each of his fingers turned sticky with guilt and he couldn't explain.

I'm not built for this – not for you – not for this. I love your letters. I do, I …

I love your love and I …

I'm not built to trot back and forth and to gather up letters – letters from you – letters like napalm and velvet and like having to take off my shirt while you watch – they feel like having you watch – which I know I could never do, or anything else …

I'm not built for letters from the other women, which I didn't mean to keep running – it's only that, on occasion, there have been letters which are not from a woman, letters that are from a journalist and that tell me where and when to leave his next dose of information. He suggests tea at the Natural History Museum and signs himself Lucy. You don't need to know this. I, myself, would rather not have to know this.

Jon had realised that he was nodding, quite hard, agreeing with her, using some part of himself which was more forthright than it should be.

I suggested the name. After Lucy our early ancestor – Australopithecus afarensis – mostly portrayed as rather fragile-looking and dismayed.

Courting.

The urge to cry had scrambled up his throat from somewhere low and hot and his voice had managed, 'You're ... You ...' His heart bailing hopelessly at what was apparently now a fluid both coarser and more taxing than blood. 'Sophia.'

You ... She's ... She was ... Nobody says I'm beautiful. And why would they? And she did that without seeing me – she does that – and I don't know if this means that her opinion is therefore more real, or therefore an especially reckless lie.

It has to be a lie. I'm not beautiful. I'm not wonderful. I'm not sweet. Who would think so? I'm not sweet.

He'd told her she was beautiful and sweet and lovely, because ... It seemed very much a kind of truth. It was inevitable, like the truth.

And it was quite horrible that these forms of address, these descriptions had stayed with him – in fact, all that they'd given and received was quite impossible to dis-remember. This truth, these facts – probably truths and facts – they couldn't help but be confusing, or a conflict of interest, or a cause for concern whether he was giving them or receiving because he'd known from experience they were the things one might say if one intended to reach in all the way and influence somebody. They were a kind of promise that things could get better.

Things can only get better.

Who would buy that?

Something you sing when you think the worst is over and you don't know how much you've still got that can be taken. It's something you sing while you steal in and start to take.

Beautiful, wonderful, lovely, sweet …

And one can't keep it clear in one's head – can't tell who is courting and who is being courted and if she gives me this strange new version of myself and I accept it as possible, then she has the power – quite naturally – to remove it.

She won me. But somebody winning means somebody else gets beaten.

'Mr August?' Her warm hand had darted in and touched his wrist while the whole of Shepherd Market blinked.

'Ah, that's not my name.'

And this desolation had passed over her face – this horror he'd kicked up in her without even trying.

You can't have that power over anyone – it's just wrong. One couldn't conceivably want it.

Jon had swallowed down this wad of both hysteria and elation.

She came for me, she sought me out and I've met her so often on paper, I've met her where it counts, where we are kind, where we can be beautiful, wonderful, lovely, sweet … Human beings are not generally kind or any of the rest. That's why I wouldn't study anthropology – too sad.

He had stumbled through, 'I … That is, it's not my name, but – I mean, I am who you would suppose me to be.' And that was his confession, admission and made him not safe … it let her know where to find him … here, in this skin. 'I am who you think, it's simply that I took another name in order to …'

'Oh, oh, I did, too.'

She was rushing her sentences, keen in a way that seems young and – yes – lovely and so forth. But what she said was a small disappointment.

I'd wanted you to be Sophia – that name for you was in my head, was there when I spoke to you in my head. I thought that I might not be able to start again and redirect all of my daydreams, readdress them … not that we should consider my daydreams … I shouldn't have them. I didn't quite want you to be called Meg.

'But I'm the man ... I am who you intend, intended me to be ...' He was almost entirely sure this would condemn him to disappoint her, but still he went on with, 'Yes.'

And her face had become happy and it had been clear this was something he wanted to see regularly, always, forever. In just a moment, after maybe a pause for reflection, she had been suddenly and unreservedly happy. It had shown him that her happiness or lack of it would now be his fault.

She'd said, 'I'm Meg. Or Margaret. I don't like Maggie. Peg ... I had an Aunt Peg – she was a Margaret, she was a ... If you don't stop me I'll keep on talking and you'll get this just bad – you wouldn't believe how wrong you'd be – this bad impression ... If you thought that I talk all the time, you should have another think coming ...' And she'd already taken his hand – left hand – in hers and the grip had been dry and firm and warm and something he wished to continue. 'My name is Meg.'

'Hello, Meg.' And Jon thinking that, Christ, she was sort of gorgeous. When you considered her calmly. 'I'm Jon.' Not a wonderful suit she's wearing and grey's a colour that can make one seem drained. Or not. Apparently not. Mainly she seems to be thinking that he isn't well turned out – he recognises the signs, sees much the same look on his own face every morning. 'I'm Jonathan, Jon.'

And I'm not well turned out.

Her skirt is a whisker too long.

Only a whisker.

But she's wearing no make-up. Thank fuck for that. 'I'm Jon.'

She is gorgeous.

A gorgeous person cannot be with someone who is not gorgeous. It cannot last. Not unless the gorgeous person is unwell – and instability of that kind is also a reason why relations between people cannot last.

She'd lightly brushed at his other hand – the one she wasn't holding, the one freighted with other women's letters which he couldn't justify.

In the course of being utterly pathetic, I'd set up a perfect cover – love letters from multiple sources.

I only kept on with the others to give Lucy somewhere to hide. I didn't need them. I had the one I wanted … I had the real …

It's me who'll be caught with my dick out in the wilderness, isn't it? Not bloody Lucy.

And now I'm caught with … Oh, Jesus, not that.

All of this had bolted through him in spasms while the woman – Meg, his Meg … it's genuinely, really, a great name, Meg, once you think about it – Meg had frowned a bit, but was also observably content that Jon should be Jon, more than content that he was there and just himself. He did seem to be all right with her.

Perhaps fairly well turned out after all – passable.

And a woman who lies in wait – gorgeous woman – should you find that her actions flatter you, or are appalling? Is it normal to discover they do both?

Meg – she had good name, though, no matter what – Meg had continued, 'I don't mean to be weird. By turning up, finding you. I mean, it is weird – has been weird – the writing to someone you've not ever met is weird—'

'I'm sorry.' Jon, it seemed, said this to women on instinct and was only occasionally wrong when he assumed that it was necessary. 'But no, it isn't the bad kind of weird. Possibly … It was … That is to say, Meg …'

I wanted to say that she looked magnificent.

Weird choice of word.

Treasure. I never called her Treasure. Nobody uses that as a term any more, but I should have – it was appropriate.

Meg had begun: 'I just …' And then she'd faltered and for a while – perhaps a long while – they had stood in the little square with nothing much going on around them, simply holding hands in the manner of people who did this on a regular basis and who were accustomed to the pressure of the contact, to the shape and safety and dearchristitssofuckinglovely of the touch: knuckles and fingers and palms and thumbs and skin.

My naked skin against her naked skin.

Ludicrous that it should feel so very … so very …

But I'd spent months, by then, telling her that she was sort of keeping me alive and that I knew the way she was inside, the tender and warm and basically perfect way she was inside – not being seedy, talking about her soul – and I'd promised her that she was ... that is to say ... that she could be ... that if I prayed, which I don't, but that if I did I would pray for her to be safe always and I would hope for a God because then she would be all right. No God could exist who wouldn't keep her bundled up and taken care of and ...

The thing is, I meant it.

So he'd finally gathered his breath and suggested, 'Well, there's a coffee place right there, we could ...'

She'd laughed a bit – first time he'd heard her laugh. 'They're sick of me. I've just come from there. I used to sit and ... when I was waiting for you and ... not all the time, I have the job, sort of, like I wrote, I work with animals ... but I waited quite often – when I could – and I bet myself that I'd know you when I saw you and I did. I did.' This deep blue look she'd given him while he felt – the only word for this – *proud* that he resembled his written self – bizarrely pleased – because the self he had posted to her was far better than he'd hoped ever to be.

And he'd told her another source of fresh and ridiculous pride, 'I sometimes go there, too. I grab a coffee and read ... Well ... We might even have ... Although we didn't ...'

And they'd walked – Jon amazed that he could walk under these circumstances – back over to the café and sat in this atmosphere of close observation from the waiters and had been given cappuccinos, because that was what she liked and he didn't mind, either way, had no opinion.

There she was.

Really.

'I didn't know that you would ... I wouldn't have ... I ...'

There was Sophia who was, in fact, Meg. She was the one who'd written back and got him, got him entirely, caught him. And here he was being caught all over again.

She wrote that she wouldn't hurt me. Which is a cliché, I'm aware. But she wrote it. I never mentioned it was necessary. I never had to say. That apparently went without saying.

There were other opinions and phrases and possibly facts. I appreciated them.

But she caught me with the promise of no pain.

The cliché every dodgy man will hand to every woman, every woman who piques his interest − 'I'll never hurt you.'

Still, it's easy to believe. What we want to be true is always easy to believe.

I believed her. Even though I do know what women can be like.

She's Meg, though − not women.

I think that's the case.

And Jon had been gripping his too hot cup but not drinking while Meg smoothed at the back of his free hand, although, of course, it wasn't free, was it? It was as caught as the rest of him, trapped all over.

He'd been incoherent throughout. 'Your eyes, they … You didn't say they …' Wanting to shake himself, but unable, he offered, 'I usually like the photographs on the walls here. They're for sale. Should I buy you one? They're …' And he'd seen that the thought of this hadn't pleased her, so he'd resteered, reframed his narrative by − again − making a confession. This time it was, 'I have to leave.'

He wasn't preparing to bolt. He was staring at her disappointment in him and how she packed it away so he might not notice if he weren't paying pathological attention. She nodded and evaporated all the heat that had been pacing and lurching about in his blood.

I wasn't bolting, though.

And he did have to leave soon, because he was late for a meeting − going to be late, there were things he had to do before the meeting − that wasn't a lie. He wasn't limiting her exposure to him so that she wouldn't find his faults.

Of course I was – the longer she was with me, the more she would see and I am too much and really not enough for anyone to have to see.

But then there had been a fairly amicable, genuinely quite a delicate and pleasing kind of rush they could share while, yes, they did exchange their numbers and, yes, also a promise they would meet up properly and, yes … In fact, he'd forgotten to leave a number … He'd only wanted to, but it had felt … inappropriate … He had wanted to … He wasn't going off into hiding or anything like that.

Yes, I took her number.

Yes, I wanted to kiss her.

But, yes, I ran away.

I walked fast away from the café and then made it to Piccadilly and bolted like fuck. Over the road and into the park and ran and ran. Unseemly.

Full tilt.

It felt so wonderful to get away.

But I kissed her first.

Full tilt.

It felt completely …

It felt like I was an overly lucky man.

And you don't want to get lucky, not too much.

And Jon clamped his eyes shut and attempted again to unrecall the darting woman, her sensibletender hands and the way they greeted him that first time.

He leaned his head back against the sofa, against his resting daughter and her pain, against his duty.

Being with Maggie felt like walking about inside music, inside maybe 'The Healer' – all those coolcool Bs and Ds. D7s are always worth it. I was walking about and then running and also being mellow and not me and – fuckit – being all right, being partially mended and all right. Something in me felt like how each thread gets fitted together on 'Stripped Me Naked': the pulse they set in to run under the riffs, the one they put out there to tell you that when you're wholly done for, when everything you could care about, or cling to, is absolutely gone – even then here's this, still this, your blood full and roaring with music.

That's not to say I was being John Lee Hooker, I wasn't. I was also not pretending that I could be Carlos Santana, I was just bloody well being me and fine, so fine, so fine. I was all right.

It was so ...

But I don't think I can any more. I don't think I can manage.

It was so completely wonderful.

A crowd has gathered in St Pancras Station. They form an arc around one of the pianos placed ready for public use. The instrument isn't absolutely in tune and it jangles slightly – loose wires – there is something sly and sideways and lounge bar about its tone.

Sitting at the keyboard is a slim young man. His entire body speaks of intent effort and also of being transported. He is both here and elsewhere in a way that makes him fascinating, illuminated. He bends forward, sways, reaches, pushing himself into a complex classical piece that leaps, tumbles, repeats, leaps and trills, tumbles again. It sounds slightly like silver and slightly like being happy in a serious manner, like a very considered response to joy. Somehow, the sidle and echo of the instrument exactly suit the character of the melody.

The people who listen share the same expression: this peaceful type of absence with faint smiles. Some have closed their eyes.

The young man pounds on. In the most polite possible way, he is ignoring all observers. This makes it easier for them to observe. They are here together for something which is not quite him, but is of him – for this surprise of music. They are inside an event which makes itself plain, announces that it will never quite happen again. Everyone enjoys being, in this manner, unique. Everyone enjoys being, in this manner, together.

The piece romps and flurries, runs.

And then the pianist is done – the violence of the conclusion, the hammering, the flourish – and there is silence. There is apparently silence clear along the shopping mall that is necessary to every major railway station. The stillness may even reach far out and touch the pausing, dozing, sliding trains.

Then, of course, there is a little applause. It almost surprises the man, seems to push him a touch off-centre as he stands and looks for the bag he set down when he started, when he chose to produce so much music. He glances at a young woman who is obviously his girlfriend and obviously pleased about him, while also being mildly protective.

Several members of his audience walk to shake his hand. An older woman wearing a large hat stops and asks him about himself. He is from Taiwan, as is his girlfriend. His English is good but very slightly laborious. He tells the woman, when she requires him to, that the piece was *La Campanella* by Franz Liszt and that it means 'The Little Bell'. He isn't a music student. He just loves to play.

17:01

MEG STARTED TO leave the AA meeting smartly, briskly, fast as fuck, as soon as it ended – no hanging around. She'd joined everybody in nodding her head down and closing her eyes and addressing the variable blur which was her Power Greater Than Herself – the weather, gravity, evolution, AA people ... today it was The Universe. Meg put in a request – another request – for help to tell the difference between the problems she could alter and the ones she was stuck with for life, then she was on her feet and dodging.

That's more than enough communal activity for the day.

Please Someone – Something – grant me the wisdom to know the difference between the soluble and the insoluble ...

Otherwise I'll spend the rest of my life banging my head off walls that won't fall down – rather than the more forgiving ones that might surrender before my skull cracks.

She was aware this line of thinking was probably making her frown, because people were giving her looks of concern and a meaningful *hello* here and there as she headed for the door without mucking in to stack chairs, or to reassure the lady who'd been crying that everything would eventually be OK.

She doesn't need me – there's a bloody queue of people all having a try at that. And I can't say I'm honestly sure if everything will turn out well in the end. We die in the end – is that a good result? Or is that an assurance that any available god sits on high with a stack of razor blades, each of them ready for use on one of us? Is all of that singing and religion just about assisted suicide?

She gathered her drunk-from polystyrene cup and threw it in the bin.

Which shows I am willing to lend a hand.

I don't have to. Like I don't have to be perpetually in the mood to talk. That's not a requirement. I have to maintain a desire to stop drinking and stay clean and sober – I haven't signed up for some low-rent social club.

Or very high-rent social club – after all, you don't get in without losing everything you cared about. The entrance fees are substantial. Dress code informal.

I didn't care about anything when I first came in, though. Having something to care about came later. Having something I might lose came later.

She made it to the door after dodging several chats and gaggles and then making a final lunge past someone with their hand vaguely outstretched, for reasons Meg chose to find uninteresting. The outside air was aggressive with exhaust fumes, but also great because pressing on through it didn't involve Meg in having to tell anyone that she was fine, thanks, and OK and just great and leaving and leaving and leaving.

She walked back towards Tottenham Court Road, the air darkening by mild degrees towards evening and shop lights becoming cosier as a result.

If I want to talk, I will talk to Jon later. That's what normal people do – they talk to the people they care about, their someone to care about, their someone in particular they don't want to lose.

I will meet you.

If he says that, if he goes to the bother of saying that, then why would he not meet me and why would I not meet him? It's only a matter of time until we're in the same place today – that has been decided – and I have time. I have all the time that's left in this twenty-four hours, just for me to do with as I'd like.

And Jon involved waiting – that seemed to be in his nature – and waiting was a pain in the arse, but also less scary than actually being with him. Being with what you care about is a little like sipping at something good, sipping half a glass of this or that in company and understanding that you can't quite cut loose yet. It's like being compressed in your enjoyment and unsure if you'll disgrace yourself later, or else drown in remarkable feelings, in joys you can't repeat and that are to do with some mystery process that meant some specific mouthful was exactly the right one to work the miracle and make you delighted – only you can't tell which mouthful. You were already drunk when you took it and so it's lost. Your miracle got lost.

It is unhealthy, I have been told, to think of the people I love – the person I love – in the way that I thought about substances and liquids. It's better to see them as humans, not drinks-cupboard treats.

As if I kept an orderly drinks cupboard … a cocktail cabinet full of dainties, decorative and unopened possibilities …

As if I feel absolutely human when I'm next to a real, live human …

I try, though. I do try.

I am very trying.

And we've made that joke and we make other jokes and we're something that works, me and Jon. I believe that.

Meg continued to be surprised by how much she believed that. She wasn't a creature of faith and yet she had spent all those hours and inexplicable hours in the little café in Shepherd Market, simply waiting for Jon.

I went there, not to be crazy, not to be a stalker, not to jump out on his doorstep – just to see where he lived. The letters all went to a Mayfair address – I wanted to see how he lived, because Mayfair is something beyond me and I couldn't match that, I couldn't keep up. It had worried me, this idea that I'd be of no use to him. Just the difference in quality between his writing paper and mine – I mean, it was clear … Sometimes his paper depressed me as much as his letter cheered me up …

Only then I went there, to Shepherd Market, and the place was a PO box and that was sort of good. I took a couple of weeks and thought things through and decided that it was good. He wrote letters for strangers and needed to be safe, so he'd taken a PO box and … He'd never given me his private address. But that could be OK. He could be cautious. I'm cautious. I like cautious people. They are like me. Not that I like me …

The thing was, I could never have waited outside his house – that would have been unforgivable. But I could wait outside a place with PO boxes, outside a shop. And maybe I would see him coming to get the letters, to get my letters, and then I would know what he looked like. I thought I needn't do anything more than have a look.

I'm a cautious person.

I knew that I'd recognise him.

I knew that when I did, it would make things all right.

I wouldn't need to meet him – just seeing who he was would be enough.

I am a cautious person.

And I'm a liar, of course.

She'd sat by the window with rationed cappuccinos and the patient waiters and read a book, or stared at a book and waited. She had imagined the company of a man, being with a man and sober. Her drinking had ended as a solitary occupation. Earlier it had contained all sorts of people … Her sober life, though, that was … It had an emptiness … It was clean, because it was empty.

Empty space and counting days and being happy, looking for how to be happy, and letters. I had letters.

And nobody gets to know about the letters – they're ours, they're mine. We write them and we read them and they're beautiful and make us that way, too, and in one of them he told me that every night at midnight he'll think of me and go to sleep wishing me excellent dreams, the finest, the ones reserved for children and animals and innocence and rest.

Every night at midnight he wishes me sweet and I wish him back. We wish each other sweet and we know what that means.

We're together. When I'm tired, or I'd rather be with him, or the midnight habit seems stupid, or it gets to be a duty – it still happens and it means that we're together.

That's not a lie.

And the certainty of this got her through how strange and tricky it was to meet and the endless guessing about which part of which day might release him and let him be with her. In the same way, their letters – *one every week, sometimes two* – could get her through those long waits in the café, before she'd caught sight of Mr August or heard him say his proper name.

I guessed that lunchtimes might be likely for a sighting, but that was going to depend on what his hours were and I knew he worked in Whitehall, but not where ... Maybe he couldn't get out to the PO box until the evenings. And that would be awkward because the café would be shut ... weekends ... Sundays would be terrible – no chance of seeing him unless ... I didn't know ... I could maybe sit on the pavement. But not really. When you've been looked at by strangers when you've fallen in the street and been looked at by off-licence staff when you've been trying to buy what's needful, or looked at by mothers who don't want their children frightened, or looked at by neighbours who might be tired of you, or sad for you, or bored by you, but who always are disgusted by you ... You've got no room left for being ashamed and exhausted. You can't be doing with it any more.

So I can't sit on pavements.

So she had sat in a civilised manner and sipped at coffee and waited as much as she could bear to and been almost relieved that her limited efforts might not work and she might never have to face him.

I wanted his company, but I thought he maybe ought to be spared mine.

Women are lousy company – they usually don't drink enough, or if they do, they get strange too quickly. They get nasty. Or they cry, which is too complicated to deal with. Men are simpler.

Men see you're not right and they find where you're soft and get in there and hurt you more. They pick who's easiest to hurt. That's simple.

But Jon isn't like that. And I'm not drinking.

Even when he was Mr August, when he was Corwynn, and he was just his letters – he still made you different. What he wrote worked in under your clothes and kept you cosy. You could be in the world by yourself, but not look alone.

And when he turned up at the PO box, I did know him. He moved in exactly the way that he wrote. He was all of a piece – that's what happens when you're honest.

That funny little drag step he does sometimes, it's got the same bounce that he slips in his voice, that he seals up in envelopes and sends me.

He wants to be an R & B man which is silly, because he already is – he has an R & B body.

Nobody told him.

But it's really clear and so I knew him.

But if I'm honest and all of a piece myself I will eventually tell him – when I'm sure he won't mind – that I dived out of that fucking coffee shop four times before I ran to him.

The first time was a sort of misunderstanding: in the letters Jon said he was 'unfortunately tall' so I caught sight of this bloke who was massive, just huge, and he didn't look a proper fit in any other way, but I had a go and went and asked if he was Corwynn. Silly – thinking some wrestler-looking creature would be him. That was more for practice than a proper mistake, I think.

The man had been startled and then amused that he might be confused with someone else. He had a small tattoo on the side of his neck. Mr August wouldn't have a tattoo. He wouldn't have a frame that suggested protein shakes and whey powder and sweating over weights.

Silly cow. Don't know what I was thinking.

I wasn't thinking – I was scared.

Then there was the one who looked fussy, somehow, and who was tallish and dressed for an office job – but I realised, once I was outside, that he'd gone in with letters and come out with none and that was probably the wrong way round. And his eyes weren't as they should be. When he looked at me, they had the wrong type of light.

She had only glanced at him and not advanced across the square and into asking him if he was Mr August.

And there was a ginger person in a very lovely suit. I wasn't sure about him. I thought gingerness would have been mentioned, if it had existed. Jon said he was going grey ... and there was no sign of grey. So I said nothing to Mr Ginger – we just stared at each other and then I ran for it, because I'd needed to get in close to check the hair properly. He may have thought that I had some problem with his crowning glory ...

My dad always talked about his crowning glory – didn't just call it hair. My dad whom I chose to know less and less as he got older and I drank more. He was delicate with himself over going bald. I did notice that. Not much else.

The idea is to notice who you love before they die.
That would be the civilised idea.

Meg had seen Jon once through the café window, stood up and made it as far as the entrance before she was foxed, pressed back by what seemed to be the rapidly congealing air. If you believed you could tell from letters and letters and letters the way that a person should be, then he was Jon. This man was neat and tired-looking, soft in the ways that he moved, careful. He was wearing a quiet suit – the relative silence of the jacket and trousers, of the unbuttoned coat both concealing and framing them, didn't stop them being plainly good. The way he'd groused about other people's clothes let you be sure that he'd watch how he turned himself out for fear of being ugly. You could guess that he hated and pondered his own appearance more than anybody else's, that he walked about inside this rawness, this sense of horror.

Another man being delicate about what he thinks are his failings.

He had a haircut that made him seem a tiny bit like a schoolboy – the haircut of someone who doesn't quite take himself seriously. He had gently, tenderly thinning hair. And he'd carried a briefcase that wasn't new, or gimmicky, that seemed to fit his hand and be used to him.

Most of all, I knew he should be Corwynn August, the man who was calling himself Corwynn August, because he seemed to be walking under something – like a man who had to be brave and walk about beneath some swinging danger, something not quite securely fastened up above. You could see that he'd stopped expecting the something would go away.

She'd loitered until he came out of the PO box office again and she could study his face. She was trying to be quick about it … She didn't want to scare him. She didn't want to spoil everything. But she did have to be sure. And would her Mr August be so tense and have a mouth kept tight with what was perhaps irritation … and also these straight-scored lines coming down from near his hairline to his eyebrows – the marks you get from being angry. These details made her doubtful.

I avoid the people who get angry, the men who do that. What might have been true, shown to be true when you saw his face, was that he had sad habits and also rage, but also this softness. The rage was mostly about himself.

The softness came first and last – it held him.

I think that's what made me believe it was him.

Her man was a fast walker, though. He'd been gone before she could guess what she should do, before she could fight the solidified air, or else give up and leave him and never come back there – surrender. Alcoholics, after all, are fond of giving in.

Self-defence. Self-harm.

And he seemed very formal and our letters weren't and I didn't want formal. Formality's just a way of not being around.

And if it was him, he was a man who worked at speed – alive and fast and with someone who rushed like that you couldn't quite be sure of what would happen …

She'd let him go and done nothing, just slipped back into the café and watched what was left of her cappuccino go cold. Then she'd gone home.

It's Jon's outside that's formal. That part of him is to do with his job, but it's self-defence, too. And self-harm. I've watched the insides of his wrists and how he hides them – where he's tender – and I've noticed his fingers comforting each other and the way he bends his knees a little to be level with you so he can speak – he doesn't want to loom – and then there's the way his intentions, soft intentions, make themselves plain in his eyes. There's this quick light that shows. It makes you think you've spotted where he really is.

I don't see him often, haven't met him often, but I have noticed him a lot. I make up for our lost time. I have studied the way that he is.

Jon's an education.

She'd kept going back to Shepherd Market, kept waiting, kept close to the time when she'd first caught sight of him.

And then he was there again and I was there and I was walking over and saying his name, calling it out so that something familiar would reach him before me – and then he heard, he realised …

The way he'd stared at her …

I was a shock. I was a shock to him. Even though I didn't mean to be. I'd made him nervous.

That wasn't only a fault, though, it proved what type of man he was – he's safe.

You'll always be safer with somebody who gets scared. That's how it works. You can be like two animals, hiding together.

But first you are scared and then you scare him and then both of you get more scared, because of each other and it hurts you and it's fast.

The way he'd stared at her.

Sorrysorrysorrysorry.

Don't hate me.

He had been definitely like an animal then: all startled and ticking and sprung.

His stride had stopped and then turned into a tiny stagger and – because she knew of nothing else to do – she'd said who she was and then hoped.

That's the terrible thing about being sober, sober in an organised way. They tell you it's to do with having hope, when that's what you've always been avoiding.

Once they were inside the café, Jon had ordered and fought down his cappuccino so fast it must have burned him. And only her hold on his hand had allowed their meeting to be real.

If you're scared you need someone to do that. And if you have trouble with hope, then giving out your hand and feeling it taken helps you, too.

She could remember the feel of his fist, hers cradling it and trying to seem sane for him and calm and safe and to touch his knuckles only as she might touch any nervous animal. They'd walked to the café with her hand on his, visibly linked. He'd dropped the contact as they worked themselves through the doorway, but then – she remembered this clearly, often – they both made this reach across the table towards something that could keep them steady – hand into hand – while apparently the tabletop and the walls and windows and so forth all shifted, all made her feel they were weathering large, unpleasant seas.

Corwynn had dropped his teaspoon and retreated from her, left her cold-handed, as he scrambled about after the thing, as if it were made of platinum, or some family heirloom beyond price, while telling her, 'They're all watching and thinking I'm a fool, I'm sure. And you're …' His face had flushed with effort and possibly shame, while his hair was disturbed − *but not ginger* − was ruffled as he surely would not have wished and he spoke on his knees, his chin almost level with their saucers. She'd thought at that point, *his height is in his legs, isn't it? He has that body, which is slim and all wires and tightness, but not long. It's his arms and legs that make him seem big − they give him the reach and the height and that speed.* She considered his legs, as if understanding his dimensions wouldn't make her …

You'd be worried that if you really studied them you'd want to touch him a lot and that didn't seem what he would want, or not yet.

You don't touch wild animals, they take it badly.

And I was trying to look just sociable and normal and not insane about his legs.

So I listened very hard when he spoke and thought his voice might be drier than I'd expected. But it was him.

And it made me want to touch him, too.

Once he'd captured the spoon, he'd stood again and fussed at the twin patches of mainly theoretical dust on his trousers where he'd knelt. 'Oh, dear. Sorry. I should have thought. I'm such a …'

And she'd taken his hand for the third time and said something she couldn't remember afterwards. She could only recall his glance at her and the horror that coloured it and also this despair and a type of exhilaration. And finally he opened out a smile, a boy's summery smile − lots of clear brightness, lots of racing and heat.

He's not simple, Mr August. He's all kinds of things, all at once, is Mr Jonathan Corwynn Sigurdsson.

He'd blinked and his mouth had worked for a few moments before he produced, 'Well … It's not really, because … If you think so, then. Yes … I don't … Thank you.' His other hand had placed the rogue teaspoon beside his cup. He'd checked his watch openly and twitched. 'I do have to, I do …' And then his fingers had been decisive and had laced between her own and had fastened in snug and hard and he'd leaned forward to be closer. 'If you knew me by looking … This will sound extremely …' His scent was here:

a harsh brand of soap and self-confident cloth and a vague mustiness – no cologne, no definable choice made beyond this old-fashioned, punishing soap the name of which she'd forgotten. She'd breathed in to gather as much as she could, in case she never saw him again.

I was declaring him a good thing and therefore assuming he'd soon be gone.

Gone in the way that doesn't come back.

'If you knew me by looking ...' He'd winced quickly, but his fingers stayed certain. 'In your letters, when you wrote, you said that I was, you used the word – the word was ... No, it's all right, it's perfectly – I'd be foolish to ask ... I have to go. I'll call. Later. I mean ... I have to.' He shook his head.

His eyes had tried hers for an instant and had appeared to be ready for some kind of blow. 'Beautiful. You said. You used that word.'

And his hand had snapped away then, as if he had scalded himself and he was standing back and picking up his briefcase and no more to be said and no attempt to face her again and then he was out and away and striding and nothing of him remaining but a warm shudder in the light.

She'd abandoned her coat and followed, sort of kept a guard along behind him as he paced, then trotted, then pelted through the shadowy narrows of White Horse Street and out towards the tall, narrow slot of sun and sky over Piccadilly. Then he was fording the swell of upmarket pedestrians and then plunging into the traffic, crossing the road in its two, equally busy instalments. Meg had worried he was dashing too unwisely. She'd worried he'd turn round and see her. But he'd not looked back, had only sprinted into the park. He was, as she might have told him, beautiful as he ran.

As he ran away from me.

I thought that was it.

Sorrysorrysorrysorry.

Walking back to the café, paying the bill, avoiding the amused concern of the waiters ... it had all made her want to cry.

I thought he wouldn't write again.

I knew he wouldn't call — it would make him too tense. And he hadn't given me his number and that was probably a cause for concern …

The way he'd stared at her.

But, after three letterless weeks during which she couldn't exactly eat — not really — or dream without being unhappy, he had sent her an envelope full of sorrysorrysorrysorry for making her wait, because he had been dithering over how to phrase things.

Only then he didn't phrase anything much — it was a very short letter, more a note.

But sorry again and here was his mobile number and I should call. Or texting would be better because he often would be busy. But I might text soon if I wanted — soon or sooner than that.

Being funny for me.

And I didn't forget that before he ran, he kissed me.

He did.

Here it is.

There are two men on a crowded Northern Line Tube train. Both are dressed stylishly in jeans and shirts a little too young for their age. They have well-tended beards and moustaches and shaven heads. One man carries a young pug dog which is wearing a small neckerchief and a soft leather harness. The man is holding the dog snug and high, protective, clearly enjoying its newness and affection.

Because the carriage is so crowded, the dog cannot help but peer out, over-close to a middle-aged woman's face. She is smiling in response and petting the dog's ears. Both its owners tell her how brave it is being – it does seem only calm and curious and contented, despite the crush. They talk about introducing their dog to other dogs and about training sessions for good behaviour and about a day-care centre where they leave him when they go to work. Although they don't like to be parted from him, they feel he should get used to novel experiences and people.

The dog is perfect, cherished, glances about himself with an air of security.

As passengers ease past it and out, or insist themselves into the crowd already on-board, the conversation continues. It is something cheery to be overheard as a mass of individuals undergo a mildly gruelling experience, pressed together.

Eventually, though, the chatting wanes and the men simply murmur between themselves and seem glad about their dog and being here and now and together. The woman withdraws into being a stranger again, her face becoming neutral and turning to examine the slide of the platform as the next station finds them, then slows and then stops alongside. For a moment she seems sad. She is perhaps considering that the men have this dog as their son and that they love him and that dogs do not live very long, not nearly as long as children are supposed to. It may be that she is surprised by how willing they seem to risk being very unhappy.

Meg was in a pub when her phone rang. 'Hello?'

She wasn't there for any terrible reason, it was only that the other places – shops, cafés, sandwich bars – they'd all looked too steamy and sticky and claustrophobic and someone can be in a bar, can sit on a stool in a bar, and still drink an orange juice and lemonade.

'Hi, yes it's …' The sound of him flared in her, the music, the breath – her anticipation that something must be wrong, or why else would he call … 'It's you, Jon, yes. I know. I can recognise your voice. Probably always …' And she tried to keep on talking, because then the bad news would not be delivered.

He's either going to tell me about a problem, or something really great. There won't be a medium option.

That's OK. Alcoholics don't do medium.

When she paused for breath, he started a fumbled, 'That's … I am. Well, Jon. Yes.' And his tone was extremely careful, somehow – both painstaking and nervy. 'I … I had to … I can't.'

So it isn't good news.

This cold unfurled through her torso and along her arms, which was disappointing because being sober and an adult meant you were supposed to get independent and not rely on other people to keep you happy.

'I've tried. But I really …' He sounds frightened. And numb. It's tough to tell if somebody is lying or in shock when they offer you that kind of combination.

She asked him – because this is what you do when you care about someone, even when that someone is man: 'What's wrong?'

'I can't say.'

Which caught Meg slightly as an impact might – not a kick, but a strong shove.

I will keep civilised, though. I will be as I think I should and not chuck everything and tell him to fuck off, just to be done with all this messing about.

She even sounded civilised, produced this fairly convincing courtesy, 'Can I help?'

And I would help. I want to.

'You can't ... I can't ... And there's a problem with my daughter and I won't be able to ... I wanted to phone because this ... The day's not over. There's later. That would be quite a lot later, but would you be able. I sort of think if I don't today and if I put it off, if we put it ... I'm so sorry.'

'It's OK.' It was not OK.

'Things keep moving and I have to move because of them and I don't want to and this has been a horrible day and I know you've had a ... another horrible day. I truly am ... I absolutely am ...' At this point there was an interruption from someone else, this distant other speaker, and Meg couldn't make out the words, but it sounded as if a question was being asked and, of course, she then heard him say, 'Nobody.'

And that was, of course, a name that suited her better than Sophia, or Margaret, or Maggie, or Meg, 'That's right – nobody. I'll let you get on.'

'What? No, no ... It's only that ... I will call you again. Later. Later today. This evening. I won't text. I will call you when I can call you and it will be today, I promise, I swear, and I will see you and we will do something and . . . '

There was a fumble of motion at his side of the call – a movement, perhaps, of hands that she knew and had liked and which were currently with him, there in his sleeves in another part of London.

I would have fucking helped.

Meg couldn't hear what he said to her next – it didn't quite sound like goodbye, but had the same effect.

She put down the silence he'd left behind himself and picked up her glass which was sticky. That served her right for ordering a kid's kind of drink.

I'll be fine, though.

Before midnight when we get to send sweet dreams, we'll be all right. Please.

I would like that.

307

I do think I need that.

Her drink was making her feel tearful, because it was unsuitable. An adult gets to move beyond orange squash and summery smiles and pretending a grown-up will help you know what to do next.

Meg waved to the barman and he stepped along to her section of the bar, ready to do what he could.

Here it is.

Jon was in his daughter's bathroom, 'I absolutely am ...' He was –
again – letting his mouth start a sentence that he knew it couldn't
end. He was also mumbling, because he knew that his daughter
was standing outside, beyond the door he'd locked for privacy and
safety and so that he could be insane without anyone watching.

'Dad? You're on the phone in there?' Accusing.

'It's nobody.' Holding his mobile phone like a warm sin.

'Dad?' This was his daughter's voice – dear voice – another
dear voice – while he listened elsewhere and couldn't say what
he had to, because he felt too ill to try.

And because I have no balls.

I can't do this. Not any of it.

'I love you.' This was his own voice – muffled blur of a voice –
and then he cut the call before there could be a reply.

I can't.

Then this noise, a hacking sort of sob, lurched up from his
chest and out and then once more and then he was bleating,
yowling.

Inexcusable.

'Dad?'

''M OK. Honest.'

'Dad?'

Jon stepped to the sink and turned both taps full on, let their
sound slightly mask his own as his arms cramped and he leaned
over and further over and wished he could be sick rather than
simply hollow.

Christ.

He cupped the water, let it be harsh against his palms, lifted it
to his face and doused himself. In the process, he drenched his
shirt, while his foot kicked at his phone, which had fallen and
was somewhere on the carpet and no use to him.

Christ.

He didn't use the mirror before he came out of the bathroom,
but he guessed that he was not at his best as he blinked down at
Becky and hugged her in, because that was the comforting thing

for a father to do and because it would prevent her from studying him like the wet, mad animal he understood himself to be.

Christ.

'Daddy's here. Dad's here.' Her arms being wiry and tight around him in a way that was a great relief and also a burden. 'Dad's—'

'What's the matter?' Her voice was a reproach against his chest, hot. 'What's wrong?' He'd made her worried, which was not his intention.

'I, ah … Bad day. Bad week. It's a funny time. And … I can't.' She was patting at the small of his back and that was nice, a kind gesture. His breath heaved a few times at the idea of it, but he kept steady thereafter. 'Becky, I'm—'

'Has Mum done something?' He loved that she sounded protective.

'What? No. No. She's on holiday, remember? No. That's completely …' He gently disentangled himself and offered her an expression he hoped would pass, while he stared off to one side at a reproduction of a poster for the movie *The Cook, the Thief, His Wife, and Her Lover* which was on Becky's wall – Helen Mirren in complicated underwear and some fruit.

That would have been Terry the wanker's choice – trying to be shocking. I pity the poor bloody actors in a piece of crap like that … Suffering all round. The indignities required of any trade. Who needs it? I don't need it. Dear God, I don't need it.

And I don't want it to have to be my fault.

'I shouldn't be bringing this here, not to my girl.' Jon kissed the top of her head – *hair smells as it always did, of love and home and peacefulness* – and he felt like a swine for planning, while he kissed, how he would get back into the bathroom and retrieve his phone. 'My girl is wonderful.' He'd forgotten it.

I'm really not in a position where I can afford to forget anything.

'You don't look OK, Dad. You look thin.'

'I am thin. I'm always thin. That's me – thin.' He felt something like a smile afflict him and then slink off before it failed close inspection. 'I know this is shit of me, but I have to go in a while. In a not very long while. I'm so sorry.'

He braced himself for her disapproval, but – rather more horribly – she provided none, led him back to the living room as if he were elderly and damaged. 'You should eat.'

'Well, no – you should. You look tired, sweetheart. And you really should eat.'

The tray was still there on her coffee table, with the untried and now congealed soup and probably slightly dried bread. Rebecca lifted it all before he could stop her and told Jon, 'I'll make this hot again and get you some as well and then we will both eat and then you'll go.' She didn't attempt to load the end of the sentence: this was simply a list of things that were going to happen.

He was forgiven, then.

Which left him to sit on the floor again, because for some reason he liked it down here, leaning back against one armrest of the sofa, and listening while there were tiny kitchen sounds: his daughter turning on the hum of the microwave, bustling, taking care of her dad.

I shouldn't have seen Rowan last night – it's thrown me off. The thought of someone cooking for me and busyness elsewhere and … I feel I am setting myself up for a fall.

He folded one hand around the other, clasped his palm over his fist, as if it were some live, clever stone that could help him.

Kneeling in Rowan's bloody garden – a ridiculous thing to build, a whole garden made out of love – you can't risk that. And I told him – stupid – told him I wanted Filya to have seen it all when everything was better and cleaned and … It's insoluble. The waste of everything is beyond me.

I can't say.

Jon rocked while some horrible shadow swung through him and he just …

I used to be, used to be a man who was all about preparing for solutions, about showing other people where solutions might be found and how they might be implemented. One can't change one's nature, particularly not if some element of it is functional and – one believes – beneficial and worthwhile. I can't stop doing what I feel is necessary, not without changing myself and …

Jon heard Becky come back, her bare feet over the boards and the little slips of the spoon as it rocked against the bowl – he could picture it all, but not lift his head. He felt her shin rest against his side and press.

'Dad?'

'Yes. Yes. Yes.' This was meant to be the start of a longer statement, but instead he could only agree to being her father. 'Yes.'

'Dad, you're crying. Why are you crying?'

And now she has let him discover that he is – yes – crying, the force of it sparks in his lungs and almost chokes him and he can't tell her why.

Even when she sets the tray down on the floor – or somewhere, just somewhere, he doesn't see where, can't see where – even when she kneels and holds him round his breathing, pins his arms in to his sides in a way that makes him drown slightly, just a bit – even then he can't tell her why he is crying.

Because nothing is soluble any more.

Because it's all ruined.

Because I am ruined.

Because an extraordinary woman called Filya is dead.

Because I never loved your mother properly.

Because I never loved you properly.

Because I am going to lose my job.

Because I am going to be destroyed.

Because I have a girlfriend.

I can't.

Because I have never saved anyone.

Because I have tried and never managed to be as I should, act as I should.

Because I have Meg, but I can't have Meg.

I can't.

Here it is.

But, really, I can't.

He kept on holding his own hand.

18:22

WELL FUCK THAT, *though. I'm better than that. My name is Meg and I'm better than that – which is what people say, 'I'm better than that,' and I'm not very sure what it means, or how they'd know, but why not think it anyway, it sounds friendly.*

I can imagine, I can assume that I am better than being in a pub and feeling lousy and wanting to do what any normal human being should do in a pub.

So fuck that. Fuck normal.

I'm not normal.

I'm better than that.

Meg had left the bar and was heading down Charing Cross Road, which was undoubtedly better than some things and some places, but not exactly at its best.

Although you never know with Charing Cross Road what its best is meant to be.

Its shops always managed to seem not quite in working order, a bit rubbish and quiet. Or else sleazy. It had an aura of louche dysfunction. Chinatown was a block away and doing its restaurants and stacks-of-vegetables-in-boxes and busyness thing, but Charing Cross Road wasn't Chinatown. And just round the corner in Denmark Street were classy guitars and hard-fingered experts and hopes and prayers for the dispensation of blue, blue coolness – so Meg was told – but Charing Cross Road just wasn't Denmark

Street. And Soho was right over there and doing its clubs and raunch and posing and out-of-your-mind-on-whatever and up-all-night and no-knickers thing – but that wasn't Charing Cross Road, either. Charing Cross Road was all shoddy offers and empty bookshops and tourist tat and places where you wouldn't eat and shouldn't drink.

It's OK, the stuff doesn't jump out and grab you, it doesn't get forced down your throat – lots and lots of grown-ups have told me that.

And there were too many theatres around here. Maybe it was the theatres that gave the place its unreliable vibe. Theatres wanted nothing to do with you most of the day and then they lit themselves bright and liked to be all straggled round by dressed-up crowds and queues. Then every trace of that got tidied away, shut in behind doors. And the same crowds were leaving, out again, two or three hours later and you'd no idea what went on in between, except that it made them seem smug and overheated. And the people who worked for the theatres leaned about across interesting doorways and looked purposeful near trucks full of equipment and mysteries and they kept odd hours and encouraged odd hours in others: late eating, early eating. They kept to an alcoholic's schedule: late drinking, early drinking. That was maybe why Meg hadn't been this way in a while.

There was a greasy-spoon place just off Leicester Square where she used to get breakfast in the tiny hours of semi-regular, irregular mornings. If you'd had to make a night of it and wanted propping up – there it was.

Charing Cross Road was built for visitors in ideas of their Sunday Best, for pickpockets and lost sheep and bookworms and the people who acted as warnings against the risks of eating through your lifestyle. Asleep in doorways, ill in doorways, can't-tell-if-they're-dead-already in doorways – they were your examples to learn from, the sketches from your future. You see the other options – the ones on the way to soup kitchens and shelters, theatrical about their misery, wearing it out loud. Charing Cross Road was always there but for the grace of God.

Whoever that is.

This evening she was glad when she could get herself down in the Underground and away.

Where no one can call me. I don't really want another call.

I mean, I do. But I don't want be waiting for it, or waiting for another failure, or …

There are things that I can't manage in my thinking. Not today.

Maybe forever.

The subway hadn't been a friend to Meg when she was drinking: the inescapable white passageways, bowing out as if she had been Jonahed, taken deep inside the whale. It had made her sweat.

Jon wrote about being Jonahed – I never thought of it before as a word.

She hadn't enjoyed the branching muddle of directions, the sudden lock of crowds around you, the delays and the fuggy trapped air – or the unexplained sudden assaults of feral pressure, gusts from nowhere which might be normal, or a sign of accidents and collapses. The roar of the tunnels once she'd got aboard a carriage could be unbearable – so much velocity, so much unnatural submersion, so many people to peer at you and find you wanting and shaking and damp.

I don't mind it now, though. Not so much.

Meg could stand on the platform and wait for a Piccadilly Line westbound train without much considering how remarkably easy it would be to step off in front of the next one that pulled in and solve herself.

Everyone thinks that a bit, though. Everyone. It lets them feel extra-comfortable, once the idea has gone past and they don't need to and won't scare the driver, won't cause delays and tutting amongst strangers. That's all you get for killing yourself in London – tutting. There's been a lot of tutting lately. We live in peculiar times.

I'm all right, though. I am. My name is Meg and I'm an alcoholic and it's not like how you see it in the movies when you say that, not like on TV, the whole room doesn't gasp and weep and stare at you like you're a unicorn and you've just started speaking French. You're in an AA meeting – it's the one thing that everybody thinks you'll say.

And my name is Meg and I'm an alcoholic and I have a plan because I am better than not having one, than what might happen if I try to improvise.

I am going to have a nice dinner later, that's all that's going on.

My shoes are the wrong shoes for all of this walking about, but otherwise I'm in promising shape.

And I have a medallion with me and it has 'To Thine Own Self Be True' on it, along with a great big fuck-off Roman numeral –

I

– for one year, because sober years are so important, you get them in Latin, and I can take it out and look at it and it will prove that I'm all right and it has that bloody prayer embossed on the other side and I can't pray – not exactly – but I can have a loud think and the words I might use are written down in any case and I choose to believe – because it's a nice idea – that having written the words down will now mean they are permanently reciting. It's like an open channel, and the words are saying themselves in my pocket the whole time.

Like a letter to Nowhere.

She put her hand in her jacket pocket and ran her thumb over the metal disc, the raised letters, let her nail read what she knew by heart, having heard it spoken so many times, by so many people.

Myself being one of those people. I can have faith in words. I like words. I like them more and fucking more. The Universe I can have my doubts about, but words can be proper and sweet.

**GOD GRANT ME THE
SERENITY TO ACCEPT THE
THINGS I CANNOT
CHANGE, COURAGE
TO CHANGE THE THINGS
I CAN AND WISDOM TO KNOW
THE DIFFERENCE.**

It says that without me, right in my hand. I don't have to do a thing.

And I'm wearing a not nice jacket. But it's the best that I can do. I have to accept my jacket because it can't be changed. I don't think I need drag a God in to assist. My clothes don't fit well, but I'd have no respect for a deity who cared. Why should it?

With the booze, you gain weight and then you lose it and you stop being sure of which shape you are at any given time and you also stop caring – which makes you resemble the high and finer type of God.

I do care now, though – about the jacket. I accept that: not the jacket, just the caring.

I am wearing the jacket as if I do not accept it. I think that's what would show to an observer, but that's also the best that I can do.

And the caring makes me feel sick, so I would rather change that. And looking bad and ugly and pathetic makes me feel sick, too. One thorough glance at me and you'd see: there's a struck-off accountant forever in a jacket and skirt that nobody could trust – which also makes me feel sick.

I would rather change the fact that I feel sick.

And I would rather not feel sick about tonight and about the meeting, or the maybe not meeting, because it does seem unlikely to me that it will happen – it does seem already too far away.

Which I want to change.

Jon seems far away.

And I do not wish to accept that.

I mean – fuck it. I can't do it, the accepting and not accepting and changing and not changing and I would ask – I don't know who – but I would ask what is the fucking point of having a prayer and writing it down and putting it on medallions as if it's important and can help when all it does is make your head hurt?

Should I apply to the God I do not believe in for clarification? The razor-blade one, the faraway one, the beard-and-a-frock one, the one of some religion I've never tried, so I would never even have a chance ...?

And then again, if God has a hurt child to help and a landslide and a cancer ward and a crashed bus full of pregnant women and jolly families to deal with and nice people who are dying – which would mean God was having a pretty quiet day – then I shouldn't be bothering God about anything.

I could leave God out of dealing with decisions about my lapels.

Jon cares about lapels. He probably cares about mine and doesn't like them. They probably make him sick.

And it's a problem, all this. And worse because he's seen this suit before — twice before. It's all she's got that's even bearable. How do you explain to someone with suits and shirts and enough comfortable things that you don't live in their world and that they're sensible and understanding but nevertheless, somewhere in their head they must be filling out this kind of temporary visa so they can come and visit you in your ugly country, examine you and then be glad they can get the hell out again.

God grant me …

Meg let the next Tube train arrive without making it kill her. The thing opened its doors kindly and let her in and then took her away while she sat on the blue, blue seat that ran the carriage's length and decided to remember lunch with Jon, because that made her happy.

I was in this bloody awful suit when I met him outside the PO box place. Then in this bloody awful suit when we managed to have lunch, a sort of lunch. I am now in this bloody awful suit and waiting. Again.

There's being busy and then there's being unwilling and then there's being evasive and then there's being Jon.

After Jon ran for the park it took months to fix another time with him, then change it and change it and change it — this bounce and apology and slip and apology and dodge and apology becoming part of what might be a process.

If somebody wants to meet you, then they meet you — that's how it works.

But you still hope, because you have been told that hoping is good for you.

I will meet you.

That's a kind of hope.

Rather than have to make any new decisions, they'd returned to Shepherd Market for a lunch which wavered and slid back to three o'clock and then four and then half past.

But in the end …

Shepherd Market had *become a sentimental place* – is what Jon had said.

Silly.

The train rocked her, while Meg pushed it to one remove and let Jon arrive in her mind – on a January Thursday, practically dark already and the day dead and the square quiet.

We were warm, though. We were ... I think I was shaking a bit, actually, and you have no idea, at the time, that something will work out, so you worry beforehand ...

He had been his formal self, talking past her. 'A lot of people don't have satisfaction in their work, I can see that and I realise I don't deserve satisfaction any more than somebody else, but there are days when one sits back and considers and ... For more than a century now, you see, I think, many sensible people think, Britain's been circling nearer and nearer the drain, all Parliament does is provide a running commentary and speed the revolutions.' And somewhere round about then, he'd properly noticed her, met her eyes, and then made this smile that was polite, or embarrassed, or upset and trying to hide it, and he'd told her, 'Not actual revolutions, not ... I do apologise, this must be very tedious for you.' Then he'd swallowed in a way that was quite loud.

Meg tried to get what she said next right and maybe didn't. 'I look after stray dogs. Part-time. And I stand near my kitchen window and watch ... Well, I watch the sky, trees, parakeets ... I don't mean my life just is dogs and watching trees grow and so your tediousness doesn't seem so ... You're not tedious.' She appeared to be waving her hands – as if somebody far away was running in the wrong direction and she was signalling they ought to turn back. 'You're not tedious. Sorry. This isn't tedious.'

Jon made a strange upward nod, almost as if he were trying to catch a biscuit in his mouth, or summon something. 'Yes, no, you said – wrote. About the dogs. And how's the goat, by the way? The original goat. Is he happy with the new goats?'

Which wasn't what she'd expected to be asked. 'He's ... I'm mainly in the office. But he's doing well, I hear. They have funny eyes. Rectangular pupils. They're these real, precise rectangles with squared-off corners, but their eyes are the usual round shape of eyes – I can never imagine how that works. It doesn't look natural.'

'Rectangles …?'

'Yes.'

'My … I never knew.'

And that was roughly when Meg had realised that she couldn't cope with this any longer, or with the post-goat silence. She was going to have to break something, or laugh, or yell, or throw a chair.

Jon had wagged his head vehemently. 'I don't know a thing about goats.' It apparently disturbed him that he lacked goat knowledge. 'They're all about … aren't they …? The sex thing, I mean, eating and symbols of, the impulse of … Maybe that's why – the eyes – why people associate them with …' He glanced about in what seemed to be moderate despair, clearly trying to find someone to take their order in a close-to-closing restaurant. He was blushing and clearly aware of it, of its rising round his throat.

Then he'd frowned at her briefly and she'd seen his real face, who he was when he was angry, and he'd leaned a touch nearer and said, 'I'm sorry, this is excruciating, but – in fact – in another way – being nervous people – we're doing well, I think we're doing well, I believe that, under the circumstances, we're managing …'

And then he'd leaned back and cooled again, snapped shut. 'I'm open-plan – when I'm in the office. Dreadful … The chosen ones who still have their own four personal walls get obsessed with floor space, size … You should see what the Home Secretary gets. Visitors have become tired and sat down to rest their horses, possibly herds of goats, during the trek across his mighty carpet. Allegedly. They fight for good furniture – the people, not the goats – they fight to be in Number 10, then they fight to be in Number 10 and close to the PM's PPS and then they fight to be in Number 10 and close to the PM … And they jaunt across the country always seeing the railway end of strangers' gardens, or regional airport cafeterias, which sours one, and they go visiting boys' clubs, hospitals, prisons – being shown that apparently problems and ugliness are caused by everyday people, and are inevitable amongst the electorate. And, conversely, all buildings, all capital projects, are offered up in a pristine state they never quite preserve for passing trade, so why on earth the everyday people have cause to complain, or fail, or be unhappy, well who knows ...' He'd breathed, fluttered into a grin that seemed ashamed of him, of his noise, his complaining. 'The world, you see, is full of people who have to stay human in intolerable circumstances because people in exquisite circumstances can't manage to stay human at all. That's the ... the thing ...'

This had caused another silence during which he'd glanced at the menu as if he was extremely used to restaurants – a restaurant expert; a not everyday person – and had quickly understood that he would have linguine con vongole. 'I like the shells – it's a craft activity for me, getting the meat out ... I harbour vain dreams that somebody saves the emptied shells back in the kitchen and makes them into those table lamps one used to see in provincial B & Bs. Or in the kitchen at my parents' house. They had two – lamps, not kitchens. Sentimental value. Holiday purchases, all the way from a place called Crail. We lived in one small Scottish seaside town and would only ever visit other small Scottish seaside towns if we went away. Provincial B & Bs. Sentimental ... The only thing my mother ever was sentimental about were those lamps. I don't even believe they worked.' His eyes flickered into a resurrection of something unclear and then he sighted the waitress at a point beyond Meg's left shoulder and signalled neatly for service. 'I'm sorry that we're so ... That we're late.' He was used to receiving service, was politely authoritative. 'It's my doing, I'm afraid – the lateness. I would like the vongole and my friend will have—' He'd halted and flushed. 'That's terrible. I didn't ask if you were ready. Or you might want a starter. I don't know what's good here, I've never been ... Would you like a starter as well as a middle? I thought we could have a pudding, but we might have both ... all three, that is ... we might ...'

Jon had offered the waitress a face suffused with the correct degree of helplessness to make her suggest that the shared antipasti platter would be excellent as a starter and Meg had found the idea of this somehow improper – it had been like letting an interloper, newcomer, barge in and make louche assumptions about them.

And thinking that made me know that I wanted to kiss him again in the way I had kissed him goodbye before he fled the café. This time we hadn't kissed hello. We hadn't done anything to say hello – not even said hello. But, even so, I would have felt strange eating with him off the same plate. He was being formal by not touching me, not starting off the ways we might do that – and I couldn't start, I can't start … I was being formal by sitting like a mostly mute idiot and avoiding sliced meat and probably olives and stuff.

And she hadn't needed bruschetta – it was a while since her life had included bruschetta, which was only messed-about-with tomato on toast, which she wouldn't fancy at any time … She hadn't fancied any kind of starter and she'd told him it was fine and she would have the pappardelle with lamb ragu, because that sounded uncomplicated – it would basically be spaghetti Bolognese, really, wouldn't it? He had solemnly agreed.

Not that you'd try spaghetti on a date – if what they were on was a date. Whatever they were on – a cliff edge, a motorway verge, their best behaviour, a date – she would have enough trouble eating without ordering something unpredictable and possibly peculiar that she couldn't manage and then seeming to be a fussy eater.

'Do you want wine?'

'I don't want wine, no, thank you.'

Always there was this moment when you had to say why you didn't drink real drinks. You think you have to give a reason, you can't just offer this unnatural denial of what everyone else gets to have: those hot mouthfuls of signs and wonders.

Fuck that, though. I am – as agreed with myself – better than that. If I'd drunk and he'd been there to catch the show – it would have been the last I saw of him. The least of his problems would have involved me

having phoney loud opinions, over and over, and then the sweating and
trying to feel his dick probably, or telling him I wanted to, or any of that,
all of that, shit like that, covering him in shit like that.

He was a clean man and he met me as I am when I am a clean
woman. That matters. It is not possible to overemphasise how sweet it is
to be with someone and clean. It is not possible to think it without crying.

Jon had ordered a single glass of Gavi and that wasn't a wrong
move on his part. She didn't want any, wasn't going to want any.
She was fine. And it wasn't as if he was downing some kind of
cheap red slosh – the smell of it wasn't reaching out across the
table and making her uneasy. When it arrived, he only nibbled at
it, anyway. Clearly he was not a drinker.

Although I didn't want him to taste of wine if we kissed.

Which I didn't especially expect, not really. The hope kept flailing for
a while and then started to tire, began dropping.

The pappardelle had, as it turned out, been a dreadful choice.
The pasta was huge and leathery. It was like eating bits of bandage
under pretentious tomato sauce.

She tried to fold the stuff on to her fork in ways that would
be controllable, while Jon dipped his head and clearly, plainly was
mortified by his efforts to manage lengths of linguine without
making a mess.

There was a lot of silence. This made the sounds of their eating
seem very wrong.

The waitress watched.

We hadn't shared the antipasti – and so we were doomed, she could
tell.

'Oh, for Christ's sake.' Jon had sat back, hiding his chin with
a napkin and breathing too fast. 'I am terribly sorry. I eat alone
at home. Or at my desk. It leads to just … My wife, ex-wife …
It has been pointed out that I don't eat tidily and, of course, I
would want to eat tidily on this occasion because I am attempting
to make a good impression, fair impression, and to keep you
entertained and … content. If possible.' He blinked at her, defeated
by himself. 'This is all there is. Of me. Is the problem. This is all
there ever is.'

Jon. That was him – a man with an anxious neck above a narrowly knotted tie in solid blue, but with a texture, one that agreed with the blue of his shirt and that rested very neatly above the white stripes in that blue. Charcoal suit: sharp, careful, thoughtful, worn by someone who seemed physically unable to cause creases. A lilac lining to the suit – this little effort at suggesting he might be more than all he ever is, more unexpected. But you know he keeps the jacket buttoned mostly so that nobody will see. Slender face, tender face, pale skin, fastidiously shaved – you believe you will never touch his face and that the world is a vile place becuse of this – and hair which is brown and tawny grey. And his eyes dip glances at you, but never rest. When you catch them fully – in those tiny instants – you can see what he's hiding. You think you can see that inside he's pulling the levers and pressing the pedals and keeping himself in the game and up and working, but close to his end. His eyes make you want him to lie down somewhere – you wouldn't insist he should do that with you – you just do, you just do, you just do want him to rest for a bit and sleep.

What he needs.

At the table, there's this ghost of holding him while he dreams. It lopes through her like a shame, like a promise, like a body in motion.

'Jon?'

'Yes.' He faces her then, focuses on her absolutely, although shaking his head. 'Do you not want to do this any more, because I would understand. I am, in fact, waiting to understand that – or I already have – and if you say now we can finish what's left of this in peace and—'

'I don't want to.'

His expression doesn't change, not exactly – it's only that the warmth dies from it as he keeps it, digs in and holds on, until he can present you with a courteous mask. And all this is done easily, as if it is a practised skill. He is extremely good at being impersonal.

Meg reaches to touch him – *fuck, I'm trying to pat his arm* – but doesn't complete the gesture. 'Jon, I don't want to not do this. I do want to do this. Why would I want to not do this? I want to do …'

His eyes changed, they lit. 'Ah.' And then they were fully themselves again: blue at the darker end of blue, a quiet shade, but something unquiet about his gaze, a fine kind of unquiet.

Meg had told him then.

The stupidest thing to say, but you do – you trust the frightened people more than anyone, you trust them like fuck, you can't help it.

She said, 'I don't drink, because I don't drink, because I'm an alcoholic. I don't drink. You should know. I couldn't have written it down for you – I wanted you to see me when I said, I wanted …'

This made him curl his hand around his wine glass as if he should hide it, or sweep it away. He was staring beyond her while he did this, maybe studying the waitress, or the wall, or nothing visible.

'Is that OK?'

He spoke to the tablecloth, laboriously. 'That couldn't be OK because it would be a horrible thing for you and I would rather a horrible thing hadn't happened to you …' He nodded at that point where she was not. 'You're an …' He picked up his glass and downed its remaining contents in one. This didn't quite work and he coughed afterwards, covered his lips with the back of his hand.

'Are you all right?'

Jon nodded again and made sure to let her search his eyes, the wet shine of them. Another swallow and he could manage, 'Fine.' He nodded definitively. 'I won't have another. I wouldn't have had that.'

'You can have whatever you like. I don't mind. It's OK.'

'I've seen it in others – the drinking. One does. Never looks fun.' Then he smiled at her, produced this cool, unhappy grin. 'My turn. My mother didn't like me. My wife didn't – and doesn't – like me. My daughter is occasionally ambivalent. I don't do well with female people, although I do like them. I have no excuse for this. I do not drink excessively, or take drugs, or have any vice that has broken me down and made me unpalatable. I was apparently born unpalatable.' His eyes busy with examining hers now, checking for who knew what. 'Probably you should give up on me now ... Because I'm thinking ... I'm thinking ...' Jon barked out a small and unamused laugh, a lonely sound. 'I'm actually – please don't be offended – thinking that maybe you only wrote to me and you're only here because you have some kind of ...' His shoulders sank.

'You think I'm here because I've drunk myself into brain damage, or – what – that I'm crazy? I'm some kind of moron?' The sounds of this tasted badly in her mouth – tasted of wine.

He cupped one hand over the top of his head, his forearm obscuring most of his face. 'I know, I know ... See ...? I'm a terrible person.' He sounded muffled and in pain, 'If it's any consolation, I find myself much more offensive than you do. Except, of course, that's an offensive assumption, isn't it? Because you're kind and a kind person ... Oh, Christ, I'm a disaster. They should take me out back to the kitchen, shoot me and serve me up with ... spring greens.' He patted at the tabletop with his free hand, as if to comfort it. 'I hate spring greens. I wouldn't go with them. Oh ...'

And what do you do when you can't write yourself out across the cream of the tablecloth and consider what you need to say for hours, before you prove to him – for sure – prove to him that you're only as much of a freak as he is and that he is nothing to hate, that he cannot be hated. How do you tell him about love?

'Hm?' His head appearing again, the arm dropping.

'I didn't say anything.'

'Oh.' And a smile which was faintly a real smile, an admission of some unfathomable kind, Jonahed away in the deeps of him, behind his restraint and all of his needs which are clearly there and pressing, but not defined.

He does want something. I could swear to that. But maybe not me.

You would understand it better if you could kiss him.

Jon had partly mumbled, 'I'd hoped you had. Said something. I have, um ...' The corner of his mouth uneasy. 'I have run out of ...'

And you realise that you should know what to say by now and say it, because otherwise you're no use at all and you want – this is what you want – to finally be of some fucking use. Writing to Mr August was supposed to make you different and ready for anything – for his anything.

Because you can think of nothing else, you try, 'Look, tell me about where you were born – not Corwynn August, where was Jon born? You tell me that and then I'll do the same – about me – and that'll mean we have a plan and we can manage and I don't want dessert, but I can't be doing with any more of this bloody ... the meal thing – pappardelle ...' This sounded like somebody else, but at least someone practical. 'And your lunch is making you unhappy. Well, isn't it?'

His voice is tiny when it answers, 'Yes.' The schoolroom expression, and he sits up straight and says, 'Linguine – it means *little tongues*, which you wouldn't ... Pappardelle doesn't mean anything much. They have all sorts of names for the shapes, even calamaretti – *little squids*, would you believe.' And now he's recited his homework, 'I'm finished. With it. Them.'

'We can have cappuccinos. That's ... If you don't mind ...'

He'd stared at her then, as if she were a startling headline, a peculiar animal, and she'd wanted to howl – perhaps – at him, or herself, or the waitress with the condescending manners, which was no manners at all. 'I do better with a plan. Birthplace, school, first job, favourite colour. You start. Tell me.'

And his amazement continues, but gently colours with happiness. The man who takes orders all day grins at you – here's someone who intends to be fastidious when he gives you all his answers for your test. 'I don't know my favourite colour. I mean ...'

'Then we'll skip that.'

'No, that's great, yes. A plan. We'll always have a plan. That's what we should do. Agree a plan beforehand. Yes.' An effort towards gladness creeping out over him. 'I was ... I was born in Nairn – well, Inverness and then they took me back to Nairn, to an area called Fishertown, which is fishermen's cottages and some slightly bigger places, Edwardian what they call villas, if the *they* happens to be estate agents. Villa would be a bit much. It's all very upgraded and extended these days ... Which is ... for the local economy ... that is ... My dad wasn't a fisherman. Neither was Mum. They did all right. But not that.'

'You don't sound Scottish.'

'It was removed – the sound. Fashionable procedure. Like docking a dog's tail, or lopping its ears to do it good. No, it was my choice. I wanted to prosper and back then an accent adjustment helped. Still would, I'd imagine.'

'I was sent away to school – birthplace and then school is what I'm providing at the moment, you will note. At the time, one wanted – one's parents wanted their child to collect educational achievements ... I first attended the little session school in Fishertown, but after that I showed an unfortunate amount of promise and so I was scholarshipped off down south. It was a shame, because the Ballerina Ballroom in the High Street had some great gigs while I was away, just when I would have loved them. The Who played there, can you imagine? And Cream. Eric Clapton in Nairn. When I was twelve, thirteen, something like that. The Beatles were in Elgin earlier, I seem to remember. I wouldn't have bothered with them, even if I'd been able – all dressing alike, it wasn't cool. It's only almost cool if you're from Detroit ... I saw Clapton, that gig, because it was in the holidays. I sneaked in. Keen. Decisive. Or something like that. Mainly I was just tall for my age.' He shrugged his shoulders as if he had just set down a pair of heavy cases and was feeling himself to be unencumbered. 'There you are – what I grew up with – seafront teas and provincial devotees of rhythm and blues with an option on rock and roll. You can shake off the sand and the accent, but not the R and B.' And his first proper grin emerged and stayed.

It wasn't so bad after that, our not-really-lunch. It was lovely.

It was the two of them drinking four coffees each and pretending the stuff tasted nicer than it did as a justification.

And Jon's mouth was flavoured with coffee and not wine and with his speaking, with his voice.

That's what I found out.

They had kissed at the table once, Meg shivering for a moment when they stopped. Then Jon had handled the bill like a man who handles bills and had taken her hand, as if he was picking up an apple, an egg, lifting up something breakable, but not broken, leading her outside.

Standing in the freedom of Shepherd Market, Meg had felt herself shy without the observing unpleasantness of the waitress to act as chaperone. On a wintery late afternoon it was dark, of course – they weren't so terribly exposed. And she'd needed a solution to the cold. Even a cautious person finally might decide that she had to be rid of the so much, too much cold it seemed she always had to deal with.

And Jon had cleared his throat, but not spoken, only raised her hand and placed his lips against each of her knuckles – hello, hello, hello, hello – finding out the details with his mouth.

So that's how that would be, that's how he does that, investigates.

And it was all right after that to hold on fast to each other and to have the flex and tuck of his breath pressed against her own. And it was all right to listen while he said, 'The shop's shut – where I collect your letters.' She could feel the thrum of his words happening inside him, while he spoke. This was the touch and the sound of his voice. 'Meg, I appreciate your … what you've …' His arms had drawn in with a tremor and then relaxed slightly. 'I would write, but I can't, so I have to say while you're here, because writing would be nonsensical and I am nonsensical, but not that much … I'll say that I want you to go home and have a lovely evening and when you go to, when you sleep … I want when you sleep, I would like you to dream the best and finest and sweetest and feel well and be well and be happy and wake up happy. I would like you to wake up happy.' She felt him press his face to the crown of her head. 'I'll tell you later. At midnight – how much I would like that.' And then he stepped back and peered at her, while there was a dim noise from the pub at the corner, a dither of feet.

Meg had nothing to say and wished she did and wished so much that she did, but she could only stand on tiptoe to kiss his forehead as if this might be what they always did. She was hoping to calm what was inside. It seemed necessary.

And he liked it. I saw how he looks when something happens that he likes.

She had held on to his hand afterwards while the seconds shone and darted and this part of their life was right here and clean and lovely.

She had wished the time could be longer and deeper and more.

I'm greedy – a greedy drunk.

And he'd sent her the midnight text and begun that habit – their wishes sculling out across those few miles between them, regular like clockwork, regular like safety and all safe things every-where – from home to home and room to room and pillow to pillow. Every night.

He might be greedy, too.

It is the late afternoon on a spring day. An assortment of children are climbing a tall street that leads to a park. They have formed a chain, one following the next, their arms pistoning forwards, or their hands resting on each other's hips. As they jog upwards and upwards they make the noises of steam engines – trains in a time from before they were born. People in their gardens pause to watch them and the children are aware of being important and delighted and an event.

Alongside them rush three women, who are more out of breath than the children and who are probably the mothers of most if not all of them. The women seem tired, but although they flag now and then, they cannot stop, because their children are racing and unstoppable, they are an inarguable joy and should not be prevented.

At intervals, the women let out steam-whistle hoots, in lieu of doing anything more taxing. And sometimes they are also swept up by this forward motion, this train which is not a train, which is better and safer and more fun than any conceivable train. This makes them run and their faces change into softness and lightness and they laugh.

There is never a point, though, when all of the women laugh together. At least one of them stays watchful, remembers herself, and becomes slower and heavier as a result. But they still run. They can't help it. Everyone runs.

The children have plainly been allowed to dress according to their own secret logic: there is a towel worn as a cape, there is a mask, there are wellingtons and sandals and a shapeless hat. One boy wears a little suit of black with white bones painted on it and clearly this running about and this being his dead self are both his most favourite things. He runs and runs – the bones of a boy.

Everyone runs.

20:55

JON WAS USHERED up the ugly stairs of Chalice's club – *East Berlin could truly not have furnished any building more unsightly* – and was then permitted to propel himself into the biscuity, overwarmed air of the Carrington Room. There were stacks of high-end chairs and a few folded tables, presumably ready for functions of some kind, but otherwise the long, low space was simply dominated by a hideous carpet and lighting of an oppressively revealing type.

Chalice was, of course, not already there. It was Jon's job to be the man who waits and who is taught, once again, that his time is of minimal value.

He decided that he might as well be comfortable and took down a chair to sit on. He set it within sight of a lumpy oil painting depicting some barricade of note in Northern Ireland: 1970s uniforms, Saracens and loose bricks, an image from what, in the light of more recent adventures, now seemed a morally irreproachable and painless campaign.

And that's how they're sold now, aren't they – the Troubles? All soft hats and assisting the civil power – hearts and minds and didn't we do well? War as a game show.

His eyes wandered over the little greenish figures designed to convey sturdy British anguish and resource. He also considered the figures designed to convey civilian treachery and threat: the classic elongated silhouette of the firebomb-thrower, those cheap estate-dwelling flared jeans, the energy of inadequately disciplined youth.

There's something about chucking a Molotov cocktail, a bottle of Rafah lemonade, that always looks low-class. The poor man's napalm.

We have to call it asymmetric warfare these days, don't we? Rather than burning despair. Depictions of the military at work have never quite been what they were since the static nature of the Western Front bollocksed their cavalry charges. People like horses. People do not like pictures of dead horses lying splay-legged and swollen in mud, being used as temporary landmarks by men who reinforce their trench walls with corpses, having nothing else to hand but an overplus of death.

For an instant he remembered watching a tourist couple posing for each other, turn and turn about, grinning for the camera in front of St Paul's annual plantation of war-memorial crosses ...

As striking a backdrop as any. No meaning required.

Once your wars have been rebranded, re-rebranded — in the end any possible meaning wears away, or simply withdraws and leaves you to it.

Teeth and smiles.

That's all you want in a photo ... Or in a war.

The portraits of current campaigns will have to show descending drones, perhaps the faces of their operators. The instant of accurate annihilation immortalised on canvas in a blossoming of flames — not the instant when the child runs out and all is beyond recalling. The soldiers won't be there, because we prefer to wage wars without them, such people being servants of the state in which we no longer believe and, likewise, a concept of nationhood we actually should abandon in favour of more exciting definitions involving areas of consumption, zones of commercial influence.

Can I betray my nation, if my nation no longer exists? What if there is no social contract and only a series of punitive arrangements forced upon me by supranational entities? What if these entities have their own, ideologically acceptable armed forces and an admirable ability to float on in glory and in light, high above any taxation or legal restraint? In that case, what is treason? One might ask that. One might.

The painting was giving him a headache, either that or his day was giving him a headache – his day in combination with his personality.

Does anyone truly believe they can outrun history, break free from reality, become transcendent, never pay any kind of price …? Running in camouflage, running in pullovers … Both sets of figures displaying the danger inherent in long memories and immoderate belief. Long hair to keep you safe on the streets, short back and sides to mark you as a target … The occasional civil servant blundering off to Derry, fretting about car bombs and trying it on in a mumble with squaddies, having a go at quoting equivalent rank … Those were the days. So I've heard.

I am the civil-service equivalent of a captain – in a fog with the light behind me.

As if …

Jon sniffed, swallowed.

Gets it all out of the system, before I need myself to seem composed.

It's best to feel I'm simply hiding a pissed-off rant and nothing more … Play the passed-over man. So many reasons that I'm passed over and I truly should be, but let's agree that it's currently down to Valerie, to women, to the mail drop, the courting and maybe one odd conversation I had with another man's wife in 1987.

In 1987 – that long ago – some woman, somebody's wife, told me things and I paid attention and I tried to …

I asked questions and was quietly told that I shouldn't, not thereafter, and also the conversation I thought I'd had with somebody's wife … Well it hadn't happened. I was mistaken.

And nothing was sexual.

Nothing is ever sexual.

Nothing is ever said or ever has been, or ever could.

So I stopped asking questions and I've behaved as a good boy ought to ever since, as far as any department oversight can know.

I am safe. Look at me, please, examine – I'm so safe.

I am not a manifestation of civilian treachery, civilian threat.

'Like it, do you?' Chalice was hamming up the military precision of his walk as he cleared the doorway and crossed the muffling depth of black and fawn carpet.

All soundless is his progress – see, but do not hear where he comes.

It's somehow terribly tasteless for the likes of Chalice to sound as if they're walking when they walk – audible effort is something for the other ranks, the boot-wearing classes.

Or it's meant for the high-heeled accompaniments to one's evening – gowns and bags and running the show when they can, grabbing their old boys by the cock and leading them round ... Not quite admirable, but I can see their point ...

Alternative sources of enjoyment for the quiet-footed gentleman – well, they're entirely silent. At all times. Ask no questions, hear no silence.

Jon didn't spring to his feet like a well-trained subordinate when Chalice manifested. For one thing, Jon was weary. 'I'm sorry?' He was inordinately weary. He didn't want to shake hands. He didn't want to interact. He just wanted to sit.

'Got your eye on our painting there, Jon. Like it? Quite an engagement at the time. Although the regiment gets no credit.'

Chalice playing up how much he was at home here, rising on the balls of his feet, stepping, swivelling.

At least Val left my cock entirely out of it in every sense. I should send her a card and thank her.

'One does hope to be better appreciated.' Harry Chalice, former man of action – although what action exactly was hard to ascertain – continued with what he surely imagined was an air of amiable dominance. 'Unpopular wars – they still have to be fought. In fact, they demand our attention rather more than the easy sells. I think the public understand that better now, don't you? Efforts to put the military view at the heart of our national conversation – they're really bearing fruit.'

He only does it to annoy.

'Hearts and minds,' Jon told him, not rising to the bait.

Chalice paused overly near Jon, perhaps in an attempt to make him stand.

Or perhaps it was an expression of disrespect. Most likely that.

You can present your crotch to me as often as you like – I'm never going to blow you.

340

'Hearts and minds, Jon. That's right. Although if you've got their hearts, you don't really need their minds, do you?'

Naturally. When you're in love you'll do anything you're asked.

'Harry, it's been a long day and I have another appointment ...'

Chalice backed away enough to simply be a man standing over his inferior colleague.

He's going to, isn't he? He's going to ...

And he did unfasten his nastily tight jacket and spread it apart, set his hands on his hips. 'One of your many, Jon?' He was showing Jon the full horror of an old-school pair of close-cut trousers: they hinted at cavalry britches, hugged the just slightly too generous thighs, while maintaining the emphatic line of their creases and deftly holding the neat little parcel where Chalice kept his sex.

An officer blithely at play in the city. The prefect at play in the biggest school on earth, the one he never needs to leave, coat pegs and name tags all the way, from prep school to the House of Lords. All the way in all suitable directions. And nobody gets expelled, not any more, not really.

Although I did hear Sandhurst nearly spat him out. In fact. Not much loved. If we were dealing with facts.

'I beg your pardon?' Jon happy to ignore the reference to Sophia, to Lucy – especially to Lucy. Jon delighted to not play along.

'One of your pen pals, Jon?'

And then, because today was today and because he needed distracting and because he could, because he could, because he could ... Jon dropped his head and tried, 'Well, you know me, Harry.' He composed the properly knowing expression, the smile that tasted of contempt – the one with which he was always eventually confronted at parties, functions, receptions – the boys'-club sign of membership, the evident assurance of the man who knows women and finds them wanting, renders them wanting. The effort was distasteful enough to make him queasy for a breath. Then he looked up and showed himself to Chalice, hoped his nausea would pass, or at least not show 'Yes ... you know me. A man has to have an interest. If it isn't the money, well then it's the honey.'

Absurd bullshit – and the bigger lies are easier, are exhilarating – keep his eyes, let him think this is your true self, the only secret you've been hiding.

Jon let his mouth shrug slightly and then added, 'We play ... And they play, too, the ladies. They do know how, always have ... They just want the rules skewed in their favour. They want it to be noted they're unhappy and put-upon. Duly noted. And then they pretend they don't welcome our attention and haven't got us on eggshells and taken our jobs.'

Steady, steady, don't be completely preposterous.

'It's all just the usual game, though.' He nodded to the painting, as if it were a beach scene, a domestic interior evoking only casual nostalgia. 'Back then – a young chap like yourself, you wouldn't remember – we operated honestly. Men and women knew what was expected and they had a sense of humour. There was the pill, the girls got that. There was Alex Comfort – she could read the manual, see the pretty drawings, tasteful. Nothing "Readers' Wives" about it.'

Val thought Comfort was grotesque – no pun intended. Sketches of some hairy European couple being happy and exchanging artisan pleasures ... not quite her thing.

Jon continued, the words dizzyingly untrue and therefore thrilling, 'No one, so to speak, tied anyone down.'

Being Chalice must always feel like this – the exhilaration of deceit.

'If objections were made, they were just signs of her paranoia – they were her hormones kicking in. What we currently have to put up with ...'

It seemed Chalice wasn't sure about this. He didn't react.

Come on. You want to believe it. Come on.

And Jon felt the pressing need for a short Scotch, while feeling also as if he had drunk one.

Then a grin emerged. Chalice had decided to be glad.

Flowering like nightshade, like hemlock, like flames.

Chalice sniggered. 'Well, Jon ... I did wonder. We have wondered ... What does he get out of it? If anything? Where does

Jon's heart lie? What occupies Jon's mind? You were a bit of an enigma. Which is never wise.'

'Now you know, then.' Jon being as brisk as he could, although he realised that Chalice wouldn't let things lie without kicking about a little.

'A man who lets his wife screw around like that, who can't stop her – that man has no balls. That man is wanking with an empty sack. Is what I thought.'

Jon setting his fingernails into the palm of the fist Chalice can't quite see. 'Open marriage. Not what you'd want to make public. Or I chose not to.' He could feel himself sweating slightly and couldn't work out how not to. 'Valerie had other opinions ...'

'You chose the dignified option.' Chalice nodding with only a trace of irony. 'Good for you.' And there was the reptile flicker of a darker smile. 'Although not good for your career. If you'd talked to us ...' And then another expression, the one Jon had wanted to see.

The one that says, 'Thank fuck, you're as dirty as me in your sad, old way. This means we can do business and that's grand, because doing business is all there can be, or ever will be, world without end ...'

Jon modulating his tone to reflect a manly desire for cooperation and common sense: 'I don't like to be beholden, Harry. But – if you wouldn't mind – I'd be very grateful if this went no further ...'

I'll tell you I trust you – when you cannot conceivably be trusted – and so you'll trust me.

That's the thing about your kind of man – you lack imagination, so you do great harm. But because you lack imagination, you can be – in the long run – easily and inexorably undone. As ruined as a Lloyd's name, as a Madoff client – remember what happened to them? There are so many breeds of mug punter. There are so many innocents. They all get screwed.

Jon leaned his legs out ahead of him and pretended to stretch, rejoiced in the fact that Chalice could not possibly know (and wouldn't, in any case, like) the speech in *Pimpernel Smith* where the quiet and mild and clever and overlooked professor of archaeology politely lectures the Nazi holding a gun on him.

Smith predicts that what is wrong must plod onwards, grind down its own wrong road until it has destroyed almost everything and can only continue destroying, can only destroy itself.

And I actually – fuck – do believe that.

He inhaled like a man who wanted to do business.

I am a creature of long memory and immoderate belief.

He wanted, actually, to shout out, 'Captain of Murderers' in Leslie Howard's 1940s English accent – one of the many you no longer hear, one filled with an English way of thinking which has also been extinguished.

Captain of Murderers ...

That's one, or both of us ...

'This Milner thing ...' Jon felt his head twitch, which was unfortunate, because it indicated stress – but it wasn't so fatal a tell now they were friendly, well accommodated, 'I really can't help you that much with him, Harry. I don't know the man and I don't see ... I may be mistaken ... what purpose my getting to know him might serve. He seems very much a spent force. In other times, he could have regrouped and been a problem, but these aren't other times. He's a dinosaur.'

Chalice licked his lips. 'Takes one to know one ... No offence.' And he strolled to look out of the window at the broad and high and dark and evening stillness of Pall Mall. 'Milner's not quite the problem, not exactly. The leaks are the problem. There are too many. And they're too targeted. They are strategic. Some shifty little shit is kicking up dust, stamping his feet.'

From you, that's a compliment – you shifty little shit. The boys – and girls – from the Darknet, the shadowy 4chan types, they called me a Moralfag.

Jon speaking as his thoughts gallop past him, 'And Milner's the contact for that?'

Moralfag's a compliment, too.

'He doesn't seem quite up to it ...'

'Milner's had none of them, but he's running with them once they're out. He seems to be actively avoiding any close connection, which seems slightly ... odd. And he's digging – we heard him spooning out his little tunnels, late at night – test shafts … And as he's the loose cannon, as he's got the big mouth, we feel he'd be the best line to pursue back to the source. He's a horny old hack, a pre-Wapping drama queen – loves big reveals and purple prose.'

'And you really think he's holding something, knows sources? That he would tell me?' This being a legitimate question, asked in a legitimate tone.

Chalice avoided making an answer, 'We'd like to know if he's holding something – other than his sweaty, alky dick, that is. We'd like you to check his hairy palms, Jon … Have a regular look at him. Just lately he's walking around like a man with a platinum knob – as if he is finding himself more than averagely precious. He broke a little something today – but not much, not quite what he seems to think he's holding.'

'Is he holding, though? Is he bluffing?'

Jon stared at the man's back, felt secure in loathing the curve of his skull, the slightly low left shoulder, the undefended view of a liar.

They never look quite the thing – the liars – not unless they can give the full-frontal view. Not even very good liars can lie with the back of their head.

'What do you think, Jon?'

'Me?' Jon sighed as a tired and overstretched public servant might. 'As I've said. I don't see that he's got a light in his eye about anything. He is a show-off, as you say, and he'd at least have hinted this afternoon – he was genuinely quite drunk. He would have wanted to let me know he was sitting on at least a straight flush before the flop.'

Chalice fancies himself at poker, yearns for the days of the Clermont Club and the glamour of white-tie losses.

Jon played his own kind of bet. 'God knows … you'd think someone would have leaked about me, that he'd have heard something of it. He'd have been bound to mention, it would make a fun story for a slow Sunday morning – senior civil servant enjoys …'

'A harem? Hot and cold running *cunt*?' Chalice turned neatly on his heel and pressed back into the room. There was no smile this time.

No. I made a bad bet. I take it back.

But I am all smooth.

But I've offered the wrong fucking bluff ...

But I can breathe easy ... visibly easy ... I'm OK.

Nevertheless, Jon's arms and legs lost their muscle tone for a horrible plunge of cold time.

Your feet go numb first with hemlock ...

Meanwhile he thought softly what Chalice said aloud, 'Ah, Jon, but if Milner *did* know about you — if any of them did — you'd be just the man to lean on for information ...'

Jon sinking into his breath, keeping his breath, still and still and still and calm. He produced a frown, an evident instant of distaste, anger. 'And you think that? Of me?'

This hunting pack kind of laugh, a hound's laugh, escaped Chalice as he patted his hands together — so, so, so — and then chuckled on with, 'We thought it a possibility. That's why — for goodness' sake — we made sure all the heavies already know about you and your sad little headfucks on paper and your sad little marriage. We told them it's no kind of news and that they all have it, so why bother running it? We stopped their guns. *Bedroom frolics* they would have loved, a man in his forties, a credible man, that would be different ...' Chalice tilted his head to one side. 'But no offence, Jon, but a thinning memo-shuffler who's outlived his hopes of promotion penning damp little letters, writing down his wanks, the scraggy old lad keeping busy ... All rather too disgusting. You're not a story. You're more a cry for help ...'

Jon kept his fists — he suddenly had fists — in positions of violent stillness, cramped at the ends of his arms. He nodded neatly, like a memo-shuffler. He kept his mind in suspension, locked away from all activity and harm.

Stillness.

I will meet you.

Stillness.

I will …

Jon kept nodding, drifting his head down so that he could not see Harry Chalice, not even his feet, and so that it was possible to say, 'I do have an appointment now, though, Harry, and I would like to keep it if you wouldn't mind.'

A pause floated in and made the air taste slightly metallic, unwholesome.

There was the sound of a jacket being buttoned — that tiny disturbance.

I will meet you.

I'm all right.

I'm a good man.

I do my best.

'All right, Jon. Off you trot.'

A young man, possibly a student, stands in a Circle Line subway train. The car is half empty and he could sit if he likes, but he may not be aware of this. His eyes are closed and he wears headphones which are leaching the ghosts of music into the space around him. He holds tight to an overheard rail and rocks only gently, slowly, with the motion of the floor under his feet, even though the passengers near him can hear the driving speed of the beat, that rapid and tinny insistence, which must be something almost overwhelming in his head.

Eyes turn to him, irritated, disapproving.

At St James's Park three girls enter the carriage, brushing past him and opening his eyes.

They also choose not to sit and, instead, gather opposite him. They look at each other. They smile. They begin dancing to what they can gather of his spilling music: arms lifting, bodies swaying, answering the thin call of what he offers, perhaps in spite of himself, perhaps as a demonstration of his general thoughtlessness.

He watches them as they shuffle-walk closer, swing and bump.

They don't meet his eye. They dance as though they had always intended to, as though they always do, as though it is only coincidental that they're keeping his second-hand beat. They shift and spin, change places, as if they have realised they are beautiful, are human beings in their twenties and therefore effortlessly lovely, unable to do anything other than shine like this and be in the world with a perfect bloom like this and show the tranquillity of easy muscle like this. They are languidly delighted, ignoring the man in a way that means he becomes so aware of himself that he blushes and a sudden jolt of the moving car makes his feet stumble, while his arm snaps up and clings to the overhead rail and saves him, lets him hang.

The young man, possibly a student, watches the girls as if they are a miracle, a wonderful humiliation that he can't mind, that he loves. It seems they have suspended his breathing. It seems he doesn't mind that, either.

21:25

Jon had reached South Kensington Station. He rose up from the platform with the purposeful frown of a man in a hurry. That seemed a hopeful choice. He mounted the escalator with fierce and obvious strides as the grey-toothed metal steps lifted beneath him, reeled him forwards to the exit and ground level. He was his own ministry in motion.

I progress.

When the treads subsided, meshed and flattened at the end of his climb, they offered the usual illusion of mildly gliding dominance and things sinking before his will, going his way.

Even though quite a number of things were not.

I ought call her. Again. Explain myself, everything, something.

I need explaining. That second time, in the restaurant … I was a disaster. I was unmitigated in my total fucking failure. And I'm aware that's a criticism framed in terms unsuited to a supportive and functional workplace.

But I am not a workplace. Or supportive. Or functional. I am only a person. I am a fucked-up person.

He coped with the station's final steps while shaking his head like a swimmer, freshly emerged.

Or maybe I'm not quite totally screwed − I'm simply not perfect at once. Even the greats, they'd have a few takes at each song. The version you finally hear, it's had work. And I need time to work. I don't improvise. I can't get away with rough and ready. I will not ever be a feasible live show. I'll always be the hideous semi-pensioner, thrashing about with his fork like some care-home resident, suddenly baffled by pasta in an empty restaurant.

Not empty – full of her.

Talking to her about goats, about tongues … As if all I could think about was … As if I was constantly in a state of …

Lurking – I was lurking somehow – spattered with olive oil and tepid bits of parsley, opposite a not-so-much-younger woman, but for God's sake there is a gap – mind the gap – a discernible gap and one feels that one has no right to expect …

I mean, the letters are one thing …

Dear Mr August

He kept at least one of them folded in his pocket when he went out and about. Always. For ever. Two folds of cream paper were in there today, snug by his heart and full of tiny, hot motion. Like a pacemaker he couldn't quite keep up with.

Sweet Mr August

Inside his jacket, held safe, were whole remarkable sentences of kindness, meant for precisely him. Bespoke.

You get me through.

And she gets me through and once I've tried a few rehearsals, I can write that to her. I have told her that truth, but she simply gives it back again. The whole process is bloody well unending, apparently – and then you have to bloody meet her.

You get me through, Mr August. And you've changed things that happened a long time before I met you. Now everything can seem to be the route that led to you. So I make sense. I never expected to make sense.

I know her off by heart. Her music.

But I can't play my own tune, not now, not under my fucking circumstances.

Heading away from the station, Jon understood he was fine on paper. A person of around sixty – genuinely, technically not quite sixty – could be, in their absolute absence, possibly impressive and – if not attractive – then agreeably lived-in.

If you're bluesman cool, any kind of cool — then you can get away with being lived-in …

I'm not bloody lived-in. My face has squatters. My premises have been ruined by moral subsidence and stress — I'm all crumbled façade and squinting little windows.

Why does the skin around one's eyes collapse with age? Exuberant eyebrows, endless sodding vigour in your ear hairs, nose hairs — but your eyelids turn entirely apathetic. Is this a type of natural mercy? Do the slumping lids join the fading eyesight and spare one the pin-sharp details of one's personal decay?

Jon's vision was, in fact, still quite serviceable. He only needed glasses for the work on paper.

Papers of colours appropriate to their function, memos, reports, emails — and letters.

I wear the glasses when I'm trying to write letters back, to match her, to correspond, to be …

Jon cradled the back of his neck with one cooling hand and stood beneath the sodium lights and tactful surveillance cameras of South Kensington. He had this sensation of weakness in his legs which made him believe that his brain was being damaged. If perhaps he could think less …

What the hell should I have said to her? What warning should I have posted in advance?

We do live in an age of prior warnings. We have less and less real safety, but there's hardly a human experience now that isn't introduced by catalogues of cautions: walking routes, furniture, sandwiches, films …

I may contain scenes of mental collapse and sexual …

This evening may end with … Myself, everything, something.

Jon spun slowly, sighting along the voluptuous, straight perspective of Exhibition Road and its central, prickling spine of futuristic street lamps. It seemed for an instant to lead his eye along towards a great emptiness, a devouring space.

I do want her to be happy.

A kind of hot cramp ran down from between his shoulders and crouched at the small of his back. Chalice's voice was somehow still rooting about and doing harm within Jon's inner ear.

Chalice, you are a thing with an inhuman scent.

Jon felt himself becoming shadowed, essentially naked and ready for display in a suitable case, exuding just the air of melancholy that would prefigure an extinction. His reflection in the window of a tiny Chinese restaurant apparently agreed. He was this stricken outline, tall but round-shouldered – this old-school monkey man lost inside a good coat.

You don't know me, though, Harry fucking Chalice. You haven't noticed we're not the same species. I'm not a modern man who's chosen to unevolve, slide back to the days of blood and territory. Your kind – you're out for wild cries and hunts through darkling forests in like-minded troupes.

Not far away in the dark was the Natural History Museum, dozing inside its swarming terracotta ornaments and creatures.

One day last year Jon had made an entirely innocent visit – no notes to leave for anybody. He'd trotted upstairs to visit the hominid cases, wanting to contemplate the skulls and faded dioramas and to be with the vanished dreams inside his forebears' skulls.

They might have imagined all kinds of humanities: strange musics, dancing and setting one's palm tight to a wall and painting around it to show the cleverness of fingers, keep a record of the tenderness that might touch other skin, might care when someone reached for care, might be their warmth and their shape of safety.

I really do want her to be happy.

He'd perhaps also liked the idea of standing with a fresh letter flickering in his hand and showing the models of his silent relatives how he had prospered and advanced.

I try to progress.

But all the displays on the origin of his species, that entire section, had been removed.

They'd been replaced with odds and ends about Darwin and a weasel-worded panel for the kids to read on evolution – heavy emphasis on the theory. The panel avoided ever stating whether we've evolved, or just been pressed out by God, like fresh little gingerbread babies. Gingerbread, rib bones and mud.

In a palace built to celebrate the scientific method and the safeguard of information in a world full of dangerous dreams ... In case they offend opinions, they tucked away their facts.

Evolved human beings had thought this was the proper course to take. In the Natural History Museum.

It was like – in a small way, a tiny way ...

I don't want to see this.

It was like coming home ...

I don't want this.

Why I think of more harm when there's so much harm loose here already ...

It was like coming home that first time ...

The picture of it was unfurling like a bolt of bloody cloth, tumbling.

It was like coming back to find one's home not as it should be and a man sitting in one's armchair in one's living room and smirking inside an atmosphere which suggested activities had been undertaken. And the man had that particular look – that special, concupiscent, lazy glance – which he turned to your wife when she came through from the kitchen carrying two fresh glasses of beer ...

I'd successfully forgotten that on occasions she did drink our free beer. On occasions when I was elsewhere.

And one would rather not believe one is a cuckold, not even in theory, yet here it is – the evidence.

As if someone tore out a hole in the side of the building and let half its contents spill out.

But Meg wouldn't do that.

He punched his fist into his palm, caught his own knuckles clumsily – not a manly gesture, only stupid. The images didn't stop.

Also like – in a small way – coming home one summer holiday and seeing one's mother as one passes the bedroom door – the carelessness of limbs when the sleeper isn't sleeping, is only passed out. The smell of sweetness and sourness and wrongness.

Post-partum depression – my fault.

She was given drugs, repeated drugs, eventually hoarded and then gorged-upon drugs – her doctor's fault.

It wasn't just me who ended up leaving Society Street. Mum went, too. Dad spent years there in the same house with her, but having to live by himself. She was intermittent. She was chilly. She was a ghost's body. She was lots of things which weren't her fault.

One cannot understand an addict when one is a child. When one is older, one reflects and analyses their inabilities, acknowledges their disease …

It makes no fucking difference.

One still feels precisely the same.

As if someone tore out a hole in the side of the building and let half its contents spill out and every neighbour suddenly was able to peep in and find your mother, undignified and overcome.

Women who have wild cries inside and get dark like forests – that isn't their fault, but I couldn't currently stand it.

Jon stopped – inside and out.

He'd been pacing – *like a captive creature* – to and fro at the back of the station. He made himself angry again about the museum, specifically the museum.

I have become a preposterous old geezer, ranting and raising my hairy knuckles against the decisions of the young.

Moralfag.

Scraggy old lad.

Defending knowledge in the face of evasions and entertainment.

He realised that he'd been holding his breath for some time.

He exhaled.

This is good, this is appropriate thinking. This is better than the thinking I cannot think and shouldn't mention, because then I'll think it.

Fuck.

As if someone tore out a hole in the side of the building and let half its contents spill out and therefore continued the process of handing the world to the humans who have stolen Darwin and portrayed him as only cruel – the ones who feel his theory must be savage, because he describes the working out of powers greater than their own. They find such an idea cruel – these men and women who can value nothing in those around them but fitness and competition, taking and keeping and blood and bone.

Which is a generalisation of a type we would avoid unless we were making an unwise and emotive pronouncement, shouting on television, on the radio, in a paper, on Twitter.

Does it really matter where? It's all shouting.

In media and electoral terms, shouting is a requirement.

One is reminded again of how much – in both senses – one hates.

But one really would rather love, if one could manage.

Jon – inhaling and exhaling as he should – crossed the slightly unnerving paved road now laid out beside South Kensington Station.

You take your luck here with the cruising cars. The aim is to promote coexistence between traffic and pedestrians by removing any clearly defined pavement. Survival of the fittest.

Children might be harmed here, I feel. That would have been one of the risks assessed and presumably discounted during the planning process.

Jon did not approve of harming children. He believed they should be always defended.

I'm also not in favour of risks.

He pushed himself past 20 Thurloe Street, home to the Polish restaurant where Cold War spies once met their handlers – Kim Philby tackling pork knuckle, or pierogies, poppy-seed cake – handing over the goods between courses, one had to presume.

I met Lucy in there once – a joke location that I couldn't find amusing.

He doesn't care if I get blown. He'd think it was funny, thinks I'm funny.

Everyone, apparently, thinks I'm funny.

Or possibly Meg doesn't and I should phone her. I need to do that. But I keep forgetting.

But instead Jon kept walking, left behind the cheerily fogged glass of the establishment where Christine Keeler once sat being stylishly traitorous, or flirtatious, or whatever else, while her Soviet lover, or client, or confidant, got down to the pierogies. Perhaps.

He went on into Thurloe Square, slipping along beside the well-maintained people carriers that would gather up well-maintained kids in charmingly retro well-maintained uniforms and then ferry them off to their well-maintained schools in the morning. Illuminated windows showed deftly arranged furniture, investment art, bright fragments of lives, meals being prepared by homeowners, meals being prepared by servants, by nannies, by au pairs: the gradations of posture, costume, comfort. Held in the dim palm of the square, a gated garden was all silences and shapes, polite leaves.

I'm sure we could have made a dead-letter drop there, somehow: got keys for access and then hidden slips of paper, little weatherproofed canisters and so forth.

It didn't matter, not at this stage, not when everything was so near to its end.

Thurloe was Cromwell's spymaster – appropriate to have his name salted round about.

In Thurloe Place, the pavement at his feet seeming to give every now and then, sinking. The rush of traffic as the road widened was both absurd and horrifying to him.

Thurloe was a survivor. Under Cromwell and then Charles, John Thurloe kept his head, because he had a necessary mind. There's hope in that.

Jon felt like running, but did not.

One ends up with a friend, that's the trouble with letters. One posts out slivers of oneself and gets these warm, these hot, these delicate pieces of someone else back and one is in their mind – they write and say they keep you, hold you in mind.

And if you sleep, you dream their body.

Fuck …

Jon reached a junction and peered to his left. Apparently he had to peer this evening, had to strain for the shapes of things with his perfectly serviceable eyes. Across the road was the Brompton Oratory: that high neoclassical mound of ornaments and pillars, that pretty heap of dirtied Portland stone.

Inside, it's a bit Vegas: lots of marble, like an upscale hotel bathroom with confessionals for light relief. I never quite took to the place. And traitorous letters died there while they waited for the KGB – the communist faithful nipping up the broad front steps to slip indoors beside the holy-water stoups, carrying codes past the mother of God in her seasonally adjusted robes, tucking secrets into the chapel for St Cecilia.

St Cecilia watching.

Oh, but that's a fucking lie. Of the worst kind – reliable information polluted by credible bullshit. If I had the strength I'd punch myself.

I have no idea who passed over what or where and St Cecilia is a statue and even if statues could see, hers doesn't watch. She's lying on her side with her head draped in a cloth – a very lovely model of a corpse. A victim of state torture in white marble, the cut to her throat not obvious ... Slim waist and noble suffering. After an original by Stefano Maderno.

I know this because I've been in, now and then. I don't visit often. The churches of my former religion always smell the same – of bad silence. It loves silent women especially. It adored my mother – in her mute phases. It was less fond when she was raucous. One would have to point out that speechless women seem popular with many belief systems.

Cecilia's only silent because she's working, listening. She's tending – allegedly – to all music everywhere: Howlin' Wolf and Dr John and E flat and D7 and every blue note and every other note. But surely a murdered virgin would have to prefer the blues.

St Cecilia, wise virgin, pray for us – that much, I remember.

The power of prayer hasn't helped me, nor my mother, nor Dad.

I mainly have faith in wearing a good suit.

Really.

Wear a sharp suit, a whistle-clean suit, and it can hold a life together. And it's possible – a suit can grant this small salvation – to be wearing one's suit in the way that Charlie Watts would, or the Kinks. One can stand out in front of the world – all silent – and no one will see that one has secrets, is a secret. They haven't the wit to tell that one's drape and one's drop and one's practical cuffs are laughing at the whole sad, bloody pack of them.

And every other secret follows on from that, the original one with the nice silk lining.

He cuddled his palm for a few paces.

But Meg knows how I'm laughing, she did notice.

Always the women.

Watching Dad trying to prove that love is suffering and suffering is love. And then I had a go myself.

As if someone tears out a hole in my thinking.

Always the women.

No.

Better to worry simply, to fret about needing a suit tonight.

Jon was loping now, fast enough to hearing the knocking of his pulse. Ahead he could see the white pimples of electric light, line upon line, that marked out the uprights and horizontals of Harrods.

The place actually looks worse than me, like what it is — a rattle bag of brassy tat. Shining out like a permanent Christmas, but locked up for the night. No more shopping. It is still sometimes possible for there to be no more shopping.

I met a woman once who, long ago, used to play hide and seek in Harrods when it was shut: sardines after lights out with the larksome offspring of the owners while Knightsbridge drew as close as it ever does to sleeping. Wild cries and hunting in the dark. Men getting bruised by complications they can't see. Everyone, I suppose, bruising.

Everything changes and nothing changes.

The law of the civil service, one might say.

Jon tried not to think of hunting. He had quit the Tube system one station early, a habit he'd been cultivating lately. Now — also a newish habit — he was threading himself along thin night streets, into mews and sideways options. It was as if he was trying to shake off a pursuit.

Not that I'd notice if anyone really was following.

The extra walking gives me space to think.

Fuck.

I do not progress.

But I know that I don't, I truly don't want to hurt her.

There is shouting on an overground train. A man's voice rises until it is audible to every passenger in the long car.

'Do you know where you are? Do you know where you are?' There is a pause during which no one answers, but it becomes clear that the yelling man is standing over someone, some other man, whose head is bowed, though perhaps not penitent. 'Do you know where you are? You're in South fucking London, where cunts like you get served. You treat a woman like that …? You fucking treat a woman like that …?' There is something lyrical, musical, about the way the standing man bellows. He is slightly enjoying himself, slightly enjoying this opportunity to make the world as it should be, sing it out right. 'Next stop when I get off, New Cross, if you want to talk about it, we can have a word, you can get off and we'll have a word … You want that? You want that?'

The sitting man seems not to want that.

'You frightened her. That could be your sister. That could be your mother. Look at – her sitting there.'

A woman is, indeed, sitting amongst the other passengers, also with her head bowed – she's across the aisle from the allegedly wicked and discourteous and certainly voiceless man. She is very still, while so much protection furies up in the air around her. It is difficult to tell how she feels.

'If you did that to my sister, if you did that to my mother, I'd fucking kill you. You understand? You don't do that. You don't threaten a woman, you don't make her scared. Big man … You think you're a fucking big man?' That coiling upward South London note kicks out at the end of every sentence, question or not. 'We can talk about that, about how big a man you are.'

The yelling has an oddly gracious air. The man has the virtuous bearing of someone deciding not to be violent, beyond making this roaring noise. He's stocky, quite short, dressed as if he may be coming back after lunch to a job of work, something dusty. With him is a younger man who nods while the lecture progresses and seems perhaps to be some kind of apprentice.

When the shouting man pauses to draw breath, the probable apprentice nudges in with, 'I've got a mum.' He is inexpert, but emphatic. 'I've got a sister.'

The other passengers cannot help but overhear what has turned into a kind of lesson in something beyond the skills of a trade, or rather something which seeks to ensure that a proper man, when he's learned a proper trade, will also know how to treat women and that such behaviour will belong to South London, and yet be extended in fellowship elsewhere.

The man turns and leans to the woman and offers quickly, 'Sorry for swearing.' Before he begins again. 'Doing that to her ...'

When the next station appears outside the windows, there is a type of fluttering change in the air. The proper man and his apprentice step down on to the platform, their point made. Another disembarking passenger shakes the proper man's hand. He becomes shy with her while they speak and the train pulls away again, unheeding, going further south.

I held her – third time's a charm – I held her and it all got simple.

Me and Meg and clarity, all hugged together in Monkey World.

Monkey bloody World. Bloody Dorset. Who'd have thought?

'Dorset? That's a bit far, isn't it?'

Her voice had been still an unaccustomed thing, raging in through his phone and making him fragment his sentences, hear his voice getting higher when – ideally – he would have preferred it to sound low and firmly masculine. 'It's not far.' Breathing and swallowing had become mutually exclusive. 'I would drive us. If you didn't mind that, Meg?'

I got married – I must have taken part in the usual preliminaries: sharing meals, talking on phones, going to Dorset.

Jon drove himself past estate agents selling impossible apartments – pointed expressions of needlessness, the otherness of wealth.

If I'm being honest, I think Val dealt with all that. The intimacy. Not going to Dorset. But the rest. I can't – it's maybe some kind of shock – I genuinely can't recall even the marriage, never mind what went before.

'Where in Dorset?'

'Monkey World.' It had been best not to varnish the news.

'Pardon?'

'Monkey World. It's my favourite place. Don't laugh.'

'I'm not laughing.'

But she had laughed, she did keep on laughing. 'Honestly, I'm not laughing.'

Biddable electromagnetic waves had left her mobile phone, undulated over rooftops and through windows and walls and unknowing skulls – or however these things travelled – and had soaked and bounced and wriggled into him, brought the sound of her laughing, because he had in some way pleased her.

One may laugh because one finds some other person ridiculous and pathetic, but that gives the voice a quite specific tone with which I am familiar.

Meg had just sounded happy. 'Is it actually a world of monkeys?'

'There are many varieties of monkey and also some apes, yes.' His voice had sounded, by this time, even more hideously adolescent.

'If you'd enjoy that, Jon.' The warm sound of her mouth.

'Well, I … It's a good place. It's a refuge … type of thing … It's sort of probably a bigger version of where you work, which would be dull for you … And the aim is for you to … the enjoying thing.'

We did the enjoying thing, though. Truly we did – I'm not wrong about that. This, this … It lets you rest. The fabric of … Everything lets you rest.

'We don't get monkeys. We get hamsters. Are there gorillas?'

'No gorillas.'

'That's a shame.'

'I know. But it's basically a primate refugee camp, so it's good there are no refugee gorillas … Or … They tend to be killed and have their hands made into ashtrays. Rather than staying alive to get evacuated. Maybe … I don't have much gorilla information.'

And there's the enjoying thing. These horrifying fucking jokes she makes.

'You're not just going to drive me to the countryside with your boot full of bin bags and a hacksaw.'

'What? No. What? No, of course not … I …'

Picking her up at London Bridge in one of Findlater's cars – SUV sort of thing named after a spice, for Christ's sake.

There had somehow been no time for finding and hiring a car, so Findlater had loaned him the Paprika, or Habanero, or whatever.

I do get tired of useful and everyday things being given names that render them shameful. And Findlater grinning at me as if I am going to use every seat for nudities and sexual congress. Probably he'd filled the glove compartment with condoms and … wipes … I avoided ever looking.

He'd set off with his own terrible joke: 'I hope I don't kill us.'

But it was OK.

And she'd nudged in at once with, 'They banned me from driving. That's all. Speeding. Quite often. And once going over the top of a roundabout – mandatory ban.'

'Christ. Or, I mean. Joke?'

'No. Serious. But no harm done. Except to some daffodils. You should know this stuff … About me. In case I ever get my licence back. I'm a rubbish driver.'

Collecting information about Meg – I could do that for the rest of my life.

'We'll go to Monkey World and it'll be nice and nothing bad will happen. Promise … And you're better now.'

And positive change can be irreversible. Yes, it can.

Maybe if I'd driven today, things would have gone more smoothly.

No. It would still have been awful, but with the additional bother of having to park.

He passed a café that seemed to specialise in crêpes and hummus, which seemed an unwise combination, but it suddenly occurred to him that he should eat.

I haven't really. This doesn't seem to be a day for eating.

In Monkey World's café – not too far from his favourite chimpanzees – Meg had sat and been remarkable despite having dressed a little as if she was going for a hike: almost-combat trousers, reinforced trainers and a fleece top.

Not obviously alluring – or not intentionally so.

Not an ensemble that Val would have chosen, or even known how to source.

Not anything other than beautiful.

Truthfully, it created an increase in beauty, because she seemed relaxed in those clothes, as opposed to that weird suit she'd insisted on hitherto … alcoholics being obviously – perhaps – uninterested in their appearance. Or unhappy because they can't buy what they'd really like, having money issues.

And trying to drive with prudence along the glitter of a wet M27 I had been picturing touring Meg about and delighting her with fittings and offerings parcelled up in tissue paper and popped in those unwieldy, stiff card bags with silk rope handles which might entertain her – or else suit carriers bearing the name of a tailor that could be her tailor.

All of which I didn't mention. And couldn't afford.

But I'd tell her about the suit, the secret in the lining. I'd open my coat and my jacket and let her see where her letters sit. Oh, Lord, I would. St Cecilia, I would.

She'd sat beside him at a bus-party-proof table. 'You need building up. Have another sausage roll.'

'I ... Do I?'

'Not looking after yourself.' Meg had delivered this with a satisfaction that was vaguely baffling.

I want to buy her shirt dresses, pleated skirts, low heels that let her walk, walk, I love her walk, blouses with a rounded collar, I want to discuss her best colours and signs of brio, sprezzatura, and I want to encourage pullovers I can hug – or those oversize jumpers that are like a wool hug in themselves.

She wants me to eat sausage rolls and look after myself.

He was beyond the hummus now – apparently it was impossible to be hungry.

By then I was exhausted by assessing too many risks – my lack of recent driving experience causing a head-on collision – the air bag coming to her defence. My adoration – fuck it – really adoration possibly lending me skills despite my legs being overfolded and my jeans – bad choice, too thick – cutting off the circulation to my legs, but still I'd manage every hazard and did manage every hazard and climbed down from the Poblano only slightly resembling a veteran of the Boer War.

I'm a born pedestrian – the faster I go, the more I'm terrified.

The houses round about him were becoming noticeably reclusive, smoothly watchful. He slipped his hands into his coat pockets.

I was wearing this coat – covert coat, slate blue. Put it across the back seat on the journey so it wouldn't get crumpled – unlike the wearer.

I want to dress Meg when I can't even dress myself.

I want to buy her clothes and then see her remove them.

To see and see and see.

Sweet Jesus ...

Doing what I always do while we crept out of London, bloody murdering her with facts.

'You'll like this when we get there. I think. They do very good work, though, and the chimps ... I mean, the chimps don't work – quite the reverse. They have all retired. Most of the chimpanzees have just had these hellish lives beforehand – forced to work, perform – and you'll see them being better now … Well, being themselves and … they seem to …'

Sounding not unlike a man upon whom no one should rely, a man unequal to the rigours of motorway navigation and with uncontrollable weeping in his inevitable future.

But she fiddled with the radio and I didn't fuck up – I let her – and somewhere, at some point, at some wonderful point between London and Wareham the fucking Piri-Piri's speakers kicked out 'Lola'.

That horrible, horrible car threw me the Kinks.

Ringing big chords to open and then that rolling, tumbling, running lick.

And then she was singing. Really. Beside me, leaning and beating out four-to-the-bar on the possibly libidinous glove compartment and letting it out – I only sing that way alone – singing along with Ray Davies – that cleversexy, playing-it-dumb, man-baby voice.

I'd kill to have that voice …

Those six, kiss-mouthed syllables in the refrain.…

Dave, the other brother, singing it raw and John Dalton there and John Gosling – that was Gosling's first record with the Kinks …

I think that's right.

Glancing over to see her lips as they would be in an opened kiss, a kiss that could taste cherrysweet and American exotic.

And wanting her to be happy.

And glad I'm a man.

I held back from telling her everything she'd never want to know about Dobro resonator guitars, as used in …

She knew the words. This girl in the silly car that is not one's own – she knows all the words and she likes them.

Bloody lovely.

And I took her to my favourite place. A little world full of outrage on behalf of the weak. To hell with the humans and rescue the innocent: there's a sense of that being the ethos when you visit and I see their point.

Wise old chimp sitting high on the level top of a telegraph pole, folded in round himself like a neat thought, like a netsuke, and I could feel him watching me, and hope he'd be wishing me well – 'Never seen you here with a friend. Go careful. Not too much about the psychiatric problems of marmosets people have locked up in birdcages and maybe just mention with charity the ugliness of the macaques and how the lemurs would be sunning their long bellies if only it wasn't drizzling and apologies for that and for the – now and then – stench of excrement and best of luck with her, my cousin, my clumsy, weak, small-handed cousin.'

'I know pretty much fuck all … sod all … about primates. We've never had them at the farm.'

I didn't know why she self-corrected. As if I wouldn't want her to say 'fuck'. As if I wouldn't have asked her to repeat it, if that might not have seemed peculiar.

'I'm not really swotted up about primates, or monkeys, beyond the obvious. I do enjoy understanding things. The trouble is, I'd rather know them already. I want all the facts transplanted in advance, just there. Being told them irritates me.'

'Oh.'

I know a number of other people with that issue. I work near a palace full of them – and more.

She nodded. 'I want to be well informed, this well-informed person at a dinner party – I hate dinner parties – in the pub – don't go to pubs any more – but anyway … I mean, I want to know to things … Mr August, he knows lots of things …'

And the touch of that name, my name, it makes me tell her, 'Fuck dinner parties.'

And kissing her, I'm kissing her – cherrysweet – heart at four beats to the bar … St Cecilia, care for me, I am like music. And I tell Meg again.

'Fuck dinner parties and people who go to dinner parties. And the ones in pubs and everyone who isn't us, frankly. Fuck the fucking lot of them.'

So that she'll hear me saying it – fuck – and the chimps watching. Showing off in front of my cousins. Because, St Cecilia, what would you know? You're a virgin.

We were in the observation area for the chimps: indoors in the animal funk and the big, broad windows, there to let us see and see and see.

In there it's always got this tang of nearly-human mayhem: it's what would happen if we shat and pissed neatly and casually on to the floor, if we were untidy and unashamed, if we never washed and always touched and held and patted and stroked and held and groomed and smoothed and fucking held each other, if we never let go and we always knew exactly where we are – even when we set off raging, flailing, screaming, we'd still know … I think we would.

'They're serious animals, aren't they. Look at the muscles in that one's arms.' *Meg murmuring because anything else would seem rude, with the chimps so close through the sturdy glass – which is sturdy glass, which is their living-room window – and they're sitting about and not concerned that I understand in my spine, in my balls, in my kind of a soul, that this is her early-morning voice, up-out-of-sleeping voice, the one I would have all to myself – sheets and cherrysweet and coffee and nonsense.*

'They'd do you harm if they didn't know you, or took offence.'

Look at them directly and they're creatures, beasts. Keep them just at the edge of your awareness and they show the forms and shifts and habits of a person, of yourself, of a more naked beast.

'They don't seem to be in the mood to take offence.'

And I can hear my own early-morning voice, saying – slow, pleased, low – saying to my treasure, 'That's Simon, the silvery chap who seems studious. And that's Hananya – the bustly, broad one with the startled fur. He's in charge, poor bastard. The two together over there are Jess and Arfur, they like each other, but not that way, because Hananya – he's the boss – would stop them from liking each other that way. He gets the executive position and the girls. Mostly.'

And Jess and Arfur touching and checking and touching – thick-nailed fingers and their fat-soled, clever-thumbed feet. Arfur kind of dusty, an oldness about him, although he's not so very old. White-bearded Simon with his bald forearms – showing his muscle, his crinkling skin. Thelma the jug-eared baby, tenderpinky Thelma who was born here, born safe, who is unscarred – incautious eyes and climbing around her mother.

'One chimp – that's maybe her – was rescued and kept for a while by royalty in Dubai. She arrived at the park once she got too old and too big, too adult to be cute – turned up with luggage, apparently, a selection of outfits … I can't imagine being around humans, growing up against yourself and then you arrive here and you take off your dress.'

Fuck.

Jon slowed on the quiet Knightsbridge street, looked up at the London sky, the dirty yellow roof it gave one instead of stars, and heard himself telling his love, 'And you never put clothes on again. You're just yourself. And you're with family, like a family.'

Hananya had slipped along, quite mellow and afternoony, and hugged some female or other and – dab – just slightly fucked her. Chimp sex being unimpressive but just … it truly is … it's carefree, it seems carefree. It happens and is all of a piece with them.

Dressing and undressing …

Such a tenderness for them overtaking … it being prudent that it should overtake … such a tenderness …

I didn't look at her because I didn't have to, because she was leaning against me and feeling like a song – lullaby, aria, anthem, this song that has never existed – and I tell her, because I can tell her things, because we can tell each other things, because fuck everybody but us: 'They get taken – most of them – out of the wild when they're babies and saleable and cute and the poachers kill their families because otherwise the families won't let their children go – they won't ever let their children go – and then the infants are caged up and alone and it must be inexplicable, unimaginably miserable, and there's travelling, aircraft or ships, and if you survive the trip then you're sold and you maybe have your teeth pulled out to stop you biting, or you're taught to smoke, or given drugs to keep you placid, because that's easier than beating you, or they teach you to drink and you do your tricks, do what you're told, you meet strangers and wear your outfits, put a suit on so you look like a person – this joke person – but you're scared and—'

She told me, 'Shush.' *A child's kind of way to put it.* 'Shush.' *Or a parent's.*

My fault for making her cry.

As if she was fighting, this soft fight, deep fight so that she could be …

She was here.

Arms inside my coat, this coat, arms all fierce and untranslatable and loving me because I am a fool and have hurt her.

I don't want to hurt her.

Body that scalds.

Beautiful.

You know where you are.

Crying with her.

You get single-minded after having a time like that.

I don't want to hurt her.

Jon tucked down his chin, absented himself from an expansive, well-manicured street and headed down the slope of a lane.

Her arms closed round the small of my back.

He turned left at a strange narrow house with ominous windows – *I never believe in that house, it seems taken wholesale from Dickens* – and entered a cobbled mews. Ahead was the mild noise of a little pub – the sort that guidebooks like to pick out and pet. He didn't want to be with people yet.

I was in her arms and I could rest.

He wanted to sit, perhaps on the cobbles, and marshal his forces. He wanted to rap on the odd house's door and ask to be taken in and welcomed at a fireplace and given charity and a pathway to his favourable conclusion.

I should call her. I should say that I am single-minded.

I should promise to keep her safe.

I should tell her how.

His hand lifted to reach inside his coat – his coat that knew her and that she liked – but before he could finish the movement somebody punched him.

21:45

MEG WAS AT South Kensington Station. For some reason, although she had left her train and climbed up a staircase or so from the platform level, she couldn't quite continue her ascent. Other passengers brushed past her as she stood, her back to the passageway, facing a vast metal grille, peering into the workings of the station.

She'd been catching and changing and catching trains beneath the city for a while this evening – for a long while, it seemed, now that she checked her watch.

The system had taken her into itself at Leicester Square, pushed her north to King's Cross and she'd let it. She had drifted up the Northern Line, then rolled back down, nudging all the while between the eddies and jolts of more purposeful commuters. Then she'd transferred to the Circle Line.

Gets you nowhere. Round and round.

It no longer was quite possible to ride the Circle Line and find yourself back where you started without ever leaving your seat. A break had been inserted annoyingly at Edgware Road and carriagefuls of humanity would wait about there to make connections which had once been unnecessary; the Edgware atmosphere was permanently thick with irritation and murdered plans.

The break prevents homeless people tucking themselves up in corners and falling asleep in their seats, simply circulating in the warm and dry for the price of a single fare. And I suppose it removes the possibility

*of depressives using the circuit to demonstrate their own uselessness —
the way that they end at their beginning and do not progress. You can
only do that now if you get on and off at Edgware Road. Which was
gloomy enough as a station in any case.*

Meg had only ridden along clockwise, dodged some more,
caught the Piccadilly Line to here – South Kensington.

Jon may well have called. He said he would.

*As soon as I come up for air I will know. I might have heard
nothing because he is a man who tends to fade and he has faded. You
can see it in him – the way he'll be. Maybe he's going to avoid me
all day and by the time I go to sleep nothing good will have happened.
Maybe I make him too scared. Broken animals scare people – although
he liked the chimps … The one who rolls sticks in her fingers and
acts as if she's smoking them when she's stressed. Messed-up monkeys.
Apes. Fucked-up apes.*

*But maybe he only likes the way we are when we're stuck behind
glass and fences, when he can walk away.*

*Or maybe I've just heard nothing because I've been underground and
I'll hit the open air and it will be fine. You can see that he doesn't want
to fade and is trying not to – that's there in him as well, the wanting
to stay. I do know what wanting looks like and he does want.*

And he's nice.

She remembered the way Jon had held her in the rescue
centre.

*Sometimes you just need a hug – there's no drama, or anything, not
really, it's probably nothing special to anyone – you just want that.*

And Jon knows what wanting looks like.

And so I got my hug.

He's a kind man – that's always true.

And I could do with another hug now.

After this morning … If we only think of that – then I'm entitled.

*I'd have smoked a make-believe cigarette in that hospital, if I'd had
one. I'd have smoked a real one.*

*I'd have shat on their floor, if it wouldn't have taken the last of my
dignity.*

They made me an exhibit, why not act as if I'm in a zoo?

Meg leaned against the grille and through it came the rush of cold tunnel air and undisturbed depths. It licked against her hugely. Beyond the mesh was this kind of broad, round shaft, lined with ocean-liner-looking iron plate – old and secretive.

It was put in for ventilation, I suppose, or to lower equipment.

The well had the authority of Victorian construction. It spoke of clambering labour, important and forgotten skills, fatalities.

Long way to fall.

The drum of space gaped above her head, clear up to street level, but showed no trace of sky. And it sank away beyond her feet – she supposed – to the depth of the lowest platform. It was usually out of sight, rendered unnoticeable by its darkness. But now there were raw white lights across the broad yawn of the drop and so she could see and see and see: the complications of metal and equipment, other grilles on the far side, structures of obscure purpose.

No one else is noticing. Only me.

Because I want something to keep me down here and away from his having left no message and this never properly working out and …

I am down here with my drunk's head – down in the shelter to keep off disappointments.

Because an alky doesn't drink St John's wort, or meditate, or phone a reliable friend, or leave things alone for a bit and relax – an alky worries. Why else would you always need to drink?

Forever.

The cold seeped and stroked around her and there was something too old about it, something beyond a human lifespan, which made it seem unreasonable. She was beginning to shiver. The sense of being shaken by her own body, the chill of shock, seemed to take her back beyond the morning's examination and uncoil memories she didn't want.

Why else would I always need to drink?

Already, she had this nervous pitch in her stomach, this straining of something intolerable nuzzling her spine, this repeating fact of emptiness. She was dealing with the symptoms of hope. Hope felt very much the same as emptiness, as panic.

Forever.

I should go. I really should go.

She turned into the flow of travellers and began the last little journey to the surface.

I have to go.

It is late on a Sunday afternoon at the end of a warm autumn. Across London, people are heading for home, for meals, for rest after perhaps the last outdoor weekend of their year.

A Northern Line Tube train is travelling down from King's Cross. Its carriages are not overfull but most of their seats have been taken.

One car holds a snug assembly of couples, families with children, individuals. They all seem to share this afterglow of tired pleasure. Some hug backpacks on their laps, a few carry sleeping bags. They stand in the wider spaces near the doors, they sit on the long, upholstered benches and face each other across the width of the carriage. And they are quiet.

A very large man is sitting tight up against the glass partition beside an exit. He is asleep.

He is both unusually tall and solidly built. His broad knees and long, substantial feet extend quite a way into the aisle. In every direction, he gives the impression of being only just able to fit. His heavy-looking hands are folded together across his stomach, rising and falling placidly as he sleeps. He is so tall that his head – which leans joltingly against the partition – also almost grazes the ceiling. Although the passengers are wearing coats, scarves, hats – responding to the little shock of winter's first real cold – the monumental man is in his shirtsleeves. It seems that he is a person of strength and above such things as temperature, weather.

As each station dashes in along the windows, as passengers arrive and leave, as each station creeps and then darts away again, the man keeps sleeping.

Behind him, propped against the window, is a huge square cushion. It is supporting his shoulders, neck and skull. It is new, still wrapped in clear plastic, and made of felt and other soft fabrics. The cushion has been marked out into sections and each one shows a simple picture of an animal, built up in embroidery and cloth. The creatures – beyond the zebra – are quite hard to identify because they have been created mainly to smile and seem reassuring, rather than to reflect any zoological reality. They are illusions to please children.

Like a vast child, the man rests and is peaceful, this peace spreading into the carriage. Everyone inside has decided to follow the invisible rule that a child – of whatever size – should never be disturbed.

No one speaks. Those who leave do so on tiptoe. Those who arrive drop quickly into a nursery gentleness.

Faces calm and smooth, books are read with tiny glances to the sleeper. The wakeful are taking exaggerated care and when they meet each other's eyes they look happy, they look like people with a happy secret. They rock together with the motion of the carriage. The man rocks, too.

'Oh, for—' Jon was apparently rolling across cobbles, this assailing weight above him.

'Hold still.'

'*What?*'

'I said hold still, you moron.'

Jon realised that both the weight and the voice belonged to Milner while worrying that his coat was going to be ruined and wondering if the lack of pain in his face was due to some kind of numbing hysteria, or the fact that Milner's blow had been glancing. 'You fucking maniac.' It hadn't felt glancing.

'That's good. Go with that.' Milner was now kneeling astride Jon's chest – the belly even more alarming in the half-light than usual.

'You stupid fucking bastard!' Jon allowed an instant of fury to lever him out from under his attacker. 'You fucking …!' And then the passion didn't stop – it yanked him up, hotly breathless, into a raggedly standing position. 'You stupid, stupid—'

And for the first time in his life, Jon was wholly furious. He swung fists that had never been guilty of such behaviour and connected with sneering air.

Jon spun round on his heel – the side of his right hand beginning to sting now, along with his right knee, likewise his left cheek – and there was Milner swaying with glossy, early-evening drunkenness.

What the hell is the idiot up to?

At the blind end of the mews they'd just tumbled across: 'You fucker!' At the end of the mews was the picturesque Victorian pub. It was once frequented by guardsmen. Now it was tucked away enough and charming enough to host a smattering of celebrities wishing to recreate a London that never was. Drinkers lingering outside the prettily painted front steps and quaint novelty sentry box might not relish an outbreak of violence.

Jon bent forward, hands on his knees, and caught his breath while Milner chuckled wetly. 'You big pansy, Jon. Gotta take your lumps, you know. It's the modern way …' He was enunciating well for someone who was meant to be fighting drunk.

'You fucking, fucking, shitting … You …' Jon was hissing now, while trying to get his bearings. 'What are you trying to do? What, exactly? Destroy me? I'm already destroyed – you're too late. I've been all over bar the fighting for years and – oh, look, *we've just had the fucking fighting*.' He suspected that he might be sick.

'I'm saving you, fuckwit.' Milner patted at Jon's back with admirably judged inaccuracy. 'This way, you're not meeting that naughty girl Lucy and giving her another instalment of the crown jewels, you've been waylaid by that terrible old soak Milner and taken one for the team.'

Jon felt Milner's clammy paws grab briefly at his hips. 'Get off me.'

Milner stood close behind Jon's thighs and made jokey thrusts at him. The feeling of that belly pressing and giving as it thumped against Jon's buttocks was entirely as repellent as intended.

Jon broke loose and stood. 'You …'

Impossible to call him a cunt, I refuse to associate him with … I'm not bloody having that used as an insult, but so help me …

He settled for, 'You fat, useless prick.' And then attempted to shake out his coat, dust himself down. 'Prick. Cock. Dick. You are a dick.'

Milner laughed like a pantomime devil and murmured, 'We'll nip into the bar – best of mates now – nothing like a little anal action to soothe you public-school survivors, put you at ease. And I will buy you a drink to make up for my joke that went wrong. There's no one about who's looking, nobody paying the wrong kind of attention. The bar's preoccupied with tonight's touch of glamour – the place is mildly famous for hosting the extremely famous: caps doffed and come in for an offbeat pint in Good Olde Lahndahn surroundings …'

'I know that – I'm not an idiot, you fucking idiot.'

'Touchy … Well, there are two blokes in tonight who stand next to Prince Whatever sometimes and who play that game with the funny-shaped ball.'

'You're not amusing.'

'Ruggah buggahs ... And there's that woman who didn't win the telly baking competition this year ... or last year ... Fame ain't what it fuckin' used to be.'

'You didn't need to do that.'

'At lunch you gave me the distinct impression that I did ...' Milner approached Jon as if he were a petulant animal, a startled horse – his hands wide and low, placating.

And Jon submitted, allowed Milner to slop one heavy arm over his shoulders, make him stoop. Then Milner guided him, like an old pal, towards the glimmer and chatter of the pub.

I can't see her like this. I'm bad enough at the best of times and ... I'll look like some cartoon idea of a tumbling drunk. I'll smell of Milner, of tepid pints and ketoacidosis because – yes – I have researched the physical effects of alcohol abuse.

All the large and little harms I would have spared her if I could.

Please let her always be safe.

Please.

Please everything, something, nothing.

Fuck.

Jon heard himself whine – *Christ, I have an ugly voice, tonight worse than ever* – addressing himself more than Milner: 'Um ... let me .... I'm running late for my next appointment and I have to send a text.'

'Go ahead.' Milner breathing this against Jon's injured cheek – the impact of his heat felt infectious.

'I need to do it alone.'

'Suit yerself, duckie. I'll get you a pint of bitter – that be all right?'

'I don't want a drink.'

I don't want my mouth to taste of drink.

'I'll get you a bitter anyway – you're a bitter man, Jon. Ha ha. A bitter man. If you don't want it, I'll take it myself.'

'Get me a cup of tea, for God's sake.' And Jon shrugged him off at the foot of the endearing and perhaps original steps that led to the pub's entrance. Then he watched the bulk that was Milner ease itself up and inside. Jon closed his eyes.

If he broke my phone on the cobbles ... If I can't ... If I don't find a way of ...

The dark in his head only made his thinking louder than he could bear, so he glanced about. The evening seemed to slither, wet patches of illumination hiding round the cobbles like signs of disease. He reached into his pocket, took out his – as it turned out – undamaged phone. He dialled Meg's number and then stopped the call before it could go through.

Text. That would be better. I'll send a text.

That actually wouldn't be better, but it's what I'll send.

His fingers were slithering suddenly and traitorous.

He felt that he might want to cry.

A text.

21:52

JON FOUND THE Friday-night fug and din of the bar offensive. It made him – inevitably – queasy and then more than queasy.

Perhaps I should develop an eating disorder.

He had to head on straight past Milner and find the gents' as soon as he was penned definitively indoors.

Oh God Oh God Oh God.

Having made it to the toilets, he coughed and heaved unhappily in an unproductive effort, then left the relative privacy of the stall and rushed water into a sink, cupped it up and over his face like a repeated small rebuke. He looked – according to the mirror – dreadful.

Like some mugged ageing householder, staring out for his headlining picture in the local paper – look what they did to me.

Look what I did to me.

Milner had drained one of the available pints on his table by the time Jon returned. The other pint was grinningly rocked in mid-air before the first of it was taken too, Milner showing his teeth. 'Now then.' He paused. 'I didn't hit you that hard, but you look like shit … You're getting on a bit more than I thought, aren't you, Jonnie? Proper grey, you look.'

'Thanks.' Jon folded himself into a seat and slid one hand into the other – maintained himself, held on. 'I don't have any figures for you. And there's no point to them any more, anyway. If there ever was.'

'Don't lose your balls now.'

'Why must everyone this evening take such a lively interest in my balls?' Jon was alarming himself. 'My balls are in place. In fact.'

'I'll take your word for it. And the figures serve a purpose – if they didn't, why would it be so hard to get them? Why are they being buried at sea? How many suicides, how many deaths, what are the increases in costs and where are they hidden? … Our hints and tips are building a tide for disclosure.'

'They're building fuck all.' Jon kept his voice as low as he could while this kick of anger jolted up his forearms. 'Nobody cares. Remember *shop a scrounger* in the soar-away *Sun*? That was ten years ago. The start of the high-octane hate.' He eyed the happy bar, its happy drinkers.

Fuck 'em all.

He continued, 'We've had more than ten years of being told about the undeserving poor. If you're poor enough to need benefits you must be doing something wrong – you must be something wrong and undeserving. Want shouldn't get – that's our departmental fucking motto. Our national credo – we all love royal babies and hate the poor. At present and for the foreseeable future. That's how it works …'

'Is it your time of the month?' Milner patted Jon's arm and he felt the man's contact as an unclean thing, as a kind of obscene comment on how Meg might have been when she was drunk.

'Fuck you, Milner.'

'Only asking, because it does seem to have taken the whole of your career for you to notice that maybe things were going off course.'

'It's taken the whole of my career for it to go, as you say, off course … I stayed in …' *Too loud.* Jon noticed he actually had been given tea – teapot, milk, sugar, cup and saucer, the petty litter of it all seeming quite confusing and pathetic, now that he examined it … He poured some out for himself – *More tea, Deputy Director?* – and added sugar.

Good for shock.

And then he settled his voice down into the murmur reserved for informing a minister while he chairs this or that committee, attends this or that occasion when the public must be faced – his warm undertone for leaning in and making all right. 'The open secret, the one at the heart of public service is – as you know – that there are facts, but they don't matter. There is knowledge and that knowledge can prove and disprove the better – if not the best – ways to do anything. Anything at all. But ministers, MPs, politicians, theorists, they have to be visible, they have to do things, and if this involves dismantling a functional system, then it will be dismantled – not adjusted, adjustments aren't sexy, not mended, mending is what tradesmen do. They must be certain, they must have strident opinions and tangible faith, the better to overpower reality. We are asked to advise them less and less – the infallible need no advice. More and more, we are required to change what worked into what does not work. We navigate a blossoming coral reef of unnecessary change and legislation and we peep out from its nooks and crannies to look at the sharky exercise of will amongst those who actually want to bring about what does not work. They want to be freed by catastrophe. Freed from logic, freed from restraint.

'And conservatives know that you can't change human nature and therefore the suffering must have been born to be the suffering; at the most fundamental level – they have brought their pain upon themselves. They could only be forgiven if they thrived and conquered and no longer need any help. And if you can't change human nature, you don't need government – it's an unnecessary burden to tax the people. It has to go – except for those posts occupied by those who believe that you can't change human nature. They have to stay. To make sure there's no change.

'And progressives believe that you can change human nature and therefore the great plunging herd of voters must be restrained and managed at all times by armies of virulent overseers. And those overseers must justify their presence – they have to make those inevitable changes very obvious and challenging and extreme, otherwise the change might look as if it would have happened anyway without their help, because you can change human nature.

'And it used to be just a little bit, you know just here and there, just a little bit more fucking sane and honourable than that. Some of them had brains ... Some of then still do ...

'But fuck both sides against the middle now. A plague on all their houses now.'

Milner killed his pint of bitter during this, eating it up while shaking his head. 'Jon ... Poor, Jonnie ...' He winked. 'Abuse and conspiracy theories ... That's my cup of tea, surely?'

Jon stirred his syrupy tea, then found the first sip revolting, 'What is a political party? A conspiracy with membership cards. Conspiracy as re-engineered by greedy children. What is Parliament? An institution designed to prevent any activist from staying active. Ask any decent MP, once the hundred days' shine has rubbed off them.' The sugar wasn't working. 'I want to give you something else.'

'I knew you were holding out on me.'

'Shut up. I can't ... I can only ...' Jon was breathing badly, stupidly, in a way that might draw attention. He pulled out a pen and wrote a phone number on to a beer mat. This was the number he kept in his head, safe with only one other. It had never been written down.

The things that you don't want to lose, you trust to no one, you hide them inside.

Jon swallowed a mouthful of unruly saliva. 'Put that in your pocket. Now.' And he waited while Milner gave him that patronising half-smile – *as if he's looking at a crack-up, at a fuck-up* – but then he did pocket the beer mat.

First you step out on the ledge. Then you just step out. You try to like the feeling it gives you – airy. Oh God and St Cecilia, oh Cecilia – in whom I do not believe – please believe in me.

'Go on, then, James sodding Bond. Left the tuxedo at home, did you? Miniature radio in your knickers?'

'Shut up.'

'I do this for a living. I don't sit about being self-righteous and wanking on about the problems I helped create. "Ooh, I am so sorry I built the hand grenade. I just never had the time to think what a hand grenade could be for – and it looked so pretty ..." You twat.' Milner troubling the sweat on his face with a broad palm. 'I actually go to places that could kill me and bring back information that saves lives. I don't piss about in an office being scared of my own paperwork, compromising my dick away ...'

'Shut up.' Jon feeling his own sweat creeping down the back of his neck like the feet of shamed insects. 'You haven't been anywhere lately – not at all – you're spent. And this, by the way, is the end. Of us. But I brought you a present – OK? A goodbye kiss.' The carpet flexing under his feet as he says this. 'This is something to make you whole again – possibly – and then you can forget me because I won't be any use to you, I'll be working somewhere else. I mean, I won't be, I will have ... It's of no importance what I'll be.'

And Jon caught hold of Milner's hand.

Because I need to – the need to cling – primate need.

The contact was hardly a comfort – *like grabbing a starfish, a squid, a dead animal* – and the grazed area on Jon's palm complained mildly, not liking the touch of hot salt.

Here I go – airy – airy and falling, I can feel the rush.

And then Jon started to talk it all out, spill it – the real stuff – gabbling because he might otherwise faint before he was done. 'That number will be burned in a week's time, but if you call it before then a man will answer and tell you a story. It's a good story. Very interesting. I'll provide you with a precis, which goes like this: the man is Mr Alex Harcourt and he once worked for a company called Hardstand. Hardstand provides IT solutions, as we have to term them: software, hardware, support, peripherals. The company has another division that deals with office catering ... which makes a kind of sense. They sell you the sandwich you eat in front of the computer they also sold you and now maintain for you, because you don't know how to.'

Milner barged in with, 'What, has he scored some dodgy emails? I'm hardly going to wet myself for that.'

'Pay attention. Please!' This syllable reminding him of a song – of some song ...

And Jon was under the impression that his heart was not right any more, that it had come unstuck – if this were possible – and would soon refuse to function – along with his ruined brain – all of which would be sad, but not much of a loss. He couldn't foresee excessive mourning. 'Mr Harcourt works for a subdivision of a subsidiary of a subsidiary of Hardstand. He is a specialist. He was. He retired. Eventually, Milner, one gets old and either does or doesn't deal with it. Harcourt isn't old. He is fatigued. He got nervous, or moral, definitely weary, probably scared. One does. He can give you dates, times, details, whatever you want on this. He is set on giving his particular game away. I won't ever speak to him again. You can if you want. I won't know ... I insist on not knowing.'

Milner by this time smiling gently and in the manner of a man who wheedles indiscretions out of imprudently relaxed Kazakh diplomats, or oil-company execs. Or fading civil servants.

'Harcourt groomed phones. His term. He wanted to talk about grooming – the only reason I met him. He turned up in an email – one email – when I was looking for something else. And I found him out because I can do that – I find out information. It's not some remarkable and exclusive journalistic skill – I do it all the time. And my stuff's pure ...' Jon paused to breathe, let his shoulders come down. He allowed himself to uncover the name, the story, the everything of Harcourt – the everything he packed away each morning in his dusty torso, under his gone-adrift heart, hidden so no one could see it unless they cut him open.

Harcourt. He was in another pub – out Walthamstow way. So I'm sitting there and facing this balding guy in a maroon leather jacket. He looked ex-army and unsuccessful – an NCO who might end up as an unhandy plumber, try driving a cab – looked as if he might enjoy violence of the bullying sort: against women, against kids. I sat and made assumptions about him along those lines ... Wrong assumptions.

Jon continued: 'To take an example – Harcourt's example – if you're a visitor to Downing Street you roll through security, they check you for secret hand grenades and so forth and then you trot up the iconic steps and in through the iconic door and you leave your phone in this nifty little rack provided for the purpose: sort of faux mahogany, it's the kind of thing you'd buy from a catalogue, or a smug ad at the back of a Sunday-newspaper magazine – thin shelves to fit your mobile and keep it while you head off without it. And anybody reasonable can see why a modern mobile phone would be unfit for the inner sanctum – guests couldn't be allowed to wander the hallowed precincts taking photos, or tweeting indiscreetly. It's partly a security issue and partly a matter of taste. Our masters can take selfies with each other at notable funerals, high-profile events, but the rest of us might lack discretion. We might put mocking snaps of their toilet or their canapés on to Facebook. We might record chats that were meant to be just cosy. Which is to say, deniable.'

Jon grabbed another mouthful of tea and felt it – he could swear – beginning to destroy his teeth. Why not add his incisors to the rest of the catastrophe, why not …? 'Once your phone has been abandoned then you're in for quite a walk – the building is oddly designed, it has to hide a family apartment and close the baize-backed door between the public and the working surfaces, very *Downton Abbey*. It's an old and complicated place. You'll find a hallway gives into a hallway and then you'll climb those wonderful stairs – photos of the previous incumbents lining its rise, a thrum of undiluted narcissism – and up you go to this or that reception room … the slight scruffiness, the tall windows with a view over the garden, over the great big blank of Horse Guards Parade, over the grey bones of St James's …

'That's just how it is.'

'And your phone is far away back by the entrance where you can't protect it. You're up above, avoiding the average catering and whatever art they're displaying to impress, or having your official picture taken shaking hands with whoever – touching your skin to theirs in this weird exchange of mutual humanity when maybe there's nothing like that available at the time. And maybe you're thinking they look peculiar, the top-flight men. You've seen them, Milner: the camera-ready, smoothed-over tribe of mannequin-faced nonentities ... They look bizarre. They're the ones who succeed, who mountaineer right the way up to the top, but they just have become bizarre. Nonetheless you're slipping in your wise little word, stating your case and feeling quite close to the heart of things, you're getting eye contact and being reassured that someone's listening – you're learning that someone you possibly thought an opponent is maybe doing their best and giving you artisanal cheese straws, or whatever the occasion may allow ... But your phone is still downstairs and lonely.

'And that's why kind Mr Harcourt takes it away and he speaks to it gently and kindly – grooms it – and then he opens it up – not so that it'll show – and he climbs inside it and leaves what he must, leaves you with clever presents you don't know about.

'Even if you rush downstairs sharpish, are unexpectedly on hand because you've changed your mind about breathing the same air as whoever's up aloft – even if you leg it back out, having urgently remembered you left the gas on ... Well, you'll be too slow to catch him ... You have to go all that long way back in this mazey old house ... And you'll perhaps need to pick up your coat, put it on, field a polite enquiry from this or that member of staff – they like to be helpful and pleasant at Number 10, they're servants, but not servile, not a bit of it. No matter how fast you come downstairs, Mr Harcourt will have the friend from your pocket back in place and ready for you and shipshape when you reach for it. It will seem the same, but it will now inform upon you in rather more ways than it did already. It will see and overhear and tattletale about your family, your affairs, your travel, co-workers, plans, meetings, flirtations, loves. You're fucked.'

Milner was no longer drinking. 'Fuck.'

'Yeah. As I said.'

'Fuck me sideways. That can't be true, though.'

Which gave Jon a scything headache. 'I'm telling you it can. I'm telling you because your colleagues who spend their afternoons dozing in the Commons Library, the ones who no longer swap treats for access, because they don't want access – the ones who are as much a part of Parliament as the Pugin wallpaper – those people who call themselves journalists missed this. And I don't think they'd really want it. It would be tasty but it would scare them. You're outside – I needed somebody outside.'

'Yeah, because you're so far above any journalist, aren't you, Jon? Nobody's lower than us. And you, you don't have opinions, you civil-service fucks, you float above it all like fucking farts – worse than fucking lawyers. You won't rock the boat but if you did … my how clean your hands would be. You help your little masters screw over strangers and you let everybody know that you'd do it so much better if you had your way – only you're too pure to be in nasty, dirty politics … You're the dirtiest there is.'

Jon just nodded and held his tongue.

Yes, fine, agreed – I don't care. Just take the hook and swallow it, will you?

And Milner did have the proper feral gleam about him that Jon had hoped for.

I can brief. I can brief better than Chalice. I can raise an appetite. I can inform and provoke forward motion … And this time it's for me, for my ministry. This time I am doing something that's for me.

'Targeted?' Milner's voice pressed down to a whisper and he pretended to lean on Jon's shoulder for support. 'Targeted grooming, or dragnet … No, there wouldn't be time for dragnet …'

We must look like a very mismatched couple.

Or like two sad bastards clinging together for warmth, for their last chance.

'You should ask him. But not dragnet, no. And it saves bumping people, break-ins, picking their pockets in the street – all that risk.'

'Just Downing Street?' Milner close enough to tickle breath straight into Jon's ear like a teenager on a date.

'Think of all the government buildings that ask you to leave your phone when you step inside. Think of all the boisterous opposition, the NGO reps and agitators, the politically involved, the uppity celebs, the potential rivals. Once they've been invited for drinks and nibbles, you've got their privacy, not just texts and emails and calls – their whole privacy – forever. Or at least until they ditch their phone. I don't exactly know who listens. I think knowing who listens would be unhealthy.'

'So I'm meant to get unhealthy for you.'

'There are so many people who already want to kill you, it will make no odds.'

I don't believe that, not anything like that. It would always make odds. Any damage is to be avoided. And I would like to conduct myself in a manner which conforms to that ideal.

'I don't believe you.' But Milner's grip on Jon's hand feels already fond and committed. It indicates a hearty boy's excitement at the prospect of a rough and tumble game – a good kicking.

'I don't care, Milner.' *I can kick a bit myself when necessary.* 'Ask Harcourt – he'll convince you or not. It's none of my business. He knows he'll be hung out to dry – so many skeletons falling out of so many cupboards – and he needs a friend. He feels the end is nigh. And if I could find him, someone else could, too.'

'Fuck.'

'He's sleeping – I think – in his car at the moment and no longer has an address. Travel plans in place for somewhere I am assured is not Costa Rica ...'

'But how did you get him?'

Jon attacking his horrible tea again as one of the chaps who slightly knows Prince Whatever goes past to the gents'. The group of chaps who were standing around the chap who knows Prince Whatever now chat like girls, high-pitched and laughing too loudly about something.

'I got him because I was looking for something else. He was an accident.'

Because I saw the words grooming specialist *and thought I'd uncovered something else. A jokey memo on a desk – something to draw the eye. I believed I had found something else.*

'I was after something else.'

That wife – the one I stood beside at that party – unhappily drunk and confiding: something not right about her husband, something not right about his finances, something not right about his spending, something not right about the way he is with kids, something not right.

When he'd seen her again, she'd blanked him, been a stalwart partner to her husband: exemplary, busy, devoted. The problem that she had implied might exist had slipped back beneath the surface.

The problem had made people go deaf – deaf, dumb and blind.

But you don't steal other people's futures, souls, bodies – you don't pick the weakest human beings you can find and do that to them. That sort of behaviour isn't meant to happen, isn't meant to be a shared joke, a delicious secret, a proof of power. It's not right.

Some of the truth about that kind of problem is there now, out and stinking in the open air. Some of it.

Even when they're dead – the rapists – they drag pieces of the truth down with them, get it buried again. Cap it with concrete if necessary.

'You can tell me, Jon. How did you get him?'

'I did tell you. By mistake. I was looking for ghosts. I have been since 1987.'

That woman's eyes – they stayed the same, though. When she was telling the truth and when she was the fond and charming figure beside and just slightly behind a statesman of genuine promise, her eyes were the same – screaming.

Milner with his pinky-doggy eyes, allowing a display of appetite that's real, that isn't camouflage. 'Secretive – silly tarts always do get secretive when you've seen everything they've got.' The hand squeezing in around Jon's fingers.

It doesn't matter. Say what you like. I was after the ghost of bad things in the seventies, in the eighties – I was looking for ghosts, monsters. I wanted to do something actually, genuinely useful before I left. But I couldn't get to them – and they kept being monsters.

Which isn't what I tell my daughter when she asks me why I stayed in post, why I haven't retired, why I cling on, still making compromises and knowing that what I do – precisely what I do – means children are more exposed than ever before in my lifetime to predators of every sort.

What happens when a school fails, a community fails, a children's home fails, a parole system fails, a prison system fails … Tired parents and absent parents and desperate parents and shattered parents and lost parents and then here we are … at the nakedness of everything, down to the flesh and bone. Human nature can't be changed and so if you're fuckable you should be fucked. Human nature can be changed and so I will fuck you until you are fuckable, just as I wish.

Who are we that we can't keep our children safe?

'Are you still with me, Jon? Don't start doing that staring-off-into-space thing – it might impress the ladies, but it irritates the fuck out of me.'

'Do you want this or not?'

'Of course I want it. This will fuck the fuckers and the fuckers should be fucked.' He says this as if it is a poem, a declaration of love: softly and with a kind of proud sadness. 'But this may not be able to make the splash you hope. Not here. It's a bag of frightening for any paper, these days. I may have to take it abroad – feed it back that way. Put it somewhere bombproof online … Shit, I may end up in Costa Rica – some non-extraditable shithole … But I love the sunshine. So yeah … Go out with a bang.'

And the pub's attention rests on the famous baking woman – the quite famous baking woman – over there by the window and it also smiles on the return of the rugby player – *sportingly fast urination* – and there's a merry glow of fake and authentic Victorian charm dutifully winking on the glass and varnish while the air sickens around you, while you sit with this journalist you barely know who may take this trouble, this burden of information, away from you – who may be competent and only pretending to be terminally tired and spent.

'Take it wherever you like, Milner – just keep it away from me.'

But probably not far away enough. And I can't bolt off to Morocco, or somewhere, because – not the only reason – but because this is my home, my complicated home, and I want to be at home in my home and I want my country to be the country that I have believed could exist.

Not the nation as a blade – the one that will always draw blood, no matter if you hold the handle or the edge. The nation as love.

Stupid.

Morocco.

Costa Rica.

But I would like love.

Why not, as a foundation – that's a knife of a different kind, keeps you right and keeps on cutting.

Milner was shaking his head at Jon like a man who could not be relied upon in any circumstance. 'I've got your back, Jon. I have.'

This is my best hope for freedom of speech … Noble disclosure of wrongs …

Twenty-first-century Britain.

Like I say – it's all unmarked vans and amateurs and paying more than anybody ought to for what you won't get.

'Milner …' Jon retrieved his hand from Milner's grasp and tried not to look down and see if it was visibly greasy.

I'm too tired to throw up again. Too tired to try.

Jon wiped his face with his palm to clarify – perhaps that was the intention – his thinking, realising too late that he'd used the wrong hand, smeared himself with Milner. He swallowed, breathed, steadied his impulse to at least flinch and then began, 'Milner, I have to go now and we won't meet again. I'll be resigning soon and all this will be … everything will be … I won't be any more use.' Jon let his head slop forwards and gazed at the carpet while his thoughts apparently slid into a clump above his eyes and forced him to end up saying, 'This is the end. That's what I understand to be the case. Because … Because …' He was being too loud and might well disturb the other honest and hard-working, cake- and rugby-loving occupants of the pub. He went on anyway – telling a story he knew Milner wouldn't give a damn about and quite possibly telling it precisely for that reason: 'A woman came up to me when I walked out of the railway station at the Junction. Where I live … It was a nice evening. Warm. And she was thin and seemed … she had that look they all do now – the face of someone who no longer understands their own surroundings. I don't mean being somehow rendered foolish by drink or drugs, I mean having the look of someone – being someone who doesn't know why everything has decided to hurt her. Wherever she faced, she seemed to be searching for some kind of answer. And – with this bewilderment ongoing – she caught sight of me and she stopped me and she said, "*I'm not going to attack you.*" '

Jon paused while Milner's attention did indeed wander – he had a fumbling, furtive expression.

The prospect of telling truth to power round the back of the bike sheds – he can't wait ... He wants to call Harcourt, probably, and get things under way. He's itchy but he won't scratch while I'm watching, while I'm here.

Jon dug in and kept on with his anecdote, no matter how unwelcome.

The political pub bore. There's always one.

But he felt the need to explain himself, even if neither of the people he might pray could understand him were actually here to listen. 'The thing was, I didn't expect that a slightly frail middle-aged lady *would* attack me – St Kitts accent, that very gentle-sounding St Kitts accent – and she asked me, this breakable-looking black lady, she asked me, 'What size are your feet? No, your girl's feet. Your wife's feet?' And she wanted to know because she said she needed money so she could buy milk for her child, but she didn't want to just take it, just have me give her money. She said that she wanted to sell me something and that she had shoes with her – women's shoes, her shoes – and I could buy them. She said she'd been asking and asking all day, but had got nowhere. The Junction is certainly nowhere ... Oh yes – and she had a hat.' Jon was aware that he was lightly damping the pub's glee and chatter.

I really am being too loud.

Jon was making what his mother would have called a spectacle of himself – *and she should know* – and strangers were finding him more difficult to ignore than perhaps they'd have preferred.

So then, listen. Although I can't guarantee you'll understand.

'And the woman ... she does, absolutely, have one of those thin corner-shop carrier bags with her and in it there is a fairly new pair of shoes and some less new shoes and some kind of winter hat and I don't want shoes or a hat. I have nothing I can say to her. I have never knowingly met someone who cannot feed their own child.'

Milner let out a derisive little huff of breath which Jon answered, 'Or else, she was – of course, because the poor are always wicked – conducting some fabulously profitable business which involved having to tell strangers humiliating lies.' Jon leaned in towards Britain's last remaining Real Journalist.

He calls John Pilger a dizzy blond who's up himself and says Greg Palast is a wanker in a hat ...

'I decide to give her some money. Less money than I could afford. Enough money for some milk, or some heroin, or some food ... but not enough, because she'll need milk, or heroin, or food for a very long time. And I tell her that I'm fine for shoes and hats and then she reaches one hand into her top – this thin top she's wearing – and she brings out her breast – small breast ... She's not drug-thin, but she is thin. This flawless skin ... Wiry little woman on her own in the street, showing her breast to a stranger and she's telling me that I'm a good man and that she thanks me.'

Jon glowered across at one rugby man who is staring at him, or perhaps only pondering thin air. *It's not as if I have much substance.* And Jon didn't say aloud that the woman had much the same build as his mother – the figure of a slim fighter, of someone who is slim because she has to fight. But he does feel that he should continue – go right to the end – hit the buffers. 'And she squeezed out milk from her breast. You understand me? There, in the street, she is explaining to me that she is expressing milk in the street to prove she has a kid. She wants me to know she's not lying. She has a kid and the kid needs milk when she can't give it, needs the follow-on stuff and also needs all of the other things kids need. Her flow of milk is proof she isn't lying. As if this is always demanded and indignity is necessary at all times, in all places.' And Jon paused and then – being overly audible again – said, 'Fuck.'

And Meg would have said that with me, before me – she would have held my hand through this, all of this, and it would have been not so bad, not quite so bad.

Jon coughs while the male escort of the cake celebrity glowers across at him for sullying the hearing of a woman whose fondant rose petals were pure as an anchorite's prayer.

He has an eloquent glower and it does seem to imply all that and slightly more.

Jon lowered his chin and prepared to continue softly, while being of the opinion that purity was something which no longer truly existed and perhaps never had.

No. Wrong. It exists. So many people wouldn't be so pleased they could destroy it, if it didn't initially exist.

Purity exists, the problem exists ... People like me – any people, just people who are people – we all suppose that purity and the problem always stay apart.

'And the woman's crying and I'm apparently a good man again – better than I was when she first said it – and she's lifting up her arms like a girl, wanting to be hugged and I can't hug her because she has her breast still there, still naked, and if I hug her like that ... I can't, can I? If I held her, half-naked in the fucking street, as if that's OK and I have the right ... That can't happen. And it looks as if maybe she'll cry because I won't touch her and it would only be the kind of hug I'd give my daughter ... That's what she wants, that level of acceptance ... But then she sort of works out what's wrong and straightens her top and covers herself ... She looks like a kid remembering something obvious and being that bit clumsy about it and ... then I do ... I do hug her. Of course.'

If somebody will hug you, will hold you, then you're not as unclean as you think, or as you are being led to believe ... You're not completely done for – you're a going concern.

Jon stood up suddenly, almost lurched up, while the floor objected, fluctuated – one, two, three – like an uneasy heart and then agreed to be flat again, under his feet. 'And I didn't want to know what actual trouble she was in – the detail – it was none of my business. She seemed to be a refugee from somewhere softer ... from somewhere that hadn't required degradation ... She seemed to be waiting to wake up still, and to find that she was OK and her kid was OK and food in the house and heat and ... objects, toys ... Comfort. I suppose. That could have been nonsense. I was only guessing. I often guess wrong, am wrong – I'm wrong. I've been wrong for years, I've been off course ... ' He shook his head back and forth and was surprised he didn't hear a noise – something like wet matter, or maybe the silly rattle of a stick running down along a fence. 'My point would be that there is no world within which you don't give money to that woman. No matter what. There are no other considerations that matter. You give her the money.'

Christ I'm tired.

And wrong and condemned and infectious.

Jon cleared his throat – *I sound raw* – and pushed himself on, his tongue heavy under and over the words: 'There is no world ...' And then the air around him got simply too clotted, too unbearable. 'Milner ... I take no further interest. I'm done.' And he turned and began what was now a long and sagging and weirdly angled walk across the few yards between him and the door. At his back there was an outburst of half-serious cheering that blurred into laughter and a few bangs at a tabletop. It had nothing to do with him.

I take no further interest, because everything is over now.

It's all done.

He released himself into the little shock of darkness, night. There was a languid straggle of smokers loitering outside at the foot of the steps, murmuring in bands and clouds of conversation and carcinogenic breath.

When I walked away from the woman, there was this guy sitting on the wall beside the jerk chicken place. He was smoking. Off duty from the kitchen. I knew him – he's called Samson, he's a nice person. We chat. I've tried his chicken. But that evening he sucked his teeth at me and laid this long stare down against me and he said, 'Ought to be ashamed.'

And I couldn't tell who he meant should be ashamed.

I didn't know who he meant.

I'm out there in my ex-council bedsit at the Junction, because that is where I chose to be, but I don't have to stay ... I have access to other possibilities and could leave at any time. But living in the Junction — really living there — has to do with having no access to choice, about having only frailties in most directions; it's about mildew and noise and lousy window frames and botched repairs and no repairs and policemen giving out crime numbers, so that victims can keep an eye on their ongoing crimes, this daily cascade of smaller and larger risk. I am not unaware of this. And at any time I can step away and leave it. So I don't really live in the Junction. I'm playing a game, acting out some kind of purposeless mortification in a scruffy patch of SW9 — tough enough, but not so very tough, not too harsh an imposition ...

And, conversely, I have submitted myself to the Junction as if it can only be a punishment — but it's a home to people and must be loved, at least liked and sometimes loved by its residents ...

I am a patronising charlatan.

Oh, and Christ knows, if I hold on for a couple of years the whole bloody postcode will really commit to being upwardly mobile — the whole of London being upwardly mobile, the cost of each metropolitan square yard of earth becoming as miraculous as unicorns and mercy. And the Junction's residents are trying to improve it, so as soon as they succeed they will be cleared and then replaced with much more palatable people. Like me. People who do not quite have to live in places — who can always manage to investigate other options.

I'm permanently elsewhere. I'm an elsewhere man.

It doesn't make me a bad person.

It's all of the other failings — they do that.

Samson was right.

And I did know who he meant.

And I ought to be ashamed.

And I am.

Of everything, something, myself.

When Jon started walking, his feet didn't cope with the cobbles as well as they should. To anybody watching he'd look drunk — like a man who'd thrown it all away and then got wasted.

21:52

MEG, I CAN'T talk and I don't think I wish to talk at this time and I can't meet you tonight. I am very sorry. I can't do this. I can't do any of this and should not have begun what I would be unable to pursue and please forgive me. It's for the best. I never intended to make you angry or sad and I know that I have and I regret it. You should never be hurt. Please don't pursue this. I am so sorry. X and I think that it would be a misfortune and that I met you tonight. I am very sorry I came up this. I can't do any of this and I should not have begun what I would be unable to manage - bad feelings anyway, if ... for this was that was intended to make an unnecessary scene and - now that I have and I regret we - you should never begin. Please don't think ill of it. I am so sorry xxxx

22:50

IT WAS BEST to expect your disaster — then you could be ready.

Meg was in Pont Street. She wasn't exactly lost, it was more that she knew exactly where she was and couldn't leave. She was walking and walking unstoppably, back and forth between the tall ranks of salmon-pink mansions, the too-much terracotta and red brick: apartments stacked up underneath their Dutch gables, Victorian window glass showing and showing and showing high rooms full of brightness and there's fresh pain on the railings … no, fresh paint on the railings … fresh everywhere … Everything here was expected to be like new — as good, or as bad as new.

I was sure that he'd end up doing this.

Brass nameplates at front doors had a rime of old polish around them after years of pressing care.

I was expecting it.

The rub of hard attention has left a stain along the brickwork — it's slightly like a greenish or greyish moss, or a smeared unease.

But I wanted to find out that I was wrong and stupid and worrying over nothing because that's what I always do. I wanted to be me and love a clean man.

He was supposed to be a man who didn't fucking …

Being sad about a man … I'm not going to again.

It ends badly.

I won't.

And fuck you and fuck you and fuck you, Jon Sigurdsson.
I bet you could afford to live here.
So go ahead and why don't you fucking live here.
You go and have everything you fucking want.
Jon Sigurdsson, you don't have me.
Jon Sigurdsson, you don't want me.

No one would want to live here, though – not if you were sensible, not even if you could – you'd have to suspend too much of your disbelief, ignore everything but the prettiness you came home to. Although Meg, of course, does not especially come home to prettiness – at least she does her best, she is a work in progress and so is her home – and so she can only make guesses about prettiness and how it would be, having no clear idea herself and – *fuckit fuckit fuckit* – she had this ... There was this ...

Eventually she would have to go back to the Hill and her street and her front door and ... It wasn't a good place to be. It would have ...

His letters were inside it.

She was going to open the door and she would know they were there and she'd have to forget them or else she would be in this pain – this ... It was like somebody reaching inside you and doing what you hadn't asked or wanted or needed and what you did not deserve. Even you did not deserve it.

I won't sleep. And If I don't sleep then I'll be ... I'll need ...

All around her there must be old money and new money, wrapped up snug indoors and being happy, or being – you never knew, but it generally happened one way or the other – being junked up, or drunk, or married, or living with someone, or being with someone in dangerous ways – all of the usual mess and disaster, like anywhere else, but with nicer carpet, nicer worries, much more expensive fixes for much more expensive mistakes.

He was too scared and once you're frightened then your plans all come apart. I fucking know that, I fucking know, but I get scared and I was trying to hold it together, I was holding it together, I was being better than I am, better than me.

I did that for him.

She'd been up and down these few Knightsbridge blocks, making a rat track, wearing this furrow between the point where Pont Street was forced to cross over Sloane Street and the junction where the pavement lost its name and had to be called Beauchamp Place.

And he fucking liked me. He said it. He said. He said love. There was … He said.

He didn't even phone me – he ran away by text.

Meg didn't seem able to go any further than Sloane Street.

I can't go back to not sleeping.

She was caught in these few blocks – back and forth – getting cold, or shivering, which wasn't exactly the same thing.

Not sleeping, you get the big bad dark and I don't know how to fill it except in the ways that I can't any more … so I won't sleep, then … But if I won't sleep.

And she was halted at the foot of this hard, high watchtower … it's a church spire, but when she looks up at it, the thing seems aggressive and more like a prison, but also … It has a simplicity … It puts up its calm and implacable weight on the corner of its street and it's making her gaze, strain, and it seems dizzying and judgemental and too big.

It's beautiful and when you don't feel the way you need to, you can't deal with beauty – it can sod off.

By text.

You don't say anything like that in a text. You don't do that.

It's acting as if I'm nothing and I don't think I'm nothing – I'm not much, but I'm not bloody nothing.

And Meg wanted somebody to take her inside the beautiful tower – *sanctuary, isn't it? A church is a sanctuary* – she wanted them to pick her up and carry her and make her in some way absolved, the contents of heart and mind washed out until the muddy water runs quite clear and then she'd be all right and she'd find someone better and not be alone.

I can't – not awake and at night – I can't – the alone is what I can't …

But the building couldn't help her tonight, because it was empty and because buildings can't help and churches can't help and nothing can help.

I'm nothing.

I can't be alone.

I was supposed to be with him and I was doing it right, I was doing it all the right way and I was going to meetings and I was being grateful and I was doing my best and I was being my best, better, and I was telling him the truth and I was loving him because that was ...

Meg walked on, this time beyond her boundary and up into Beauchamp Place.

This isn't supposed to be ... There aren't enough people like me for me to be with, I won't find another, I'll be ... I'll just sit in rooms and listen to strangers telling me all about the wonderful fucking stuff they do now they don't drink and I'll fucking be alone, I'll fucking be alone, I'll fucking be alone.

Shopfronts winked and glimmered, full of things women with men would wear to be with their men and to be successful with their men, full of things worth more than she ever could be.

I think he is sorry and this doesn't make sense if he's sorry ... He said he was sorry and why bother to say that if you're telling somebody goodbye and you needn't be kind?

You're not being fucking kind, so why try to be kind?

If he's sorry, then he shouldn't have ...

I think he is sorry.

Everything she could see was laughing at her.

Fuck him fuck him fuck him fuck him fuck him.

And it wouldn't do to fold herself up here and sit on the kerb.

I can't feel like this. I need to stop feeling. I need to feel something that isn't this, or else I'll bloody die.

There is a certainty – calm and high – that she will be killed by her own emotions, that it could be possible this will happen.

And there is no room on the kerb because of the nice cars parked up nicely beside it and there is no corner to hide in because of the nice lights and the glitter from the nice windows and the shapes of the nice people outside the nice cafés with their shisha water pipes and the nice smell of sweet tobacco, hot fruit, is swaying along the nice pavement, narrow pavement, and Meg is not a creature that belongs here. She isn't nice.

Fuck him fuck him fuck him fuck him fuck him.

Meg is thirsty. She is so thirsty. This is in her like a law of physics – this rule that governs her actions and sometimes sleeps or fades but never leaves her.

Fuck him fuck him fuck him fuck him fuck him.

Inside the café – this still-open café – they have things which are things to drink. When you are thirsty, you have to drink. This is simple, like the edge of a cliff, like the edge of a knife, like the edge of this happy pantomime you were acting out when really you didn't belong there – you belong with a drink.

Meg opens the door and goes in because this is better than going home.

A family sits in a café: mother, father, child – an infant child. They are happy.

This is a weekday afternoon and the place is quiet. Outside there is drizzle and greyness, viewed through a window which is stacked and lined and mounded with perfectly manicured cakes. The display is impressive, even when viewed from behind, and it seems to keep the weather, the grey day, at a bearable distance. And the premises are bright and warm, the staff independent and talkative. Being here feels unusually pleasant. It feels like a treat. The decor, the ambience, the glistening cakes: they are all designed to make any customer feel they are in some generous person's home – the front room of a jolly and energetic baker – and that now they are getting a treat.

At the end of their stay, they will pay for the treat, but they won't mind.

The mother is breastfeeding the child, which seems very tiny. The father watches while the small body rests against his wife, completely surrendered to peacefulness. The mother sometimes drinks her tea and sometimes chats to her husband in a low, sleepy voice. Both parents seem sleepy, not so much in the sense of being tired, but in the sense of dreaming. They appear to be alive inside a large and agreeable dream.

After forty minutes, perhaps a touch longer, the baby – still slightly lost in her new clothes – has finished feeding and the father lays her on the table and begins wrapping her up for the outside air, then fitting her into the harness he will wear to carry her.

Now that the mother is no longer preoccupied, the woman next to her discusses babies and the children she already has. This is the mother's first time – she tells the woman that she worries, that she finds everything so strange. She does not look worried – she looks illuminated. The woman tells her, 'You'll do fine.'

The father is now standing and has the baby strapped in neatly, tight to his chest. He smiles. The other occupants of the room turn to him, perhaps because he is so noticeably content. They smile, too.

And he walks to each of them and shows them the baby, his daughter, and some of them smile at her and some stroke her hair or her cheek and she watches them with clever eyes, hungry for everything. And the father says, 'This is Nina.'

People tell her, 'Hello, Nina.' And she listens to her name and, somehow, this inspiration of her father's has become a little ceremony.

His daughter is being introduced to the world.

And the world likes her. And she likes it back.

Even when she has left with her parents, the room continues to be filled with this.

23:02

'SWEETHEART, I'M REALLY sorry.' Jon was apologising into his phone – or trying to – sitting in his second gridlocked cab of the day. Outside he could see the night's tally of supercars barging themselves along beside him, heading the other way. Their absurd engines were shouting, overperforming for any high street – even Kensington's. It all aimed to make one look. So Jon didn't look.

Why would you want to own a car with a predator's face, a silhouette that speaks of sharks and bullets and a lack of imagination? And they have to be too low-slung for comfort. Why would you want to be lying down when you drive?

'Darling, I wanted to call and ... This is so that you can know I'm sorry.'

Tinted glass, ungenerous windows – they're a kind of wilful blindness – the usual menu of sharp-muzzled toys: Lamborghini, Aston Martin, Porsche, Audi, Ferrari, I don't care, I wouldn't know ...

I do know I'm in favour of comfort.

I truly am.

He was leaving a message, calling out to a phone which was possibly turned off and possibly broken and possibly lost and possibly owned by someone who would not currently make him welcome.

I am not a bad man.

'I just … I know it's late and … I hope you're OK. I hope you're resting. I didn't mean to …'

I never mean anything – trained not to and now I can't help it. Or something like that.

'Becky, look, I'm sorry I had to run and I did want very much to ring before you went to sleep, but I've missed you … obviously … I am glad if you are asleep. That's good. Do rest. And I am thinking of you and wishing you well and I will call you in the morning, not too early and maybe we'll … It's a Saturday, that's a day off.' He felt this swing of pressure, this lighting of pain in his face. 'And you're right, I do need to … retire. That's the thing. Retiring. Leaving. But I …' His words coming out childish, foolish, selfish …

All the things that I am.

'Night night, darling, or good morning, or hello. I love you. I do. I do.' This last was a dash at sounding functional, being useful. It left him clammy and the sound of it seemed to pull out through the height of him, as if he was being unthreaded, unstitched in some terrible way.

I am not a bad man, but I can do bad things. A good man may quite easily do bad things.

And a bewilderment slapped at him, as if he were eight again and back in Society Street and trying to understand why his Christmas wasn't being a Christmas and why his father was out in the garden, sitting on a lawn that was silver with frost in the light from the living-room window and why Dad was staring out at some kind of unseeable something and why his mother was in the kitchen and cooking pancakes and using up all of the flour and all of the milk and why this was happening in the absolute dark of the night. It turned the dark into a new place he had never heard of, a box you were dragged up into where time stopped and stared and hated you and made you little.

I love her.

And Jon was, of course, by now crying and people spoke of tears as a relief, but they were mistaken.

Being accurate – because I am accurate – I would state that if I tell someone I love that I can't do, or be, or want, or offer anything with regard to them … To their love … Not anything, not love, not anything … If I do that on a day when I particularly should be there for them … And I do that, not in person, or by speaking to her, but by throwing out this scrap, an underhanded bloody text, this piece of electrical cowardice … If I have told her something and been electrical and unkind and without warning … Then after that she will be permanently disappointed in me. She won't want to contest my decision, or get back in touch. And I would agree with her – she ought to have no more to do with me, because …

Around Jon, his current box of night was apparently being shaken. Whenever he glanced out through the cab window, the glitter of headlamps phantomed and jarred. It wasn't just that his eyes were wet – there was something not right about Kensington High Street, there was something fundamentally unnatural happening underneath the fabric of things.

She has sweet hands, hands that are … And the way she … When she's stood against me and her head has been rested at my chest and my arms go round her, right round with room to spare, round this little person, I can hold her all up tight and it makes her happy. It makes her happier.

And I wake in my bed the following morning and I don't exactly want her, but I am aware of … I do need, would prefer if she were there and also I can't breathe.

I want her, but I cannot breathe.

I want her.

I want her, but the thing is that I do also, I really do need peace.

And what if they find me, catch me, fire me, throw me to the journos, charge me and bang me up in some horrible suicide factory of a jail – out of those, which would be the best option?

There is no good option.

What if somebody finds me somewhere, no longer breathing and naked and folded up tight in an airline holdall and suddenly somebody else is making statements to the police and is some kind of expert about how I always did like to take these horrible, self-harming, sexual risks.

And what if she drinks? I believe that she hasn't drunk and isn't drinking, but I might be wrong and she might be dangerous and crazy and she might be dry now but she might start drinking at any time and I bloody well can't deal with that.

And what if she's the sweetest human being I've ever met and not anything that I deserve?

And what if the men in the authoritative suits might go out and get her — the blokes with the little earpieces who talk into their sleeves, the ones with those Special Branch faces that tell you they understand how the world's really worked and perhaps they are right and there's no shelter or sympathy anywhere and why would I let her be at risk of that?

And what if I hurt her, which I already have? What if I hurt her, which I wouldn't forgive in anyone and I don't forgive in me? What if I shouldn't be allowed anywhere near her?

His head ground itself into a sicker and sicker ache.

I am a good man, but I do bad things.

And I didn't tell her goodbye and that I'm sorry because I want her to be safe — it was just because I can't ... I can't ... I'm a man who can't ... I never really could ... Valerie — yes, she was dreadful, but I picked her precisely because she'd be dreadful. I chose someone who would manage to be with me, but also not — someone who would therefore not terribly mind the way I am.

And it was proper for him to cry now and to continue crying. He could weep all the way along Coldharbour Lane until he reached the Junction, paid off the cab and then unlocked his door on the sanction he had imposed — to be there and not there and this failed little man and to know it.

I am Jon Sigurdsson.

I love Rebecca Sigurdsson.

I love Margaret Williams of Telegraph Hill.

I love Meg Williams.

I love Meg.

These are the best things I do, but I can't do them.

Beyond him, London was gleaming and offering its ways to pass the time and Jon faced the city and felt it shudder — was sure that he felt it shudder — as if it might break.

23:02

THE WAITRESS SET down a full glass, a tall glass, a cold glass, and where the air touched it there was misting at first and then beading and then the downward roll of fat, condensed water drops. Meg looked at it and decided that it was kind because it wept like a living thing.

She sat by herself which was the old habit, and here was this drink and here was Meg with it, here because she was thirsty.

Much further away than Meg's drink, other human beings were perhaps talking and food was being ordered and there was laughter which was not intended to prickle on Meg's skin and mark her out as ugly and angry and sad and ridiculous. Much further away than Meg's drink, there were possibly other waitresses and also waiters who carried dishes and glasses and baskets of bread and it was maybe they who were smiling too much and who were raising up that kind of Lebanese/Mediterranean atmosphere that was meant to feel like being family and being welcomed and which resulted in this – distant, very distant – sensation of being orphaned and a gatecrasher, a freak. And much further away than Meg's drink there was probably conversation of the kind that arises between people who are friends and people who are lovers and people who are going to be lovers – there were voices sounding these unmistakable notes of familiar and opening and rising affection. And much further away than Meg's drink it seemed there was this continuation of life. That was very likely. Somewhere shallow and inexplicable and just beyond Meg's reach there was everything else which was not this drink.

Between her and the glass, though, there was nothing but a peaceful understanding and privacy. She imagined that she was so still by now that she must have become almost invisible. In the late bustle of meals and arrivals and calls for the bill and glowing goodbyes – the palaver of other people – she was practising transparency. She imagined that if she lifted her head and studied herself in the mirror – there were many mirrors available, these sheets of lights and echoes – if she was careful about how she looked then she'd find the real truth which would be that she had succeeded in disappearing.

I used to love anticipating. It almost made what would come next unnecessary.

You open your mouth to it and first it's nothing and then it burns and by the time you swallow it's ready to heat you and colour you all the way through and makes you the opposite of nothing and that hit – that big hello hit – just swings you back on your feet and you make sense and the world goes simple and easy and you can get through it because you feel the way – you feel exactly the right way to go and to do anything and you grin that special grin which is about having a secret that nobody else could ever understand and if they have to ask, then fuck 'em.

This glass. Here is this glass. It is upright and smooth and watchful and here with her.

And then you open your mouth to more and that idea you had which was very good and was going to solve every problem, that slips past you again and you can't catch it and you open your mouth and there is more of the burn and it makes your skin uneasy and the only way to soothe yourself is to move and stand and be in the room and be bigger and you open your mouth and – between swallows – there's so much you want to say and it's important and fascinating and you are important and fascinating and you have to rush because you also have to open your mouth and get more in – more of your friend – more of the friend who is making you more friends, because now other people are noticing you

*and they are paying you attention because you matter and you're funny
and you're clever and you catch the eye and you open your mouth and
the world is sliding — you notice this — the planet is sliding instead of
revolving, but you can cope and the speed goes wrong on actions and
motions, but you can cope with these things, too — you are so good at
coping, it's something to admire — and you open your mouth and having
sex would be good now and fitting and you won't be scared about it this
time — except then the fear leaps up at you because you've mentioned it
inside yourself and so that makes the nasty in you wake — and you open
your mouth and you do want to hold somebody, though, even if it's
frightening, and you open your mouth and you're the centre of where you
are, other people can't help giving you maximum space and turning heads
to you and watching and you do want to hold somebody and be safe and
warm with them and cosy but you open your mouth because that makes
you cosy, too, when there is no one who is there for you — which isn't
sad, because you will cope with this as well and you need no one — and
you open your mouth and the faces you are facing with your face are
unfriendly because human beings are bastards and that always comes out
in the end, except that you are a bastard and the faces are being sorry for
you and being angry and being disgusted and being not right, being like
animals, or bad ghosts, and you open your mouth and you haven't remembered until this why you don't drink in public any more — you have
forgotten again that the reason is because this happens, these things happen,
these breaking-glass and falling and shouting things happen and this being
an animal, or a bad ghost, keeps happening and you can't stop.*

Meg looked at the glass and the glass looked back.

I can't stop.

The everything slides and I can't stop.

It was a tall drink in front of her: cool, no ice, but still cool
and still the dapper little drops of moisture were sleeking down
with quiet purpose, just as they should.

I asked for it specially.

And fuck him.

Fuck him.

Although I won't.

And I never would have.

This glass, this drink, which was closer than any person to her.

I would have made love.

I would have tried to do what I never have.

This glass contained a liquid of a complicated colour which was made up of blended pineapple and melon, banana, mango, beetroot, and when she drank it down in one, down in one, this thick and sweet drink, it tasted like not dying and like being very so tired.

And everyone in here is lucky and they don't know it. They have no idea how I might have spoiled their evening, who I might have been.

Meg feeling that she could grin because of this good secret.

They haven't got a clue and I won't give one and I won't be anyone's accident tonight – not even my own.

And if I don't save me, then no one else can.

And I didn't expect Jon to try, but also – fuck him – I didn't expect him to make things worse.

Her mouth was sweet just now and she was still thirsty – only simply and innocently thirsty – but the drinks here were expensive and it was late and really she should go.

And I didn't expect him to hurt and be a coward and unimpressive and not himself.

Fuck him.

Fuck him so very much.

And I wouldn't drink for him if he paid me, I wouldn't drink for anyone, I wouldn't fucking drink if somebody came in here with a gun and set it right to my head – I don't fucking do that any more. I am sober. He can't fucking touch that. I am sober.

Meg allowed herself to glance across at the mirror and see what looked like herself – this smallish, dullish person in bad clothes that would disappoint a sensitive observer – and she had anticipated that she'd have this triumphant expression and some kind of a brave grin, so now she was disappointed, as a sensitive observer would be.

I look like a kid who's lost and out too late.

There was no grin, no smile.

She looked sad, in fact.

She was crying, in fact. She did have to admit that.

And her crying made one of the waitresses come over – friendly gesture – and offer another juice on the house, because perhaps there was nothing to be done, but someone of decency could give you a little something that might cheer you – you were a guest – or maybe a few sweets could help you, honeysweet kindness.

Don't take sweets from strangers.

A coffee?

And Meg was shaking her head and leaving unsteadily and being a spectacle, sniggered at, just exactly as she'd hoped she wouldn't be.

23:29

'EXCUSE ME.' JON was – now that he considered himself – pushing and pushing his hands up away from his forehead and through his hair. 'Excuse me.' The cab driver paid no heed and Jon pushed and clawed at his hair again. He cleared his throat. 'Excuse me, but I think I would like it if you could take me to London Bridge.'

'That's not where you said.'

It seemed Jon had found a driver of the less helpful type. 'Yes, I know that's not where I said, but I've changed my mind. I've had a call and – that is – I will be making a call … ' Jon could feel hair actually coming loose and adhering to his fingers, then dropping off softly like insect wings or tendrils or some such against his face. 'Which is … I just need to be at London Bridge.' He had – it would appear – sticky fingers and was hauling out his own hair by the roots.

'It'll cost you.'

'I don't mind. I have to be at London Bridge. Getting to Coldharbour Lane was going to cost me, anyway.' Jon not intending to snap, or to sound like an arsehole in a pricey coat, but there it was – he managed anyway. 'It's all going to cost me.'

'All right.' The cab driver sounded aggrieved in the way bullying men seemed bound to when confronted. 'It's no skin off my nose.' His head shook visibly in an expression of passive-aggressive exasperation. 'I can get you there. What time's your train?'

I swear to God, they get a phrase book they have to learn, along with the Knowledge: fastest route from Mayfair to Loughborough Junction and clichés to recite as we plough ahead.

Jon focused on being glad that the taxi's radio was only playing pallid semi-pop, rather than some kind of pretend election phone-in, or a preacher.

I couldn't stand it, not tonight. The amateur approach now indistinguishable from the professional: the magisterial generalisations, the scared mythologising, the shrill defence of whatever, whatever, whatever … ideology, faith, obsession … with fragments of last week's headlines and fragments of next week's hate …

Actually, just …

Fuck it.

'I'm not catching a train. Is London Bridge a problem?'

'No, no, not a problem.'

'Then if we could do that, thanks.'

'Yeah, we're doing that – I can't just turn here, though. I gotta wait until those lights, you know?'

'Change of plans, you know? Change of plans.' And Jon's hands fell to his sides, resting ungracefully on the seat, this sensation about them which gave the impression they might be emptying, letting something drain away from them, something a little like sand in texture. He felt also that his shins and torso were being emptied – *socks overflowing with sand, like a POW dumping excavated earth, like a corpse being mobile, shoes dirty with grave traces.* He imagined that if he unbuttoned his coat and jacket there would be a tumble of grains – perhaps grey – which would seethe down and away from him and leave him only … He wasn't sure of what this process might achieve, how it would leave him.

Even more empty.

Light.

I could be light.

I feel …

And, of course, this was the moment when he reached his absolute zero and there was nothing left to feel. His awareness bumped and jolted inside his vacated body, responding to the motion of the cab, and it found not a spark of any emotion.

I'm all done, absolutely – I've wasted myself away.

He'd expected some form of terror – galloping pulse – but he might as well have been sitting and planning to do nothing much, quiet night on his little futon sofa, back in his bedsit – the futon that he didn't always bother making up into a bed, because a bedsit looks much bigger without a bed and because he could sleep anywhere and sheets and pillows didn't matter, did they? No, they didn't matter.

It's quite likely that nothing matters.

So it is pressingly important to do what is necessary, anyway. One does – in the end – what one understands to be right. One does this whether it makes any difference and whether it alters anything and whether it's possible, or not.

One does this because one has to.

One does it.

And Jon raised his hand – such a weightless extremity now, it drifted up almost without him – and reached it into his inside pocket and brought out his phone and dialled a number and listened to it ring and felt as still as water, as still as the soul of water somewhere deep, as still as one 3 a.m. moment when his infant daughter had stopped crying, had been awake but settled in his arms and been alive and with him and from him, but better than him.

Which was the first time I really knew her as a person, an identity, a human being who liked being with me and warm against my chest.

And now he was still again.

The miles-away number kept on ringing.

In a café filled with after-school children, there is snacking and mild rioting after the school day's restraint. Adults drink coffee and address each other with the practised focus of parents who are used to ignoring the din of their young. Two boys sit on the floor in a far corner, eating toasted cheese. It is clear that being on the floor and together makes everything different and more glorious.

A mother and daughter sit opposite each other, intent. The daughter – about five – is dressed to combat the outside cold: thick tights, bright pullover, little boots. Her coat – red to chime with the pink pullover – is hung on the back of her chair. The girl's hair is a wild, soft frizz of brown. Her mother's might be the same were it not bound up in an adult and responsible manner.

The girl leans forward and extends her hand in a fist, then in a blessing, then a blade: 'Rock, scissors, paper ...' And again, 'Rock, scissors, paper.' This repetition seems to press the child full of amusement, which escapes her in smiles, shivers, laughter. Her arm wavers with giggles as she repeats, 'Rock, scissors, paper.'

Her mother is also leaning forward and also sketching the shapes of a rock and a pair of scissors and a sheet of paper. Neither of them makes any attempt to play the game through and so no one gets to discover what might happen beyond this cycling rehearsal where stone meets stone and metal meets metal and paper meets paper. There's no competition, the two just dance their hands through the forms and grin at each other, their voices quietly reciting in unison, 'Rock, scissors, paper.' And then the child says, 'Again.' And they do it again.

Over by the door, a father is addressing his son: 'That's funny, isn't it?' While the boy picks the sausages out of a sausage sandwich with apparently absolute concentration, the man goes on, 'Yes, it's funny because Amanda was here when I had coffee after I took you to school and we've known each other for years and we're friends and now she's here again. Isn't that funny?' The sandwich is more interesting than this strange definition of funny. 'She's waving at us – do you see? And I …' The father stands, 'I think I'll go and ask her if she'd like to sit with us, because that would be nice, wouldn't it.'

The boy's dad moves across the unpredictably bustling café, carefully patting heads and waving at a woman as if he is in a train, or else a black-and-white movie about leaving. The boy watches him go. The child's face flickers for a moment through an expression which belongs to adult life – he seems for an instant to have stopped indulging his father by pretending to be young and to be fooled. And then the boy returns to being a boy and making a mess of his sandwich and the sausage and the ketchup, because he is worn out after a day of lessons and is mostly only a primary-school pupil, a son, a child, someone for whom all meetings between grown-ups – married or unmarried – are much the same, someone for whom food is important. He's growing, he needs to eat.

The daughter and the mother keep on rehearsing the introduction to a game they never play. The daughter is almost savagely focused, this gleam of enjoyable secrecy in her eyes, an inrushing surprise. She says, 'Again.' And her mother nods, perhaps slightly bored by this point and sipping from a mug. The daughter recites, louder than usual, 'Rock, scissors, paper … VOLCANO!' She makes a little pyramid with her fingers at the last word and then bursts it apart and sways her arms high.

'Volcano?'

'That's when you can do anything.' The girl explains this as if she is leading her mother gently out from arithmetic to calculus, or else explaining the operation of gravity. She speaks slowly and clearly and with an energetic type of seriousness, because she is passing on important information.

Your name is Jon Corwynn Sigurdsson and you are ...

Your name is Jon Corwynn Sigurdsson and you are speaking and ...

Your name is Jon Corwynn Sigurdsson and and and you are not you – you are Mr August, you are Dear Mr August, you are Very Dear Mr August and you are ...

Your name is Dear Mr August and you have made a phone call and she has answered, actually answered, when you didn't think she would, because you are no longer deserving and never were and always were caught in two minds, caught between your two minds and ...

'Yes, I know.'

And all you can hear is your darling's voice – your baby's, your sweetheart's, your best girl's voice. You can hear her voice.

And you can't hear yourself – only her. Warm at your cheek as kisses would be and you know enough, remember enough, of her to know about her – Dear God, Dear Mr August – to know about her kisses.

'Yes, I know it's you.'

And she is very far away.

'What do you want?'

And this is going badly.

'What is it that you want, Jon?'

And what you want is horrible, horrible, wonderful, really obvious, dreadful, too much and it's in you, inside you and working changes, breaking out in ripples, in waves that lash from cell to cell to cell.

'You should have called me. If you wanted me to stop. If I'm supposed to stop. When you hadn't said that you wanted to stop. You said you were happy. Why would I want to be something that doesn't make you happy? Why would I want to bother with ...'

And she does not say *a waste of time like you, an ugly fuck-up like you,* but she is audible all the same.

'You don't say goodbye in a text. If you want to go, I can't stop you – you do what you want. You do what you fucking want, but you tell me, you bloody tell me. You call me and you tell me – at least that. You should tell me to my fucking face. Fuck.'

And you like this about her, love this, anger being a form of passion and therefore she had passion and this passion is still for you, about you – double-minded and pathetic and useless Dear Mr August, she still has this passion of hate that's for you.

'I though you were—' And her voice fraying with this fury you have given her. 'I thought you were a human being. You're just a fucking man.'

And you want her to shout more vehemently. You are of the opinion that her doing so would help you both.

And you have this heartfelt ... *like a cup of hot metal rocking there under the ribs.* You really are wishing that you could tell if you're shouting back – you don't think so. *Not sure.* You imagine that you would hear it or have the sensation of it in your chest ... *with the spill of metal.*

You think that you are praying – *sort of* – and whispering – *Sigurdsson, don't mumble. You are not in bloody Fishertown now* – and you are maybe smoothing – *I hope* – smoothing your voice towards her, smoothing it like sheets, like almonds and milk and the sheets of a fresh-made bed, like altar cloths and the silk skin at her wrists, like the sheets of a fresh-made bed when you have pulled back the coverlet and are getting ready.

All of these things which are so very clean and so very sweet and so ...

'Well, I do! I fucking do! I never said that I didn't!'

And here it is – she's shouting. You like the way this hurts you, are contented by it, warmed in your bones.

'I'm tired!'

And it's so good, all good.

'I'm fucking tired!'

And once it is done – *please, please* – you can start again. You will be able to start again. You will, won't you?

'Jon, I'm tired!'

And this is true and you are too and this is only fair.

'That's not fair! You're not fair and I ... Look, OK. OK.'

And you understand – *ridiculous at my age* – you have come to this kind of fundamental understanding after all this time you've wasted in being alive, but not really alive, and in knowing so many other, useless things. All of a piece and sudden, you can see that love, that loving, that being in love is a fundamentalist's occupation. Your beloved is your beloved and there can be no other, not like her, like this. And the world must love her also and always, for ever, and if it does not then the world is wrong.

'You won't be there, Jon. No, you won't be. You're going to make me go there and wait for you and then you're not going to come. You won't.'

And you don't do ideology, never have.

'OK.'

But now you have your articles of faith. Deep.

'OK.'

But now you are not hollow. You are burning, you are filled with burning. Your metal heart has spilled and turned you molten and your creed is screamed and lashing in you, it is like rage and like wine.

'Jon.'

But now you have the love you chose – the love that chose you back – the love which is a blessing in your body and upon your body and which excuses it.

'Jon, goodbye … Goodbye. I know. Goodbye. I have to go. I will. I'll be there.'

But …

But …

There is this possibility that opens up as soon as you can tell yourself, your world, your love, darling, sweetheart, treasure, your sweet, your serious sweet – when you can tell everything. 'But …'

You want her not to go, not quite yet – *dearsweetmybaby* – and you do wish that you could have heard – *allthatIcould* – what you managed to tell her – *allthatIam* – you really do wonder the words you could have picked and offered, the ones which let her no longer hate you when you deserve to be hated. You are all unsure.

But you think most of what you said was just the one word – *please.*

And also the other word – *but.*

But and then please.

Please.

Please.

And you hear it like Stealers Wheel singing 'Stuck in the Middle with You' – that's the song you were thinking of before – Gerry Rafferty singing *Plee-ee-eease, Plee-ee-eease* in this high, long dog howl of need. It's like that.

And it's like sweetness and like fury.

23:55

LONDON BRIDGE.

In the end it is – *please* – possible to reach.

Jon had asked the cab to drop him just a little before the station, his intention being – perhaps – to catch his breath.

He steps out of the cab and pays his fare while experiencing this flapping and plummeting sensation – as if he has opened the door of a plane, stepped out bravely.

He walks up the narrow street that will lead to the station, his body progressing while other parts of him seem to be scuttling low and then lower, keeping to the cracks in the pavement – lizarding along.

The route he has to take shoves him past a succession of restaurants where it would now be completely pointless to try and dine.

Too late.

I don't think I'm hungry.

I hope she's not hungry.

I hope that she has forgiven my unforgivability.

The air is unsympathetic against his face. He presses the heels of both hands to his eyes and rubs. He guesses this might look to sensible observers as if he is newly arrived in a country he does not know, a country where one's surroundings may blur and shine and turn to a wide pelt of light, spines of light.

There are no observers, not as far as Jon can tell.

At the head of the street the architecture seems almost entirely composed of glass: slabs of bright, high glass.

It's like walking up the throat of a closing box, or into an aquarium, terrarium ...

It feels clear to him that he is a clumsy-handed, apeish man, soon to be trapped in this huge and over-elaborate case. He is about to be absurd and lonely – *please, Meg, do be here, be with me and see me* – and then afterwards he's going to have the memory of that – *of waiting while she doesn't turn up*. And at some date, as yet undisclosed, when he's sacked, arrested, punished, destroyed – at that point he will have nothing to sustain him.

I did the best I could in the end, but doing it in the end wasn't quick enough. I wasn't fastidious, not as I should be. I wasn't who I thought, not a properly tuned man.

How to tune oneself to the relevant scale.

Usually it's E-A-D-G-B-E. Elephants And Donkeys Grow Big Ears ...

But I tune to open G, I tune to D-G-D-G-B-D because I like the repetition, because repeating known things which have done no harm is always a comfort, or should be a comfort.

I taught myself to remember it with my mnemonic, my very own.

Do Good Do Good Be Determined.

Do Good Do Good Be Despairing.

Do Good Do Good Be Deserted.

No.

Do Good Do Good Be Determined.

I did try.

The pavement is echoing under his shoes as if it is tensed above some vast and peculiar nowhere. Still, Jon proceeds. Above his left shoulder rises the new and ardently modernistic head office of a rebranded newspaper group.

They wouldn't let Milner over their threshold: all of those shiny surfaces he'd smear. And the place would make him look Cro-Magnon, look like me.

The building's vast foyer – glistering and mainly transparent – does manage to have one solid wall, which is blocked across with dark, impressive letters, capitalised words that build into phrases of fugitive, yet stirring meaning. They provide just enough to

occupy a reader without embarking on any kind of communica-
tion – a wash of elevated intentions.

I think I have real intentions. I think …

He tucks his head lower and pictures the shades of all the
pubby, grubby, digging old hacks gone on before, the ghosts who
still knew about subbing and sources, there to doorstep the premises
and haunt – *if they could be bothered* – chucking about lead type
and pissing into corners.

At the end of the high-concept, low-content display are four
last words.

THE BUSINESS OF STORYTELLING

*The Four Last Things, I was taught, are Death and Judgement and
Hell and Heaven. I like to close the list with Heaven, although others
may not choose to.*

The foyer gives itself a dashing exit line, truthful as death and
judgement and nobody's ever too clear about the hereafter so
never mind.

Here it is.

THE BUSINESS OF STORYTELLING.

*Which is now all the business there is, all the truth there is. No goods,
no services, nurses, teachers, doctors, artisans, soldiers, warders, guardians,
leaders, technicians, experts, knowledge, justice, privacy, safety, dignity, mercy
and so forth.*

This is what we have instead.

THE BUSINESS OF STORYTELLING.

And I am in this business.

I was in this business.

I think I have decided to retire.

Fuck the lot of 'em, I say.

Yeah.

Shining directly ahead is the tower that blades up into the soft
sky above the station: overmastering height and bleak windows,
illumination that gives an impression of festive threat. The thing
is too big to be comfortably visible, even comprehensible, once
you have drawn this close.

Here it is.

The open piazza beneath it is blighted by its influence and even on a sunny day those who pass under its glimmer and shadow tend to scuttle anxiously, rather than linger, rather than wait.

But Jon is going to wait.

She isn't here.

Beyond him is even more glass: the walls and doors to the station concourse – another wide and immanent space.

She isn't here.

Peering through he can see – *of course* – no rush-hour crowds, no heads raised to watch the indicator boards, intent like worshippers, like animals standing ready to be startled.

She isn't here.

Without its people, the place seems burdened, packed with a strange energy, on the verge of being reckless.

She isn't here.

One of the late, of the final, trains must have straggled in, because now a small wave of passengers appears. They amble, or rush towards the Underground. They head out of the exit that leads past him and walk in the outside air, gravity serving them nicely. A man by himself and draped in, no doubt, significant colours trots by and lets loose the kind of cries that end a Friday and start a weekend. The man's calling does not summon companions, does not stir up echoes of agreement, as he seems to expect. He shakes his head and sways on.

Jon studies the angles of backs and shoulders, the differences of walks and hair, bags, coats and ... *I've no reason to bother – they're not her.* Jon doesn't know these people: they are strangers, they are irrelevant to his purpose, they are in the fucking way.

If this were a film, they would be the crowd. You don't need to care about the crowd when it's a film – the crowd is only there, all dressed up and shifting about, to make the world look real and populated. The people aren't people, they're scenery, the backdrop.

She isn't here.

This entire experience is becoming very much like watching a film, or dreaming a film, or discovering a film has opened up and folded one inside its working.

Jon can't tell if this is good or not.

She isn't here.

He wraps his arms around his chest. And it is past midnight and they haven't wished each other sweet dreams and this fact seems terrible and sad.

But I can fold my arms and I can feel and believe this is me. I am holding on.

And all of this fucking glass and all of this fucking waiting and all of this fucking ...

Please. Please.

The pervading emptiness of an almost closed railway station has started to invite a weird ascension, to demand that he drift up, unanchored, clawing at glass to slow himself until he breaks into the depth of the night and becomes all lost and gone.

No, no, no. Feet on the ground.

He clings tighter to his own ribs – caught in the arms of someone he does not love and who cannot love him.

I am stressed. This is simply stress. I am not in danger, I only feel as if I am in danger. A feeling is not a fact.

Men with unnamed professions might arrive soon to ask him questions he can't answer – soon, or this Monday, or this week, tonight – without making a proper appointment, without warning – in four minutes' time, or in no time at all – and disgrace and disgrace and disgrace will follow after.

But I am not currently in danger.

He moves, still hugging this invisible parcel of nothing, palms on his shoulder blades, and he eases into the actual station precincts. This is not an effort to put a solid roof over his head, not an attempt to prevent any type of yanking levitation, a wildly floating display of guilt.

Like the test for witches.

There he is – the informer, transgressor, traitor, coward, the too-little-and-too-late man.

Another train deposits a scatter of travellers. He knows none of them. He loves none of them.

*It would take a while – if I can be logical – for Meg to get here and
I'm not sure – night bus, night train, Tube – how she would be arriving,
if she is arriving …*

*The city's provision of public transport, while not ideal, still offers a
varied and flexible …*

It wouldn't be that hard. She has choices …

I should have offered to send a cab …

I should have said I would come to meet her wherever she was …

I should have arranged to be somebody else …

He wasn't even sure which direction he should face: outside
for buses or inside for trains, for the subway … The tiny, repeated
bewilderments of his situation, the turning, the shuffling, the
knowledge that he was so extremely, pathetically obvious – *a
man expecting someone who never arrives* – these factors combined
to mean he was viewing the world – again – through a wet
haze of splitting light.

*A man expecting someone who never arrives and therefore makes him
weep.*

If she finds me like this …

Infantile.

If she finds me with my back turned …

Discourteous.

He has so many worries, like dogs scratching at a door.

He has so many pleasures and they scratch too and he does
want to let them in, in, in.

I like the way she shouts.

*I am of the opinion that hearing her shout has made me a different
shape.*

Jon blinks to regain his composure and then rolls his gaze back
and forth and round and round, scanning.

His briefcase should be set down neatly between his feet.

But he can't recall when he last had his sodding briefcase. It
has gone absent without leave. He has maybe left the thing at
Becky's flat. If it is genuinely lost, gone astray, abandoned, this will
be both a professional failing and a shame.

Additional disgrace.

Before he can avoid it, he recalls another time – *lost, gone astray, abandoned* – a previous wait on a railway platform. The memory falls on him like water, soaks in.

He was in the big – *it seemed big* – main station at Inverness and holding his dad's hand and they were both standing to meet a train, because Jon's mum was coming back on it from somewhere, from her own mum's perhaps, or else perhaps she'd been at Auntie Bartlett's. And the whole occasion had been not as advertised.

Dad had said the expected and inevitable things – *We'll be glad to see her, won't we?* He'd gone on about tiredness in women and the need for pleasant resting and a quiet house and Jon being a good boy for ever to keep the Sigurdsson household free of further tiredness. Jon had not exactly seen, but certainly perceived this threat of illness in his mother as a kind of smoke, black and thick around everyone's ankles, eager to trip them up. *We'll all go to the pictures tomorrow, would you like that?* Other treats were suggested as possibilities – Jon's mother not being herself exactly a treat – and every offer was only a promise that showed what came next was going to be appalling.

Inverness Station was where, for the first time, Jon had been able to watch while what someone said and what was the truth were peeled right apart from each other, like skin from muscle, like muscle from bone. This was proper lying, important and adult lying. This was the kind of lying that meant reality hung about them in sticky shreds and that it was ugly and made no sense.

Dad's face smiling but not happy and his hand being almost violent around mine and I was thinking that we'd enjoyed ourselves while we were being alone together and that it had been different from how it was with Mum in a way that I'd liked – different from the stuff before which I couldn't quite remember, but which was bad. Dad told me the badness would never happen again. He told me so unconvincingly that it was almost not a lie. Mum always brought the badness in with her – we knew that. We couldn't please her. We did try. I did try.

Dad told me how wonderful everything would be. His eyes were frightening while he spoke to me, because they looked scared and that made me scared. He dropped us both inside the whale, let us be Jonahed.

I am the spineless son of a spineless man.

Jon had done what his father plainly wanted and believed several unbelievable things, as hard as any heart could. There on Inverness Station, he had agreed that sadness would be happiness and badness would be right and that all would be well. Because Jon was a child then and children understand such matters absolutely, he had been certain that make-believe never works.

Jon had caught sight of his mum – one little case with her, small and serious woman, wiry, and approaching him along the round-shouldered, metal perspective of the train. The big carriages, just arrived, seemed to be lending her stability. When she reached him, Jon was already crying. The tears had been open to multiple interpretations and had therefore suited the occasion.

She will be here. Meg will be here. She almost, mostly said that she would. I asked her to.

Please.

A dog howl of wanting her lacerates along his spine. He paces for a while to create a distraction, his feet paddling at the unfriendly floor, seeming bizarre. The whole building offers him far too many opportunities to see himself, reflections of reflections.

Here it is.

Jon Sigurdsson: no fool like an old fool, tall fool, stooped fool.

But please. Please.

His watch shows that midnight has passed and this is tomorrow.

And his image shows that he is empty, a hollowed man with gangling feet and heavy fingers.

Taptaptaptap.

Nice coat. Awful trousers. A shirt that would feel gentle if she touched it.

Taptaptaptap.

Please.

I used to think nobody waits in the way that a child waits for something good, anything good, for something to be mended.

And Jon's weight is on his left heel as he turns, slowly. He is trying make sure that somebody catching sight of him would not see a clumsy figure, an unpalatable silhouette.

Taptaptaptap.

He is certain that his expression is unsuitable and that his mouth is ugly.

Taptaptaptap.

And there's this noise which is not in his head – *taptaptaptap* – it's a fact and it's coming from somewhere to his left and it sparks towards him, quick across the great, big floor – *taptaptaptap* – and it's the sound of footsteps.

Oh.

It is the sound of footsteps because somebody immeasurably lovely is walking and now walking closer and now she is here.

Oh.

Meg halts beyond Jon's reach, but not so very far beyond it.

Oh.

'That's ...' Jon's voice tumbles out of him like stupid pebbles. 'I'd ... I thought ...' And his arms fall, ungainly, to his sides.

I thought I would die.

Which is melodramatic.

But really I do think that without you I may die in every sense that matters to me.

Which isn't something I can tell you, of course it's fucking not.

'I thought you might take the bus.'

Oh, fuck. Well, that made her trip worth the effort.

'I don't like buses.' Meg folds her arms. 'The Tube's warmer – at night.'

They call it small talk because it's smaller than you should be and so it strangles in and snuffs you out.

'Is it, I mean, is it safe, though? I mean, on the Tube at night are you safe ...?'

Meg is clearly dressed for the meal they haven't shared – for making one straightforward journey and then sitting and giving him a good impression. That she'd do such a thing, try to do such a thing, is impossibly moving.

And I'm getting a good impression, I am impressed – but I always would be, no matter what – but thank you for making the effort – thanks.

By this point, though, the hours have passed and she isn't dishevelled, not that, but her finish has faded, the effect she must have wanted is no longer crisp. She looks weary, too.

Poor darling.

'It's my fault.'

'What?'

'I – sorry – keeping you up so late and no dinner and being on the Tube at night ...'

I want her to look the way she would when everything's fine and all right and she can relax.

Jon raises his hand to flatten his hair, or smooth it, discipline it in some manner, only then he doesn't bother and this makes him probably appear to wave when there is no need to because she is here, absolutely here, terribly here.

Oh.

He makes fists and puts them into his overcoat pockets. He regrets this at once – it seems to put such a limit on his options, 'Oh ... But you ... Because I was facing the bus stop and expecting ... That's why I didn't see ...'

Oh.

He wishes to be unconscious. He wishes to be on his knees, or curled on his side – plainly incapacitated instead of standing and being this apparently capable shape.

Oh.

And then she steps in a pace and reaches out to him and pauses, offering.

Oh.

And there is no way to signal how altered he is by this, with this – *more all the time* – with this baying and coursing happiness.

Oh.

And up and out of his pocket he lifts one fist and loosens it, loses it, as if this is simple and easy to do and ...

Oh.

She takes his hand. 'And when you're on the Underground you get a better view. I think. Of the people. You can see the people more.'

Oh.

She is here, Meg is here and keeping his hand safe and this means he will not have to fly away.

He finds himself telling her, 'That's ... very sensible.' And he squeezes her palm and her fingers answer, squeeze him back, and this is perhaps how they'll have to speak for at least a while, because he sees no hope in talking when he cannot speak, only make these small noises. 'Quite the right choice, I'm sure. Good evening, I mean, good morning, I mean hello. Hello, Meg.'

He's been waiting like a child until he can say the right thing to make her seem happy, even slightly glad, about being here and seeing him. 'I'm cold, Meg. Sorry. I'm really cold. I—'

Oh.

And this is what makes her come to him completely, right in, until she is fitted to him, locked, makes his whole skin ask for more of her so that he nearly stumbles.

Oh.

She is alive, alight, astonishing, her head worrying at his breast-bone, his shirt above his breastbone, shifting.

Oh.

And these are her shoulder blades and these are the quiet, small knuckles of her spine and this is the swoop to the small of her back and this is when she slips her arms – *feels determined, feels entitled* – pushes them inside his coat and inside his jacket – *the way that I have to remember and couldn't forget and she did once before, inside, inside* – inside until she has caught his waist and he is so delighted that his shirt must be tender for her while her touch burns in.

Please.

They stay like this.

Please.

They stay.

Here it is.

They catch each other's breath and mend it.

A man and a woman sit in a living room. The walls have been recently repainted in a warm shade of cream, the skirting is also immaculate in a slightly darker shade of cream. Someone has taken up the carpet and sanded the floorboards in a way which makes them look slightly rough, but also clean, scrubbed. A large rug – obviously new – glimmers with oriental patterns in dark blues and reds at the foot of the sofa. These efforts at refurbishment make the furniture – a nondescript bureau, two armchairs, a low table, a bookcase, that leather sofa near the rug – they make the furniture look both slightly tired and slightly relieved. Each item has the air of an object which feels that everything may be all right from hereon in.

It is late, past midnight.

The tall, red curtains have been drawn and the room's only light spills from a small lamp – perhaps a family favourite, perhaps a lucky find from some market – this dusky-pink glass shade suspended from a polished brass stand. Art deco.

It is tomorrow.

But neither the woman, nor the man has slept – not in almost twenty-four hours – and so they are both, in a way, insisting that it should still be yesterday.

It is yesterday.

The man is wearing a navy overcoat with a lighter blue jacket beneath and has his hands caught deep in his coat pockets. His knees, in navy corduroy, are crimped together, legs angled away from the woman who is beside him on the sofa. His shoes are long and dark and glossy and seem ashamed to be set on the rug. The woman is also still dressed to cope with being out of doors – she's in a charcoal skirt suit, rather dated, and a black trench coat.

The man gradually drops his head further and further forward, letting his torso follow after. He folds at the waist until he is resting along and over his own thighs. His forearms and hands reach up to wrap around his neck and the back of his skull. His posture suggests that he expects to be attacked soon, or that he is a passenger bracing himself to survive an emergency landing.

The woman leans back and covers her face with her palms. They both stay like this for some time.

01:12

IT WASN'T THAT the kissing didn't work. The problem was more that it did.

Oh.

The cab had swallowed them into its dim interior and the driver had been cheerfully silent while they …

Oh.

They were on their way.

Oh.

Meg opening her lips because of course, sure, this is the kind of stuff that happens and how you find out who he is when he does these things, these things which are what men, in the end, will always ask for.

Oh.

It's beautiful, though. Being with him is beautiful and this, this, this stuff that you're doing is beautiful, too – the kissing. He feels just the same as he is on paper and also different but not in bad ways. He is careful. The way he licks and flickers is careful, it's delicate. But here he is, more of him, truly, and now here he is being with you in your mouth. His tongue is speaking to you in your mouth and he feels kind and funny and as if he's making it up as he goes along – there are these pauses while maybe he does some thinking about what's next. And he also seems pleased. You would say he felt happy.

You have to get used to him, but it's OK.

He tastes serious, if that makes sense. He tastes like a person who means what he's doing. And then his mouth tastes like your mouth which tastes like his.

You're not scared. He doesn't make you scared.

Oh.

And Jon is aware that he is breathing as if he is running, as if he is labouring along in mud and weather and making the long loop back to school with no cheering because he always was the straggling lad, left out at the end of the pack – *this is, this is, she's letting me and I'm allowed and* – but no running is required. He is kissing her and hearing how it sounds, like eating peaches in sunshine, and this is so much the place to be.

She's silk, glad silk, playing silk, but I can feel her being cautious, too. Jesus fucking Christ what did that man make her expect? Jesus, gentle Jesus. We have to be – me and Jesus, we have to be – the two J.C.s, we have to be careful of her, for her. We won't hurt her.

And the heat of her is what will keep him warm for ever, this is a fact.

If she feels shy, if she feels worried, if there's this … the absolute aim is to not hurt her.

And he slows and eases, almost shuts up shop and simply rests, puts small moments of his lips on the crown of her head, on her worry. But she tenses her spine, herself – *sideways, the cab seat … it's awkward, this is awkward, I'm awkward* – and she finds his mouth and the opening shape of hers insists – *but this isn't what we should do, not for much longer, not yet, this is for in the house* – and here is the flavour of her smile while she presses into him, laps and tickles – *safe, so safe, so safe, be safe* – and she breaks out a sweat on him, and she turns his head, turns him, lifts him.

But lifting is for when we're in her house, her flat, with her bedroom, with her bed, Christ not yet. The place with her bed. But not her bed tonight. Jesus Christ, not yet. Not that.

She draws him in until the roots of his tongue are tensed and she's lovely and she's something else he can't quite place, there's this shivering sense of her, and – *you taste of love.*

464

Margaret Williams, you taste of love.

Oh.

The cab's dark had bumped and jogged and leaned them fast against each other and then eased them just fractions apart – it moved them as it seemed to wish and they let it. And Jon had looked out once and seen Peckham High Street – *regal magnificent fucking bloody gorgeous Peckham High Street* – and Meg had tested the warm crook of his neck – licked so she could understand it – and rocked with him and with the journey. And the Queens Road Fire Station was oblivious as they passed. And Meg had told Jon, 'We're nearly here.'

Oh.

And his body had flinched at the news while he answered, 'Oh. Not as far as I'd thought.' And he'd withdrawn from her and sat straight-backed as a good schoolboy, slim as a heron, and looking ahead, looking about, as if he were anxious to remember his surroundings and take in the details offered by New Cross Gate, as if he should be visibly admiring every detail, because this might please her. He reached back to her and patted her thigh, elongated the touch, before he broke away and sat like a formal stranger on a midnight sightseeing trip.

Which I virtually am.

Fuck.

His hands hunched in his lap. 'Thank you, Meg.'

'What for?'

'For, for …' His voice blurred and small as a sleeper's. 'For being kind.'

'I wasn't. I'm not.'

The last few minutes of their journey had seemed to be wrong and emptying out and beginning to echo.

And when they'd reached the flat, it had resisted them. Meg's key had been foxed by the lock and this didn't seem amusing and Jon's offer of help didn't seem to be helpful. Meg snapped at him and when she'd finally made the lock's levers work, she burst Jon and herself forward and into the hallway as if she was furious and she didn't quite manage to prove to him that she wasn't. 'Sorry.'

She ushered Jon along too quickly. 'Sorry.' And as they went along she left the lights off because she knew her way and because the hall hadn't been repainted and it had been an alcoholic's hall so it didn't look great. Still, the living room was cleaned up and sober and was really her best bet to impress him and was, anyway, the place you would offer a guest.

When she'd stood with him at her side, though, halted by the sofa and switched on the lamp – had his unease close up next to her and her sofa – then she understood that everything she had was past its best and a fresh coat of paint wouldn't fix it, would only make it worse. 'Sorry.'

'Why? Don't be sorry. What for?'

'If I could afford a decorator ... Someone who could paint, or ... I kind of ... It's ...'

'No ... Meg.' Jon had examined the room, slow-footed about – *like a visiting heron* – and he'd sounded – maybe truthfully – as if his surroundings had somehow been less alarming than he'd thought and Meg couldn't tell if that was to do with what he'd expected from a drunk and a drunk's home.

After his over-laborious tour, Jon had returned to her and nodded, rubbed his ear. He then bent in and held her to him perhaps in the way an explorer might seize a colleague before they set off on an arduous ascent, some risk to life and limb.

And then kissing had flared again while they stood, not quite daring the chairs or the sofa.

Oh.

John's back had rested itself against the door frame – *how did we get over here?* – and her weight – *like the best responsibility you could discover, like the only duty you could long for* – her weight had rested itself, in its turn, against him and he'd been fine, entirely fine, absolutely fine, swimming and smooth all over in fine.

And then it was not fine.

Then it was not.

Fuckfuckfuck ... I can't be like this, not with the day she's had and the way it's been for her and she'll think I'm just the same as all the fucking, fucking fucking ...

His unforgivable body had begun prickling and stiffening unpreventably and he'd had to recoil his hips and also – *ungallant* – fend her off mildly – *fuck* – and the feel of her taking this badly and being insulted and worried when he didn't want to worry her, only wanted to please her – it was beyond what he could …

I'm a shit. I'm a shit with a hard-on. I knew this would happen.

He dumps this half-crouching mess that he is on the sofa and tries to think.

Oh, fuck this.

Absolutely, it wasn't that the kissing didn't work.

01:16

LOCKING HIMSELF IN the bathroom seems the intelligent thing to do.

Of course it's not intelligent, it's imbecilic, appalling.

'Is your …? Where is the …? If you'd excuse me, I'll just …' And Jon is lurching from the sofa and then thumping along a passageway and upstairs, hands scrabbling at the banisters. On the landing he peers into an airing cupboard – *scent of clean sheets, of her sheets* – and this is a box room – *don't look, could be a bedroom, could have a bed* – and here is what he needs – *bathroom* – frosted-glass panel in the door and he opens it with pathetic, monkey fingers and in he goes, here he goes, and pulls the toggle to let him have light.

I don't want light.

And he shuts out the rest of the building and slots the bolt in fast behind him and then sits, slides, lands on the floor with his legs crumpled out before him and his back against the lower panel of the door – *wood, substantial* – and this is absolutely not good.

I want to be, I want this to be – later, in the end this will be … We'll remember – please, we might – we'll say, 'Oh, and that time when you ran like a spineless, time-wasting git and hid yourself in the toilet, because that's where shits belong. Or some such. Less abusive phrasing, because we'd be laughing about it. Please. Later this would be funny. Please. This would be the funny thing that stupid Jon did. But there won't be a later, we won't have one, so this won't be funny. There won't be later, there won't be us.

'Jesus fucking idiot Christ you bastard.' He tells himself this in a voice that he has never before produced. He sounds oily. 'You fucking moron.' The voice of a man who always had no value and who is no longer even plausible. He sounds like Sansom.

The feel of her body and how it apparently wants to be with his ... she's on him like pokerwork, cauterised through to his bones and he'll never shake that, never be repaired.

It's my ... it's just that my ... I don't know how, Meg ... and when you've had the hospital ... and your life and the way it was and mine and when we hardly really ... I don't see that it would be possible ... I don't want or intend ... And if you think I do intend ... My dick intends, but it's a dick, please can't we ignore it?

Fucksake, how can a man be afraid of his, of his ...

I'm not afraid of my penis, of my cock, of my dick, of my fucking Neanderthal dick.

I am not afraid of it.

I hate it.

I need it to stop. I need it to leave me be and ...

She isn't going to want it, she isn't going to want me – I don't mean because of today, of what happened today – I wouldn't want her to even think of it today, but I mean she shouldn't have to want it ever.

He thumped the back of his head softly and over and over against what he guessed was the small rise of the frame holding the glass panel. It was pleasantly uncomfortable.

And even if I wasn't a screw-up ... I mean, she's a screw-up, she's an alcoholic, she's ... I don't know what that would involve ... You can be great in writing, it doesn't follow that ... Once they can move you, once they can thicken you and they own you that way, because they own you when they've got your dick, you don't think straight, they have you ... You end up ...

He hit his head harder and wanted it to bleed so that he could go downstairs in a bit and tell her, 'I have to go because my head is bleeding and you need to forgive me and let me go.' He would do this – he would consider doing this – because he was a lying bastard and a man of the type that he found most despicable.

She doesn't fucking own me.

Say anything for an excuse to bolt, won't you?

Fucking Bolter.

She loves me.

That's worse.

That's wonderful.

Worse.

Once they love you and they make you love them and you miss what they are and you look forward to … and you think when you wake up, when you first wake up … and there's this part of your day, this line through your day which is coloured in a way that nobody ever provided and so when she goes …

I don't want her to go.

That's the thing.

I don't want her to go.

So I'll go.

Jonathan Corwynn Sigurdsson, this absurd man who is ashamed of himself and should be and who wants to lie on this linoleum for a while, just curl up and maybe he could cover himself with a towel – *her towel that knows her body, dear God* – and maybe if he slept then he would feel better after and he could …

'Jon?' Her voice with his name in it comes walking through the door like an animal he can't face, like some transgression of the laws of physics. 'Jon? Are you all right?'

And Meg has no idea why particularly she's saying this, because it's obvious that he isn't all right and it's stupid probably to try and speak to him and she isn't stupid.

'Are you not well?'

Meg feels bad for hoping that he isn't well and yet she does hope it in this hot, sudden rush of asserted will that's almost scary. Illness would give him a reason for holding her and then running absolutely away – something apart from getting disgusted by who she is and can't help being.

Jon and his disgust, his hating her, his doing whatever thing it is that he's doing – they would all mean, would have to mean, if she was sure of them – would all mean the end for what had been this sweet thing. And there's no drink in the house but, fuckit, there's always drink somewhere, you can always whistle and find that supplies will come rolling up and shining.

But it wouldn't help.

There is not a bad situation that my drinking will not make worse.

And why bother to have the thought. I can't. I am stuck with this – this – this shit.

'Jon.' She knows that she shouldn't sound angry, because that will also make a bad situation worse. 'Jon.' Why not be angry, though? Because he's not allowed to do this, he's not right when he does anything like this, whatever this is. 'JON.'

And she tries the bathroom doorknob and it turns but – of course – he's thrown the bolt and there's no getting in. *Maybe he is ill, maybe he's got some stomach thing, some … Maybe he's embarrassed by some …*

The whole mess, the whole bloody mess makes her kick the door hard, twice, and then realise that she is furious at just about the exact same time she realises that she's hurt her foot.

Ridiculous.

'No, I'm here. I'm sorry. I'm well.' Jon sounds small.

A tiny heron.

Nerves and wildness and no way of getting used to people.

You want to wrap him up and cure him of whatever this is.

'I, ah … Meg, I just can't. I can't. I'm scared is the thing and that's …'

He also sounds as if he would like her to be sorry for him.

You want to wrap him up with a cloth put over his eyes like you do with birds to make them calm and then strangle him.

'JON!' And she kicks the door another three times and doing this is only painful and frightening and pointless, but it seems unavoidable in her mind.

Each time she hits the door, or kicks it – Jon is guessing that Meg is delivering kicks – the impact jars through his head and neck and hurts him. This makes him happy.

Meg, darling, sweetheart, baby, all those words – I'd be angry, too.

I'd give up and leave a hopeless case like me to rot – let me deal with whatever policemen, or troubles, or silences, or waits come my way. Let me be alone.

If she'd just even get away down to the living room again, or anywhere else, then I'd have a chance. I can wait until she's gone and I can dodge outside probably ...

I don't want to, though.

I could dodge out and head off to wherever, to New Cross Road, to some road, there are roads. I could walk for a long time and when the sun came up I could flag down a cab. I'd be tired enough to stop my thinking by then. I could ask the driver to take me home.

Except there isn't home.

Not if there isn't us.

The bathroom smells of her perfume and her soap. It's a nice bathroom, a good one. Neat.

'Meg, I—'

'No, shut up! Fucking shut up!' The wood at his back shudders softly as she undoubtedly sits down and rests against it.

When she speaks again, the words seem to slip and drift out from her, they emerge strangely.

Jon feels them glide under the door and then pool round him, being sad. The way he has made her sad soaks into him ...

The cause of this fuck-up is me, because I am a fuck-up, because of my cock.

And a brief yelp escapes him, rather than a laugh, and he tells Meg – he turns his cheek to the bolted door and he tells her, 'Unparliamentary language. Not out loud. In my head.' And he breathes and his lungs fill with more of how she would smell after a bath, in the morning, in the evening, before bed. 'Oh, Meg ...'

'Open the door, you fuckwit.'

'I don't think I can.' Jon has the sound of a person surprised by himself and beyond his own control and the certainty of this works along Meg's skin and chills it.

He's lost. I've lost him.

'Meg, I ... I do want to ... I really do. There are all kinds of things that I would ... You made me very happy. You do make me very happy. It's only that I ... There's no point to me and please hate me, it's the only way. I can't think that anything would be enough, or work, or be worth your while, or—'

'Shut up!'

'OK.'

'Shut the fuck up!' Meg's tongue feeling disabled by unknown influences and wanting more than words to touch and making her sound like a bully, like the thing she would never want to be. 'Sorry. I'm sorry, too, Jon. Honestly, though. Do shut the fuck up. I'm not going to hurt you, I'm not going to do anything terrible to you. Do you think that anyone who meets you, or just looks at you, anyone at all, can't tell that you shouldn't have anything horrible happen to you? You're something that no one should hurt. Like with animals – you're meant to look after them.'

When he hears this, Jon is surprised to find that he's not at all unhappy to be classed as an animal.

'It's like with kids, Jon. There are things you don't hurt ...'

He also likes being a thing – it sounds simple, almost effortless.

She stops and he can hear the fall of her breath and wants to fit himself around it, wants to feel it on his neck, feel it warming him through his shirt – *soft shirt* – wants to feel it on his penis, cock, dick – wants her to be kind to his inexplicable self there and to not hate it, not laugh at all the other places about him that are horrible when you see him, the mess of him. He wants to be with her.

He tells her, 'People hurt kids. They do it all the time, they—'

'I know!'

And there's the dunting of possibly her head, lower than his own, drumdrumdrumming on the wood until he worries about her for a new reason, wants her to stop, be safe, be careful.

'I know, Jon!' It sounds as if her throat is getting sore. 'I know!' This huge sound she's throwing out, this volume that you wouldn't expect from a small person – startling person. And he does love her very much. It would be unforgivable to say, but loving her is everything he knows or can remember at the moment. That's why he can't stand and can't open the door.

'Meg, I am sorry.'

'Jesus, I know that, too! I know you're sorry all the fucking time – you say it often enough. Almost as often as I do. And now you can stop. And I know people hurt each other and they hurt animals and they enjoying hurting whatever they can reach, but that's not everyone, not me and not you and that's who's here, that's the only fucking people here and we're us, we're just us, we're us ...'

'Meg, I—'

'You think I don't know about being hurt? You think I don't get scared? You think it's a mystery to me what complete cunts people can be? You think I would ever, ever, fucking ever want to do anything to you that would hurt you, when I know you and I fucking love you and I'm me! You know me! You fucking know me! I can't hurt you!'

And she shifts her position against the door and Jon feels the change in his cheekbone and that's OK.

'Jon. Listen. You sit and you listen, right?'

'Meg, I—'

'Shush. Shush, baby.' Meg is peaceful when she says this.

Nothing to lose, because everything's gone: that's a peaceful way to be.

And she leans the side of her head up close to the door, and believes the gloss-painted wood is warmer than it should be, because Jon is on the other side of it. She makes that true in her head and decides to be glad about it. She begins quite softly, speaking to his heat, 'When the cab was driving us up here, you saw that couple – you noticed them, I could see. There was a man walking after a woman and yelling and she'd got two of those shitty, thin carrier bags they give you in corner shops and both bags were full up with cans – beer or lager or cider or something – and I could feel you thinking – because alcoholics can do that and we're usually wrong, but not always – I could feel you thinking this was a reminder of what drunks look like. And the woman was a mess and in heels she couldn't manage and you were thinking that's what a drunk woman does on a Friday night, that's how she is and how she dresses, and that's the way a couple would act if it involved her – the guy trying to hit her and her trying to hit him back and the pair of them screaming, about … Well, you don't know what it's about and they probably don't, either.'

'Meg—'

'Shush.' She has to press on and not let him slow what she needs to say, or steer it, or interfere – this is her fucking story and she'll fucking tell it. 'Shush. Please. The point about all that is – fuck you, actually, because I'm sober now. I am sober today. What you get, what you've got, is me sober. And we never, ever would chase each other along a pavement at night and scream and slap and … we wouldn't, Mr August. We're us. And I'm me and today was a long, long fucking day. Not the worst I've had. I'm not going to make you listen to the worst I've had – I don't want that day, or the days like that day, to come anywhere near you. Or near me. But I've been stuck in nights, in times when a man's shouted and the hands come in at you, Jon, and I've kept my head down and it's made no difference and where you live, your home – it isn't where you *can* live any more, after that – if that stuff happens even once, even only a little bit, then you've lost your home, because he could always do it again. The fucker could always do it again. Couldn't he? The guy. The guy whose name I'm not going to remember. And I don't want his name anywhere near your head, it would be like putting something dirty in you, if I make you hear it, you know? Jon?'

'I think I know. I think. I'm … Please don't be upset, Meg.'

'Too late. Way too late for that. I am fucking upset.' Although she only mentions this flatly, keeps it as a statement and isn't loud – nowhere near screaming. 'I am upset. I don't understand what you want, Jon, and this is all … I'm upset. You can't do things that are the kind of things that would make a person be upset and then ask that person to act as if you hadn't and to not care about them … and just shush, please, shush.' She can hear him shift behind the barrier he's fixed to keep her out. 'I don't get why you're bothering with the door – it's not like you don't have a great big fence around you, anyway – you don't need an actual … Anyway …'

Meg pats at the glass panel above her head – *taptaptaptap* – touches it in the way she might touch his arm to reassure him and, after a while, a small while – *taptaptaptap* – back comes the reply.

Like prisoners in adjoining bloody cells …

'What the guy – the one who doesn't get a name – what he liked wasn't violence. What he liked was the other thing. I said a little bit about it, I wrote to you and said a little bit about it. He would do the other thing. Afterwards, I would bleed.'

'Christ.'

'I don't think about him. I haven't, except on days when there's medical stuff, gynaecology stuff, examinations … Which is me taking care of myself and doing what's right, let them check that I'm well – but it pisses me off that it makes me remember him. And I do … I …'

She pauses while something empties her lungs, and her lips stop being clean and a seal that can rest on proper loving. Her mouth stops being something she'd want to give – like a present, like a present that can hold a present.

'Meg?'

'I'm fine.'

I'm Fucked-up Insecure Neurotic and Emotional.

F.I.N.E.

Smug, fucking rubbish.

'You don't sound …'

'I'm as fine as I need to be, Jon.' She clears her throat and swallows and would like some water. Meg would like to be drinking cool water. 'Today was one of the days for an examination and you have to book up weeks in advance and if I could have met you on any other day, I would have, but it's—'

'That was my fault.'

'All right, it was your fault.'

'Oh.'

'If you want it to be. I don't think it's anyone's fault.'

Oh.

'I have … I get busy, Meg. I only understand about work, I do my work and the rest of … I don't do the rest of my life. I'd

479

rather not.' Jon's hands are clasping each other, slipping with worry when he grips too tight, unreassuring and ungentle. 'I get busy – I prefer to be busy and once you're geared up to be someone who is busy … Today was a day – that is, yesterday was a good day when there would have been a fair chance that we'd make it.'

Hearing himself use the past tense when describing their fair chance – *oh* – simply drops him into silence.

Meg calls to him, 'Jon, I was the one who assumed that I could cope if all of this happened in one day. I could have told you no. I could have anticipated that I'd end up pretty much insane.'

'You're not insane.'

'You're not exactly best placed to judge.' And this sounds cruel, which she doesn't intend to be, but then she hears Jon make a half-laugh in response and that's a fine sound, a lovely sound – one of the best. 'I just … Jon, I'm going to tell you about something from last year. From about six months ago. It's a story – my dad would do this, he'd come upstairs when I was a kid and if I couldn't sleep because I was worried, he'd give me something else to think about. He was no use at fairy tales or those kinds of things, but he could talk about things that had happened to him. He could give me his life. In pieces. That's what he did.'

'He sounds like a good father.'

'You'll have been the same.'

'I was away a lot. Too much.'

'And you're doing better now.'

'I don't know.'

'I'm sure it's fine – this is where I talk, though. About me. Self-obsessed alky. I talk and you, you don't have to stop worrying, or doing whatever you are doing in there, but you listen and that's all you have to do. No duties otherwise. OK?'

'OK.' Something young in his voice, something of being peeled back to his child self.

'Six months ago, I went into hospital—'

'You didn't say, love.'

'Shush, for fuck's sake. No. I didn't. I couldn't work out how to tell you and it was just a small thing, day surgery, and I assumed that I'd be fine. Like I always assume that I'll be fine. Or that I'll be dead. No intermediate positions. Just those two. Even if somebody sawed my head off, I would probably assume I would be fine, that I'd get by … If there's no threat at all, then I'll fold flat and just wait for the Four Horsemen, order a coffin … I'm wired up wrong – backwards. If there's something horrendous and dramatic and it's only going to ruin me – nobody else – then it seems to sound reasonable. I probably could deserve it, I probably could survive it. Something like that. I tell myself I'll bounce on through it and hardly notice. It makes planning a bitch.'

And this faulty wiring is perhaps why Meg is thinking that Jon will leave tonight and not come back, but that she won't be destroyed by his loss.

She tells herself *shush*.

And then she says, 'They tell you to be at the hospital with a little bag – as if you're just taking an overnight trip, Paris and back, and you go with that as a nice idea. You can't bring anything with you that might get stolen while you're off in theatre, or unconscious. Which makes the journey sound like a pretty tough trip.

'I mean, I hid money in my knickers – and put my phone inside my sock, inside my shoe … childish. You do need your money, though, and you do need the phone.

'Or at least money. You'll have to get away at the end.

'I've no clue when this will all be done with, when a cab could be called in to pick me up, when I could stroll out, apparently unscathed, hardy … But I'm not concerned about that, I'm saying in my head that I have my little bag and I'm checking into this hotel – a big hotel that smells of bacon and gravy – there's a lot of catering places as you go in and it's breakfast time, powerful aroma of toast, pale toast and disinfectant and the smell of people who aren't well. Not a great hotel. Hand-sanitising bottles all over the shop and great big metal lifts. You have to not size up the lifts and work out you could get a trolley into any one of them, or a coffin.

'It's really early. So no one's about except for a few of the staff heading off for toast and coffee and the other people who are checking in with their little bags.

'You go to the desk – not exactly a check-in desk – and you say your name and date of birth and then you sit on a chair – it's always chairs and waiting – and I had a book with me in my little bag, one about polar explorers, because those bastards had it worse than anyone. Their teeth shattered in the cold – that doesn't seem fair. The frostbite and starving and snow blindness and all that is horrible, but it's not – I'm saying this is my opinion – it's not unexpected. Walking along in a snowstorm and dealing with that and then having no bloody teeth, that's fucking unreasonable.

'And I'm sitting on the chair and being outraged about these fuckers in the snow with no teeth and that's cheering. I reckon I've made a wise choice with the reading material. I like finding out about the suffering and the sledges and mittens and portable stoves and tents. It's letting me feel comfortable. They made it back, this particular team, so that keeps it calm and not depressing.

'So, after a while, you've just about persuaded yourself that you're in a hotel for real, on a holiday in this place that reeks of dead people and pies – you're ignoring that – but you're breathing in faith, or frost, or adventure – something that's bearable – and you're being thankful that you've got your little bag and that you still have access to health care, that you don't have to pay extra for it when you've already paid for the NHS – even though you shouldn't be thinking of health, because this is meant to be a hotel – but then a nurse appears – makes the hotel vanish – and she's got a list of names and there's something about a list of names which is a bit ... It's never good, is it? You never can tell ...

'She wants you and all the other little bag people to follow her and – like mugs, like a bunch of mugs – you just do tag along. You go along these corridors that you'd never find your way out of and they seem kind of yellowy-faded and not quite ... You'd want them cleaner ... And then – which is a surprise – you're round a corner and here are the beds. Not a ward, precisely, just in a fat bit of corridor where there are beds. There are no swing doors you have to go through. You maybe wanted swing doors.

'And the nurse with the list sends you off to your bed – the number of the bed is on the list, too – and your position is right by the wall, this whole wall which is just radiating coldness. It is colder than the weather was outside, which isn't fair.

'And then you end up sitting on another chair which is beside a bed and you're reading about the sledges again and waiting and pretending that you're a well and normal person visiting someone, because that's what people in their everyday clothes are doing if they're sitting on a chair beside a hospital bed.

'But another nurse comes by and says you should take off your clothes and put on the gown she gives you and your dressing gown, which you have because it was on the list of things to put in your little bag.

'So you pull round the curtain that hangs down from a track in the ceiling which circles the bed and doing this makes that chattering sound and that swish that it always does in films and soap operas – so you can be glad about that. You can be a film star, or just someone in a television series. Then you undress and put on the gown which isn't yours and then the dressing gown which is.

'You can be glad of the dressing gown because it keeps in a bit of heat – the hospital gown is hardly there, it's just this shape-less, odd shroud of a thing, designed for the convenience of others, made out of cloth you'd imagine using to polish your car and then throwing away. You do wonder if it's meant to be disposable and if the fact that clearly it's quite old and has been washed often means that corners are being cut. You worry. Not about the operation – just about the gown and the missing corners.

'You're also glad of the slippers you've brought – they were on the little bag list, too – the slippers which make a small place under each of your feet belong to you and your home and not to where you are, which now does not smell of death or gravy, but of other things you can't identify and don't exactly take to. One of the smells makes you think of embalming.

'And even though you're glad of the comforting things, you're also thinking that hospitals are full of really ill people. And the ward is full of probably slightly ill people who are also pulling their curtains and changing themselves into patients – strangers in dressing gowns with bare shins. They all look much iller than when they came in as soon as they've undressed. You suppose that you do, too, if it comes to that. And you're wondering if your dressing gown and your slippers aren't getting covered in illness and strangeness and if you won't have to throw them away once you're back home. And you liked your dressing gown.

'And you're getting colder and colder. Beyond the wall, you could swear there are ice fields and white bears and unrusted ancient cans of meat. There are penguins with sloped shoulders waddling across these pale spaces like patients in contagious slippers and they're shaking their heads.

'You're shivering.

'Another nurse asks you again who you are and when you were born and where you live. And it makes you feel doubtful – this is the third or fourth time you've been asked. You want to imagine that they're being extra careful, but you end up being sure they can't keep hold of information and can't guarantee to remember what patients they have from one minute to the next.

'Would you want them to cut you or burn you, or do what they have to do when they can't keep safe hold on an address?

'You talk to your anaesthetist for a long time. He checks who you are again and your address and that stuff, and you don't care if he knows who you are, or could come round to where you live with a fucking Christmas card, you just want to be sure that he knows you're the alcoholic. You're the alcoholic who doesn't drink and who never wants to feel as if you have and that means no sedative. No feeling out of it, no recovery from feeling out of it – no chemical ripping about in your blood.

'The specialist said this was possible and that the pain wouldn't be too bad and you could get injections and this topical cream as well, which can be a bit of a joke when you say it to yourself – like the cream is keeping up with the news ... You would like to trust the specialist. She visits you next and doesn't check who you are, or where you live, or how long you've been alive and this seems slapdash. But she does remember that you'll have no anaesthetic. You can see she's thinking hospitals aren't arranged to deal with conscious people.

'You wait for an hour and you take the tube of anaesthetic cream – topical, that's funny – they've given you and go with it to the bathroom – you worry about the cleanliness of the bathroom – and you fill the urine sample bottle you've been given and you wash your hands and then you put the warm little tub on the edge of the sink – which seems unhygienic of you – and you apply the cream where you're guessing it should go and you hope that it works.

'You wait for another hour, which is an hour longer than you were told you would have to be here.

'You shudder with the cold, you try and hide yourself in away from it and you stop reading your book. You go and apply more cream.

'You wait for another hour and other people have left for their procedures and have returned, flat-out, and they've got dreaming faces. The anaesthetic has made them happy. You go and apply more cream and you can't feel anywhere down there now – it's all dead. This is what you wanted, but it crosses your mind that maybe it will always be numb and you think this is funny and you want to tell the man you're in love with about it so that he can think it's funny, but you can't tell him because you can't use your phone and because he doesn't know you're in hospital and because it's all ugly and you don't want him to think you're ugly and because being numb was what you wanted a lot before, it was what you needed, and it's a joke and the wrong kind of joke that you've got a whole tube of numbness now – when you don't really need it as much. Or maybe you do, though.

'You hope it works.

'It's three and a half hours before they come and get you and say you should lie on the bed. Even though you're not unconscious, they want you to act as if you are. The porter wheels you to a small room full of cupboards, like a kitchen, and a very young nurse takes away your dressing gown and puts it somewhere you don't see and you wait a while longer. You're just in the hospital gown. And this room is colder than the ward.

'You can't stop shaking.

'Then you're pushed from the kitchen room, through into the theatre – at least you get to see swing doors – and it's not right. It looks half-abandoned – all white space and not much equipment and it's freezing, the air's freezing.

'You help them to strap you into the special chair – legs in thick Velcro, held tight, held up and tight and parted. This means that the porter sees you. He can see you while you're naked. He must probably do this all the time, but the naked women he sees are asleep and that makes it more OK for him, you can understand that. He is nervous and upset. You're nervous and upset. And you're cold.

'From a door in the far corner, a man walks in – you're not sure who he is – and he glances at you. He seems surprised that you can look at him back. Mostly, though, he's strolling towards another door, a far door, and out. It seems you'll be having your operation somewhere which is used as a short cut.

'Your specialist, gynaecologist, is fussing with an extension cable – there is a problem with the power supply in some way – or the room's hugeness means that the laser she will use isn't near enough to a fucking plug. You decide not to let this disturb you. You're thinking that can be a joke, too.

'And she puts in the expander and winds it open and you're not doing that well, already – the cold has stolen away how you move and you can't keep control of yourself – these tremors happen. And the cream was good cream, working cream, not a failure, but you hurt and you remember other times that hurt and you can't fucking believe you could have thought this would be reasonable and something you could fucking deal with. You're a fucking moron, obviously. And the gynaecologist who said this would be a breeze is also a moron, because there's this huge pain, but maybe that's your own fault and you're weird and you're not going to tell her any of this, because she's closing in with a a needle in her hand and you're watching that syringe dip in – you don't want to – a needle between your legs. I'm thinking to hell with that. And it hurts and it hurts again and all this is hurting – the biopsies, the looking around, messing you about, this crap that she's doing – and she hasn't even started with the laser.

'The specialist talks to her student about you. She doesn't talk to you. Even when you talk to her, she gives her answer to this really young guy beside her and then he passes it on to you. She can't seem to deal with you being alive.

'Then she starts the lasering.

'It smells of burning. That's you burning. And you know that because it feels like you burning.

'More injections don't especially help.

'You shut your eyes and you go somewhere else for a while, way down where your breathing runs away to – you know how to do this, you go there to get warm – the only place that's warm.

'Then there's this metal, rattly noise and you get yanked back into what's happening, because your specialist has kicked over some kind of bowl that was on the floor and you can't feel pleased that she's this clumsy, or that bowls in operating theatres get left on the fucking floor.

'The laser takes forty minutes, probably because you're moving, you're shaking because you're so cold – the creak of the frame you're strapped to, the way it's rattling, is mostly what you can hear – even though you're trying to be still and numb, really numb. You're saying that over and over.

'It's fucking horrible.

'And afterwards you get yourself on to the trolley because you don't want the porter to touch you, even though he seems a nice person and wheels you very carefully back to your place by the wall and he looks at you with this still face, still brown eyes, he's such a still guy, and then he looks at your chair and he sees your book on it and he goes and picks it up and gives it to you and he says, "Now you can read your book." He talks to you as if you're a person.

'You tell him, "Thank you."

'And he goes away and you hurt like fuck, exactly like fuck.

'But you did it, you got through, you made it. And you walked in with your little bag and you walk out the same way and nobody can see that you had no dignity, because now you do, because you're sober and you can fight this shit and be OK, even though it was humiliating and it hurt and it brought down so many different kinds of crap on you that you'll have nightmares for a week. You walked in and you walk out and you deal with it. If you have to, you can probably deal with other crap that's worse.'

And Meg stops there. He'll either understand that she knows about being scared, or he won't. He'll either understand that she doesn't need any more trouble, or he won't. She really does understand being scared – it's not like he's so fucking special.

She flattens her spine to the door and rolls the curve of her skull against it, back and forth, back and forth. When he doesn't say anything, she stands up, slightly stiff, and she goes downstairs.

Leave him be.

Jon unfastens the bolt.

Huge clack and grind it makes – enormous warning signal that here I am, hopeless man, on my way.

And he opens the door which isn't technically a hard thing to do.

Nothing else will ever be like that for her, not ever again. Promise. I'll see to it.

His arms and legs work passably well.

If she'll let me, I'll make sure of that.

He knows where the living room is – it's down the stairs.

She doesn't need me to, but I will.

My girl.

'Meg?' His feet – big, ridiculous, guilty things – bring him downstairs.

The girl I didn't help to make.

The other girl.

The girl I choose.

There's no one in the living room.

You can hear crockery, soft motion. There's a spillage of light from under a further door.

Kitchen.

And you follow her to where she's gone, walk through the air that her body has already pushed aside, head along the corridor and down three little steps – they're all the same these Victorian houses, you needn't expect surprises, you just shouldn't.

She's there at the far end of the kitchen and her face is to the window, so you can't see it.

And you can hear when your voice says, 'I'm hungry.'

She tells you, low and even, 'Yes, well, so am I hungry because some fucker stopped me having lunch and stopped me having dinner and I haven't felt like ...' Meg with her back to you in the dimness and leaning on the counter by the sink. 'It's not good if I don't eat. I get a bit crazy.'

The kitchen smells nice, like being in a home with established habits. 'Meg ...'

'What? Don't tell me you're scared.'

'No. I won't. At least ...' He presses on into the room and is aware that Meg can watch his reflection approaching her. 'I made the rules, you see, the rules for the letters and I was, you see, surprised when you ... The idea was that I would never meet anyone and that ... I was surprised.'

She brushes her hands through her hair and sighs and he doesn't know if this is a sign of disgust, or tiredness, or something else, and he doesn't feel able to ask, but then she tells him, 'There aren't any rules. We aren't playing a game. I'm not a bloody game, Jon. I don't have time to be a game.' Meg turns, looks at him and her face is so gentle, soft, secret-looking – as if she is dreaming him. Jon would like her to be dreaming him – she would do that very well and undertake many improvements, he is sure. She asks him, 'You want a game? I'll tell you a game. We'll play *rock, scissors, paper, volcano*. That's what we'll fucking play. That's all anyone needs to play.'

And Jon's head wags, 'I don't know what that is.'

'You said you're hungry – I'm starving, I think. Yeah ... I've got ...'

Meg paces about from shelves to cupboards and back and this is all right, this is perfect – he watches her, each shape that her body reaches and then passes through, abandons. He asks, 'Do you have honey? I think I would like bread and honey.'

This makes her, for some reason, smile, 'You'd … Well, I do have that. All the ingredients for that. Bread and butter and honey. The butter's on the table – butter dish, see? You slice the bread, I'll get the honey.' She pauses, as if testing whether he will take instructions, whether he likes them, whether he – in this context – is pleased, so pleased to do one thing after another and be uncomplicated and know where he is – in Telegraph Hill, in a kitchen, with Meg Williams.

'While you're doing that, Mr August, I'll tell you about rock, paper, scissors, volcano. This little girl was talking about it and I made sure I remembered it. Every time I see something good, or kind, or silly, or worth collecting, I remember it. Every time the city gives me something sweet, I remember and I write it down.'

And Jon goes and collects the butter and lifts out the bread and his hands do not stammer. He might have been in this same kitchen for lifetimes and worked with Meg to make plates of bread and honey and to end their hunger. He might have done this over and over again and always loved doing it. It's beautiful.

02:06

A MAN AND a woman are asleep in a living room. The art deco lamp shines on without them, makes shadows.

The couple are lying together on an old leather sofa, their bodies released into careless shapes, their faces unguarded. The man's coat lies on the rug beside them, as if it might have covered them at some time, as if they have turned in their dreams and it has fallen from them.

The man's shoes are together by the door, neatly parallel, the woman's are under an armchair, also tidily paired. Beyond having stockinged feet, they are fully dressed, wear jackets, their clothes disarranged now, creasing.

Because the sofa is quite narrow, the pair are snibbed together – the man lying on his back and the woman's weight resting partly across him. Her head is turned on his chest so that she seems to be listening to his heart, perpetually making sure that it continues.

This is something the woman would wish to remember, that she would collect along with all the other incidents, moments, presents that have seemed valuable and something to sustain her. But instead she sleeps.

04:18

'YOU SHOULD REST, darling.' He says this as if they have made love.

'I am rested, sort of.' She says this as if she doesn't find him ridiculous and as if she is speaking from somewhere still perfect and unpreventably possible, somewhere which is a dream.

Time falls on them quietly and gentle as dust. The house is full of silence, a well-disposed silence.

They are lying on the old leather sofa together – Jon loves the old leather sofa – and Meg is waking against his chest – she also now loves the old leather sofa. They are both discovering hurts of the sort they can find entertaining, of the sort that make them proud.

Meg's neck is cricked from being trapped at an unwise angle by Jon's arm and something about one of her ankles isn't right – it's been jammed in hard between a cushion and the sofa's back … that feels like what's happened … she can't move to get up and find out, or else won't move to get up and find out.

Jon is coddling Meg – as he intends it – like dozens and dozens of eggs, enjoying the pressure her weight puts on his breathing. His one arm, laid safely over her, is cold but not uncomfortable – the other is bent beneath him and filled with jarring and shooting types of tension. His knees have been folded over one end of the sofa and this has made his knees ache and cut off the blood supply to his feet.

I might get gangrene, because of falling asleep while holding my baby, my sweetheart, my girl.

'Meg?'

'Hello.'

'You should rest, though. You should go up, go to bed.'

'Can't.'

'Why not?'

'Rather be here. With you.'

Which he's not unhappy to hear, but it does mean that she doesn't expect him to follow her and keep her just as safe in her bed – she doesn't want that, or doesn't want that yet – doesn't want that today, or wouldn't take him and keep him there, ever.

She moves in tiny ways against him and this feels like lava, like delicately boiling oil that runs over him, breaks. She gives him the explanation he wouldn't have asked for, 'I could tell that you weren't resting, because you were staying awake to check that I was asleep, so I can't go upstairs and go to sleep, because you won't sleep when we're there.'

Thank you.

We.

When we're there.

Thank you.

He retrieves his lost arm with some difficulty. 'I slept.'

'Liar.'

'I don't lie to you. I won't. I did sleep in the end quite significantly and parts of me are sleeping still.'

And here's to them staying asleep.

I haven't woken up with an erection in years, I haven't.

There would be reasons for that.

I don't have those reasons any more.

'Jon.'

'Yes.'

'We're a lot of bother, aren't we? One way and another, we're a right pain in the arse.'

He laughs – this tight punch of sound – and when his torso flexes beneath and beside her, Meg finds that she wants to kiss him and so she does – *dab* – brush her lips to his cheek.

The warm disturbance of his voice is under her, is something she would seek out, this being wrapped but undefended, this feeling which was what she always looked for after the first sip and which was not provided, not when she'd passed her early, early drinking days. Jon swallows – *I am fond of his throat* – and, 'We're not, as far as I'm aware, any kinds of pain in the arse. I believe that my arse is my only pain-free area.'

'Do you want to sit up?'

'Well, no. But I may have to, Meg.'

'My suit's all crumpled. I don't know if it'll recover. It didn't fit, anyway. You'll have noticed.'

'I didn't.'

'Jon Sigurdsson, you are lying. And you said you wouldn't.'

'I'll buy you a new one. Suit ...' His hand pats at her – *dab dab dab* – in immediate apology, immediate reassurance, the touch of someone anxious to be understood. Or simply anxious, or else simply not and simply speaking with his fingers, 'Sorry. But I could, if you wanted. I'd buy you something you might not buy for yourself.'

'A rah-rah skirt and a wimple.' She kisses him again. It's good, this kissing, this way of intruding upon someone who likes your intrusion and who is contented and so you're no intrusion at all. *People do this. It's normal. It wasn't normal for me, but I can have it, I can.* 'You need a shave.' *I can be someone who isn't anxious.* 'Sorry. You do, though.' *I can try that.*

He produces another small laugh, this relaxation clearly flowing up and down the body that she can read beneath her, being alive and with her and all right, very all right.

'Of course I need a shave. I am a manly man and have grown bristles overnight.' And he rushes on into, 'I do love you. Meg. I mean ...' His voice irregular when he tells her this and as soon as he has, he begins to untangle himself from her, to pat and hug at her, while slowly easing away. 'I'll shave when I'm home.'

There's probably no reason to panic when he says this, but she does, while his hands ask her to move, steer her, delicate, until they are sitting side by side. The freed blood in her limbs sings and throbs and sets up bites and twinges of discomfort. And she's cold. The places where he rested close – touched – now they're cold. 'I don't know how to do this, Jon. I was with someone … There were people I was with, but … This isn't the same … You'll have to … If you're going to.'

He kisses the top of her head, 'We will both get this wrong together and we will both not mind getting this wrong and we will continue and improve our performance – not performance – well, why not performance? We'll rehearse and we'll …' He coughs, 'No one will ever do anything to you again that you don't like. No one. I will fucking kill anyone … I will … I will …' And he thinks …

I can't actually say, 'I'll be the man who keeps you safe.' Because that is laughable as a statement and especially laughable from me.

Fuck it, though.

'I'll keep you safe, Meg. What we do will be safe.'

Special Branch thumbing my file while I say this, probably, but I do promise. You will be safe.

His fingers seem more biddable and useful now they've been with her, they're interested in her, they want to rest against her and take note. 'I've spent all my life being someone who tried to help and that's not actually … trying to help is not the same as helping and in the end it can be the reverse and that's very obvious, but I ignored it for a long time. And I've made – professionally speaking, really, in a way – not helping, I've made that palatable. And I've read about really terrible things, I've read about Pol Pot and how governments were really so polite to his legitimate government – murdering, fucking annihilating but legitimate government – which forces one to redefine legitimate in ways that aren't possible, tenable … It's a way of not getting involved, all that shit – legitimate … And about massacres in

Ruhengeri and Bentiu and Rekohu, Dersim, Kuban, Volhynia …
And all the other places and the other ways of killing people:
starving them to death, marching them to death, working them
to death … I read to learn, because I am in favour of learning,
but I read to prove I care, I care very much, only I don't act as
if I care very much, I don't fucking do anything … Sorry, my
daughter says I go on about this too much … But … I'm naturally boring, yes I am … But … Once you're inside a system, an
institution, then … it's like … When you're a kid, you have a
face for visitors, you have a face for the world and it's not how
you look at home, the way you look when you're at home is …'

*She knows about that. I'm telling her things that she knows – as if
she's an idiot.*

His hand – before he asks it to – reaches and finds her hand
and cuddles round it, makes a nest for it, makes sure that he is
gentle as he should be.

*If we can't be tender, if I can't be tender, then it's not possible to be
anything. I believe that and my hand believes that also.*

'Meg, I've told things to the press. I've broken the rules about
that. But the rules don't work and I should have probably –
definitely – broken them before. But I didn't say the things I most
wanted to tell – what I could find out wasn't enough. There were
things about children and … No one was interested. No one ever
managed to keep the information, to keep what I passed on about
the children from being lost. Everything always got lost …' His
hand moves, leads his arm, lets it curve around her shoulder and
he says, 'Meg, good morning. Hello. And what comes next might
be quite complicated, but it will be better than what was before.
In a way. Is how I would say it. I mean …'

And Meg watches him make his sideways and frowning smile.
'Quite complicated.'

'I'll keep you out of it – only out of that … Safety, you know …'
And he takes her hand again, holds it like a quite complicated
and delicate present and he kisses it for a while in tiny ways and
tiny ways and tiny ways.

'Jon?'

His mouth answers, still close to your fingers and so what he says brushes and gloves over the back of your hand, 'That's me, yes. I'm here, yes. Your boy is here, your mannish boy, like it says in the song.'

'I would like a walk.'

'That's ... Then we'll have a walk. I'll make myself – if you don't mind – more presentable and then we'll do that.'

The temperature of this stays on your skin.

04:38

HER SHOWER — good God — still damp underfoot from where she has showered — have to let her go first, that's obvious — damp from where she must have stood and you are naked, naked, naked in her house and the steam which is touching your body is here and the steam which has touched her body in traces here also and — ape hands scrabbling — and this is her soap which has been ...

Inevitable, really.

Farcical man that you are, wet-headed and ignoring your erection while it ignores you and ...

But it insists. That's what it's for.

It is not a demonstration of anything that's ...

I'm not doing wrong.

Oh, Jesus.

I'm not being wrong.

Oh, Jesus, Meg.

Eyes shut and the water running and monkey fingers and don't let her hear and don't let her know and she mustn't know, you think, about this, unless at some other time you might tell her, but you're being ...

And later ...

Perhaps.

With her.

Later.

With her.

In some way.

In some gossamer fucking way.

Jesus ...

Please.

Please.

Like a dog howling, a monkey howling – it feels like a howl through your muscle, under your skin which is in the steam, which has ...

And the tilt back of the head.

The small pummel of the dropping water, the small pummel.

For you, for you ...

And in behind your eyelids there is black and there is red.

Anarchy and revolution.

For you, for you ...

And the world beyond, shaken.

And this sweet that you can breathe and be and you're not so dead as you'd thought, you're still standing.

Solid and standing.

And ...

And ...

Here it is ...

Oh.

And there's this shiver all through you, but you're happy and there will be a plan, some kind of plan, there will be sweetness.

Oh.

Subsiding.

Not quite.

Oh.

We'll kiss now. We'll always kiss.

And you're stepping out for her towel, for the folded and ready and gentle thing she left you.

And you'll dress in clothes that are already warm with her scent. You'll dress in whatever order you feel is right. No tie to wear this morning – you're let out of school.

Stepping out from the bath like a big chord just opened, like it's kicking, like you could be the mannish boy who'll do all right.

It's only love. There won't be anarchy or revolution, there will be the other thing which is harder, which is love, which is the practice of love.

I am not ideal and my position is not ideal, but it is also not impossible, surely.

05:25

THEY WALK OUT together, climbing a touch higher than her house is, strolling on the Hill.

The air is still dozing, cool, it presses against their faces and has the taste of greenery in it and of the moving world. A few windows shine along her street – in early-woken houses, stayed-awake houses, ready-for-work houses, worried, or ill, or loving houses. They may be shining for any of the reasons that can put an end to sleep. There is a small trace of music from a basement, it drifts.

They don't speak.

Jon hums something under his breath and the small sounds of their feet keep time and cross time and syncopate as they go.

The Top Park is waiting for them, full of sky.

When they have dipped through the gates, taken the dim path past the empty tennis courts, Jon begins, 'There was this myth …' He leans momentarily towards Meg so that their shoulders meet and this makes her decide to set her arm around his waist, to keep him closer, deal with the stride of his long, heron legs as best she can.

He continues, 'A medieval story about beavers – don't laugh – and beavers were meant to be extremely intelligent, because they built things, I suppose, they were architects of a kind. Apart from their clever brains – which nobody wanted – and their pelts and meat, which were both popular at the time, people found that the beavers' – excuse me – testicles were of immense value. They contain musk. And the poor creatures would get hunted sometimes mainly, you know, for their testes. And the story went that, being ingenious animals, the beavers would see any hunters approaching and – to save themselves – they'd look their pursuers in the eye, then bite their own balls off and run away, leave them behind. No balls, but alive.'

'Fuck.'

'Mm hm. Cautionary tale. "*He has the sagacity to run to an elevated spot, and there lifting up his leg, shows the hunter that the object of his pursuit is gone.*" Is how they put it, if I recall correctly … It's nonsense, of course.'

And they are clear of the shadows now, off the path and out on the hilltop, walking across the wide curve of grass towards the gleam and shimmer of the city, its night shape.

'The story made me laugh when I was a student and then I would think of it later. Later it would be a story about me … But now mine have – I think – grown. Back. I think. Inconvenient.' And he laughs in his way that isn't quite laughing and slips his arm to her waist – this mild rearrangement of arms – and they stop, stand.

And there is London, staring at them, broad in the dark: the coloured prickles and restlessness, the gape of emptinesses, blanks.

Jon hasn't quite seen it like this before, 'Oh.'

'It cheers me up.'

'Oh.'

She can feel the clifftop breathlessness racing in his lungs, it moves against her arm, speeds her, too, 'That's where we met.'

'Which makes me like it more than I did.' He shifts away from her and removes his coat, puts it down on the grass, with the lining uppermost, that dull gleam of silk. 'Let's sit and watch it wake up.'

'There are benches.'

'I don't want benches, I want to sit on watered silk with you.'

'You'll ruin your coat.'

'Necessary sacrifice for the occasion.' He duly sits, above him the lack of stars, the hiding of stars. She can make out his outline, can tell that he has crossed his long legs and that his knees are almost up about his ears and a little comical. 'And dry-cleaning is a wonderful thing. Come on. Be with me.'

She joins him and together they see and see and see the bright traces of the lives upon lives that are burning, floating unsupported in the thoughtless dark. She kisses his fingers and speaks to them: 'Down there I saw a kid have someone play a saxophone, only for him. And a man who caught a balloon instead of ignoring it. And two women who helped another woman when she was upset – this disabled woman on a train. They'll be there tonight, this morning. Or they'll have passed through and gone home, gone to wherever was next. But they'll still be who they are.'

'These are, these are people from your collection?'

'Yes, I'll show you – if you want. I have them all written down. They would make you cheerful.'

'I'd like that. I think I … Cheerful is appreciated.' And his hand, the knuckles of one hand, smooth at her hair.

She leans back slightly towards the touch. 'The other day this older lady was riding a bus with this little boy and resting her chin, just over the top of his head, hugging him – her grandson, maybe. You could see in her face this was the best thing she could imagine doing in the whole of her life. There was nothing better. She was shining. And he was only sitting and a bit bored and didn't notice, didn't realise at all that he was making someone so beyond herself, just by living.'

'Isn't that sad?'

'I don't know, Jon. It's only sad if love is always sad in the end.'

'Oh.'

And they pause and neither of them says what they believe love might be in the end, perhaps because they aren't sure, or else because they're superstitious about it. They may be afraid it can hear and will listen and then contradict. That could be the case.

And somewhere a blackbird begins a tumble of song, too early but very lovely and alone.

'I was walking on a Sunday afternoon, about a block away from here, and up in a window this boy had a toy pistol and was aiming it out and someone down on the pavement noticed and put her hands up – he started smiling then and she's smiling and it's terrible in a way, but the gun isn't a gun and he isn't firing, he can't fire, and he's laughing. They were both laughing ...'

And Jon moves very quickly – those levering arms and legs – and he kneels up behind Meg and his arms are locking around her and clinging and his face is pressing, his mouth is pressing, at the side of her neck. He searches in at her skin. 'You collect all the people I can't help.'

And the dawn is coming, this greyness flattening out the night's possibilities. The park begins to be only a park, the grass muddy. 'You collect all the people I can't help.' His voice not loud, but hard. 'You collect the ones who will be hurt. You collect the ones who are hurt. And ... Operation Circus and Operation Ore and Operation Hedgerow and Operation Fernbridge and Fairbank and Orchid and Operation Midland, Operation Enamel ... I tried at least to look after some of the children, to make people know what happened to them. Not because anything happened to me. No one harmed me in that way.'

She can feel the tremor in his muscles as he holds her faster, closer. 'If a human being will not help another human being, just because that's meant to happen, if they don't understand the truth of the necessity of that – every time, every time – then what is the point of us? We're not worth the bother.' The words beside her ear and in her hair and he's talking to her and not talking to her at all. 'In the end, you see, in the end, it's all violation, it's all the abuse of children. The actual child abuse, it simply fits with all the other abuses of people who were children, who had innocence, people who are powerless, or trusting, or weak, or just alive – alive will do. When you make food impossible, when you steal away shelter, when you make someone abject, what's that? I mean, what is that? When you do that you put something filthy, unspeakable, you shove that inside someone's days and their mind and their soul ... or not soul, spirit ... without even being there. Isn't that a kind of rape?'

After this he breathes and breathes and cradles Meg's head with his hands, puts his palms over her ears, as if he is afraid of what else he will make her hear. 'Sorry. Sorry. Sorry.'

'Don't be.'

'I'm sorry. Because of you ... because the ... I don't want to ...'

'Don't.' She whispers this, so the world cannot listen to her, only him. 'Be whatever you need to, but not sorry. Fuck that.'

'I've never been so fucking furious. And so fucking happy.' He breathes again. 'That's how I feel.'

And they sway their heads together, they nuzzle and smooth each touch and strong light comes intruding, comes screaming up from beneath the horizon and unfurls and it's today and Meg and Jonathan rock against each other, they just rock and that is all there is for them at this moment – the knowledge that they are unsteady and together and unsteady and together – and new birdsong begins in skeins and bursts, while they taste salt and they believe they are saving each other, that two people are being saved, which is two more people saved than yesterday, and a handful of parakeets makes its first pass overhead – *tsseuw, tsseuw, tsseuw* – in those unasked-for colours that never were here before.

Then Meg lifts Jon's right hand.

My hairy-knuckled, miswired animal hand.

She kisses it as if it were spun sugar, or a model of his soul, and he nods and is single-minded.

Here it is.

Love.

Here it is.

06:42

AN ILL-KEMPT COUPLE are sitting on a hill above a well-known metropolis.

They are side by side and laughing.

They are side by side and crying.

They would rather be here and die of it than have to be anywhere else.

Here it is.

penguin.co.uk/vintage